MAINE

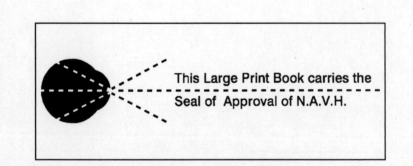

MAINE

J. COURTNEY SULLIVAN

THORNDIKE PRESS

A part of Gale, Cengage Learning

GALE
CENGAGE Learning™

Detroit • New York • San Francisco • New Haven, Conn • Waterville, Maine • London

GALE
CENGAGE Learning™

ALL RIGHTS RESERVED

Thorndike Press® Large Print Core.
The text of this Large Print edition is unabridged.
Other aspects of the book may vary from the original edition.
Set in 16 pt. Plantin.

LIBRARY OF CONGRESS CATALOGING-IN-PUBLICATION DATA

Sullivan, J. Courtney.
   Maine / by J. Courtney Sullivan.
      p. cm. — (Thorndike Press large print core)
   ISBN-13: 978-1-4104-3837-9 (hardcover)
   ISBN-10: 1-4104-3837-6 (hardcover)
   1. Women—Family relationships—Fiction. 2. Family secrets—Fiction. 3. Maine—Fiction. 4. Large type books. I. Title.
PS3619.U43M35 2011b
813'.6—dc22   2011011191

Published in 2011 by arrangement with Alfred A. Knopf, a division of Random House, Inc.

Printed in the United States of America
1 2 3 4 5 6 7 15 14 13 12 11

For Trish

Alas, a mother never is afraid,
Of speaking angrily to any child,
Since love, she knows, is justified of
love.
— ELIZABETH BARRETT BROWNING,
Aurora Leigh

Just do everything we didn't do and you
will be perfectly safe.
— *a letter from F. Scott Fitzgerald
to his daughter, Frances*

ALICE

Alice decided to take a break from packing. She lit a cigarette, leaning back in one of the wicker chairs that were always slightly damp from the sea breeze. She glanced around at the cardboard boxes filled with her family's belongings, each glass and saltshaker and picture frame wrapped carefully in newspaper. There were at least a couple of boxes in every room of the house. She needed to make sure she had taken them all to Goodwill by the time the children arrived. This had been their summer home for sixty years, and it amazed her how many objects they had accumulated. She didn't want anyone to be burdened by the mess once she was gone.

She could tell by the heavy clouds that it was about to rain. In Cape Neddick, Maine, that May, you were likely to see a thunderstorm every afternoon. This didn't bother her. She never went down to the beach anymore. After lunch she usually sat out on the screen porch for hours, reading novels that her daughter-in-law, Ann Marie, had lent her during the winter, drinking red wine, and watching the waves crash against the rocks until it was time to make supper. She never felt the urge she once did to put on a swimsuit and take a dip or muss her pedicure by walking in the sand. She preferred to watch it all from a distance, letting the scene pass through her like a ghost.

Her life here was ruled by routine. Each day, she was up by six to clean the house and tend her garden. She drank a cup of Tetley, leaving the tea bag on a dish in the fridge so she could use it once more before lunch. At nine thirty on the nose, she drove to St. Michael's by the Sea for ten o'clock Mass.

The surrounding area had changed so much since their first summer in Maine, all those years ago. Huge houses had gone up along the coast, and the towns were now full of gift shops and fashionable restaurants and gourmet grocery stores. The fishermen were still around, but back in the seventies many of them had started catering to tourists, with their breakfast cruises and their whale watches and such.

Some things remained. Ruby's Market and the pharmacy were still dark by six. Alice still left her keys in the car at all times. She never locked the house either — no one up here did. The beach had stayed untouched, and every one of the massive pine trees dotting

10

the road from her door to the church looked as if it had been there for centuries.

The church itself was a constant. St. Michael's was an old-fashioned country chapel made of stone, with red velvet cushions in the pews and brilliant stained-glass windows that burst with color in the morning sun. It had been built at the top of a hill off Shore Road so that its rooftop cross might be visible to sailors at sea.

Alice always sat in the third row to the right of the altar. She tried to remember the best bits of wisdom from Father Donnelly's sermons to pass along to the child or grandchild who needed them most, not that they paid her any attention. She listened intently, singing out the familiar hymns, reciting the prayers she had recited since she was a girl. She closed her eyes and asked God for the same things she had asked for all those years ago: to help her be good, to make her do better. For the most part, she believed He heard.

After Mass on Mondays, Wednesdays, and Fridays, the St. Michael's Legion of Mary met in the church basement and said the rosary for ailing members of the parish, for the hungry and needy around the world, for the sanctity of life in all its stages. They recited Hail Holy Queen and drank decaf and chatted. Mary Fallon reminded them whose turn it was to bring muffins next time and who would accompany Father Donnelly on

11

his weekly trip to the homes of the infirm, where he prayed for a recovery that usually never came. Though it was terribly sad, watching strangers her own age dying, Alice enjoyed her afternoons with Father Donnelly. He brought such comfort to everyone he visited. He was a young man, only thirty-four, with dark hair and a warm smile that reminded her of crooners from the fifties. He had chosen a vocation from another era, and he was thoughtful in a way she didn't know young people could be anymore.

Alice felt a sense of deep dedication watching him pray over his parishioners. Most priests today didn't make time for house calls. When they were done, Father Donnelly would take her to lunch, which she knew for a fact he did not do with the other gals from the Legion. He had done so much for her. He even helped her around the house now and then — changing the high-up lightbulb on the porch, hauling away tree branches after a storm. Perhaps this special treatment was only a result of the little arrangement they had made, but she hardly cared.

Father Donnelly and the seven members of the Legion of Mary (no fewer than five of them actually named Mary) were the only people Alice interacted with on a regular basis at this time of year. She was the lone summer person in the group, their foreign exchange student, she called herself as a joke. The year-rounders were suspicious of outsiders. But they had agreed to let her join just for the season after the archdiocese shut down St. Agnes two years back.

St. Agnes was her church at home in Canton, the church where Alice's children were baptized, where her husband, Daniel, was eulogized, where she had gone to Mass every day for the past six decades and run both the Sunday school program, when her children were small, and the Legion of Mary once they had grown. She had co-chaired the campaign to save the church with a young mother of four named Abigail Curley, who had translucent skin and a soft, childlike voice. Together, they gathered five hundred signatures; they wrote dozens of letters; they petitioned the cardinal himself.

At the final Mass, Alice cried quietly into her handkerchief. These closures were becoming common practice; you read about them all the time. But you never thought they'd impact you. At St. Agnes, Abigail Curley and some of the other congregants refused to leave. Thirty months later they were still occupying the church around the clock, holding vigil even though there was no priest there anymore, no lighting or heat. Alice started going to a new church in Milton, but she felt no connection to the place or the people there. Now her summer church was her main link to her faith and her past. The Legion members seemed to understand as much.

They were mostly widows who had let themselves go. They wore sweat suits and chunky white sneakers, and their hair was a uniform disaster. Alice was the sole one among them who had kept her figure. Only her deep, deep damn wrinkles even hinted at the horrifying fact that she was eighty-three. But like the rest of them, she was alone. Sometimes she wondered if they all took their morning prayer sessions so seriously because they each needed someone to bear witness to their presence. Otherwise, one of them might have a stroke at the kitchen table some morning, and simply go unnoticed.

Her husband, Daniel, won the property in 1945, just after the war ended, in a stupid bet with a former shipmate named Ned Barnell. Ned was a drunk, even by the standards of his fellow navy men. He had grown up in a fishing village in Maine, but now spent his time squandering his paychecks in some of Boston's finest barrooms and underground gambling clubs. He made a fifty-dollar wager with Daniel on some basketball game, which absolutely enraged Alice. They had been married two years then, and she was pregnant with Kathleen. But Daniel said the bet was a sure thing, that he never would have made it otherwise. And he won.

Ned didn't have the money to pay him.

"Surprise, surprise," Alice said when Daniel came home that night and told her the news.

He had a wild grin on his face. "You'll never guess what he gave me instead."

"A car?" Alice said sarcastically. Their twelve-year-old Ford coupe sputtered and pooped out whenever she started it. By then, they were so accustomed to gas rations that they mostly walked everywhere anyway, or took the streetcar. But the war was over now, and another New England winter was coming. Alice had no intention of being one of those mothers on the train, shushing her screaming newborn while others looked on with disapproving stares.

"Better," Daniel said.

"Better than a car?" Alice asked.

"It's land," Daniel said gleefully. "A whole big plot of land, right on the water in Maine."

She was skeptical. "You better not be joking, Daniel Kelleher."

"I kid you not, Mrs. Kelleher," he said, coming toward her. He pressed his face to her stomach.

"You hear that, jelly bean?" he said to her belt.

"Daniel!" she said, trying to push him away. She hated when he talked directly to the baby, already attached.

He ignored her.

"This time next summer we'll be making

sand castles. Daddy got you your own beach."
He straightened up. "Ned's grandfather gave
all his grandkids some land, but Ned's got no
interest in his piece. It's ours!"

"For a fifty-dollar bet?" Alice asked.

"Let's just say it was the last in a long line
of fifty-dollar bets that may or may not have
gone unpaid."

"Daniel!" Despite the good news, her blood
boiled a bit.

"Honey, don't worry so much, you married
a lucky guy," he said with a wink.

Alice didn't believe in luck, though if it
existed she was fairly sure that hers was lousy.
In two years of marriage, she had already
miscarried three times. Her mother had lost
two babies in infancy before the rest of her
children came along, though Alice wouldn't
dare ask her about it. All her mother ever
said on the topic was that she assumed God
had taken away the things she loved most as
some sort of test. Alice wondered if in her
case the children simply vanished because
they knew they weren't quite wanted or, more
to the point, that she was no mother.

She was used to the routine — no dark
spots on her delicates at the usual time of the
month, followed by a few weeks of nausea
and vomiting and headaches, and then the
sight of blood in the white china toilet,
another soul gone.

She had overheard a gal in the elevator in

16

her office building whispering to her girl-friend that a doctor in New York had fitted her for a diaphragm.

"Such a relief!" the girl had said. "Lord knows Harry's not doing anything to make sure I don't get knocked up."

"If the men had to push the babies out, then they'd take the precautions," her friend said. "Can you imagine Ronald, huffing and puffing?" She closed her mouth and filled her cheeks up with air, squinting her eyes until they both began to giggle.

Alice wished she could say something to them, find out more. But they were strangers to her, and it was a vulgar thing to be talking about in the first place. She didn't know who to ask, so she went to a priest before work one morning — someone a few parishes away from her own. Everyone acted as though penance was an anonymous process, but you could see the priest before he went into the confessional, and he could just as easily see you. This one was old, with pure white hair. FATHER DELPONTE, it said on a plaque on the outside of the box. Italian, she supposed. Everyone knew Italian girls were fast. She hoped he wouldn't mistake her for one of them. She was married, after all.

In the dim box, she knelt down, closed her eyes, and crossed herself.

"Bless me, Father, for I have sinned. It has been one month since my last confession," she began, the same words she had uttered so many times before.

Her cheeks blushed a fiery red as she told him about the babies she had lost.

"I wonder if perhaps now isn't the time for me," she said. "I wonder if there's something I might do to hold off. My sister died a couple years back, and I'm still not myself. I'm afraid of being a mother. I don't think I have it in me to love another person enough, at least not yet."

She wanted to say more, but then he asked, "How old are you?"

"Twenty-four."

Alice could swear she saw him make a baffled face through the screen.

"You're more than old enough, my dear," he said softly. "God has a plan for each of us. We have to believe in it, and do nothing to put it off course."

She did not know if he had understood. Perhaps she should have been clearer.

"There are ways I've heard of to delay," she began, fumbling for the words. "I know the Church frowns on it."

"The Church forbids it," he said, and that was all.

She cried for a moment in the parking lot and then set off for work. She never told Daniel what she had done.

This pregnancy had lasted six months so far. Alice was terrified. She tiptoed everywhere, afraid to breathe. She had to drink half a glass of whiskey each night to get to sleep. She smoked twice as many cigarettes as usual and paced around the block in the afternoons — she had been reprimanded by her boss three times now for being away from her desk when she wasn't supposed to be. Mr. Kristal was downright wretched to her, probably because he recognized her condition, and knew from experience that she'd be giving her notice soon enough.

The Saturday after Daniel won the land, they took a ride out to Cape Neddick. Alice didn't know what to expect. She had been to Maine only once before, on a day trip with her brothers and sister when she was a teenager. All six of them were jammed into their father's Pontiac, barreling along with the windows rolled down. They ate lunch at a clam shack and then drove east until they found a slip of beach to relax on. The boys skipped rocks into the water, and Alice and Mary sat in the sand, talking. Alice did a sketch of the dunes in her notebook. They didn't know what town they were in, and they didn't linger for long. They couldn't afford to stay overnight, not even at one of the cheap roadside motels that lined the highway.

Only a few years had passed since then, but it seemed like another lifetime.

Daniel drove the car through downtown

Ogunquit, past a motor inn and a dance hall and Perkins Drugstore, and the Leavitt Theatre, where *Anchors Aweigh* was playing at two o'clock. They went straight, past the stone library and the Baptist church and a row of grand hotels, until they reached the tip of town, where fishermen's shacks and lobster traps stood on the land, and fishing boats bobbed up and down in the harbor. There was water on three sides: the Atlantic's rocky coastline to the left and in front of them, and to the right a small inlet with a footbridge leading to the other side. Carved into a stone at the base of the bridge were the words PERKINS COVE.

Alice raised an eyebrow. "Gosh, is everyone in this town called Perkins?"

"Just about," Daniel said, clearly excited to have a bit of inside information. "According to Ned, that family owns half the land around here. They're fishermen, like his people. Ned went with one of the Perkins cousins back in high school."

"Lucky her," Alice said.

"Now now," Daniel said. "Hey, Ned even taught me a little poem one of them wrote. You ready to hear it?"

Before she could protest, he was reciting it, almost singing, in his best James Cagney voice:

A Perkins runs the grocery store
A Perkins runs the bank
A Perkins puts the gasoline in everybody's
  tank.
A Perkins sells you magazines
Another sells you fish
You have to go to Perkinses for anything
  you wish.
You'll always find a Perkins has fingers in
  your purse
And when I die, I think that I
Will ride a Perkins hearse.

Alice rolled her eyes at her husband. "Okay, darling, I catch your drift."

They turned the car around and pulled onto Shore Road. Daniel drove slowly, looking this way and that. Through a long bank of pine trees on the left, you could see the ocean. Here and there, clapboard houses with American flags out front dotted green lawns. Cows grazed in fields of grass.

"It's somewhere off of this road," Daniel said.

They had brought a map, which she held unfolded in her lap. Daniel expected Alice to know how to read it, but to her it looked like a mess of veins and muscles she had seen in her high school biology textbook years earlier. She half expected him to snap, "Oh, give me that!" But Daniel wasn't the type. He only laughed and said, "I guess we'll have to follow our noses, since I clearly chose a day-dreamer for a co-pilot."

That was when Alice saw them, a small assembly of women and men in smocks, sitting up on a hill, painting at easels.

"There's an artists' colony here," Daniel said. "Ned told me bohemians are buying up the lobstermen's shacks. I thought you'd like that. They have a summer school. Maybe you could take a class."

Alice nodded, though she felt her body tighten. She willed herself not to grow dark. But she could already feel her mood shifting. She stared out the window.

Off to the right was a plain wooden saltbox with a sign out front that read RUBY'S MARKET. To the left was a small green building that she might have taken for a house were it not for the word PHARMACY inlaid on a plaque above the porch.

There was no sign for Briarwood Road. Ned had told Daniel to take Shore for two miles, until he came to a fork. Then he was to turn left onto a dirt path, and follow it all the way to the ocean.

"He says we'll think we're driving straight into the woods, but we're not," Daniel said.

Alice sighed, preparing herself for what was probably a patch of overgrown brush that Ned had decided to call his own.

They passed the entrance twice and had to turn around. But on the third try, they turned at what hardly seemed like a fork. Alice gasped. The road was from a fairy tale, a long stretch of sand inside a tunnel of lush pine trees. When they reached the end, there was the ocean, sparkling in the sun, dark blue against a small sandy beach, which was nestled between two long stretches of rocky coast.

"Welcome home," Daniel said.

"This is ours?" Alice asked.

"Well, three acres of it's ours," he said. "The best three acres, too — all this land along the water."

Alice was elated. No one she knew back home had their own beach house. She could not wait to see her best friend Rita's face when she came here and saw it.

Alice kissed Daniel smack on the lips.

He grinned. "I take it you like the place."

"I already have the curtains picked out."

"Good! I'm glad that's taken care of. Now we just need a house to hang them in."

On the way back into town, he stopped the car at the fork in the road and carved a shamrock into the soft trunk of a birch tree. He added the letters *A.H.* and said, "Now we'll never miss the turnoff again."

"A.H.?" she asked. "Who's that?"

He pointed at each letter slowly, like a teacher leading a lesson. "Alice's. House."

Daniel and his brothers built the cottage with

their own hands, laid every beam, one by one. The five rooms on the first floor made a loop: The narrow stone kitchen leading into the living room with its black piano from J. & C. Fischer New York, and the iron wood-burning stove in the corner, and the dining table that could comfortably seat ten, though they often had sixteen people crammed around it. That led straight into a small bedroom meant for a couple, which led into the sun-yellow bathroom, which led into the next bedroom, which was as big as the rest of the rooms put together, with two single beds and four bunk beds. There was a lofted space up above it all, the only private spot in the house. Off the kitchen stood a screened-in porch, and off the living room a deck. Beyond that was an outdoor shower full of cobwebs, from which you could gaze at the stars while you washed your hair. That was it. Their little piece of Paradise, where the Kelleher family had spent every summer since.

In the fifties, wealthy out-of-towners started buying up plots of land all around Ogunquit and Cape Neddick. But no one ever built on Briarwood Road, so it felt like the long stretch of glorious trees that led to their home on the beach was all theirs.

They went every June and stayed for as many weeks as possible. If Daniel couldn't get off work at the insurance company, Alice would invite Rita to come. The two of them

24

would poke into antique shops in Kenneb
unkport, each with a baby slung over her
shoulder, and then they would drink Manhat-
tans on the beach in front of the cottage. On
rainy days, they went to the movies or for a
drive up the coast. Tallulah Bankhead did a
four-week stint at the Ogunquit Playhouse,
and they saw the show twice, even though it
really wasn't any good. The town was a
strange blend of fishermen and locals, tourists and actors and painters. Everywhere you
went, someone was sketching a seascape, a
sunset, a stack of lobster traps arranged just
so. Alice avoided the artists when she could.
In town one morning, one of them, quite
handsome, had asked if he could paint her
picture. She smiled, but kept walking as if
she hadn't understood.

Some weekends Alice's and Daniel's families visited, and everyone would stay up late,
eating and drinking and singing Irish songs
while Alice played the piano. After she went
to church each morning, Alice and her
sisters-in-law might lie out on the sand in a
row for hours while the sun beat down
against their bare legs. Alice always brought a
book along since they weren't the most
entertaining gals; they were morally opposed
to gossip and clearly jealous of her figure.
She wished like crazy that her own sister,
Mary, were there. Alice would almost forget
about what had passed, expecting to see

25

Mary turn the corner at any moment.

Before dinner, the women shucked corn and boiled potatoes in the kitchen with a Dean Martin record playing in the background. Meanwhile, the men gathered outside around the grill, fanning the hot coals as if it took eight of them to get a fire going.

Later came more children — Alice and Daniel's three, and forty-two nieces and nephews between them. For years there was an army of kids in the cottage, and Alice gave up on even trying to make the place look presentable. By the time the Fourth of July arrived, all the children would be bright red and freckly from the sun, their brown hair ever-so-slightly lightened, especially the girls, who squeezed lemon juice over their heads after breakfast each morning, same as their mothers. On arrival, everyone's feet were smooth and soft, but after weeks of walking barefoot out on the stone jetties and across the dunes, their soles toughened up. Daniel joked that by summer's end, they could walk over broken glass without feeling a thing.

In Cape Neddick, Alice was distracted, surrounded by smiling people, all of them grateful for the invitation. The children ran in a pack with their cousins, demanding nothing. She watched the sky over the ocean turn pink in the evening, a reminder that God created beauty, every bit as much as He created pain. She became a different person there in summertime.

Back home in Massachusetts there were so many memories; left alone in the house with the children, she often felt like she was losing hold. Her thoughts took gloomy turns without warning, and she got terrible headaches that forced her into bed all afternoon. Her life there was by its very nature boring, and she could not stand to be bored. She never cottoned to gaily cooking dinners and folding laundry and scrubbing the kitchen floor, as if that were all the world had to offer, no matter how hard she tried. She had been meant for more. Her cottage in Maine was the only thing that set her apart from everyone else, the only unordinary thing about her.

When her older daughter, Kathleen, ever the wet blanket, turned twelve or thirteen, she declared that she hated going to Maine. The air was too buggy, she said, the water too cold. There was no television and nothing to do. From then on, from the moment they arrived each summer until the inevitable morning when they packed up the car to head back to Massachusetts, Kathleen would complain: "Can we go now? Can we?"

"It's strange," Daniel had said once.

"Oh I don't think so," Alice replied. "She must have picked up on how much I love this place and instinctually decided to hate it."

Much later — it amazed her how time sped up more and more, the older she got — the

27

grandkids came along. Daniel retired. Her children drove up to Maine whenever they liked, and no one bothered to call ahead. They'd just bring extra hot dogs and Heinekens, cookies, or a blueberry pie from Ruby's Market. All summer, she and Daniel were the constant. Other bodies piled into the cottage and slept wherever they happened to drop: children under blankets on the hardwood floor in the living room, teenagers on inflatable mattresses up in the loft, her grandson Ryan's playpen wedged into the narrow kitchen.

In the mornings while the rest of them slept, Alice would brew a pot of coffee, toast English muffins, and fry up a dozen eggs and bacon. She'd set a basin of warm water out on the porch for the children's sandy feet, and later, maybe help Kathleen and Ann Marie slather the kids in SPF 50, which by then they understood was essential for Irish skin. Even so, they got burns. Red, painful, blistering burns that they spent long evenings dousing in Solarcaine. The grandchildren, like the children, mostly resembled Daniel's side — a half hour in the sun and their faces were six pink little pools, covered in constellations of brown freckles.

A few years before Daniel passed, their son, Patrick, had offered them a gift. He was having a house of their own built for them on the property, he said. A real, modern house with high-end appliances and fixtures and a view of the ocean and no kids screaming, next to the cottage, but worlds better. They would have a big-screen TV with a sound system that was somehow wired through the walls. In the cottage there was only a small radio that picked up Red Sox games if you put it on the windowsill at the right angle.

"I think it'll be wonderful," Alice said to her husband after Pat told them his plan. "Our own hideaway, no squirrels in the rafters or mildew smell in the bathroom. No leaky old refrigerator."

"But that's what a summer place is," Daniel said. "If we wanted to be alone in a souped-up house, we'd have stayed home in Canton. Why do I feel like this is a way to get rid of us?"

Alice had told him not to be ridiculous, even though she partly agreed. It was extravagant, and seemed a bit beside the point of a family retreat. But Patrick had already had the plans drawn up, and he sounded so pleased when he told them the news. Plus, as he pointed out, adding another house to the property would only increase its value.

"Like in Monopoly," he had said, a comparison that made Alice laugh, though she could see through Daniel's tight smile that he found the comment patronizing.

After the house went up, Patrick had the

whole place appraised. When he told her that it was now worth over two million dollars, Alice nearly fainted. Two million dollars for land that had been handed to them for free half a century earlier!

"See? Our boy is a smart one," she had said to Daniel then.

He shook his head. "It's dangerous, talking about money this way. Our home is not for sale."

She looked into his sad eyes and gave him a smile. She wanted to hold on to it all every bit as much as he did.

She put a hand on his cheek. "No one said it was."

Of their three children, Patrick, the youngest, had done the best by far. They sent him to BC High. His last year of high school he dated Sherry Burke, the daughter of the mayor of Cambridge. Sherry was a sweet girl, and her family exposed Pat to the finer things. Alice always thought those years with her might have been what motivated him to make money later on. (She still saw Sherry — a state senator in her own right — in the newspaper now and then.) Pat went on to Notre Dame, where he finished sixth in his class. He met Ann Marie, who was studying at his sister school, Saint Mary's. They were married the summer they turned twenty-two. They had a strong marriage, and three wonderful children — Fiona, Patty, and darling Little Daniel, Alice's favorite of all her grandkids. Pat was a stockbroker; Ann Marie stayed at home. They lived in an enormous house in Newton, with a swimming pool out back and matching blue Mercedes sedans.

Alice's daughters called them the Perfects. Well, by comparison, yes. Alice was always quick to point out that Ann Marie was a better daughter to her than either of them was. Ann Marie included her in weekend activities; they got their hair done together at a fancy place in town. They had long lunches and traded recipes and thick hardcover books and fashion magazines. Alice's own two daughters could barely manage to call her once a week and update her on their lives. Clare made up for it every now and then with nice presents, but Kathleen didn't even bother trying.

Clare was Alice's middle child, born two years before Patrick. When they were young, Alice had worried the most about her. She had a shock of red hair, the color of autumn leaves; an unfortunately round face; and freckles (Daniel's side). She was a tomboy, and she was smart, perhaps too smart for her own good. In high school, Clare acted as serious as a nun, cloistered away in her bedroom, reading her textbooks by the open window, sneaking cigarettes when she thought Alice wasn't looking. She never had many friends, no more than one or two at a time, and never for longer than a few months. Daniel said it wasn't very motherly of her to say so, but Alice feared it was something Clare was doing that kept chasing people off, rather than the opposite.

After graduating from BC, Clare worked with computers, doing something Alice still didn't quite understand. She was completely devoted to her job, and never went on any dates as far as Alice knew. In her late thirties, she met Joe, through work, of course. His family business was a religious goods store in Southie that sold ornate Bibles and prayer books to true believers, and crosses and Infant of Prague statues to children making their First Communion. Joe's father gave him the company when he retired and Clare put the merchandise on the Internet somehow.

They had done well for themselves. They lived in an old Victorian house in Jamaica Plain, a neighborhood that they claimed to love for its diversity and public victory gardens. (*Those sound like the sort of traits you'd use to praise a slum,* Alice thought each time they mentioned them, though she knew the house had not come cheap.) Their neighbors on either side were black.

Until she went to work in downtown Boston at the age of nineteen, Alice had hardly ever seen a black person. Today, you couldn't drive

down the street she had grown up on in Dorchester without locking the doors and holding your breath and saying ten Hail Marys. There were gang members and prostitutes on the corner where her brothers used to play baseball before dinner. But you weren't allowed to comment on such things. If you did, according to Clare and Joe, you were a bigot.

The two of them were a perfect match, so in step with all that liberal hoo-haw. So in love that Joe didn't even seem to notice that Clare was downright plain and she didn't seem to care that he was embarrassingly short. Their son, Ryan, only seventeen, was a student at the Boston Arts Academy. He was a gifted little singer, a real hot ticket. A bit of a brat sometimes, but that was how he'd been raised. Alice had warned them against having just one child. When Ryan was small, he would ask her to play the piano for him and he'd belt out "Tomorrow" as pitch-perfect as any girl on Broadway. Alice and Daniel had gone to so many school plays over the years that eventually Daniel invested in earplugs so he could nap in the auditoriums. But Alice loved watching those shows. She had saved all the programs. Clare and Joe kept Ryan away from her so often now. They were always too busy with auditions and meetings and travel and *life,* as if that were any excuse.

Kathleen, her oldest, was the one with

Alice's black hair and blue eyes — the prettier sister when they were young, though only by default. Kathleen's features were terribly round. When she was a teenager, her full hips and breasts hinted at the weight she would gain later.

Daniel said that Alice never really took to Kathleen, that she didn't treat her like a mother should. He, on the other hand, spoiled her rotten, making no secret of the fact that she was his favorite. It was true when Kathleen was a little girl, and true when he offered her the cottage during her divorce, even though it wasn't strictly his to offer, and it was true right at the end of his life, a fact that Alice could never forgive.

After Kathleen's divorce, she went to graduate school for social work. Her kids were still young then, they needed her. But Kathleen stayed out late studying and attending AA meetings as if they were handing out bars of gold there. Later, she started working as a school counselor and began to date all sorts of unsuitable men.

Her two kids, Maggie and Christopher, had become the kind of adults one would expect from a broken home: Chris had anger issues. As a teenager, he once punched a hole in the bathroom wall because his mother grounded him for sneaking out. In contrast, Maggie always tried too hard to make everything perfect. She was too polite, too inquisitive. It

put Alice on edge.

After Daniel died, Kathleen moved to California with a loafer boyfriend named Arlo, who she had known for all of six months at the time. They had a plan (or rather, he did) to start a company making fertilizer out of worm dung. It was a preposterous choice that still embarrassed Alice nine years later, especially because Kathleen had used Daniel's money to finance the whole boneheaded plan. Kathleen had borrowed plenty of money from him before he died too. Alice didn't want to know how much. She had once thought of Daniel's money as *their* money. But if it were hers as well, then she would have had some say in how he spent it, and that was certainly not the case when it came to Kathleen. Each time she made some foolish romantic mistake, there was Daniel, ready to clean it up.

Even as a teenager, Kathleen had always been popular with boys.

"Why don't you invite your sister to come to the party with you?" Alice would say to her on a Friday night. Or "Can't you find a nice fella for Clare?"

But Kathleen would only shrug, as though she couldn't hear her.

Once, they had argued about it, Alice feeling so enraged at her uncharitable offspring that she shouted, "You're lucky you even have a sister, you wretch. Do you know what I would do if I —"

"What would you do?" Kathleen had interrupted. "What? Take her out to some club and then leave her there to die?"

Alice was shocked, and instantly livid with Daniel for telling Kathleen. That was the only time in her life that she ever struck one of her children.

Usually, especially when they were young, she left the physical discipline to Daniel, for fear of what she might do out of fury or frustration. They had agreed that he would hit the children with a belt when they needed it, and Alice had never felt bad about this. She and her own siblings had endured much worse.

"Wait until your father gets home," she'd tell the kids when they acted up, and their eyes would grow wide with fear.

When he arrived, Daniel always made a big show of dragging the offending youngster to his or her room, and closing the door. Alice would hear him say sternly, "Now, you brought this upon yourself and you know it. Take it like a grown-up."

Next came the sound of his belt lashing against a soft backside, and then the child's dramatic scream. This sort of behavior was highly out of character for her husband, and it always thrilled Alice a little, for the children could be monsters and she felt like he provided the exact buffer she needed to cope.

After Daniel died, the kids told Alice that in fact he had never once struck them, only taken them upstairs and thwacked his belt against the mattress a few times, instructing them to shout as soon as they heard the sound.

Alice rose from her spot on the porch now, and went to the kitchen. She poured herself a glass of wine. Surveying all the dishes and silverware spread out on the counter, she sighed. She had wanted to get a bit of reading in before dinner, but the contents of her pantry were staring straight at her, begging to be dealt with.

There was a big roll of bubble wrap there, and she began by cutting off several thick sheets. Next, she wrapped the plates, one by one. Newspaper would have been quicker, but it seemed a shame to risk staining the china gray, even if she was giving it away. She had briefly considered asking Clare or Ann Marie if they wanted it, but she knew that would only raise their suspicions, and she didn't feel like arguing.

Lately, the one thing her three children had in common was a real love of nagging her.

They wanted her to quit smoking, and were forever citing statistics about the bad effects or pointing out that her white ceilings were tinged orange, so imagine how her lungs must look. Last spring she had somehow left a lit cigarette burning on the edge of an ashtray on her kitchen table when she went out shopping with Ann Marie. Her daughter-in-law helped her bring in her bundles afterward, and saw the still-smoldering cigarette, which had rolled onto the tabletop and left an ugly burn. The kids all went crazy over it, even though nothing bad had happened.

They thought she drank too much. Well, honestly, who gave a fig about that? She had abstained for more than thirty years for heaven's sakes, and only to appease her husband. Patrick had given her a stern lecture at Thanksgiving about driving the car after a few cocktails, which made her laugh. She wanted to say that she had driven a car after more than a few lousy cocktails throughout her twenties; when she was pregnant with him and his two sisters; when they were screaming brats in the backseat of her station wagon; and everything had worked out fine. Alice assumed they were thinking about the accident back when they were kids, even though that was a onetime slipup, ancient history. With all that was painful in the world, she wondered why on earth her children felt a need to focus on unlikely hypothetical disasters that might or might not eventually occur.

They said she wasn't watching her diet carefully enough, monitoring her salt intake like the doctor said she should. Ann Marie called over and over with cautionary tales about her own mother's ever-worsening diabetes or an article she had read in *USA Today* on the subject. Alice had to bite her tongue to keep from saying that though Ann Marie's mother had once been pretty enough, she now looked a lot like Winston Churchill in a swimsuit, while Alice herself had never weighed an ounce over 119 pounds, other than during her pregnancies.

They said Alice should be smarter with her money, because in the wintertime, cooped up in her house with a Manhattan or a glass of cabernet, she enjoyed buying items off the television every now and then — Time Life music collections, hand blenders that promised perfectly thick soups in minutes, even a replica of Lincoln's log cabin for her granddaughter Patty's children. But she never spent much, not more than $19.99. She went to the department stores in the mall after church one Sunday a month, and made herself feel better by trying on silk scarves and lipstick or mascara at the Chanel counter. But she certainly didn't buy any of it. She just memorized the feel and the look, and then went to Marshalls and bought the closest knockoff. She followed the sales at Macy's and Filene's like a hawk. She clipped coupons every morning, and called Ann Marie to let her know about any really good deals.

Still, it was hard to keep much money in the bank just between her pension and Daniel's. A couple years back, when Patrick looked over her taxes, he frowned and said, "You're shelling out a heck of a lot more than you're bringing in. You need to reverse that situation, pronto."

Her very first thought was that perhaps she ought to sell the property in Maine. It surprised her that she would even consider it, but there it was.

Alice wasn't particularly attached to the big house, but she still felt sentimental about the cottage, with its familiar details, and stories from their past tucked inside each cupboard and under every bed. On the doorway leading to the kitchen, hundreds of dates and initials had been written in by hand, chronicling the heights of her children and grandchildren and nieces and nephews over the years. This was where Clare had learned to walk, and Patrick had broken his arm one summer, trying to jump off the roof of the screen porch and fly like Superman. Where her grandchildren had first stepped in sand and had their tiny bodies dipped into the ocean. Where she and Daniel had taken countless strolls to look at the stars, hand in hand, not a word spoken.

But those were only memories. The place wasn't moving forward anymore, not for Alice. In recent years, her children had even created an asinine schedule for the cottage: One month per family each summer. Kathleen and her kids got June; Patrick, Ann Marie, and theirs got July; Clare, Joe, and Ryan got August.

It made Alice nervous, unsettled, to have to see her children one at a time like this. The joy and spontaneity of summers past were gone now. Daniel's death had ended them as a family. Each had pulled away from the others, and at some point without realizing it, Alice had gone from the matriarch — keeper of the wisdom and the order — to the old lady you had to look in on before the day's fun could begin.

She got the feeling that none of her children particularly liked one another, or worse, that they had no use for each other. So why keep the old place? And why bother coming up, year after year, when it only made her feel lonely, longing for something she'd already had?

It seemed to Alice that everyone these days was out for themselves. The sort of families she and Daniel had grown up in and tried to carry on no longer existed, not really. Her mother had had eight children, including the two babies that died. Daniel's mother had had ten. Though she had hated the noise and the chaos and the sacrifice this implied back then, now Alice saw that it gave you something, being part of a family like that. Her own children and their children would never understand it. That was why they were so comfortable splitting up their summer home, or living a few miles apart but only seeing one another every couple of weeks. Or, in Kathleen's case, moving clear across the country for no good reason. Worms, for Christ's sake.

She gently laid the plates in a cardboard box on the floor. The box already contained the second teapot they had kept around forever, and some old dish towels, and a *Kiss Me, I'm Irish* coffee mug that had once belonged to her brother Timothy. Alice took the mug out and placed it back in the cabinet.

She missed her brothers more now than she had when they died, years earlier. And lately, she was haunted by memories of her sister; of what might have been had Mary lived. That past winter had marked the sixtieth year since Mary's death. On the twenty-eighth of November, Alice had thought to go to the grave site. She hadn't been since she could remember. Her parents were buried there, too, all three names on a single headstone, as well as the names of the two babies who were lost back in the twenties. But Alice knew that if she went, she would hope to feel some part of them floating in the air around her, and she knew just as well that they weren't there.

She tried to put it from her mind, but when

she opened her copy of *The Boston Globe* that day, she found a full-page story about the anniversary of the fire in the Metro section, complete with photographs. There were recollections of all of the most famous victims: The old Western film star Buck Jones had been taken to a hospital and died minutes before his wife reached his bedside to say good-bye. The body of a young woman was found in the phone booth, where she had tried in vain to call her father to come save her; a couple married that day in Cambridge both died, along with their entire bridal party. And then there was the one they called Maiden Mary, the woman who perished without knowing that her beloved planned to propose the very next day.

Alice had read her sister's name and, remembering that night, she was gripped with the sort of guilt she had not felt in years. There was no one she could tell. None of her children would understand. Daniel was dead, and if he had been alive, she still probably wouldn't have dared to say a word.

She willed herself not to think about it, but minutes later she was sobbing uncontrollably at the kitchen sink. Her chest seized up. She wondered if she was having a heart attack.

Alice wished she could go to church — her own church, which had been the comforting backdrop to so much joy and sorrow. The fact that she couldn't made the pain all the

43

worse. She hadn't been able to save the place, she knew that. Yet the fact of the closure still surprised her from time to time. Her priest from St. Agnes had been shipped off to a parish in Connecticut, and she had no idea how to reach him. She felt utterly alone.

She thought then of her summer priest, Father Donnelly. She called him with shaking hands, unsure of what she'd say — she had kept the secret for sixty years. She knew that confession meant telling it all, but for now, she told him some version of the truth, the parts that Daniel knew.

He was impossibly kind to her, and said that she needed to forgive herself, the same as her husband had always said.

"Please," she said over and over. "Give me a penance. Give me some way to fix this."

She didn't know how to say to anyone, even a priest, how terrified she was of Hell. But she knew that soon it would be too late.

"Alice, we all need to focus on doing good work with the time we have left," he said. "There's no reason to dwell on the past. Just think about what you can do now."

In Alice's day, a priest would absolve you of your sins by making you pray or go without. For Lent, you should deprive yourself of candy or perfume or gin, whatever it was that you liked best in life. But nowadays, it seemed that they wanted you to do something good instead: Paint a house, or collect money

44

for UNICEF, or volunteer with troubled children. Something.

After they hung up, she could breathe again. It felt somewhat relieving to say the words out loud. But even so, she poured herself a glass of wine and got into bed before six.

A month later, right after Christmas, Father Donnelly came to Boston to visit friends, and stopped by Alice's house for lunch. He asked if she was feeling better after their talk, and she said she was, though it wasn't really true. Thoughts of Mary had been with her ever since, and his words had lingered: *Just think about what you can do now.* There was nothing she could do to bring her sister back or to redeem herself.

She served the priest a defrosted chicken potpie she had made weeks earlier. They sat in her kitchen and spoke of other things, while outside, snow fell on the rhododendron bushes. At some point the conversation turned to St. Michael's by the Sea. Alice watched the worry lines that crinkled around Father Donnelly's eyes as he spoke. Funds were dwindling. The rectory was falling apart. The church roof was in bad shape, and there was mold all over the cellar, which filled up with water every time it rained.

"We'll be lucky if the place lasts ten more years," he said. "There just isn't any money for upkeep."

Alice couldn't bear to see it lost like St. Agnes had been. Suddenly, she knew what she ought to do — "Father, it might put you at ease to know that my family and I have decided I should give my property in Maine to St. Michael's when I die," she said. "Between the house and the cottage, there's enough room to sleep probably ten or twelve men comfortably. Or you could sell it. It's worth over two million dollars."

Father Donnelly turned red, just as Daniel had when he got embarrassed as a young man.

"Oh Alice," he said. "I certainly wasn't asking —"

"I know," she said. "But really. We had already decided."

"I can't impose on your family like that," he said.

"I've been going to St. Michael's every summer since before you were born," she said sternly. "It's given me plenty. It's only right to give back. Besides, it's not like my children cherish the place."

Once she said it she realized that all of the kids, especially Patrick, would be furious with her for not consulting them. But why should she? It was her property, after all. They had certainly never asked her opinion about the cottage schedule. Clare and Patrick didn't need any of the money. And Kathleen had spent most of Daniel's savings already. Every time she thought of this, Alice was forced to remember the way she had cast aside her pride and asked Kathleen to help her talk sense into Daniel when he got sick. Kathleen had refused, a fact that Alice could never forgive. Daniel might still be alive today if not for his decision and Kathleen's willingness to go along with it. But Alice was powerless to change that now.

"You should take some time to think about it," Father Donnelly had said. "Talk it over with your family. It's a huge decision, Alice."

She knew it was as good as made.

"I already spoke to my family about this and we're all in agreement," she said.

Later that week, she met with the lawyer and changed her will. The three acres and two houses in Maine would go to St. Michael's.

She called Father Donnelly to tell him that it was finalized.

"Oh, thank you," he said, his voice filled with relief. "Please tell your children how incredibly grateful we are."

"I will," she lied.

Alice had decided not to tell the kids. They should be able to make their memories the same as always, without feeling the weight of an ending coming on. Plus, she didn't want to face their reaction if it was bad. They could be angry with her once she was dead and buried.

MAGGIE

It was the first Sunday in June, the day before she and Gabe were set to leave for Maine. Maggie had taken two weeks off from work. Usually, before her annual trip, she felt that same giddy excitement she'd had as a child, when she watched her father packing up the car to head to Cape Neddick. But today she felt terrified.

Tomorrow they'd be at the beach; tomorrow she would finally tell Gabe the news. She imagined taking his hand and leading him down to the stone jetty. She would start off simply, not a lot of beating around the bush: "Honey, there's something I have to tell you."

Soon thereafter, they'd start their real life together — their two-year anniversary, their two-bedroom apartment in the East Village. Or else he'd panic, and none of that would come to pass.

She woke him up with a flurry of kisses all over his face and neck and chest, which she hoped would disguise her nerves.

"Let's get you packed!" she said.

Beside the bed stood her own stuffed suitcase, the hand-me-down Louis Vuitton her aunt Ann Marie had given her for study abroad over a decade earlier, angering Maggie's mother but delighting Maggie herself. She had brought it from her apartment the night before. She would be staying with him again tonight, and they would leave around noon the next day, after he wrapped up an early shoot. He wanted to spend two nights in a row with her before the trip — this in itself was a good sign, since Gabe was the type who needed his space. Until recently, she had gotten used to having to lobby for their time together, but maybe that was changing now.

He laughed into his pillow. "Maggie, it's dawn. We're not leaving until tomorrow," he said.

Really it was almost ten, but she decided to leave it, getting up to make coffee. Usually he woke before she did, and often had breakfast ready by the time she got out of bed — Denver omelets and hash browns and sausage and waffles, all served together, as if they were a couple of truckers. She had gained seven pounds since they had started dating two years earlier, though he didn't seem to notice.

In the kitchen, she looked out the window at a homeless man dragging his cart along the sidewalk, a group of hipsters in tight dark jeans sharing a cigarette on a graffiti-covered stoop across the way. She had never been able to see the beauty in this neighborhood, no matter how much Gabe praised it. She wondered, not for the first time, how it was going to feel to leave her lovely tree-lined Brooklyn Heights, with its streets of perfect brownstones, the view of the Manhattan skyline and the Brooklyn Bridge from the Promenade, the Sunday farmers' market where she and Gabe had so often gone in early autumn to buy fresh vegetables, and apple crisp, and dahlias for the fire escape, which she could never manage to keep alive for long.

It was hard to imagine living here, in a neighborhood meant for young late-night partiers, a neighborhood full of dive bars and concrete. Especially with a child. Or maybe they would move again by then, someplace quieter and more kid friendly. Park Slope perhaps.

Somewhere in the back of her mind, she thought that maybe they wouldn't ever have a life together, and this whole situation would turn out to be an extension of her foolish history with men — huge, impossible hopes that eventually came to nothing.

Maggie hadn't told anyone that she was pregnant, even though she had known for nearly two weeks. There were plenty of moments when she panicked and picked up the phone to call her mother or her best friend, Allegra, but she resisted. Gabe should be first.

Never in her life had her emotions run so hot and cold — she could talk herself into the possibility of this being a superb idea and feel at ease for all of three minutes, before completely freaking out and deciding she'd made the biggest mistake of her life.

She knew exactly how it had happened. For months, she had been thinking about babies. Suddenly, almost out of nowhere, she wanted one, and understood for the first time what women meant when they talked about biological clocks. She found herself gazing longingly at toddlers on the subway or at brunch. At certain points in each month, she thought she might kidnap the closest person in a high chair.

Maggie knew that she and Gabe weren't exactly ready. But one night in mid-April, they had a long, winding freshman-year-of-college-type talk about the way events unfold, how, as her mother often said, life is what happens when you're busy making other plans. They were both artists in their way, and they ascribed so much meaning, too much, to how they'd met. Gabe said that their next chapter could likely be as random, as accidental, as fated, however you chose to look at it. That night at eleven, when she was supposed to take her pill as she had done every night at eleven since her first year at

Kenyon, she left it in the package instead. She did the same the next night and the next, before panicking and swallowing all four pills in one gulp on the fourth night.

After the initial shock of it, this crazy, exhilarating game of Russian roulette, she waited, without telling Gabe what she had done. Her period never came. She took a home pregnancy test. Even though she probably shouldn't have, she felt stunned when the result was positive. All you heard about in New York these days was how impossible it was to get pregnant. How could she have accomplished it in a single try?

Hiding the pregnancy test from Gabe was one thing, but she knew there was something truly, deeply, wildly wrong with her when she found herself making a doctor's appointment, sitting across from her middle-aged female gynecologist in a paper gown calmly talking about prenatal vitamins, and then going to meet Gabe for dinner afterward as if none of it had happened. They had even had sex that night.

On average, they did it six times a week, a fact that stunned her group of friends from back home in Massachusetts, most of whom were married, as well as Allegra, her best friend from college, who considered herself exceedingly liberated in every way, but found this amazing even so.

There was an electricity between them that

never diminished, even when they were fighting. So Maggie couldn't be sure when it had happened. For some reason, this seemed important, a real omission on her part. She remembered them having sex in the shower that second day with no pill — she was bent forward with her foot up on the edge of the tub, and he stood behind. She cringed thinking about it. That was no way to make a child. She knew this was the least of her problems, but it seemed like a sign of just how unfit they were to become parents.

Then again, they weren't teenagers. It wasn't exactly a scandal for two people in their thirties to have a baby, even if it wasn't planned. They could do this. She thought she could, at least.

She decided that she would tell him in Maine. There, he'd have time to process, time to get accustomed to the idea. Maybe he would be happy.

Gabe knew she wanted children someday in some abstract way, though they had never really talked about kids. But Gabe was impetuous. He made decisions on a whim, and managed to be happy with them — *move to New York, leave New York, come back to New York.* She herself had never been that way, but he brought it out in her, which perhaps accounted for that business with the pills. She hadn't been sick at all so far and she took this, at least, as a good omen.

Maggie turned away from the window and pulled two mugs from the cabinet over the sink. She filled Gabe's with coffee and poured cranberry juice into her own. She had stopped drinking caffeine two weeks earlier, and no one had noticed. She wasn't drinking booze either, but she hardly ever did that anyway. She was mindful of the family history around drinking — her mother had dragged her along to enough AA meetings as a child, presumably because she couldn't find a sitter, but more likely as a sort of cautionary tale. As a result, all these years later Maggie rarely had more than a single glass of wine during the course of a night. She had never been drunk in her life, aside from two or three times with her extended family at Christmas.

For months, she had been looking forward to Maine. She could almost smell the ocean. The cottage and her grandmother's house next door were built on three acres of grassy land. Beyond those was a stretch of sand and miles of dark blue sea. You couldn't make out a thing on the other side. As a little girl, Maggie believed that the world dropped off out there, that if you swam far enough you might fall into a starry sky.

She and Gabe had had a marvelous time the previous summer. They did all the activities Maggie had loved to do with her family as a child. They lay on the beach reading for hours; they canoed through Penobscot Bay while loons serenaded them from the shore; they watched fireworks in a field in Kennebunkport, sitting on an itchy blanket in a crowd of families sitting on itchy blankets of their own. They brought a picnic dinner — turkey sandwiches, cheese and crackers, a thick slice of chocolate cake, and a bottle of wine. Children ran here and there, shaking glow sticks in the darkness, eating Popsicles that melted too fast and dribbled red, white, and blue down their chins. When the display started, a young father near them lifted his excited daughter up onto his shoulders, while his wife consoled a fearful younger brother, bribing him with a whoopee pie.

"That'll be us someday," Gabe had said. She had felt joyful at the thought.

They always seemed to do better outside of their everyday environment, as if away from the stresses and distractions of New York life, they were suddenly able to imagine themselves as different people.

In Maine last summer, Gabe had patched the screens on the cottage and helped install an air conditioner in her grandmother's house next door. He had taken her grandmother's photo, falling in love with Alice as people outside the family often did, taking notice of her beauty and her charm, not sensing the iciness that lay beneath. The picture — a stunning portrait in which Alice looked like an old movie star, with a highball glass in one hand and a cigarette in the other — was taped to Gabe's refrigerator, along with dozens of others he had snapped. It was slightly disconcerting, meeting her grandmother's gaze every time she went to get an orange, or milk for her tea.

When Gabe finally emerged from the bedroom, sleepy-eyed and gorgeous in just his boxers, Maggie blurted out, "I wish we were leaving today."

"I wish I didn't have to work tomorrow morning," he said, coming toward her, wrapping his arms low around her waist, sending a current through her, even though he had done it a million times before. "Should I blow off the assignment so we can leave sooner?"

She felt a nervous twinge when he said it, in spite of herself. He hadn't had a job in weeks.

"Nah," she said, trying to sound breezy. "We'll wait. Anyway, this is pretty nice, too, having a quiet morning here together."

A while later, she led him back into the bedroom, and placed his open duffel bag on the bed. They filled it with his swim trunks and T-shirts, sunblock and books they both wanted to read. Maggie's whole body felt filled up with light, as it always did when things were good between them. At the same time, she felt a trace of trepidation: when they hadn't fought in a while, there was the chance that a big one was coming, and she needed him in a good place for the news she was about to deliver. So she tried to step around problems, tried not to agitate, as he said she tended to do.

Maggie found three sundresses hanging in the closet, left over from the previous summer. She put two of them in the bag, but left the third on its hanger.

"You want to take that to your place?" he asked.

She shrugged. "Only to bring it back here in two months?"

"By then, summer will be two-thirds over," he said.

In August, when the lease was up, his dopey roommate, Cunningham, would be moving out and Maggie would move in.

Gabe had asked her in the middle of May, not long after she found out she was pregnant. They were having an argument, which had started off as a discussion about marriage: He thought it was a stupid, outdated institution. She halfway agreed, but also thought people said that only when they hadn't met the right person yet.

"When are you going to start believing in us, huh?" he asked, in a wounded tone of voice that made her all but forget about the fights they had had, the lies he had told. Maybe they had finally turned a corner.

"I'm one hundred percent committed," he

57

said. "I've even been thinking about asking you to move in."

Though her gut told her this was a consolation prize, that it didn't necessarily mean he was ready to be a father, she felt elated by the thought. He wanted to live with her; they were one step closer. Maggie knew her mother and her friends would tell her she was crazy, but she said yes, she would love to live with him. She took the offer as a sign that it would all work out. She had never been one to believe in signs, but then, she had never needed one quite so much. Maggie pushed any doubts from her head that night, running a flat palm over her flat stomach as he slept beside her. Soon enough everything would change.

The next morning, she asked him if he was sure, and he said yes; he loved her, wanted to wake up next to her every day. She asked if his roommate would be okay with that. Ben Cunningham was one of Gabe's two best friends from childhood, along with Rich Hayes. Gabe mostly referred to them only as a unit: "Cunningham and Hayes," or more often, "the Goons."

Gabe said he was the one who had found the place, so it was his call. Besides, Ben, like Gabe, was thirty-four, and had been making rumblings for some time about the fact that he was getting a bit old to be living with another dude and should probably bite the bullet and move in with his girlfriend of seven years, Shauna. No matter that he had cheated on her countless times since leaving their hometown in Connecticut, where she still lived.

Maggie believed the move would improve their relationship, in ways small and large. No more arguing about who was going to spend the night at whose place, no more schlepping her blow-dryer to and from the office three days a week. No chance that she might be standing in his kitchen cooking pasta, hear the door open, and see a man other than her boyfriend walk through.

In the past, she had felt like she was pulling Gabe along in her little red wagon, but not anymore. He wanted them to live together. They hadn't had one of their nasty blowups in months.

Now, his suitcase packed and stacked neatly beside hers in the bedroom, they sat on the couch, eating pancakes and bacon that Gabe had made. She watched TV and he read *Sports Illustrated.* Cunningham hadn't come home the night before, and she willed him to stay in whichever girl's bed he had landed, not wanting him to shatter their nice day. He often clambered in after a basketball game with a friend or two in tow, eating all the groceries (which she had bought and paid for) out of the fridge without asking, and switching the channel to ESPN, even if they were watching a movie. It was his apartment, so she couldn't really complain. And Gabe — always annoyingly passive and laid-back when it came to his friends — never said a word.

Once, she and Gabe had hosted a dinner party, and she had gone to extravagant lengths: a linen cloth on the big table in the living room, roasted chicken and strawberry pie, bottles of champagne they couldn't afford. Cunningham was supposed to be in Chicago that weekend, but at the last minute he had decided not to go. After the salad course, he bounded in in his sweaty gym clothes and sat down on the couch, two feet from their dinner guests.

"Can I get you a plate?" she had asked him reluctantly.

"Sure," he'd said.

Not *Yes, please* or *Thank you,* just *Sure.*

He didn't join them at the table. Instead, he ate off his lap on the couch. He filled a coffee mug with Veuve Cliquot, and turned on Sports Center, muting the volume since they had music on. Maggie felt enraged, giving Gabe a pleading look.

He was drunk, watery-eyed, and just laughed.

She mostly disliked Cunningham because he was Gabe's partner in crime, the person Gabe was inevitably with when he lied about where he'd been or drank so much he had to call in sick to a job the next day. Cunningham brought out the bad teenage boy in Gabe, as she imagined he had in high school, when they'd sneak out of chemistry class together and go jump in the old stone quarries that, years later, their hometown filled in after some other fearless teenager accidentally fell to his death.

Now she imagined what it would be like here, after Cunningham had gone: her pale blue couch and love seat in place of his two oversize pullouts. ("Why do straight men always make it their mission to fit as many sofas into a room as possible?" her friend Allegra had said when she first saw the place.)

Maggie clicked through the channels — a Woody Allen movie, a roundtable of political pundits, an infomercial about closet organizers that could change your life for the low, low price of $29.99.

She stopped at the infomercial.

Gabe looked at her with a raised eyebrow. "Really?" he said.

"It's my hour," she said. "At one you can switch to baseball."

"I don't know about that," he said. "It depends on whether I can tear myself away from watching the Storage Saver 5000."

She grinned. "Now I know what I'm getting you as a housewarming gift when I move in."

She found infomercials strangely soothing,

61

the way they made it seem as though a piece of plastic might actually eliminate all chaos and uncertainty from your life. She had been watching them since she was a kid, though she never bought anything. Her grandmother seemed to have developed a slight home shopping addiction since her grandfather's death, a fact that Maggie's mother and brother found hilarious, while she herself thought it sad.

She imagined Alice and other lonely old ladies and frazzled young housewives and overworked co-eds all around the country watching at this very moment, picking up the phone at the promise of "no more lost shoes, and no more lost hours — instantly get more time with your loved ones, more precious time to do what you *want*."

"We should make an effort with my grandmother when we're in Maine this week," she said. "Invite her out to dinner with us and really refuse to take no for an answer."

"Sounds good."

"I should probably make plans to visit my mom in California soon too. Maybe this fall."

By then she would know the outcome. She imagined them all sitting around Kathleen's picnic table, discussing baby names while the sun set over the mountains.

"Absolutely," Gabe said distractedly.

He and Kathleen didn't get along as well as Maggie might have liked. Her mother thought

Gabe had a lot of growing up to do, and he in turn had no shortage of worm-farm jokes in his arsenal. Maggie sometimes got offended when he mocked her mother's job, or the fact that her house was always a disaster, even though she herself made similar comments all the time.

"Do you want to come?" she asked.

"Sure," he said. He squeezed her shoulder gently, kneading his fingers into her skin. "But maybe we can stay in a hotel this time."

A while later, Gabe dropped his magazine onto the floor. He got up to take a shower, kissing her on the forehead when he passed.

"I can't wait to be at the beach, where a dunk in the ocean is all you need to wash off," Gabe said as he walked toward the bathroom.

"You know, some people do still bathe in Maine," she said with a smile.

"Yeah, but not me, baby doll."

"Well no, not you, of course not you."

He closed the bathroom door and she heard the water start.

Maggie stretched out on the couch and began to read over some draft pages of the novel she was working on. She had vowed to spend at least four hours a day on it in Maine. She had been neglecting her real work lately, and phoning it in somewhat at her day job too.

For the past two years she had been doing

background research and writing copy for *Till Death Do Us Part,* a true-crime cable show about women who murdered their husbands.

Her boss, Mindy, was very relaxed. She didn't care if they worked from home or in the office as long as they got their stuff done. Maggie went in all the same, afraid that too much time at home alone would make her depressed, or that she'd watch nine hours of television every day and eat the entire contents of her cabinets by lunch.

Maggie enjoyed the job mostly, but some days when she sat around a table with those other bright, creative people, she thought for a moment or two of how they all dreamed of being somewhere else.

Other than her mother, no one in her family mentioned it when she published a short story in a literary journal, even if she told them about it in advance. But when they saw her name in the credits for *Till Death,* they'd call her immediately.

Her stepmother had been the last to call, breathless with excitement: "I just saw the one where the woman shoots the husband after she sees his Visa bill, and it turns out he wasn't even cheating. He really *was* sending all those flowers to her, but the florist got the address wrong. The poor guy! Your father says to tell you that thanks to you he's never buying me roses again."

On the weekends, Maggie worked from

home, trying to finish her novel, and occasionally writing other people's online dating profiles for extra money. She had written one for a friend as a favor a year earlier, and then that friend's sister had asked her to do one, and then a co-worker of hers.

"You could actually make some mad cash on this," Gabe had said to her once, and she had told him to stop being crazy.

But she kept getting offers, and had even been asked by a friend at *New York* magazine to write a step-by-step guide to the perfect profile. (She had declined, as few things seemed more mortifying than being known as an authority on online dating.)

Maggie had briefly joined Match.com before meeting Gabe. She went on four or five dates, but every one of them felt artificial, as if she and the guy were two characters going out to dinner in a play. Maggie could never remember their real names and thought of them exclusively by their screen names — they were always WarmLover10 or BookNerd-SeeksSame, instead of Alex or Dave. And she quickly tired of translating their profiles: A guy who said he was six foot two was most likely five foot eight. If a guy actually claimed to be five-eight, it meant he was four and a half feet tall.

Now the door to the apartment opened and shut with a slam: the unmistakable sound of Cunningham arriving home. She cringed, wishing she had gone into the bedroom so she wouldn't have to talk to him.

Maggie heard Gabe turning off the water in the shower. She was grateful at least that she wouldn't have to be alone with Cunningham for long.

"Hey there," he said. "What's happening, lady?"

"Just hanging out," she said.

"I thought you guys left for Maine already," he said.

"Nope. Tomorrow."

"Cool, cool. So, what's the word?"

"Not much," she said, always unsure of how to answer that particular question. "How's Shauna?" Her reliable fallback.

"She's okay," he said. "She took a new nursing job in Westport."

"But I thought she was moving here soon. She's going to commute to Westport from New York?"

He shook his head. "No ma'am, and thank God for that. I'm not ready to give up our bachelor pad yet."

She started to say more, but Gabe appeared then, wrapped in a towel from the waist down.

"What up, my man!" he said, giving Cunningham a high five.

"Honey, Ben says Shauna got a new job in Connecticut," she said, feeling her words heavy with implication.

"Yeah? Good for her."

She tried again. "Shauna's not moving to New York then."

Gabe walked into the bedroom, and she followed behind. She closed the door. Her chest tightening, she said, "Gabe, please tell me that you've already told him I'm moving in."

"Keep your voice down," he whispered.

"You haven't told him yet," she said, weighing in her head whether this was simply bad or worse than that.

"I wanted to wait until after Maine to talk to you about this whole living together idea," he said. "Do you really think we're ready?"

She sat down on the bed. Heartburn rumbled up into her throat. She pulled a couple of Tums from her purse on the floor and chewed them slowly. She wanted to tell him she was pregnant, then and there, but she knew she could say it only once and the moment needed to be perfect. Instead she said, "You asked me to move in."

"Whoa," he said. "All I said was I had been thinking about it, and then you ran with the idea."

She breathed in deeply. "Please tell me this isn't happening," she said.

"Babe, chill out. You haven't given your landlord notice yet, right?"

"Right. But Jesus, Gabe, I was just about to."

She wished that she already had.

"But you didn't! So we live apart one more year. What's the big deal?"

The big deal is that I've already told everyone I know — every person at work, every friend, both my parents. I've already started redecorating this goddamn apartment in my head, and told Allegra's cousin that she can have my place as of August first. The big deal is that in seven months, I'll be giving birth to your child.

"I don't understand," she said. "We've been talking about it all the time."

"You've been talking," he said. "I didn't want to ruin our vacation, but when I talked to Cunningham about it, he said he wasn't ready to move out yet, and I can't abandon him. Hey, you're always telling me to follow through on my commitments, right?"

He could not follow through on finding steady work or taking care of her when she got sick as he had promised, but she was supposed to be dazzled by the fact that he felt compelled to keep living with Ben.

"So Cunningham knew I wasn't moving in before I knew it," she said.

Anger filled her, anger that she knew would turn to sadness and fear as soon as Gabe was out of her sight, and for that reason she wanted to fix this, to make some sense of it.

"I have my own place. Maybe you should come live at my apartment. Or we can find a brand-new place, and Cunningham can get a roommate off Craigslist," she said.

"A total stranger?" Gabe said, as if most everyone in New York didn't live with total strangers. "Why do you want to live together so bad anyway? What's the difference between that and what we have now?"

Because I'm thirty-two years old. Because my cousin Patty is the same age and already has three kids and a house. Because I want to know when you come in at night. Because I love you.

"You're the one who suggested it in the first place," she said.

"I thought that's what you wanted."

"It was!"

"But it's not really what I want. I feel like a big part of the reason you want to live together is just to keep tabs."

She shook her head. Was this really happening?

"Damn right," she said. "I thought maybe the possibility of living together meant you'd stop being such a liar, but I guess I was wrong."

"Guess so," he said. "Hey, this time you didn't even need to go through my e-mail to find out."

She knew all her snooping was wrong, though it never felt wrong when she did it. It gave her a weird high, looking at his e-mails while he was in the shower or out for a run. Maggie told herself that she only wanted proof — just once — that Gabe wasn't doing anything inappropriate. But she'd always find something: acknowledgment that he had lied about where he was, or an overly friendly e-mail exchange with an ex. And then she would be devastated and unable to explain her sudden sorrow to Gabe.

"Like Ronald Reagan said, trust but verify," she had told Allegra once to explain why she checked up on him this way, and Allegra had widened her eyes: "Jesus, we're getting our moral relativism from Reagan now?"

He was still wearing the towel. He let it drop to the floor and pulled on a pair of boxers and jeans.

"We're done," he said. "I'm gonna go watch the game. Come out if you want."

"You're gonna watch the game," she said, feeling suddenly hysterical. "You're going to watch the fucking game? I don't think so."

"I hate fighting like this," he said. "I can't stand it."

"We haven't fought like this in a long time," she said, getting to her feet.

"Yeah, because you got what you wanted," he said.

"I thought it was what we both wanted."

"Look, you don't trust me," he said. "That's what this living together thing is really about. Maybe this needs to be over. Maybe we should take a break."

"A break?" She felt desperate. She wondered if there was someone else. "Are you kidding me?"

"Nope, starting now. So we're not together at the moment, and I'm gonna go watch the Yankees."

"God, you're horrible, Gabe. You're so self-ish."

"If I'm so horrible, why don't you fucking leave?" he said.

"No," she said. "I'm not leaving. Jesus. Let's calm down. We need to talk about this."

Sometimes this sort of fight — the sort where she accused him of lying, and he got all hot and indignant over the accusation, even though he had, in fact, lied — could fade quickly. But not today: He left the bedroom, and she trailed behind him into the kitchen. He screamed at her to go. She refused, and they were shouting louder and louder, until he actually grabbed her by the shoulders and shoved her toward the door leading to the outside hall.

"Gabe, let go of me," she gasped, her heart pounding. She thought of the baby. She wondered where Cunningham was hiding, that coward. Gabe's hands were too tight on her. She recalled the tender way he had touched her an hour before. Their most brutal fights always came on like this; quick, unexpected, and fierce.

"I don't want you here," he said.

"Too bad. There's something I have to tell you. We need to talk."

71

"I don't need to do anything. This is my place. Now go."

"Gabe — if you won't talk to me now, then it's over," she said, terrified.

"It's over," he said. He let the door close, and she stood alone in the hallway for a moment. Then he reemerged, and her heart soared pathetically until she noticed the suitcase in his hand, her aunt Ann Marie's old Louis Vuitton. She thought of how all of this misery was their own construction — there was nothing stopping them from ending it now if they really wanted to, just going back inside and watching some baseball, and being happy, making a family together, making a life. And yet.

"Have a great trip," he said, putting the suitcase on the ground at her feet and letting the door slam.

An old familiar feeling washed over her, the one she'd get every time they had a fight and she walked out of his apartment, slamming the door behind her; or every time she gave him an ultimatum that he brushed aside by telling her to leave. The act of leaving felt empowering. But then she'd stand in the lobby of his building for ten minutes, make circles around his block for twenty, hoping he'd come after her, feeling the weight of her gesture, her penchant for the proud and the dramatic screwing her as usual.

"You've got moxie, butterfly," her grand-

father used to tell her when she was a teenager.

Yeah, well. In the end, moxie always seemed
to come back and bite you in the ass.

KATHLEEN

Kathleen woke to the synchronized impact of a fat, speckled tongue running over her nose and a heavy weight pressing down against her right thigh.

"Get off me, you savages," she said, opening her eyes. They kept at it, the tongue now slobbering across her chin, leaving behind a trail of drool. Kathleen wiped it away.

"Okay, I'm up."

Mack and Mabel were full-grown German shepherds. He weighed eighty-two pounds, she weighed sixty-eight. But they danced about the bed like a couple of puppies, scratching her bare arms, mussing up the sheets.

"Cool it, you two," she said in a fake stern voice. When it came to business matters she could be tough, but she had never had a knack for discipline, not with Maggie and Chris, and not with her dogs.

They calmed down after a bit, lying side by side in the now empty spot where Arlo slept.

It was Sunday, but he had left at the crack of dawn to give an eight o'clock presentation to a town's worth of Junior Girl Scouts in Paradise Pines, two and a half hours north.

Mack and Mabel panted, despite the fact that the room was cool, a swivel fan aimed toward the bed. Kathleen felt momentarily sad. She had rescued them when they were days old, from a litter of pups someone found abandoned on the side of Route 128. What kind of person would do that? To this day, she couldn't fathom it. Now her babies were somehow fourteen years old and completely worn out from a few minutes' worth of play.

She rolled over and burrowed into Mack, who burrowed into Mabel, for a sort of three-way spoon. This was how they had slept every night before she met Arlo. When he came along, he insisted the dogs sleep at the far end of the bed or, preferably, on the floor. Which explained why Mack still snubbed him, even ten years later.

From the time she was a kid, she had had a fondness for strays and lost creatures. How many evenings had she taken home a dog she'd found wandering around, only to have Alice say she'd have to let the dog go? Kathleen would tell her mother fine, and then she would set him up in the shed out back anyway, with a bowl of water and the contents of her dinner plate and a soft blanket and the big flashlight they kept for hurricanes switched on to its highest setting. The next day, her father would help her post signs around town, and soon enough, someone would come along to claim their Toby or their Duke or their King.

Arlo could take or leave the dogs, but they had a policy of indulging each other's passions, no matter what. Hence the fact that she lived on a worm farm, and had once allowed herself to be filmed having sex while a concert recording of "Sugar Magnolia" played in the background.

Her ex-husband, Paul, was allergic to dogs. That should have been a sign right there. After the divorce, she adopted a retired greyhound named Daisy, who nobody liked, poor thing. ("I know how you feel," Kathleen would tell her when Alice came over and turned up her nose.) She had had at least one dog — more often two or three — ever since. The dogs were partly responsible for keeping her sane. The relationship she had with them was pure joy. No ulterior motives, no spite, just love and care and kindness, exactly the emotions she wanted to cultivate.

Kathleen rose from her bed now and went into the bathroom to pee. On the other side of the closed door, two wide mouths hung open, eager to start their day. It was almost ten. Arlo always let her sleep as late as she wanted, perhaps for his own well-being more than hers. She was definitely not a morning person. Lately she had been having trouble getting to sleep at night. She was stressed about the farm and all the extra work they'd taken on. And, even more than usual, she was worried about Maggie and the way the Kellehers were treating her.

Maggie and Gabe were driving to Maine to join Alice tomorrow. Kathleen often wondered why her daughter felt such a sense of belonging and trust when it came to their relatives. She herself felt nothing of the sort, especially now that her father was gone. She loved her family, in that way that you have to love your family. But it saddened her to see Maggie let down by them, over and over again. The latest was that obnoxious phone call from Ann Marie. Kathleen couldn't get it out of her head.

She made her way downstairs with the dogs underfoot. In the kitchen, she opened the back door, and they bolted out to begin their daily ritual of eating bluebells and terrorizing innocent butterflies. Kathleen stood in the doorway for a moment, as she did most mornings, taking it all in — the view of the mountains, the border of giant oak trees far off in the distance, their gorgeous flower beds (proof positive that their products really worked), the vegetable patch, and the two red barns separated by a swath of green, green grass. If you drove for a few minutes, you were in the heart of a vineyard, with grapevines in every direction.

Two dry drunks in wine country! That was how Arlo had described them to the group at their first Sonoma Valley AA meeting. Everyone laughed, since they too were part of that strange contradiction.

They had met ten years back at a meeting in Cambridge. He invited her to go for coffee and she said yes, despite the fact that he wasn't at all her type. Arlo was an aging hippie with shaggy silver hair who had spent his early thirties following the Grateful Dead. He had once revealed in a meeting that before he joined AA in 1990, it wasn't uncommon for him to down a bottle of whiskey and smoke three joints in a single day. He had never really had a job, outside of coffee shops and bars. Despite having gone through her own ugly addiction to alcohol, Kathleen was still on some level judgmental of drug addicts. And her father had always hated hippies.

But Arlo had been sober for four years when they first went out. He made her laugh. They both enjoyed meditation, though Kathleen thought he was more indulgent about it — it was all very *let the sun shine in* with him, whereas for her it was about staying rational and trying not to turn into her mother. She liked his passion for gardening, and the fact that he volunteered at a nursery. He told her he dreamed of running his own composting business one day, comprised of feeding trash to worms and making grade-A fertilizer from their droppings.

Arlo was six foot four and lanky. He was sensitive and mellow and kind, and when he laughed, the sound could shake furniture. People always fell in love with him. Well, people other than her family, but that was no surprise. Kathleen thought (she hoped) that Maggie genuinely liked him, and her sister, Clare, too. The opinions held by the rest of the Kellehers were irrelevant.

When people asked her what she did, Kathleen told them she and Arlo were in the vermiculture composting business and hoped they would not ask her to elaborate. In layman's terms, they sold live worms and a spray fertilizer known in the trade as worm poop tea to small and medium-size nurseries all over California. They always had worms at each stage of the process: worms being born, worms just taking their first infinitesimal bites of banana peel, and worms that had finished composting, leaving them with a magnificent pile of fertilizer to sift through. Their three million worms made three thousand pounds of castings each month.

They had bought the farm ten years earlier, site unseen, six months after they met. The house sat on five acres in Glen Ellen, a tiny farming town outside of Sonoma. They sold both their homes in Massachusetts to buy it, and with the addition of the money Kathleen had inherited after her father died, they could almost afford the place. Almost. Maggie had been alarmed when Kathleen first told her about the idea all those years ago, but after considering several hours of conversation and a thick folder's worth of research, even Kathleen's worrywart daughter had agreed that Arlo's plan had potential. He needed only the financing to get it off the ground, and someone to believe in him.

This year, the company was thriving. Arlo's special orchid tea had been written up in a national magazine about organic living and orders were through the roof. Best of all, they had been profiled in the *Los Angeles Times* and the *Sonoma Index-Tribune* that spring, leading to an account with a chain of gardening stores that had operations in three states.

Kathleen had surprised them both with her business savvy. It was her outreach that had earned them all the press. It had been her idea to work with local schools to get the steady supply of garbage necessary to run their company. She was even able to channel the pushy, Alice-like parts of herself into getting nurseries to take more product than they might have, or securing Arlo a better deal on bottling fees.

Her mother and her brother, Pat, made it clear that they still thought the whole endeavor was goofy and extravagant, never mind that Kathleen had turned a profit of more than two hundred thousand last year. She understood how they might have thought the idea was suspect in the beginning, but she wished that just once they could give her credit for her success.

She'd show them this coming year, anyway.

In the early winter, she was taking their business to the next level. The tenth anniversary of the farm was in November, and she planned to present Arlo with a surprise: a worm gin, which would potentially triple their monthly output. The gin cost twenty thousand — most small farms like theirs couldn't afford that. But she had carefully saved two hundred dollars every month since they had arrived here, no matter what.

She knew Arlo would be overjoyed, and when she pictured his reaction, she felt elated. Kathleen imagined car commercials from the eighties — a man gives his wife a Lincoln wrapped up in a big red ribbon for Christmas. Perhaps she'd be the first person to ever tie an oversize bow around a machine designed to mass-produce poop.

She stood in the middle of the kitchen for a moment, and then called the office in town where the orders were processed to make sure that a bunch of invoices had been sent out on Friday. She spoke to Jerry, their faithful assistant, who was there seven mornings a week. When she hung up, she glanced around at the room and sighed. The windows were streaked and the dishes stacked up. The trash was overflowing.

The entire house was a mess. She and Arlo could never manage to get the dirt out from under their fingernails, no matter how much they scrubbed. They left smudges on clothes and walls and book covers. There was dog hair everywhere. The bathroom probably hadn't been cleaned in months. She blamed it on the business, but really she had never been one for housekeeping. In theory she'd love a tidy home like Ann Marie's, but when she set that desire against all the other possibilities for what she could be doing if she weren't inside with a mop, well . . .

Kathleen put two pots of water on the stove to boil — a small one for her ginger tea and a large lobster pot for steaming the worms' food. One of many facts she had learned about worms along the way was that just because they ate garbage didn't mean they weren't discerning. They loathed orange peels, and weren't fond of citrus in general. They preferred their food soft and mushy, so when she had the time she over-steamed banana peels and vegetable scraps and hunks of carrot tops and apple cores before loading them into the worm bins.

She pulled a ginger root from the cupboard and set to peeling it in front of the window. Outside, the dogs were lying side by side in the grass. She chopped the ginger into cubes and dumped them into the pot, leaving them there to simmer. Then she returned to her spot at the table, soaking in the quiet.

She opened the newspaper, which Arlo had set out for her. She flipped past the front-page news and the Arts section, landing finally on the Sunday circular. She didn't clip coupons, but the women in her family had always been so obsessed with them that she could never shake the habit of looking them over, just in case there was something amazing to be found, though of course there never was. One ad offered free floss with the purchase of five tubes of toothpaste. As if floss had ever broken the bank for anyone. Human beings were strange about free stuff. Her mother was the queen of it — *I got four bottles of ketchup for the price of one,* Alice had bragged over the phone a few weeks earlier. Who needed four bottles of ketchup?

Kathleen made a point of speaking to Alice once a week, even though when she did this she often felt as though she had been roughly awakened from an exquisite dream. From this distance, it was easy enough to pretend her mother and the rest of the family didn't exist. Well, all of them except for her children, who she missed every minute.

Kathleen worried about her son, Chris, about what kind of person he really was. He didn't seem to have much ambition or enthusiasm: he drank a lot of beer and got into fights with his girlfriend, after which she ended up in tears and he ended up out at a bar with friends. In short, he was terrifyingly like his father.

She had to admit, at least to herself, that she felt jealous watching Pat and Ann Marie bask in all of Little Daniel's professional success. That kid seemed to get a promotion every year, while Chris could barely find work. Maybe if he had had a real father, it would be different. She wished she had seen it sooner, done more for her son. But Kathleen's attention had always been drawn more naturally toward Maggie.

Her daughter had turned out so well, despite Kathleen and Paul's best efforts at completely fucking up her life.

Kathleen had taught her to be her own person. When Maggie was a kid, wanting desperately to fit in, Kathleen repeated a single phrase to her, over and over: "Don't be a sheep." She wished someone had said it to her when she was young. She couldn't stand the thought of her remarkable daughter living out some ho-hum life like everyone else. And Maggie had taken this advice. She had made it as a writer in New York City, the sort of big, bold, independent existence Kathleen had realized too late that she herself wanted.

By the time she figured out that she was no

Kelleher, not really, that she didn't want to spend her entire life watching college football at Patrick and Ann Marie's every Saturday while the kids played outside and the women made pasta salad and talked about laundry detergent — by then, it was too late. She was married with two children. Discovering that you craved independence when you were a young mother was about as convenient and feasible as shooting a man in cold blood and then deciding you didn't feel like being a murderer after all. So she drank far too much and fought with her husband, and fought with Alice, and was generally an absolute mess. Once, she had stumbled drunk into Chris's first-grade classroom for a parent-teacher conference, scaring his teacher half to death. Most days, she had started drinking at lunchtime. She carried on like this until the spring she took her kids to Maine and really hit rock bottom. She knew now that sometimes a person needed to sink that low to be able to get up again, and she didn't regret it. She had changed after all that, and somehow become a woman she actually liked.

She got through the rest of her children's years at home by telling herself that once they were off at college she'd be free, and that had proven more or less true. In the meantime, she had focused on staying sober; she planted an organic garden in the backyard. She learned that yoga and long walks could help her relieve stress better than chardonnay, and that there was real value to knowing about herbs and vegetables and ways to heal oneself that didn't come in tiny plastic vials. Her father lent her the money to go to night school and get her master's degree, after which she worked as a guidance counselor in a private high school full of self-loathing overprivileged girls with eating disorders. She went on lots of dates, which Ann Marie and Alice thought made her the whore of Babylon. A mother shouldn't be sexual, God forbid. She should have her vagina sealed over with plaster and declare herself closed for business, no matter if she was thirty-nine years old and only beginning to realize who she was.

No one had told Kathleen about the dark parts of motherhood. You gave birth and people brought over the sweetest little shoes and pale pink swaddling blankets. But then you were alone, your body trying to heal itself while your mind went numb. There was a mix of joy and the purest love, coupled with real boredom and occasional rage. It got easier as the kids got older, but it never got easy.

"After I had you, I understood for the first time why people shake their babies to death," she had told Maggie on one of her long trips to New York.

"Thanks a lot," Maggie had said.

"Oh no, that's not what I meant," Kathleen

said. "It wasn't you — you were the best baby I ever saw. It's motherhood in general that makes a woman nuts. All those hormones rushing around inside you. You can't sleep. You can't reason with this little beast. Before I had kids, I thought those people who shook babies were monsters, with some sort of inorganic urge. Then I realized that the violent urge is totally natural. It's the stopping yourself part that's inorganic, that takes real work."

She wanted her daughter to know this, to have all the information up front. If she herself could have had that, so much of life might have been easier.

Kathleen's mother had never understood the value of sharing one's pain. Not for her own good, or for anyone else's. If Alice hadn't covered up her drinking, but had talked about it instead — the way it consumed her, the fact that it had caused her to drive them straight into a tree when they were kids — perhaps Kathleen never would have gotten into the same mess years later.

Kathleen and Maggie had a completely open relationship; she had made sure of that. They were best friends. It had just about killed her when Maggie went off to college in Ohio, and she was an adult then, a mother. And it was still torturous now, each time she went to New York for a visit and then had to say good-bye. Kathleen told her daughter everything and Maggie in turn could confide in her. Kathleen took great pride in this, though she knew Alice saw it as a failing.

Her phone vibrated on the counter. A text from Arlo: *A success! Heading home!*

He was always revved up after one of his presentations. He liked the school-aged kids the best, since there was no other segment of the population who appreciated conversation about feces and slimy worms quite so much. They called him Mister Worm Poop. On the occasions when Kathleen went with him, he'd introduce her to the crowd as Ms. Worm Poop. Arlo usually brought a couple thousand worms along each time he spoke to a crowd, which sounded like a lot, but amounted to only two pounds' worth. The children screeched with delight as, one by one, they got to dig their hands into the bins full of slithering creatures.

Kathleen was terribly proud of him. How many people had a vision and actually saw it through? The business was the perfect reflection of their relationship. Arlo was a dreamer, an optimist, a big-picture guy. And Kathleen was a realist — she told it like it was. Together, they just worked.

She smiled now, and thought briefly of changing out of her drawstring pajama pants and Trinity T-shirt into something sort of sexy to surprise him, but what was the point? He had seen her naked a thousand times and she had seen him. She was pushing sixty, and he had passed it four years ago. The jig was up. That was what she appreciated about her sex life with Arlo — the refreshing feeling of not giving a damn. Not out of apathy but out of comfort. He was the easiest man she'd ever been with, sexually speaking. She knew it had lots to do with his warmth and kindness, but another part of it was a function of age. You stopped caring so much about every last lump and bump at some point, you just flat-out refused to suck in your gut while you were trying to have an orgasm. At least she did.

She had spent years worrying about what men thought of the way she looked. These days the only person whose opinion on the matter really touched her was her mother. Alice had a pathological need to discuss everyone's weight.

Kathleen had last seen her at Christmas, five months earlier.

"You're looking good, you've lost a few," Alice had said then.

Kathleen hated the fact that she felt pleased by this. "We've been taking a lot of hikes in the mountains. Our place backs right onto the foothills. Remember those pictures I sent you?"

It irked her that her mother had never visited. The only ones who had were Maggie and Clare.

"That's good," Alice had replied. "Make sure to keep it up now. Winter always makes everyone want to stay inside and get fat."

"I live in California," Kathleen said.

"So? They don't have winter there?"

"No, not really."

"Anyway, keep hiking."

It was a special kind of curse, having a beautiful mother, when you yourself were just average. Alice had gotten a reputation in the neighborhood when Kathleen and Pat and Clare were kids for being rather odd because she ran around the block several times every morning in a tennis dress and trench coat. Twenty years later, this would be called jogging. Alice was still careful about her figure, and she never let Kathleen forget those thirty pounds she'd gained after her own two kids. She had gotten more active when she met Arlo, but her love of sweets and cheeses kept her plump.

"You have such a pretty face," Alice would say. Or, before Arlo came along, "I can say this because I'm your mother. You might find it easier to meet a nice fella without that enormous gut."

Kathleen had felt tremendous amounts of guilt for leaving Massachusetts, but most of the time she was glad to be free. Here, no one based their knowledge of her on what she had done thirty years ago. No one made her feel guilty for missing a family party, or tried to tell her that by declaring herself an alcoholic she was only looking for attention. People in the organic gardening world and at AA treated her with such respect and even admiration that she almost felt like an imposter.

Kathleen didn't like the person she became when she was around the Kellehers. She reverted to that weaker version of herself, the bitter woman she had been in the past. She grew short-tempered and easily angry; she lashed out at the slightest provocation. There were things she was deeply ashamed of and they would not let her forget.

Arlo believed that life was short and you should interact only with people you enjoyed. He also believed that loyalty was earned — sharing a bloodline didn't mean you had to be close. He saw his father and brother every few years, when one of them happened to pass through the town where another one lived. When Kathleen asked him, he said he felt no remorse about seeing them so rarely. "We have nothing in common," he said. His brother was an accountant with three kids who had moved to Des Moines when he met his wife, a former Iowa beauty queen.

"What on earth would we talk about?" Arlo asked, as if most people interacted with their families for the riveting conversation.

The Kellehers considered it sacrilege that

Kathleen went back East only twice a year. Whereas Arlo, when she told him she was planning another trip to Massachusetts, just said, "Why are you such a glutton for punishment?"

Needless to say, he had not been raised Catholic.

"You're lucky there's no such thing as Presbyterian guilt," she had told him once when they were discussing it.

"What do you mean?" he asked.

"Never mind."

"It would be a different story if you didn't let them get under your skin like you do, but they seem to make you so stressed," he'd said. "Around your family, you never act like yourself."

"I know," she replied, though sometimes she feared that the opposite was true, that her real self was that dark, angry one she had shoved in a box years ago, the one that emerged only when she was home.

When Ann Marie called a few days earlier, she practically bit Kathleen's head off about the fact that Maggie and Gabe were going to Maine for just two weeks this year. Ann Marie had apparently decided that Alice couldn't be alone up there for the remainder of June, despite the fact that Alice was alone all fall, winter, and spring, and managed just fine.

Kathleen tried to take deep breaths and to

channel Arlo's calmness. Her sister-in-law was only a person, after all. Why shouldn't they be able to talk rationally? But when it came to Ann Marie, Kathleen could never help it. Her temper flared. Did Ann Marie actually think she could drop her business, her dogs, and Arlo, because she said so?

When Ann Marie realized that Kathleen refused to entertain this ludicrous concern, she told her to forget it. Translation: it wasn't a big deal in the first place; Ann Marie had just felt like making a fuss. This was typical of her sister-in-law, who might as well have had the word MARTYR stamped across her forehead.

Ann Marie called Alice Mom. Kathleen still found this jarring, more than thirty years after the first time she heard it. Who, if given the choice, would want to claim Alice for a mother?

Back in Massachusetts, Kathleen had occasionally pretended in her head that her AA sponsor, Eleanor, was her mother. When they sat in the coffee shop below Eleanor's apartment in Harvard Square, Kathleen would drink tea and talk about her day — another fight with Paul over money for the kids, another meeting with Chris's principal that had ended in tears.

Eleanor had always told Kathleen that a sober life didn't mean a perfect life. You could do everything right, and still, things might not turn out the way you'd imagined. She herself had been married three times. The first two were booze-soaked, dramatic, passionate, stupid. Just like Kathleen's marriage to Paul had been. Just like she feared Maggie and Gabe's relationship might be, if Maggie didn't end it soon. Eleanor's third marriage was a sober one. Even so, it ended in divorce. Then she met a wonderful man, and two years later she was diagnosed with terminal breast cancer. You never knew where a day or a year would take you. Kathleen hoped Maggie understood that.

She also hoped that Ann Marie wouldn't try to guilt her daughter into staying on in Maine any longer than she wanted to. She herself certainly wasn't going to mention Ann Marie's silly concern to Maggie, but who knew? Ann Marie might have already gone straight to the source. When it came to the Kellehers, Kathleen hated that Maggie was an adult now — someone they could call or advise whenever they wanted, independent of her.

"Technically, June is your month," Ann Marie had said during that call a few days earlier, as if this was a prize that had been bestowed upon Kathleen, instead of what it really was: the raw end of the deal.

It hadn't escaped Kathleen that when Patrick decided they should divvy up their time at the cottage, he had assigned the worst month to her. Who wanted to take their summer vacation in June, when it wasn't even hot yet?

She had called him one night a few years ago after an AA meeting focused on standing up for yourself rather than internalizing your anger.

"You gave me the worst month for Maine," she said into the phone.

"Excuse me?" Patrick said. "You haven't even been there in years."

It was true that she had avoided the place ever since her father died, wanting to forget both the good and the bad of it. With few exceptions, she had never really liked going there. The act of vacationing in beautiful surroundings always made her turn melancholy, as if in the absence of external annoyances to displease her, she suddenly realized her own inferiority — her fleshy upper arms, the sun spots that had worsened with age, and just how little she wanted to return to her day-to-day life. (No doubt, picturesque Sonoma Valley would be intolerable if not for the fact that her industry was worm shit.)

But this wasn't about that. It was about fairness, about her children's rights too.

"Anyway," her brother went on, "I wasn't aware that there was a bad month to take a free beach vacation."

Oh, he had to add that word, *free*. As if she wasn't well aware that he had been paying the property tax in Maine since Daniel died. (Only to stake his claim to the place, she assumed.) Never mind that he hadn't offered her a penny after her divorce, when she and her children were practically on the verge of living on the street.

"It's easy to be generous when you have cash coming out of your eyeballs," she said, which was actually kinder than Patrick deserved. The truth was he wasn't generous, not toward anyone who actually needed help. He never donated in a big way, or volunteered, or assisted anyone outside his immediate family. Patrick was the kind of person whose worldview made him think he was the whole, rather than a part of it.

"What is that supposed to mean?" he said in such a measured, almost jolly, tone that she wondered if he was standing among his rich yuppie friends, maybe in the middle of a cocktail party or a round of golf.

The Serenity Prayer floated through her head: *God, grant me the serenity to accept the things I cannot change, the courage to change the things I can, and the wisdom to know the difference.*

Why was it so much easier to buy all that in an AA meeting full of strangers than when she was interacting with her own family? She had learned techniques for coping with almost anyone, but the Kellehers still aroused such anger in her, such terrible behavior.

"What was I thinking?" she said, unable to stop herself. "Questioning the boy king, Jesus Christ himself. Apologies."

She hung up. There was a pull from inside her then, which she recognized as the urge to have a drink. She sat with the feeling for a moment, letting it be, observing where it manifested itself in her body: smack in the middle of her chest.

The resentments had piled one on top of another over so many years, so that Kathleen couldn't think of her adult brother's arrogance without remembering in anger how her parents had sent him to an expensive Catholic boys' school while she and Clare went to public school, how Alice had always bent over backward to tell him how gifted and smart he was, though she had never done this for her daughters.

Alice had grown up poor, and though she had raised her children middle-class, she always let it be known that she still thought she deserved better. Not the rest of them, necessarily. Only her. She put on airs and was ridiculously vain about her appearance. She thought of herself as some sort of sophisticate trapped in a world that wasn't her own, even though in fact she was a Dorchester girl from a working-class Irish family, who knew hardly anything about the way life worked.

Kathleen had often joked with her sister,

97

Clare, that their mother liked Pat's wife better than either of them because Ann Marie was an imposter, just like Alice.

Even in college, her sister-in-law was unabashedly square for the most part. Before he met her, Pat had a bit of a wild streak — smoking lots of dope, bed-hopping all around St. Mary's. When he met Ann Marie, she gave him the full June Cleaver treatment. Pat was on the golf team, and Ann Marie actually organized bake sales so the team could get matching jackets, as if she were his mother. Pat bragged about this revolting fact when he came home that Christmas, and Alice had put a hand to her heart and said, "She sounds positively wonderful."

Ann Marie came from a part of Southie that Alice had always referred to as "the wrong side of the tracks," but like Alice herself, when asked where she grew up, Ann Marie would fudge it a bit. "Right on the Milton line," she'd say, even though there was no line between Southie and Milton. When they met her, her brother was in trouble with the police and had recently disappeared. He was an underling in the Winter Hill Gang and he had dabbled in all kinds of crime — run drugs, trafficked guns to the IRA, and possibly even helped to murder a businessman in Oklahoma in the mid-seventies. It was Patrick who had told Kathleen all this. Ann Marie herself would never acknowledge such a scandal.

Ann Marie wanted so badly for everyone to think she was a goody-goody even though deep down she was no different from the rest of them. The only time Kathleen had ever seen her truly let loose was when she visited Pat and Ann Marie in South Bend after they had graduated college. Pat was killing time that summer, waiting for business school to start. Ann Marie was waitressing and making noise about getting a nursing degree, though she never actually did it. One night during her trip, Kathleen drunkenly watched from the backseat as a twenty-year-old Ann Marie pulled off her blouse and stuck her head out the car window, bellowing "Hey Jude" at the top of her lungs, hammered beyond comprehension. *"Na-na-na-nananana!!!"*

Pat was behind the wheel, probably ten beers into the night himself.

"Get your hot ass back in here," he said, pulling at his then-girlfriend's back pocket.

"No-no-no-nononono!!!" Ann Marie screamed, to the tune of, well, just guess. A few minutes later, she slid into her seat and then over to Patrick in only her bra and skirt, licking his ear as if Kathleen weren't there. The next morning, Ann Marie said sheepishly, "I hope I didn't do anything too disgraceful last night. I really have no memory of it. Pancakes?"

Kathleen would never forget it. Later, she

wished that she had thought to take a picture. She dreamed of mailing it to Alice without a note or a return address.

Even back in college, Pat and Ann Marie acted like perfect angels around their elders, a practice that irked Kathleen to no end. As soon as they were married, Pat straightened up in earnest, and they turned into a couple of pod people. Once, in Cape Neddick, when the kids were small, Ann Marie had had one too many glasses of rum punch, and proudly divulged to Kathleen that Pat was the first and only man she had ever slept with. As if women who saved their virginity were somehow better than the rest; as if anyone was keeping score.

When Ann Marie addressed you now, she'd say, "How are you doing, good?" as if to direct you toward the correct answer: *No negativity, please. It's distasteful.* Kathleen thought that if she would only show some sign of weakness, some signal of being human, then she might stop being so hard on her sister-in-law. But after thirty-something years, that seemed unlikely.

Ann Marie used the family's place in Maine as a sort of status symbol to impress her vapid country club friends, which, Kathleen knew, was why she and Pat had built that showy house next door for Daniel and Alice. Ann Marie probably kept a file on which pieces of furniture to buy for which rooms in the

Maine house the second Alice croaked.

She spoke mostly about numbers — volume, distance, temperature, price — having nothing more interesting to talk about than the fact that it was seventy-four degrees in April, or that her mother was turning eighty-one this year; or how absolutely insane it was that red bell peppers could be priced at four dollars a pound.

Ann Marie had her children believing they'd been born to a saint — a sexless, guiltless saint, who might need a bottle of white wine to get through a stressful day, as long as no one was watching, but hey, what was wrong with that? She cooked elaborate dinners for Pat every night, even if she was going out, as if he was incapable of using the stove. She took classes in flower arranging and cake decorating.

Kathleen worried about Ann Marie's older daughter, Patty. It pained her to see the poor girl always in a state of panic, no doubt wondering how the hell she might ever measure up as a mother or a wife. Kathleen often thought of letting Patty in on the secret that many people thought her mother was insane. She had wanted to rescue her from that stifling home when she was a kid, but now Patty had gone the way of so many young women — she was trying to do it all. She was a lawyer and the mother of three small children by the time she turned thirty.

Kathleen's brother and sister-in-law were grandparents! She tried not to think about it, since it was an uncomfortable reminder of how horrifyingly old they had all become. Her pulse quickened, and not in a good way, when she entertained the idea of her children bearing children of their own.

Kathleen had never liked the way Ann Marie treated kids, no matter how maternal everyone thought she was. She'd bake cookies with them after school and take them ice-skating and make clothes for their dolls, putting other mothers to shame in that way. (Some women were created to make other women feel like shit about themselves. Ann Marie was one of them.) But she also controlled every move her children made — she told them what to wear, which classes to take, who they should and should not date. She wouldn't let them have so much as a goldfish in the house even though they begged for a puppy, because she couldn't stand the mess associated with pets. Fiona, her youngest, had wanted to play the tuba in the high school band; Ann Marie insisted that the piccolo was more appropriate.

Who could say what Ann Marie's children might have become if they'd been allowed to just *be*?

Kathleen remembered an afternoon when Chris was small — he couldn't have been more than five. She had left him with Ann

102

Marie while she took Maggie to a doctor's appointment. Arriving to pick him up, Kathleen found her son curled up in a ball in Ann Marie's front hall, crying.

"What happened?" she asked, and Chris uttered those unforgettable words: "Aunt Ann Marie hit me."

Kathleen's anger unleashed, she marched toward the kitchen, where Ann Marie stood at the counter, wiping it down with a sponge.

"You hit my child?" Kathleen shouted, startling Little Daniel, who was playing with his trucks on the floor.

Ann Marie smiled, and said, as if by way of explanation, "He was talking back. I kept telling him to be a good boy and sit down, and he kept throwing a fit. Then he hit Little Daniel with a Tonka truck, very hard. I think it's going to leave a mark."

Kathleen raised her voice even louder. "So you decided to hit him to teach him that hitting is wrong?"

"It was hardly a *hit*," Ann Marie said faintly. "I spanked his bottom with an open hand. I'm sorry."

Kathleen knew Ann Marie could not stand conflict. Already her eyes were welling up. Good.

"Let me make this clear," Kathleen said. "Open hand, closed hand, whatever — you may never touch either of my children for any reason, ever again. Got that? If you do,

I'll report you to the authorities."

Later that night, her sister, Clare, called. "I heard you're considering turning Ann Marie in to Social Services," she said. "Apparently at this very moment she's trying to pick out the right potpourri for her prison cell."

"Who told you about it?" Kathleen said. "Oh, let me guess."

"Indeed. Alice told me to tell you to apologize."

"Apologize!"

"You're too hotheaded. No one knows where you get it. And apparently you take Ann Marie for granted. She's the best babysitter you'll ever get, as far as our mother can tell. You leave your kids with her all the time, but don't accept that she's their aunt, not some sort of hired help. Oh, and also, according to Alice, kids need a slap every now and again. It's good for them."

"Well, take it from the mother of the year."

"Why I'm now in on this, I have no idea."

"Why the hell does Ann Marie always run to Mom?"

"Because she's the daughter Alice never had."

Kathleen had forgiven Ann Marie or, if not forgiven her exactly, she had not mentioned the incident again. They were a foursome back then — Patrick and Ann Marie, Kathleen and her husband, Paul, frequently going to outdoor concerts at the Hatch Shell together, driving up to Maine, taking the kids to the Marshfield Fair, or out to dinner at Legal Sea Foods. And much as she hated to admit it, it was true that Ann Marie sat for her kids often, probably two or three times a week, while Kathleen was never asked to reciprocate. (Ann Marie had her own sisters for that, and anyway, she didn't have a job.) Even though Kathleen didn't find Ann Marie particularly interesting, smart, or enlightened, they were family. It was impossible to stay distant for long.

A few years later, it was this sort of closeness that Patrick used as an excuse for why he had helped Paul cover up his affair.

Two nights a week for a year, the two of them, her husband and her brother, had claimed they were together — Tuesday night poker, Friday night Kiwanis meetings. Paul was gone other nights, too, inexplicably coming home after midnight, never bothering to give Kathleen an explanation. She sensed that something was happening, but she stuffed the feeling down deep, wanting and not wanting to know.

One Friday night after she put the kids to bed and downed half a bottle of red wine, she called Ann Marie, to ask if they'd be going to Alice and Daniel's for a barbecue the next day.

Ann Marie turned her mouth away from

the phone and said, "Honey, are we going over to your mom's tomorrow?"

"Tomorrow?" came Patrick's unmistakable voice.

"What's Pat doing there?" Kathleen had said. "I thought he was at Kiwanis."

Ann Marie might have said something convincing if she wasn't such a dimwit — *He has a cold,* or *Patty had a ballet recital so he skipped the meeting* — but instead, she was silent for a moment, before saying, "What do you mean? Pat's not here. I was talking to Little Daniel."

Kathleen took a deep breath. "You're full of shit, Ann Marie. Now do you want to tell me what's going on, or do you want to put Pat on?"

Ann Marie's voice quavered. "I think you'd better take it up with your husband," she said. "I'm sorry."

Kathleen was still awake when he came in, the rest of the wine gone. She sat at the kitchen table, watching *Letterman* on the black-and-white set, waiting for the back door to swing open.

"You're up late," he said when he saw her.

"How was Kiwanis?" she asked calmly, though her heart was racing.

"Eh, dull," he said. "But we went for a few beers after and had a pretty good time."

"Did my brother mention a party at my

106

parents' house tomorrow?" she asked.

"He might have," Paul said tentatively. "I honestly can't remember now. I love the guy, but he never shuts up, you know? He rambled on so much tonight, I can't remember half of it."

Kathleen drummed her fingers on the table. "Don't lie to me," she said.

"What?" he said, taking a beer from the fridge.

"I know where you were," she said.

"What are you talking about?"

"My brother told me everything," she lied. "He told me all about her."

Paul squinted. "Lower your voice," he said. "The kids are sleeping."

"Oh! The kids. The kids!" she yelled. "Now you're worried about the kids?"

"You're drunk," he said. "I can't talk to you like this."

"You're pathetic!" she said. She could tell from his face that she had rubbed him raw with that.

"Fine," he said. "There's someone else. Is that what you want to hear? Pat and Ann Marie saw us out once — a million years ago. It was his idea, you know, the Kiwanis crap, the poker. I wanted to tell you, flat out."

Kathleen was stunned. "Well, aren't you a sweetheart?" she said.

He had been looking straight at her, practically glaring, but now he turned his eyes to a spot behind her, and his face broke into a big fake smile. Kathleen followed his gaze. Maggie stood there in the doorway in her cotton nightgown, her eyelids still heavy from sleep.

A string of painful revelations followed, and Kathleen drank more with each one: Paul had been seeing the other woman for over a year. During that time he had loaned her ten grand, but he hadn't paid his own mortgage in nine months and now the bank was ready to foreclose. Kathleen might have suspected an affair, but she'd had no idea about the money. Her father offered to help, but there was nothing to be done. In March, they lost the house.

At her father's urging, Kathleen took the kids and went to the cottage in Maine.

She fell into a fog that spring. She would forget to feed Maggie and Chris their dinner, or she'd lock up the cottage and climb into bed early, only to realize a while later that her children were still outside playing on the beach.

It was her father, as always, who saved her. He came to Maine from Massachusetts one night and gave her the same ultimatum he had given his wife decades earlier: find a way to stop drinking, or he'd take the kids away.

"Remember how much your mother frightened you," he said, the first and only time he had ever put it that way. "How on earth can you sit here and do the same to Maggie?"

That had been enough to get her to her first AA meeting. She drank again three days later, a quarter of a bottle of gin. Drunk and desperate, she called Paul, begging him to come back. She woke up horrified and went to another meeting the next morning. She hadn't had a drink since.

Though Paul was the one who had cheated, her family — besides her father and her sister, Clare — acted as though Kathleen were to blame for their marriage coming apart. Patrick said Paul would outgrow the affair, that they should try counseling, try *everything,* because divorce was plain wrong. That was why he had helped Paul cover it up, he claimed, because their family meant too much to let this destroy them. Kathleen suspected that, as usual, he was thinking only of himself: no member of the Kelleher clan had ever gotten divorced, and Pat took a certain weird pride in that.

Alice insinuated that perhaps Kathleen was to blame for Paul's infidelity, and said that she couldn't walk away from a perfectly good marriage.

The funniest part of her mother's defense of her ex-husband was that Paul had never liked Alice. He had taken to calling visits to her house "Escape to Bitch Mountain." He was unfailingly polite to her face, but that was only because she terrified him.

109

■ ■ ■ ■

The first time Kathleen took Paul home to meet her parents, the four of them were sitting around the kitchen table eating spaghetti when someone knocked at the back door. Through the window in the door, Kathleen could see her uncle Timmy and his wife, Kitty. The previous Thanksgiving, Kitty and Alice had gotten into a screaming fight over the proper weight of a turkey meant to feed twenty people. Alice thought her sister-in-law was accusing her of being cheap. She had hardly spoken a word to Aunt Kitty since. Or, for that matter, to her own brother, who was being punished for marrying such a monster.

Alice came from a family of six siblings and Daniel was one of ten. Kathleen had forty-two cousins altogether. When she and Pat and Clare were growing up, their house was a revolving door of people. You might be sitting down to dinner on Sunday, and Uncle Jack and his wife and seven kids would come bounding in, and Alice would sigh and whisper, "Fill up on the potatoes." Kathleen always hated this, and vowed that when she had kids of her own (no more than two!), her little family would be snug and solitary, an island unto themselves.

Now Aunt Kitty gave an exuberant wave

and Paul instinctually waved back. It was a normal reaction when you were in a suburban kitchen on a Sunday night and a little gray-haired lady was smiling at you through the window, but Alice hissed, "Paul, don't look at them! Pretend we're not in here."

Paul chuckled, and then, seeing the serious look on Alice's face, he turned to Kathleen, confused.

"Mom, they can see us," Kathleen said, not looking up.

"Be quiet and they'll go away," Alice whispered. "You don't show up at someone's door at dinnertime unannounced."

In fact, their relatives did this all the time, but now Alice had something against Kitty, and she couldn't let it drop.

"Who are they?" Paul asked in a hushed voice.

"My brother and his wretched wife," Alice said. "Don't worry, they'll get the hint."

They looked down at their plates and kept eating. Kitty knocked harder, as if they might not be able to hear from just a few feet away. She jiggled the doorknob, but it was locked.

"Jesus, Alice, enough already," Daniel said finally. He rose from his chair and went to the door, ushering them inside.

"Hey, you two," he said in his usual cheerful tone. "Hungry? It's spaghetti night."

"Gosh no, we wouldn't want to impose!" Kitty said.

111

"Sure you would," Alice said tartly. "But knowing me, there won't be enough."

"That's my Alice, always a lady," said Kathleen's uncle Tim. "How about a beer?"

Alice didn't move to get him one, so Uncle Timmy opened the fridge himself and pulled out a Schlitz. He was a funny, kindhearted guy, a lot like Kathleen's dad. He had once told Kathleen that he was the one who introduced Daniel and Alice, back during World War II.

"We were visiting with Kitty's cousins a few blocks over and thought we'd stop in and say hi," he said. "And don't worry, because they fed us and we're full to the gills."

"Good, because as you can see, we have company," Alice said.

Timmy raised an eyebrow. "Kathleen and her boyfriend qualify as company?" he said.

Alice still hadn't risen from her chair.

"Daniel, I didn't slave over that stove so you could eat cold food," she said. "Sit down!"

He sat.

Paul drank several beers at dinner. Kathleen couldn't blame him. On the drive home that night, he said, "Honey, I love you, but I am scared shitless of your mother."

Any other girl might have been insulted, but Kathleen felt drawn to him more than ever in that moment. It was so easy for Alice to fool people — most strangers thought she

112

was simply delightful because she was pretty, larger than life. But Paul knew better right away.

"Please promise me you're not gonna become her," he said.

"Jesus, I promise," she had said. "If I do, you're completely within your rights to kill me."

ANN MARIE

Ann Marie was up early, even before the alarm. The room was silent, and through the sheer curtains, she could see that the streetlights were still on. She looked at the clock on the nightstand: five fifteen. Her whole body fluttered with excitement. She closed her eyes tightly, thinking of children on Christmas morning.

She got to her feet and slid into her slippers and robe. There was a lot to do before she left, so she had better hop to it. She had vacuumed all the carpets before she went to bed, and emptied the dishwasher. She usually gave the whole house a good cleaning on Sundays. But today she would be away until late afternoon at least.

It was finally June second. All spring she had been counting down the days until the Wellbright Miniatures Fair. For the first time in twenty-five years, the English festival was coming across the Atlantic for a United States tour, beginning right here in Boston. She had been reading online about the different exhibitors for weeks. She planned to attend a ten o'clock workshop on how to wire your dollhouse with real electric lighting. She had already picked out a chandelier for the dining room, with opaque bulbs that looked like pearls.

After the workshop, she would take her time walking from stall to stall, finally seeing in person the objects she had long coveted through a computer screen. Minnie's Minis from Staffordshire made the most gorgeous little cakes, with frosting that looked like real marzipan, and tiny ceramic strawberries on top, each berry no bigger than the head of a pin. A slice of cake could even be removed to show the chocolate and raspberry filling inside.

Puck's Teeny Tinies produced intricate silver beer steins, the size of your pinky nail. She thought one of these might be a funny tribute to her husband, Pat, and the trip they'd taken to Germany a few years back.

Home Is Where the Heart Is was her favorite company. She probably spent eight or nine hundred dollars a month on the website. And now perhaps she'd get to meet the owners — Lollie and Albert Duncan, a married couple who had put themselves on the map with kitchenware items, almost all of which Ann Marie had purchased (gorgeous spatulas and whisks, a blueberry pie baked in a beer bottle cap, a stainless-steel fridge that hummed with the help of a single D battery).

At the end of the day, if she could keep her nerve up, she'd bring some of the photographs she had snapped to the Judges' Circle booth, and submit them in the annual Dollhouse Designer Showcase. Winning was a long shot, she knew that. Most of these people had been competing for years; some were even professionals. But when she looked at her photos, she could swear she was staring at a real house, not a replica. Pat said he agreed completely.

She had gotten interested in dollhouses a year ago, with the intention of decorating one for her granddaughter. She bought a Victorian kit in a toy shop — three bedrooms, with a wraparound porch. Ann Marie spent a week lovingly putting the house together, piece by piece. She painted the outside a pale yellow with white trim. She hung curtains using a hot glue gun and scraps from her sewing basket — heavy green floor-length velvet in the living room, short red-and-white gingham in the kitchen, a fabric covered in multicolored polka dots in the nursery. Next, she added furniture: little blue-and-white painted bunk beds and a matching crib. A white rocking horse with silky hair. A toy chest. What looked like a real Kohler toilet in the bathroom, and fluffy hand towels she had made by cutting a facecloth into two-inch strips

116

and sewing a white ribbon around the edge. She bought a sofa and an armchair for the living room. A grandfather clock. Side tables. A canopy bed for the master bedroom. A full kitchen set, complete with pots and pans, and teensy boxes of Cheerios and Tide.

She sometimes sat with a cup of tea and stared in amazement at her creation for half an hour, or longer. By the time she completed the project, she couldn't bear to give the dollhouse away to the children, who would treat it like just another toy. When her granddaughter, Maisy, visited and brushed her grubby fingers against the white bedroom rug in the dollhouse, Ann Marie — known for her patience, especially with youngsters — had said in a rush, "Wash your hands first!" Afterward she felt silly, but it wasn't such a ridiculous request.

The kids teased her about her new pastime, everyone but Little Daniel's fiancée, Regina, who said she thought the dollhouse was beautiful. Regina was a sweet girl. She had been baptized and confirmed at Gate of Heaven in Southie, the same as Ann Marie. Of course, she *had* to be nice, since she was an outsider wanting into this family. Ann Marie knew how that went.

She had had plenty of hobbies before — scrapbooking and flower arranging and even quilting for a while. But nothing had ever grabbed her heart like the dollhouse. When she was growing up, her mother had run a motley household, with people in and out all the time, women from the neighborhood always clustered around the table playing cards, drinking whiskey, smoking cigarettes, filling the kitchen with gray clouds of cigarette smoke. They talked loudly over one another. Most of their sons were derelicts, bound for prison. If they were smart, like a few of her cousins had been, they became cops. Once in a blue moon, one of them made it to the mayor's office or city hall. Those ones were remembered the longest, them and the criminals. (The Bulger family — perhaps the most famous in the neighborhood — had raised one of each, a major politician and a crime boss.)

Ann Marie's own brother, Brendan, had gotten caught up in it all. They called him a mobster in the newspaper, but it seemed an overblown word. He was only a baby, doing what he was told. They said he had helped Whitey Bulger murder a man, and maybe it was true. But when Ann Marie thought of him, all she could envision was a boy in short pants, sitting in the grass at Castle Island, with Boston Harbor stretched out in front of him, and the gray buildings of Southie behind. In her memory, he was eating a hot dog from Sullivan's, his very favorite treat. His face was smeared with ketchup.

No one had heard from Brendan in twenty

years now, at least as far as she knew.

From a young age, Ann Marie had vowed to marry someone from outside of Southie, someone with a bit of money in his pocket. She wanted to create a life with order and beauty to it. She was the first in her family to go to college, putting herself through St. Mary's in the hope that she might find a nice Irish boy from Notre Dame. Patrick was exactly what she had wished for, and when she met him she worked hard to make him see that he needed her, that it was time to say goodbye to all the other girls.

When her mother met the Kellehers, she said they were lace curtain snobs as far as she was concerned, but Ann Marie ignored her.

Until recently, she thought she had done well. But the uncertainty of raising three children could wear on her, even now — especially now. When she thought about that unpleasant business with Little Daniel and his last job, when she thought about Fiona, she wondered if she was somehow to blame for all of it.

Where were her children at this moment? Were they wearing seat belts? Did they still believe in God? Did they understand not only *how* to keep house, but why? Had she done enough? Could a mother ever do enough?

She padded down the hall, careful not to

make a sound as she passed by the door at the top of the stairs, even though she knew Pat could sleep through a tornado.

They hadn't shared a bedroom since Fiona went off to college ten years earlier. At first, it had been a temporary thing: his snoring kept her up nights, and she wanted a break. But time passed and it felt comfortable, really, to be able to spread out, to not have to elbow him every hour and tell him to roll over onto his side. They went on that way, neither of them ever suggesting that they return to sharing a bed.

Ann Marie had seen an entire episode of *Oprah* devoted to the topic: *What happens when a couple starts sleeping in separate bedrooms?* But it didn't bother her. That part of their marriage was done, that was all. She still loved her husband. They had a beautiful home and three wonderful children. They got along fine and had loads of friends to socialize with, and they never fought. That was better than a lot of people could say.

No one knew about the sleeping arrangements. They still slept together when the kids came home, though there had been one embarrassing incident when Fiona brought a couple of friends from Trinity for Thanksgiving, and found the bed in the guest room rumpled and unmade. Ann Marie improvised, and told them that she had spent a night in there the week before, when Pat had a bad cold.

"He insisted, so I wouldn't catch it," she said in a rush. "I can't believe I forgot to change the sheets."

"Watch it, lady, you're really starting to slip," Fiona said jokingly, suspecting nothing.

In the kitchen, Ann Marie flipped on the overhead light and ground up some coffee beans that a client of Pat's had sent as part of a gift basket. She shook them into the coffeemaker, taking in the rich scent. She added water from the pitcher in the fridge.

She had pulled out her collection of Belleek china yesterday and set the tea service on the counter, in preparation for a tea party with little Maisy tomorrow. Ann Marie would bake scones, and tell her granddaughter about the village in Ireland where the dishes and the teapot were made — each of them creamy white, and etched with elegant shamrocks. She ran her finger over the stack of saucers.

She sat at the table, where she had left her list of chores the night before, as she did every night, with one column for her (*Defrost lamb for P., pick up prescriptions, get the pool guy to come look at the filter*) and one for Pat (*Send money to Little Daniel, get your oil checked?, pay water bill*).

She flipped the list over now and realized

what it was: the country club newsletter, reminding them to weigh in on new admissions.

"Rats, rats," she said. The deadline was tomorrow and they had almost forgotten. She made a silent vow to write only in notebooks from now on.

At the top of the page were the words: *The individuals listed below and their families have been proposed for membership. The Admissions Committee and the Board of Governors invite your comments, which will be held in confidence.*

Her eyes scanned the list: William and Karen Eaves she did not know. Tom and Susan Devine she had met once or twice, but she didn't have any information about whether they'd make good members for the club.

She and Pat had sponsored the Brewers that past summer. They were longtime neighbors of theirs who had more recently become friends. Ann Marie had been amazed at some of the comments people sent in anonymously. Someone said Linda Brewer's bathing suit had been too tight at the Prospectives Picnic. Someone else said she took too much from the buffet. They got in anyway. Ann Marie and her husband had been members since 1987: no one would dare challenge a nomination of Pat's.

It had been his idea to invite the Brewers along to Maine. Usually they brought George and Laney Dwyer for the Fourth of July week, but this year they were off to a family wedding so Pat and Ann Marie had to search for a backup plan for the first half of the trip. (The second week, Patty would be there with Josh and the kids, and then Ann Marie and Pat would leave and Patty's brood would have a week on their own. For the last week of the month, Ann Marie would drive up every two or three days to check on Alice until Clare and Joe arrived in August.)

"Why don't you guys go by yourselves? Have a romantic getaway before your grand-children arrive and shatter the peace and quiet," Patty had said when Ann Marie told her the Dwyers couldn't make it.

"That doesn't sound like much fun," Ann Marie said. "We're by ourselves all the time."

She had planned to ask her sister Susan, even though Susan's husband, Sean, was a real know-it-all, and Pat resented him because he never offered to pay for dinner, always do-ing that awkward, labored wallet reach, unfolding every bill as though he were in slow motion, until Pat couldn't stand it anymore and just said, "This one's on me, bud."

Susan always made sure to let Ann Marie know that Sean's plumbing business brought in plenty of cash. Since she was so intent on bragging about it, it seemed that he could at least pay for dinner every once in a while.

Anyway, Pat returned from work one night

in May and said, "I saw Steve Brewer at lunch and I asked if he and Linda wanted to join us for Maine. He said he'd have to check with her, but it sounded great to him."

"Oh, well, imagine a man checking with his wife before making a major decision," she said.

What was Steve thinking? Could this be a good idea, or was it too risky?

"A major decision?" Pat said, reaching immediately for a box of Cheez-Its on the counter.

She had meant to hide those. He wasn't supposed to be snacking between meals.

"Jeez, honey, it's not like I came in and told you we're moving to Tokyo."

"Well, what if I don't like the Brewers?" she said.

"You love the Brewers," he said.

"I know," she said. "You're right. I'm only teasing."

She hoped the guilt didn't show on her face.

Ann Marie had been fantasizing about Steve Brewer since the spring fling charity ball at the club in early April. She imagined the two of them getting to know each other better over long candlelit dinners, holding hands across the table. It was more about romance than sex — that part, she really couldn't imagine. But a courtship sounded perfect to her, something to transport her away from all her worries.

She could sense that he felt the same way. They had been together before that, at group dinners and block parties over the years. But they had never really talked one-on-one before. That night, he had asked her about herself: where she grew up, what she had done before having kids. ("I had a job in the restaurant business," she said, like always. It sounded better than saying she was a waitress. In college, she had wanted to be a nurse or maybe a teacher someday, but her first baby came before she got the chance, and Pat didn't think the mother of his children should have to work.)

His hand brushed hers as he refilled her water glass, and he left it there until the glass was full.

"What do you and Pat like to do for fun, other than come here to the club?" he asked.

She told him the usual — they drove out to Maine a lot, where they had a cottage. They took long walks and played tennis in the summertime. Then she told him about her dollhouse. Maybe she had had too much champagne, but she found herself getting as worked up as she might if she were talking to a fellow enthusiast.

"I've just ordered a tiny set of Hummels for the mantelpiece," she said. "They're very rare. Antiques."

"Miniature miniatures," he said with a smile.

"Exactly!"

"What got you interested in all of this?" he asked, sounding genuinely curious.

"My grandchildren," she said. "Or maybe it goes back further than that. Do you remember when Jackie Kennedy redecorated the White House, and then she led the camera crew through? *This is the gold room, this is the green room . . .*" She was using her best breathy Jackie voice.

He chuckled. "Yes! I remember that."

"It made me want to design my own perfect house someday," she said, only now realizing the connection. "Don't get me wrong, our real house is lovely, but with a dollhouse, everything stays pristine; there's no worrying about kids spilling grape juice or getting shoe scuffs on the floors."

"Well, that's really neat," he said. "Linda likes those little light-up porcelain houses at Christmas — you know the ones I mean?"

She felt slightly distressed at the sound of his wife's name, and she almost wanted to say that dopey porcelain Christmas figurines had nothing in common with dollhouse design. But she only smiled in response.

A few days later, a card arrived. It was a thank-you note addressed to both her and Pat. Inside, Steve had written: *Thanks for vouching for us at the club, you two. We promise not to make you regret it! Next dinner is on us. P.S. For your research on the gold room, the green room . . .*

Inside the envelope was a magazine, no bigger than a postage stamp. It was a miniature issue of *Life* from 1962, with a photograph of the young first lady smiling radiantly in a pillbox hat on the cover, over the caption "Mrs. Kennedy's White House Makeover."

Ann Marie held the magazine between her thumb and index finger, and felt herself tingle with excitement. She placed it on the side table in the dollhouse living room. She didn't mention it to Pat when he got home.

Ever since, when they hugged hello, even in front of their spouses, Steve always held on a moment or two longer than seemed natural. He never failed to compliment her dress or to ask her about her charity work at the church, and he was genuinely interested, not just making conversation like everyone else. Sometimes in the afternoon, when she was cleaning the house or about to start dinner, Ann Marie would pour herself a glass of wine, go to the computer in the home office, and type in the website address for Steve's law firm, Weiss, Black, and Abrams. When the page loaded, she knew exactly where to click — the staff directory on the left. There was his picture, a broad smile on his face, above the words *Stephen Brewer, partner.* Below that was a description of his areas of expertise, which she had practically memorized by now: *Stephen Brewer is a partner in the firm's Boston office. He has extensive experience with securities offerings and transactions in the United States by non-U.S. companies, representing issuers as well as underwriters.*

"What does your husband do?" a new neighbor had asked Linda at book club one night.

Linda had responded, "He's a lawyer."

"Oh? What kind?"

Linda shrugged. "The kind that works all hours."

Everyone laughed, but Ann Marie rolled the words around in her head as if they were part of some secret language she shared with Steve — *Securities offerings and transactions, that's what he does. His experience is extensive.*

Ann Marie had been looking forward to their annual Cape Neddick trip for months. At some point in the dead of winter, she had written the word *MAINE* on a Starbucks napkin and stuck it up under the visor in the Mercedes, so that all she had to do was flip the mirror down and there it would be, a reminder of what awaited her.

After Pat announced that the Brewers were coming along, her vision for the trip shifted, and now she was excited in new ways. Nervous too. She had already bought four new Lilly Pulitzer dresses and a white cashmere cardigan, imagining Steve's face when he saw her in them. She pictured herself and Pat riding caravan-style with Steve and Linda Brewer close behind. The four of them would stop at the Press Room in Portsmouth for a glass of wine and a lobster roll, and then they'd drive on until they reached the cottage, with its familiar old wood beams and the smell of the ocean drifting through the window screens. Later, while Pat and Steve drank a beer and got settled, she and Linda would drive to the gourmet grocery a couple miles up the road in Ogunquit and load the cart with white chocolate cookies, Brie and salami and olives and water crackers, croissants and organic apple juice, raspberries, and a case of champagne. She would make her signature trifle, even though it wasn't the right season. At the neighborhood Christmas party several months back, Steve had said it tasted like heaven.

They weren't supposed to go to Cape Neddick until July first, four weeks from now. But a few days earlier, their plans had changed. More to the point, her sisters-in-law had shirked their responsibility and somehow, as usual, Ann Marie was the one who got left holding the bag.

On the previous Friday, Alice called to chat after supper.

"Clare's ignoring me," she said.

Ann Marie was sliding plates into the dishwasher. "What? Why?"

"I don't know! I was watching that *Broadway Babies* series on PBS and there was a whole piece on the history of gays in the theater. Terribly interesting. Apparently there are lots of them, even that one who wrote *West Side Story.* So I happened to mention this to Clare —"

Ann Marie poured herself a glass of wine from the open bottle on the table. This was not a topic she wanted to discuss. She didn't much want to know what Alice thought about having a gay grandchild.

At least she figured that was where her mother-in-law was going. Clare's son, Ryan, starred in all those musicals. Sitting through a single one of his performances, knowing that Clare usually saw his plays several nights in a row, Ann Marie thanked God that none of her children had gotten the acting bug, but had instead gravitated toward sports (Little Daniel) and Irish step dancing (Patty and Fiona). You could bring your knitting along to a hockey game and not seem rude, and she loved the sound of Irish music; it was a connection to her ancestors that stirred something in her heart.

"Anyway," Alice went on, "I asked her — joking really, that's all — I asked if she ever worries about Ryan being exposed to that, and you know, getting it. She snapped at me,

'Mother, homosexuality is not asbestos; you don't get *exposed* to it, you don't *get* it.' "

"Plus, Ryan has that sweet girlfriend," Ann Marie said. "He's been with Daphne since freshman year. I wouldn't worry, Mom."

Little Daniel jokingly referred to Ryan as a "fairy boy." But he was just kidding around. It was because Ryan had worn green tights in a production of *A Midsummer Night's Dream*.

"I know it," Alice said. "That wasn't even what I meant. But since then, I've called Clare twice and she hasn't called me back. I realize it's her busy season, with all the First Communions and confirmations. But still, is it too much to ask that my own daughter return my calls?"

She was getting riled up now. It made Ann Marie nervous when Alice acted that way. Best to change the subject.

"How are things up in Maine?" she asked.

"Chilly, but nice," Alice said. "There are four bunnies living under the cottage porch, I think. A mother, a father, and two babies."

"Oh, sweet."

"Sweet my foot. They're eating my tomato plants, and the green beans," she said. "I'm trying everything I can think of to get rid of them. My garden is gorgeous this year. I don't want them wrecking it."

"Better than last year?"

"Yes! I finally tried that fertilizer poop spray of Kathleen's. God help me, I think it actually works. Though why can't they come up with a snazzier name for it?"

Ann Marie laughed. For years, Kathleen had been sending Alice her fertilizer products and Alice had been hiding them in a box in her basement rather than use them, because she didn't understand how worm feces could be a step up from Miracle-Gro.

"Good question," Ann Marie said. "When do Maggie and Gabe get there?"

Ann Marie wasn't fond of her niece's boyfriend; he seemed a bit too slick for her. And she had heard from Alice, who heard from Kathleen, that he might be mixed up in drugs. She had always been glad her own children had the good sense to date decent people. Patty had married a sweetheart, Josh. And Little Daniel had found Regina, a real doll.

Her youngest, Fiona, was almost thirty and still off in the Peace Corps in Africa. She was a passionate girl, serious in her convictions, which had always made Ann Marie proud, though in recent years she had begun to think it was high time for Fiona to come home and settle down.

Having a child is one way to save the world, she had written in a letter to her daughter last year. She told Pat this after she mailed it, and he said affably, "White wine and letter writing might be a bad mix for you."

Then, this past winter at Christmastime,

Fiona had asked Ann Marie and Pat if she could take them to dinner, just the three of them. Ann Marie was delighted. It seemed a very grown-up thing for Fiona to do, and she could be terribly childish at times. Ann Marie wore her sweater with the poinsettias embroidered across the front. She imagined Fiona was going to tell them she was coming home at last, but instead she uttered those unforgettable words: "As you probably know, I'm gay."

She had thought over the events of that night so many times since — had she been naïve not to know what was coming? At the table after Fiona's announcement, Pat had said he had suspected as much, and that he was happy for her. Just like that. Ann Marie had cried. She felt awful about it now, even all these months later. Back at home, Pat cried too. But at least he had the good sense not to let Fiona see.

"I don't know when Maggie will be here," Alice had continued. "Kathleen basically told me to mind my own beeswax when I asked her that simple question. Should be any day, I suppose."

Then she casually mentioned that Maggie was coming up to Maine for only the first two weeks of June. After that, Alice would be by herself until Ann Marie and Pat arrived in early July.

Ann Marie was peeved. She had been told

early in the spring that Maggie was going to be there for the entirety of June. (Who had said so? She couldn't recall.) A huge part of the reason Pat had created a schedule for the cottage was so that Alice would never have to be alone up there for long. It wasn't simply a pleasure, going to Maine; it was a responsibility that they all ought to share. Alice was an old lady, whether her daughters were willing to accept this fact or not. Her memory was failing. She didn't always remember to turn off the television or take her keys out of the ignition. She needed looking after.

"Mom, let me call you back," Ann Marie said.

She was booked to the gills that second half of June. She had to make the arrangements for a luncheon she was helping to organize at the club. There was a meeting of the Lucky Star Fund on the twenty-seventh. She had purposefully overbooked herself in June so that she could be at the cottage in peace in July. She wasn't sure she'd have the time to go up to Maine and check on Alice.

Two whole weeks. What kind of women left their aging mother alone for two whole weeks?

At the end of June, Clare and Joe would be on their annual buying trip in Taiwan. (Who knew Taiwan was the place to go for vestments, statues of the saints, and crucifixes on silver chains? And how could two atheists run a business based on peddling sacred objects? If you asked Ann Marie, there was something blasphemous about it.)

A ball of anger lodged itself in her stomach. She didn't usually do things like this, but without thinking, she dialed Kathleen's house in California.

"Hello," Kathleen said flatly. She had probably recognized the number on her caller ID. Ann Marie was surprised that she even picked up.

"Hi there, it's Ann Marie," she said, feeling uncomfortable, wanting to lighten the mood even before there was a mood to lighten. "How are you, good?"

"Sure," Kathleen said. "I'm good."

"Great. Well, I wanted to call because Alice told me that she's going to be alone up in Cape Neddick for the last couple weeks of June, and I feel like that's a long stretch of time for her to be by herself. It's bad enough she's alone all May, but Pat and I have at least tried to see her on the weekends this past month. I have a very busy June ahead of me and I can't be going back and forth."

"Who asked you to?" Kathleen said.

She tried again, putting it simply. "Alice will be all by herself for two whole weeks."

"Ann Marie, she's by herself all year long."

"Well, yes, but it's different when she's here in Massachusetts, close by us. I worry when she's all the way up there at the beach."

"It's an hour and a half drive," Kathleen said. Then, her voice intensifying, "Why are you calling me with this?"

"Technically June is your month at the cottage. I thought maybe we could come up with a plan to —"

"You realize I live three thousand miles away," Kathleen said, like this absurd fact might have slipped Ann Marie's mind.

"Yes," she said. "But I thought maybe Maggie or Christopher could go, even if it's only for a couple extra days to break things up."

"They have lives. They can't pick up and go to Maine for half the month."

As if she and Pat didn't have lives. "No one said half the month."

"Maggie and Gabe will be there for the first two weeks. I think that's plenty," Kathleen said.

Ann Marie could feel her resolve fading. As always, her eagerness to end this unpleasantness would override her desire for what was fair. She had been raised in a family full of fighters. When she met the Kellehers, she was all too familiar with the slamming doors, the accusations, the hang-ups at the other end of the line. Familiar too was the manner in which they always seemed to find their way back to one another. She recalled a time when she was a teenager and her mother discovered that her father had had an affair with her childhood friend. Ann Marie's mother had chased her husband down the block with a frying pan. Afterward, she swallowed a bottle of pills, hoping to die. Two days later, it was as if it had never happened. He came home and sat down to supper, and after a few drinks, she was in his lap.

Then there were deeper grudges, the ones against family members who simply disappeared after some unforgivable altercation — their photographs taken down from the shelves, their names never uttered. It seemed ludicrous to her.

Ann Marie promised herself that when she got older, there would never be so much as a raised voice in her home and that she would conduct herself with decorum at all times. Pat agreed — he said his sisters, especially Kathleen, were so intent on dredging up the past that he'd already done more than his fair share of reflecting and arguing by the time they met. Kathleen was the sort of person who labeled herself an alcoholic for sympathy, and perhaps also as a way to criticize the rest of them for enjoying a drink every now and again.

(Last Thanksgiving, when Ann Marie opened a bottle of champagne to serve with the pie and said, "Just a taste!," Kathleen had said, "You know, people in families with a history of addiction should treat that stuff like rat poison.")

"If you're so concerned, why don't you go?"

Kathleen was saying now, and Ann Marie wished she had the guts to say, "Why don't you or your sister try lifting a finger for your own mother for once?" Instead, she did the usual — caved to Kathleen's demands, and jumped to pick up the pieces.

"Never mind," she said. "You're right. Forget I brought it up."

Kathleen softened her voice a bit before they said good-bye. "Sorry if I sound like an asshole. I'm overwhelmed right now. The farm is crazy. We're busier than ever."

The farm. Ann Marie and Pat found it terribly amusing that Kathleen always referred to her home that way, as if she were raising chickens and cows and goats. A filthy garage full of worms was not a farm, it was just a spectacle.

Kathleen continued, "And I'm worried Chris is floundering."

"I'm sorry," Ann Marie said, and she genuinely felt it. "I'll tell Little Daniel to give him a call. They should talk more, maybe have a beer sometime. Or lunch! Lunch would be good."

"Thanks," Kathleen said.

"It sounds like you have a lot on your plate," Ann Marie said. "I'll handle Alice, don't worry."

She cancelled her plans for late June and arranged to head to Maine on the twentieth, her frustration rising as she made each call,

138

every single excuse. She normally sat for her grandkids on Tuesdays and Thursdays after school, until Patty or Josh got home. Now they'd have to find a sitter.

Her sister Tricia sounded annoyed when she shared the news: "I thought you were taking Ma to her appointment on the twenty-second," she said.

"If you do it this one time, I'll take the next three," Ann Marie said. "And I'll do all the runs for her medicine until I leave."

She wanted to call Kathleen and say, "By the way, I have my own mother to think about too." But of course she wouldn't do that.

It wasn't that Ann Marie minded caring for Alice; she didn't. She was brought up to believe that you looked after your elders, no matter if they sometimes tried your patience or weren't exactly who you expected them to be. No one was exactly what anyone else expected.

She genuinely enjoyed spending time with Alice, though her mother-in-law could be a handful. For all her good manners, Alice occasionally behaved atrociously in public: She wrapped up dinner rolls and butter pats in a napkin and smuggled them out of nice restaurants, as if she were a pauper. Recently, while they were having lunch at Papa Razzi, Ann Marie had returned from the ladies' room to see her stuffing a saltshaker into her purse.

Ann Marie was forever afraid of ticking Al-

139

ice off, since her mood could change on a dime. Though for the most part, they had fun together, getting their hair done, driving into Boston to shop. Alice was an interesting woman; her daughters never seemed to appreciate this. She followed the news and read lots of books and always had an opinion on the latest PBS series. She reminded Ann Marie of herself in this way — they had both come from humble beginnings and made something of themselves. Ann Marie's own mother, God bless her, just sat in front of the tube all day, every day, watching some faraway bishop say Mass over and over on a loop. She had always been a caretaker: From the time Ann Marie was six years old, there was some bachelor uncle or down-on-his-luck second cousin living with them. Her mother never said no to anyone. Now she was morbidly obese and diabetic, two facts that filled Ann Marie with shame.

Alice had stayed lovely and petite. Without ever telling anyone as much, Ann Marie considered her a sort of role model in the looks department. She met with her personal trainer, Raul, three times a week. And she and Pat walked six miles on the track behind Newton North High School every Sunday after church.

Alice came to dinner at their house on Sunday nights. Ann Marie made sure to send her flowers from Little Daniel on her birthday and Mother's Day. (The girls were good about handling those things themselves.) Pat took care of the taxes and the insurance on the property in Maine, and he looked after the place during the winters — driving up every so often to make sure the pipes hadn't frozen, or that trees hadn't fallen during a storm. No doubt, the Maine property would be passed down to them when the time came. And then they would be able to go up to the beach for the whole summer, uninterrupted.

Clare and Kathleen didn't appreciate the place anyway.

Her own sisters were Cape Cod people. Early in her marriage, Ann Marie had resented the fact that Pat's family's house in Maine kept her away from them all summer, but over the years she had come to love Cape Neddick. Besides, her sisters always had to rent.

And her children were devoted to Maine now — they wouldn't want to go anywhere else. They each had their favorite beach and lobster shack (Fiona and Little Daniel loved Barnacle Billy's. Patty and Josh and the grandkids liked Brown's.) They had their traditions. The kids always drove out to the twenty-four-hour L.L. Bean store in Freeport at eleven at night, and climbed up the giant two-story hiking boot out front, just for fun. In the early morning hours, they fished for bass off Popham Beach in a boat owned by one of Pat's clients. They went to a Portland Sea Dogs game, and Little Daniel brought his glove along to catch foul balls. Even now, they still devoted one night every summer to sitting in the car eating cold chicken sandwiches and watching grizzly bear cubs climb into the Dumpsters behind Ruby's Market. This always gave Ann Marie a little scare, though Patrick said his own father had taken him on foot when he was a boy, and it was perfectly safe.

Next spring, Little Daniel would get married at the Cliff House in Ogunquit, as Patty had. (His fiancée, Regina, had been hesitant, citing the cost, but Ann Marie made it known that Pat insisted on paying.)

Ann Marie imagined a time in the future when she and Pat would replace Alice and Daniel in the big house, while next door in the cottage her children and grandchildren slept, safe and sound.

A couple days passed, and Ann Marie got used to the idea of heading to Maine early, even a bit excited. She had never been anywhere by herself for so long. Life had been rather heavy lately, between Fiona's news and Little Daniel's horrifying mishap at work, which she could hardly bring herself to think about. Some time away might do her good.

She wasn't leaving for three more weeks, but she had already started making a mental list of what to pack: the good beach chair and umbrella and a bag full of sunblock and magazines, and the sweater she had started knitting for Maisy with a pony grazing on the front. She'd be looking after her mother-in-law, no doubt. And there were plenty of wedding chores she could tackle for Regina while she was there. This wasn't a vacation. But still, hopefully she'd get to spend at least some time relaxing by the ocean.

Pat had to stay behind and work, but it was only ten days. In July, he and the Brewers would join her, as planned. She imagined greeting Steve Brewer at the cottage door with a pitcher of iced tea.

"You were so sweet to come up here by yourself and be with your mother-in-law," he'd say. "Can't really picture Linda doing that."

She would wave the idea away, saying, "Oh my gosh, it's nothing. Come on inside."

ALICE

On Sunday morning after Mass, Alice sat out on the screen porch and sipped a Bloody Mary while she waited for her laundry to dry. She stayed very still, keeping her eyes peeled for the rotten rabbits.

She had put a two-foot wire fence around her garden and the rabbits had simply dug right under it. She had gathered human hair from the local barbershop and spread it in the dirt, and they had continued undeterred. She had sprinkled the plants with ground pepper, which rabbits apparently detested, and they had chewed away as if it were honey glaze. A woman in line at the nursery in York had said that the only real way to get rid of them was cayenne pepper mixed with water. The clerk had piped up that that tore up their bellies and was awfully cruel, but now Alice thought she might have to try it. She refused to feel bad about this, since those creatures were nothing but rats with cotton-ball tails. They had gotten two of her tomato plants and the green beans. She'd be damned if they were going to get the best of her summer flowers too. And so, she kept a careful watch.

It was Memorial Day weekend, the unofficial start of the season. In town the streets were bustling with hopeful tourists, peeking into shops that had just opened and dipping their toes into the still frigid sea. But here on Briarwood Road, it was as quiet as it had been a month ago when Alice arrived, still wearing her winter coat.

Up here, most days she didn't see anyone from noon onward unless she drove out to the Shop 'n Save on Route 1 or walked up the road to Ruby's Market, where she could get a whole jug of wine for five dollars. (*Rotgut,* her son, Patrick, had pronounced the stuff after taking one sip, but Alice thought it was fine.) On occasion, she went to Ruby's even if she didn't need anything, just to make conversation with Ruby and Mort, the elderly couple who owned the place. Their favorite topic was how disappointing young people were nowadays, and Alice had plenty to say about that.

Ruby and Mort were real Mainers, salt of the earth. Everyone in the southern part of the state knew them, and they knew everyone. They were pleasant enough to Alice, unlike some. The Kellehers would always be considered outsiders here. Six decades of summers meant nothing to the locals. Occasionally Alice might be driving along and someone, recognizing her face, might give her a hearty wave. Then his eyes would land on her Massachusetts license plate, and the arm would drop.

Ruby was only twenty-nine when Alice first met her back in the forties, and she had struck Alice as old even then. Almost sixty years later, she and her husband still opened the doors each morning at seven. Mort still stocked the high shelves with canned peas and corn and paper towels. He had always worn a flannel shirt over dungarees, still did. In the fall, he went moose hunting — they'd eat the spoils all winter, selling the best cuts of meat right there in the market. Ruby washed the whole store with bleach every morning. She baked brownies and hermits and cookies, and wrapped each one in blue cellophane, putting the lot of them in a basket by the register. Ever since their kids moved out, they had had a cocker spaniel named Myrtle. When one Myrtle died, another nearly identical Myrtle popped up in her place.

Alice envied Ruby and Mort, still having each other. When she visited them, she liked to imagine that no time had passed, even though she knew old age was creeping in, in ways that were manageable, if annoying. She had trouble remembering the names of women at her golf club and the priests at her new church. She could picture the wallpaper that had hung in her childhood bedroom, but she no longer recalled the titles of books she had read three months ago. She was eighty-three years old, and hadn't had a real health problem to speak of in her life, though she had seen so many specialists in the past few years — one for her sight, another for her hearing, another still for her crummy knees — that every time she had an appointment, she'd joke to Ann Marie, "I'm off on yet another date with a handsome young doctor." She was what they called a lucky one, which meant that she got to watch every person she loved — her parents, all four of her brothers, her husband — grow old and die, without even the luxury of a little senility to dull the pain.

Alice's mother had been a lucky one too. She had lived to be ninety-six. Each morning in those last, dark years of life, her mother would dress in a good skirt and flats, and read the *Globe,* circling the names of the dead men and women she knew, from grade school, from the neighborhood, from church — her peers and first loves and even friends of her children, who were, impossibly, somewhere around seventy years old. (Alice's father, dead more than twenty years by then, had always referred to the obituaries as the Irish sports page.) Near the end, her mind began to slip. She would show up to the funeral parlor in Upham's Corner and forget which wake she had come for, so she'd stop into each of them. Some mornings she would go there without even looking at the paper, reasoning that she was bound to know someone being buried that day, so she ought to go down to Kearney Brothers and pay her respects. When she finally died, hers was one of the smallest funerals Alice had ever seen — only Alice's brothers and their kids and grandkids, Patrick and Ann Marie and their brood, Clare and Joe, Kathleen and Maggie. She didn't have a single friend on earth to see her off. She had outlived them all.

At Alice's house in Canton, junk mail still arrived addressed to Daniel. It amazed her how a person's death had no impact on these practical matters. The bank statements and pay stubs and old report cards he had filed so neatly in his basement office didn't vanish into the ether as she wished they would. Nor did the plaque he had received from the insurance company when he retired, or the framed picture of President Kennedy, both of which he had hung in a place of honor over his desk. All of it remained, a constant reminder: *He existed, then he didn't. The world spins on, indifferent to the mess.*

There were parts of living alone that she hadn't gotten used to, probably never would, even though her husband had been dead nearly ten years. She would never learn to cook for one — she still poured the whole box of spaghetti into the pot, or made a five-pound roast that took hours to brown up, with onions and potatoes and carrots and turnips in the pan, despite the fact that she didn't care for vegetables.

She would never get used to the quiet that settled in gently, pleasantly once the kids were gone, and then with a ferocity after Daniel. They were married for forty-nine years, and every day of it, much as she loved him, Alice wished he would shut the hell up. He read the headlines of *The Boston Globe* out loud over breakfast. He sang "The Wild Colonial Boy" and "Molly Malone" in the shower. He whistled as he raked the lawn, and bellowed into the phone when the grandkids called, telling them the same jokes he had told his own children decades earlier: *A three-legged dog walks into a saloon, hobbles up to the bartender, and says, "I'm lookin' for the man who shot my paw."*

Or: *Well, Chrissy, I'm afraid your grandmother's Irish Alzheimer's has gotten quite advanced — she's forgotten everything but her grudges.*

Now she missed that joyful way he had, especially in summertime, when she was up here at the beach.

Alice took a sip of her Bloody Mary, taking care not to let the condensation drip onto her blouse. That was another thing she hadn't gotten used to: dressing down in play clothes, like old ladies were supposed to. She never changed after Mass. Today she wore white linen slacks with a white shell, a black short-sleeved silk jacket, and sandals. She still put on a full face of makeup every morning, same as she had when she was nineteen and working at the law firm in downtown Boston. She still wore her hair in a straight bob, and colored it black. (Her daughter Clare had once commented in front of company that it was a miracle how Alice's hair had actually gotten darker as she aged, instead of turning gray like everyone else's.)

No one, not a soul, knew exactly how old she was. Her children loved to say that one of these days they would sneak a peek at her driver's license, but none of them had ever dared, as far as she knew.

As a girl, she had watched the old women of Dorchester, with their thin hair and their housecoats, and vowed that she would never become such a frump. She hadn't. But now she looked at her three granddaughters — none of them much older than thirty — and realized with alarm that she felt the same way about them. They were slobs. When they came to Maine later in the summer, they would trounce around the property in sweatpants and bikini tops, letting their little bellies flop out. They'd tie their hair back while it was still wet, and never put on so much as a coat of lipstick. Ann Marie said that it was the beach that brought this out in them. But Alice could never be sure. Maybe it was true of Ann Marie and Pat's two daughters, Patty and Fiona, but if she came upon her granddaughter Maggie eating Sunday brunch at a café in Manhattan, she was willing to bet money on the same damp ponytail and cutoff jeans Maggie traipsed around in up here. Both Patty and Maggie had inherited the Dolan leg from Daniel's mother's side — thick, shapeless stumps that were as wide at the calf as they were at the knee. Fiona, the one who cared the least about her looks, had been Alice's only lucky granddaughter, possessing the long, lean legs of a Brennan woman.

Through the open door that led into the house, she heard the dryer buzzing into the off position. Alice emptied her glass and then went to the laundry room.

The AM radio was playing, though she didn't remember turning it on. A young-sounding fellow whose voice she rather liked was interviewing a professor about post-traumatic stress disorder among the soldiers coming back from Iraq.

"It's more important than we can possibly say to get it out, to talk to someone," the professor said. He cited a study.

Alice shook her head. It was all the rage

now to talk, talk, talk, though she couldn't
see how talking about real tragedy did much
good. What would her brothers have to say
about it? Probably that those boys ought to
man up and shut up, though now she'd never
know for sure.

Her daughter Kathleen had once said that
the fellas who came back from World War II
might have been saved if only they had been
allowed to tell a professional about what they
had seen. But that's not how they were making men back then, and so you ended up with
an entire generation of sad secret-keepers and
angry drunks. Alice thought that sounded
more like Kathleen's cohorts than her own. A
cousin Kathleen was fond of from Daniel's
side, Bobby Kelly, had returned from Viet-
nam to a party full of balloons and ice cream,
looking like Errol Flynn in uniform, and
then, two days later, shot his wife and himself
to death.

What Kathleen never seemed to understand
was that World War II was a different sort of
war. Everyone was a part of it, every last boy
you knew. Now, when Alice asked her grandchildren if any of their old schoolmates were
fighting in Iraq, they all said no in an incredulous sort of way, as if she were an idiot to
even ask. When she was young, there was a
sense of pride among so many of the boys, a
sense of duty and honor. They wanted to
serve their country. They wanted to fight.

When Alice's brothers came home on leave, they were always trying to set her up with their buddies from the army and the navy. Alice went along with it, though she never took those boys seriously. She had no interest in settling down with any of them.

Back then, people said she was beautiful. They complimented her narrow waist and long legs. She had bright blue eyes, fair skin, and dark hair that reached halfway down her back. She wanted to be Veronica Lake — adored by all for her beauty, her art, her general joie de vivre. She believed that she deserved better. That she, Alice Brennan, was one of the most special young women out there, just waiting for someone to take notice.

The six Brennan children had grown up more or less poor, but they could always be certain of having a roof over their heads and a bit of food on the table. Then, when they were teenagers, the Depression hit. Their father's job with the police force came and went and came and went and came and went again. He alternated between working long hours, terrified of the certain lean period to come, and being at home, unemployed, angry, and drunk. He had often spoken to them harshly, especially when he was drinking, and he had hit them as kids, Timmy and Michael always getting the worst of it. Alice remembered bruises, blood. Before they were born, there had been a baby named Declan. One night, their father fell asleep with the infant in bed beside him. At some point, he unknowingly rolled over onto the child and smothered him. He was devastated. "Never the same," their aunt Rose had said. He blamed himself, and perhaps as a sort of penance or protection, he never bonded with another one of his children.

Alice's parents prided themselves on being the first homeowners in their family: both sets of grandparents had immigrated to Boston from Ireland, both grandmothers died young, and the grandfathers were mostly useless. Her parents had been raised in boardinghouses and the spare rooms of charitable but not altogether kind cousins. Now they grew frightened of not being able to make the mortgage each month.

Everyone in the family had to contribute. Alice and her sister, Mary, babysat for all the neighborhood kids, making fifty cents for a full day's work, which they then had to turn over to their mother for the Christmas club. Mary was better at it — she had infinite patience, and she actually liked children. Alice only enjoyed sitting for the Jewish ones, since their parents had money. The fathers worked all hours and the mothers just wanted to play mah-jongg in peace. So they'd send Alice and the children to the movies, always the movies. They handed out dishes at the

Magnet Theater in those days. A cup on Monday, a saucer on Tuesday, a soup bowl on Wednesday, and so on, no matter that hardly anyone had the food to fill them. Between the two of them, Alice and Mary got their mother five complete sets.

Their brothers took on odd jobs after school. Timmy waited tables and Michael cleaned floors at city hall. Even their mother worked for a time — selling fruitcakes and embroidered handkerchiefs door-to-door like a proper hobo. Alice burned with embarrassment at the sight, hating her father for letting it happen. Their mother had been a school-teacher before she married, but women were banned from teaching now, since so many men needed the work.

The four boys were made to move into one bedroom, so that the family had a spare room to let. Alice and Mary shared a tiny room already, so at first Alice was pleased to see their brothers similarly cramped together. But the lodgers who came were often frightening: Some cried and moaned over what they had lost. There were women with infants who shrieked at dawn, and men who drank and pawed at Alice and Mary on their way to the bathroom at night or scratched at their bedroom door late, whispering to them to open up and give a guy some happiness.

Mary would whisper back pleadingly from the other side of the closed door to those drunkards, telling them to get some sleep, sir, please call it a night. Alice would shoo her into bed, and then say gruffly, "Listen, you bastard, get away from here now or my father will cut you to pieces like he did the other one before you."

Their father had done no such thing. He'd hardly care if those men came in and dragged his daughters off by their fingernails.

Mary's eyes widened: "Gosh, you're brave!" she would say with a sort of awe.

At eighteen, Mary was older by two years, but even so, Alice felt protective of her sister. Mary was shy and sweet and well-behaved. She waited on their parents like a maid, considering it her duty. She even did Alice's chores sometimes. She wanted to have a dozen kids someday, and she didn't mind caring for their bratty brothers.

Alice, on the other hand, just wanted to be left alone. She loved to paint and draw. She could escape into a picture for hours if allowed. Whenever she could, she sat by the window in their shared bedroom at the top of the house, painting the street below, their mother in the garden, Mary wearing her Christmas dress and muff. She'd hold her breath, waiting for someone to yell out and ruin her peace — telling her to do something, wash something, mend something.

Her brothers protested when they were left in Alice's care. She made them eat their dinner one at a time, all off the same dish she had eaten from first, so that she'd have to wash only one plate instead of five and would have more time to sit on the stoop and chat with Rita, or to go upstairs and draw.

"The food's always cold by the time the plate gets to me!" Timmy would complain to their mother, who would then give Alice a lecture on the virtues of etiquette and cleanliness.

"You'll make an awful housewife with an attitude like that," her mother said once, and Alice felt almost proud. She couldn't imagine herself as a mother or a wife. She had never taken to children, and she had too often been forced to care for the ones in her house — to look after them, to feed them, to scold them. By the time she reached high school, she was done with raising kids. She had begun planning her escape. Or, if not planning it exactly, then wishing for it.

No respectable lady Alice knew had done anything but have children. The only single adult women in their family were nuns, or Aunt Rose, who had divorced her rumrunner husband and moved to New York City, where she now worked at the makeup counter at Macy's in Herald Square. Their father referred to Rose as "that selfish harlot" whenever her name came up. He wouldn't allow their mother to see her. Alice wanted to run away to New York and live with her aunt, but

Rose had told her in a letter that she slept in a boardinghouse full of derelicts and drunks, and that was no place for a young girl.

When she was fifteen, Alice was painting pictures with a babysitting charge one evening when his mother came home from work. Mrs. Bloom was a sophisticated Jewish lady with dark hair and eyes, and rumor had it she had married down. She and her husband owned a frame shop in Upham's Corner, which always seemed to close for the day right after lunch.

She put her purse on the table that night and looked at what Alice had done.

"You're very talented," she said. "You know that? With the proper training, I think you might really blossom."

Alice perked up at the comment, but immediately shrugged it off. She imagined her father and brothers laughing when she told them. She left the picture behind on the table when she went home, to show how little she cared.

The next time she came by, Mrs. Bloom said, "I showed that painting of yours to my husband, who may not have an ounce of business sense in his head, but what he does have is an excellent eye. He agreed with me. You're good, Alice. You should study art."

Mrs. Bloom gave her a quarter to take the boy to the Gardner Museum on the trolley. He fussed all afternoon, but Alice hardly noticed: she had never been there before and she was mesmerized. A plaque that hung in the vestibule revealed that Isabella Stewart Gardner, a great patroness of the arts, had built a mansion in Boston made to look like an Italian palace. Later, her home was turned into a museum and named in her honor. She had been painted by John Singer Sargent, and she threw the most elaborate dinners, full of great thinkers and artists. She traveled the world and studied in Paris.

This was the sort of woman Alice wanted to be. Right then and there, she decided that one day she would become a famous painter. She would attend college in Paris and sell her paintings to wealthy Frenchmen. She could get an apartment on the Seine and live in peace, without a hundred little boy feet rumbling around downstairs.

A year passed. The Bloom family moved to Brookline. When they left, Mrs. Bloom gave Alice a beautiful sketch pad with a real leather cover. "Don't give up," she said.

Alice promised she wouldn't, though Mrs. Bloom's tone sent a chill through her. She filled the entire pad with drawings in the span of two weeks. She went to the library and checked out the only biography they had about Isabella Stewart Gardner, which she had already read twice. She used her brother Timmy's card to get another book, which she had no intention of ever returning. It contained black-and-white photographs of Paris. Alice ripped them out and stuck them to the wall behind her bed.

Her main window onto the existence of the single gal was through a woman named Trudy, who she had never actually met. Their household and Trudy's apartment shared a party line. Most every night you could pick up the phone in the Brennan family kitchen and hear Trudy gabbing away on her sofa in Beacon Hill. Sometimes Alice's father would need to call in to work, and he'd try eight or nine times, eventually saying, "Pardon me, miss, but this is not a private line. Please keep your conversations brief or I'll alert the telephone company."

Trudy was undeterred and Alice was glad of it, since her favorite pastime was listening in. Mary said she shouldn't eavesdrop, but how could she resist? Trudy was better than any radio soap opera.

Trudy spoke to her girlfriends about all the dates she went on to fine restaurants, and the flowers her suitors sent the next day. She once went to an office party and ended up dancing on a rooftop in Kenmore Square with her married boss, Mr. Pembroke. She hated her hips and had allowed herself to eat only a hard-boiled egg on dry toast for each of the last fourteen days. She was going to Los Angeles in April if her stepfather would cough up the cash already. She had read a book called *Live Alone and Like It* and decided to decorate her apartment all in lavender and start stocking cocktail ingredients, even though some people thought it was tacky for a woman to do that.

Alice listened silently, taking it all in.

One night Trudy mentioned that Mr. Pembroke had brought her along to an art opening in the city, where paintings of naked ladies had graced the walls and waiters in white gloves had handed out tiny pickles and nuts.

"Honestly!" her friend had said. "Your boss is quite fond of you, isn't he? I guess he's just impressed with your typing skills."

"Those, and my impeccable manners," Trudy had said. "It must have been the childhood cotillion classes my mama made me go to."

Alice was tempted to speak up and ask Trudy what cotillion was, but instead she asked her sister, and when her sister didn't know, she asked the lady next door.

"Lessons to make you more sophisticated and polished," her neighbor explained.

Alice stole a few dollars from her mother and enrolled in cotillion immediately. Most of the other attendees were years younger than she was — only twelve or thirteen, the sons and daughters of wealthy lawyers and businessmen. Alice hardly cared. Each Saturday morning she took the hour-long streetcar ride into Cambridge and learned the rules for holding a knife and fork, the right posture for sitting and standing, and the proper way to speak, even a few French words.

After class, she brought her pastels to the banks of the Charles River and sat in the grass, sketching the passersby. She had swiped the pastels from Sister Florence, her high school art teacher, and they were usually a crumbling mess by the time she pulled them out, having been hidden for days in her coat pockets, where they made rainbows on the satin lining. In her imagination, some wealthy benefactor would stop in his tracks — *You're too talented for this place,* he'd say. *You have a gift, my dear. Let me take you away from here. Let me show you Paris.*

But no one ever asked what she was doing, and when she brought her pictures home, only her sister, Mary, ever praised them. Eventually, Alice got the guts to ask her father if she could go to art school one day, and he said yes, sure, if she kept her grades up and did as her mother told her. Alice reminded herself of his promise every morning and night from then on.

She was shocked that he had agreed. Usually, whatever she asked for, he refused. Everyone in the family, other than Mary, seemed to think that Alice was greedy, trying to live beyond what God had given her.

She liked the finer things, and had her ways

of getting them every now and then. She would occasionally order a nice dress from the Lord & Taylor catalog, cash on delivery. As soon as the courier arrived, she dashed upstairs and watched from the second-floor landing as one of her younger brothers — Timmy, Jack, Michael, or Paul — fought with the kid, saying they hadn't ordered any god-damn dress, and they sure as heck weren't going to pay for it.

They'd shout, "Alice! You know anything about a new dress?" and she'd shout back, "Ha! I wish!" as innocent as a lamb.

The delivery boy would insist he had the right address, tough and unwavering because he knew the fate that awaited him if he returned to the store without the cash. On two separate occasions, her brothers had been so flummoxed that they'd actually paid up, and Alice had gotten a brand-new dress for free.

In her heart, she knew that she was sinning every time she assumed she was entitled to another, better life. She knew it because her mother told her so, and because the Bible preached modesty and sacrifice. She had written a quote from Philippians on the inside of her nightstand drawer, and when she opened it to put her rosary away before bed each night, she read the words slowly: *Do nothing from selfishness or conceit, but in humility count others better than yourselves.*

If only it were that easy. Alice believed in Jesus and knew that he would save her if she could try harder, pray more. She prayed to be selfless and content, like her sister. But the selfish parts of her seemed built in, every bit as much as Mary's kindness.

If Mary ever got a new dress, she was more likely to donate it to the church clothing drive than she was to wear it. Once, she had baby-sat for a neighbor's kids for twelve hours and been paid with a hard-boiled egg. Alice was livid on her behalf, but Mary just said, "I suppose it was all they could afford."

Mary had always been plain. She wore a long gray cotton skirt and a simple old blouse to school every day of the week. She never went on dates, staying home to read a book while Alice and her girlfriends went to the square for ice cream with a group of boys from their class. Alice would suggest that Mary come along — she'd even tell her date that she'd go out only if he'd find someone for her sister. But Mary always refused.

"I don't want to be anyone's pity date," she'd say. "Besides, all the guys are younger than me. I'd feel ridiculous."

When Alice came home at night, she would tiptoe into their darkened bedroom, pulling her stockings off as Mary whispered, "How was it?"

Alice hoped the stories might spark some-thing in her sister, but Mary would always respond, "I can't imagine what I'd say."

After Mary fell asleep, Alice would pray for her: *Let my sister come out of her shell, Lord. Let her be happy.*

Once she finished high school, Mary got a typing pool position at Liberty Mutual and started to bring in a bit more money for the family. Their parents were glad, though Alice, still a junior, thought she would die of boredom at such a post. And she believed that the money her sister earned should belong to Mary, not to everyone else. Imagine what the two of them could do with those paychecks! But when she spoke these words aloud, Mary said, "Oh, I wouldn't dream of keeping it for myself," which made Alice feel rotten, all the way through.

Alice saw less of her sister once Mary began working. She liked to go into Boston and pick Mary up at the office on Friday nights. Afterward, they'd go see a movie or split a sandwich in the Public Garden. Sometimes they would walk into a dark bar and drink a beer before heading home, though Mary had to be persuaded to do that.

When Alice's graduation came around two years after her sister's, her mother told her to put on a dress. "I'm taking you into town today to look for jobs."

Alice shook her head. "Pop said I could go to art school."

Her mother sighed and whispered quietly,

"Now, honestly, Alice, don't be such a child. You know your father wasn't serious. We don't have the money for that."

So Alice started working at a stuffy law firm in a job she despised, pouring coffee and answering calls for Mr. Weiner and Mr. Kristal, a couple of pudgy, balding blowhards. She made it through the days by socking away a bit of money for herself (she had lied to her mother about the pay) and sketching cartoons on the back of her notepad — Weiner behind the bars of the monkey cage at the Franklin Park Zoo, Kristal being forced to walk the plank of a pirate ship.

The war began. Soon the too-bustling rooms in the house stood empty, all four of their brothers gone off to fight. Even her beloved Paris was under the thumb of the Nazis, and Alice thought she'd have to go somewhere else. With so many young men away, their father's job grew steadier, and with the extra money coming in from the girls, they were able to stop taking in boarders. They left the boys' bedrooms untouched, as if they might come home any day.

Their father's angry drunken fits worsened. He terrorized Alice and Mary some nights, demanding that they give him more money for the rent, calling them lazy, fat, just screaming and screaming until they ran upstairs in tears, or he passed out on the love seat.

"If the boys were here, he'd never have the guts to speak to us that way," Alice said, though she knew her strong brothers were scared of him too.

Alice went to church at five o'clock each morning to pray for their safe return. She recited Hail Holy Queen in a dramatic whisper as many times as she could before someone came along and signaled that it was time for Mass to begin: *Mother of Mercy, our life, our sweetness, and our hope! To you do we cry, poor banished children of Eve, to you do we send up our sighs, mourning and weeping in this valley of tears . . . Oh clement, oh loving, oh sweet Virgin Mary! Pray for us, Holy Mother of God, that we may be made worthy of the promises of Christ.*

She believed in God with all her heart, and knew that He would keep the boys safe if she prayed hard enough, if she could only learn to be good. She tried to stuff down all the bad feelings that came so quickly to her — envy, greed, anger. Something first-rate was coming, she told herself, if she could only wait for it and keep believing.

She kept up with her painting when she could. Mary was always telling her that her work was every bit as good as the Degas drawings they loved at the Gardner Museum, which Alice had copied time and time again, sitting before them, sketching each soft line for hours. Alice was flattered, but sometimes she didn't see what talent had to do with it. Degas had been born to a wealthy French family, and besides, he was a man. So he got great love affairs and Paris, while she got life at home with her sister and parents, each day no different from the one before.

"The only way anyone in this family sees Europe is if they enlist," she told Mary one night, and Mary laughed, but then they both fell silent, remembering their boisterous brothers, the peril they might be facing right this moment, while they, Mary and Alice, sat on their beds in cotton nightgowns, their hair still damp from the tub.

The streets and the dance clubs and the movie theaters looked like the house, hardly a young man in sight. Only the Coast Guard boys remained in Massachusetts, and everyone said they were a bunch of cowards. None of the girls in town wanted to date them. Alice and her best friend, Rita, sometimes went to dances without a single male in attendance. They'd laugh, dancing up a storm with each other, doing a sort of foolish and full-hearted jitterbug that they'd never dare to do in front of men. Rita was newly married, her husband on a navy ship, off at sea. She was only biding her time, waiting for him to come back. After that, she'd be truly married, poor thing, the fun over for good.

It was that winter, when men were as scarce as lilacs, that Alice's sister, Mary, finally met one. Henry Winslow had walked into her office for a meeting with her boss late one morning and asked her to have lunch with him that very day. Mary said yes.

When she told Alice about it at home afterward, Alice gave her a look.

"What?" Mary said.

"That's not like you."

"Isn't it?"

"He could be a murderer for all you know!" Alice said. "He could be from a family of gypsies. All the boys I've tried to set you up with and you've refused. Now you'll suddenly go out with any old stranger?"

Mary stuck out her tongue. "Maybe I wanted to meet a boy on my own. He invited me to dinner on Friday night."

"Why hasn't he been drafted yet?" Alice asked, suspicious. "Is he terribly old or something?"

"He's thirty," Mary said.

"Thirty! That's positively ancient. Gosh. But still, why hasn't he gone to the war?"

"He's 4-F," Mary said.

The same classification as Frank Sinatra. Their brother Timmy said he didn't respect Sinatra anymore since he'd avoided the draft. ("Listen to that voice! Does that sound like someone with a punctured eardrum to you?")

This Henry seems like a coward, Alice

thought. *Like a flat-footed weakling.*

"Do you know why he's 4-F?" she asked.

"An old injury from a bus accident in his Harvard days," Mary said. "He walks with a bit of a limp."

Alice's ears perked up. "Harvard?"

She could tell Mary was trying to suppress a smile. "I get the impression he's rather wealthy."

They went out on Friday, and Alice tagged along with the understanding that Henry was bringing a friend for her. The friend, Richard, was a real flat tire — too old and perspiring, with badly yellowed teeth and a pocket watch that he kept checking every few minutes, as if to make it clear that the tepid feeling between them was entirely mutual. Even though it would have been more trouble had he liked her, Alice felt offended by the reception. She had a policy of never eating on dates, but that night she ordered a martini and a steak.

It was true that Henry walked with a limp, a characteristic that Alice wasn't sure she'd be able to tolerate in a date. And he had little specks of gray hair here and there. But he was handsome enough for someone his age. He worked for his father, an honest-to-God shipping tycoon, and was soon to inherit the whole company. Alice watched closely as he interacted with Mary — what did he see in her, anyway? She wasn't beautiful. But Henry

170

seemed smitten. He laughed at all her corny jokes, and he ordered for her when the waitress came.

When Henry asked about Alice's job, Mary interrupted, "She's an artist. Very talented. You should see her work."

"I'd love to see it," Richard the dud said, perking up. "I'm a budding collector."

It turned out, by his own whispered admission after several more cocktails, that he was also light in the loafers. But three days later, Alice sold him her first painting. Falling madly in love with Richard couldn't have brought her half as much joy as watching him hand over the cash that morning on her front stoop. Someday they might hang a plaque: THE ARTIST ALICE BRENNAN LIVED HERE FROM 1921 THROUGH 1941.

"It's beautiful," he said. Then he lowered his voice as if someone else might be listening: "Alice, I've adored Henry Winslow since he was my freshman-year roommate, but please watch out for your sister with him. She seems like a sweet girl. And he's a bit notorious for breaking hearts."

"What do you mean?" she said, feeling like she wanted to punch Henry all of a sudden.

He shook his head. "I shouldn't have said anything. Keep an eye out, that's all."

In a matter of weeks, Mary and Henry were inseparable. They went out to dinner and went dancing. Mary seemed filled with a sort of confidence she had never known. She started to wave her hair and began dressing properly. She rubbed a bit of blush on her pale cheeks — all the things Alice had been telling her to do for years.

In her more charitable moments, Alice was pleased to see her sister so well matched, so happy at last. But sometimes she felt jealous of Mary for finding him. Not that she wanted Henry for herself; she didn't. But someone like him maybe, a bit more handsome, a bit younger. His existence had changed things. Mary had so much less time to spend with Alice now. Occasionally, on the streetcar and sitting at her desk at work, Alice imagined ways she could break them up. Afterward, she'd say the Lord's Prayer for forgiveness, burning with shame when she thought of how devastated her sister would be if the relationship were ever to end.

After six months, Henry still hadn't introduced Mary to his family, and this caused her great distress. He said he was only waiting for the right time, but Mary was convinced it meant something more. Alice wondered if this was what Richard had been trying to warn her about.

Finally, he brought them both to what he called his father's beach shack in Newport for the day. Mary baked his mother a blueberry cake and spent an hour fixing her hair. "The shack" turned out to be an enormous ten-bedroom home, complete with its own staff and a tennis court. But Henry's parents weren't there. It was just his sisters and a few friends, one of whom had brought along a pair of chubby, grubby two-year-old sons. On the terrace that afternoon, Henry introduced them as, "My sweet girl, Mary, and her sister, Alice, the artist."

Henry had been to Europe as a child. That day, when Alice told him how badly she had always wanted to go to Paris, he said, "Tell you what, kiddo. I'll take you and Mary there as soon as all this mayhem ends." She believed that he would. Alice pinched her sister's arm, imagining the world that was about to open up for them.

Later, the group walked down to the beach. Mary, predictably, ended up with the children. She held the fat hand of one in her left palm and the other in her right.

"Has she always been so perfect?" Henry asked.

Alice grumbled. "Yes."

"I take it that bugs you."

"It's just that sometimes next to her, I look like a monster, that's all."

"I think you and I are alike," he told her. "We both need to be the stars."

Perhaps that explained his feelings for Mary. Henry was the type who liked a nice stable girl, someone who'd take care of him and cook for him and fret over him whenever he got so much as a sniffle.

"I suppose so," Alice said, looking down at the glorious white beach. The rich, it seemed, could even improve upon sand.

"I'd be lost without her," Henry said. "You'd be amazed how cruel women can be. We're all fragile, but we don't like to be reminded of it."

"What do you mean?" Alice said.

He pointed at his foot. "I played baseball at Harvard, and every girl at Radcliffe wanted to date me. But after this happened — I felt that my chances for happiness were gone."

Alice shook her head. "Someone like you? I can't believe it. There must be a million girls out there who would gladly have played Florence Nightingale."

"But that's just it," he said. "I wanted someone who would look at me like women used to look. And that's what Mary does."

Alice's jealousy faded then. He was right, of course: her sister never even complained about the limp, or the horrible pains Henry suffered from time to time that rendered him immobile.

She might have said that her jealousy vanished completely after that, if not for the presents. Alice tried not to feel envious over the fact that frumpy old Mary thought nothing of wearing a brand-new mink stole, a silver bracelet with a heart-shaped charm, or a pair of dove-gray suede gloves with fur trim and heels to match, even though such items had never interested her in the slightest before.

"It must be nice, having someone to buy you whatever you want," Alice said, watching her sister dress for work one morning.

"Oh, you know I don't care about all the fancy things he gives me," Mary replied, making Alice seethe.

"You shouldn't brag," she said.

Mary looked perplexed. "I wasn't. Was I? Besides, the gloves I bought myself, with my own money. They're the only objects I really care about. Otherwise, it's just Henry that I want."

Six more months slipped by without a proposal, or even an introduction to his parents.

"My old man's business is taking a bad hit," Henry told Mary. "I know he'll come to adore you like I do, but now's not the time to rock the boat."

She loved him terribly; her moods fluctuated between undiluted joy and pure sorrow, always, it seemed to Alice, dependant on him. Mary tried to act calm about it, but she was certain his family would never accept their marriage. Sometimes she wept in bed, and Alice wondered if this was really what being in love did to a person. If so, love seemed downright dreadful.

Alice worried too — she wanted her sister

to marry him, perhaps as much as Mary herself wanted it. Once Mary married Henry, she would give their mother grandchildren. Then maybe Alice could go off and do as she liked. Henry and Mary would give her money when she was starting out, and Henry might have more friends like Richard, who wanted to buy her work.

Somehow Mary kept up with all her duties around the house — cooking dinner and sewing and cleaning up the parlor. She rarely invited Henry over. Alice assumed this was because their home wasn't grand enough, and also because of the way their father was likely to behave. On the one hand, she understood. But on the other, she couldn't help but feel a bit insulted. Mary cared so much about what Henry thought. It was as if she lived in two worlds at once, and Alice just happened to be a part of the world Mary was trying to leave behind. Still, she reminded herself of what Henry had said: One day they would all go to Paris.

Alice had begun to see her friends grow giddy and joyful about their weddings. Even Trudy from the party line had met a nice young army doctor and was moving out to a house in Winthrop (this felt almost like a betrayal to Alice, though she knew her reaction was foolish).

Alice wanted no part of being a wife, cooped up in some house full of rug rats, constantly serving a man you liked less and less with each passing year. But she was twenty-two, and it seemed once a girl reached a certain age, that's what everyone expected her to do. Dating had become a chore because of it. She had always had suitors, and she still went on dates. But the boys who courted her now were mostly the same old ones she had known in high school, and they came through only briefly, on leave, or else there was something plain wrong with them — a vision defect or a skittishness that meant they weren't even fit for war.

Plenty of boys wrote her letters. A few, who she had been out with only once or twice, now wrote to tell her they were in love and wanted to make an honest woman out of her when they got home. She'd do her duty by writing back, but always remind them that absence made the heart grow fonder, and it had never really been all that rosy when they went to the movies, or to the ice cream parlor, way back when.

In the bedroom closet, Alice had stashed a paperback copy of *Live Alone and Like It,* the book she had heard Trudy raving about over the phone. She often riffled through its pages, reading a line aloud to her sister: living alone, according to *Vogue* editor Marjorie Hillis, was "as nice, perhaps, as any other way of living, and infinitely nicer than living with too many people or with the wrong single individual."

One night Alice read to Mary in bed in an exaggerated, glamorous voice, a bit like Trudy's: "You can, in fact, indulge yourself unblushingly — an engaging procedure which few women alone are smart enough to follow. Even unselfishness requires an opponent — like most of the worthwhile things in life. Living alone, you can — within your own walls — do as you like. The trick is to arrange your life so that you really do like it."

She looked up from the pages smiling, imagining an apartment full of clean linens, pink bath towels, and untouched canvases ready to be painted, all hers.

"Can you imagine?" she said to Mary.

Mary shook her head, looking a bit sad. "I wouldn't like it," she said. "I want to live with someone, always."

Alice sighed. "I know you do."

Her sister grew silent, and after a moment Alice realized that she had begun to cry.

"What is it?" she asked.

"Never mind, go to sleep."

"Mary. What?"

"You wouldn't understand."

"Go on."

"I've done things a woman isn't supposed to do," Mary said. "I've sinned in the worst way. But I'm in love, and I don't understand how it can be wrong to — well, never mind, Alice; go to sleep."

Alice didn't respond. Her body shook with anger. She had kissed her share of boys, but she was saving her virginity until marriage. Everything to do with sex frightened her — the mechanics of it, the risk. One girl in the neighborhood, Bitsy Harrington, had gotten pregnant in the back of a Plymouth by a sailor who told her it was the only way for him to touch her heart. Rita and the other girls had made terrible fun of Bitsy, but Alice thought that she herself might not have known any better. Things in that department were a mystery to her. When she started her period at the age of fourteen, she had believed that she was dying and run home from school in tears.

Her sister had always seemed similarly foggy, but now here she was, saying that she had gone all the way with Henry. Mary was leaving her behind, making her feel like a stupid heel, when everyone knew that Alice had always been the more sophisticated of the two. More important, there was the issue of eternity to think about — her sister was sinning in one of the worst ways, damning herself, and for what?

Alice wanted to know where they had done it. Would he ever marry her sister now? It made her feel queasy, just thinking about it. Mary might have ruined everything for them both.

Alice went to Mass the next morning and

in addition to praying for her brothers, which she always did, she lit a candle for Mary.

A few weeks passed. It was October, the first cool evening of fall. They sat down to dinner with their parents after work as usual. Mary had made a roast chicken and mashed potatoes. Alice was eager to get through the meal so she could pick up the extension in the pantry and find out what had happened at the office today when Trudy broke the news to her boss that she was moving to the suburbs to start a family and would have to quit working soon. Trudy had told her friend the night before that today was the day, and she was terribly nervous that he'd blow a gasket. Why, Alice did not know. How hard could it be to find another secretary?

She turned to Mary. "Trudy told her boss about Adam's proposal today."

"How did he take it?"

"I'm waiting until after supper to find out."

Mary grinned. "I can't believe you didn't bring the phone right to the table."

Alice took a bite of chicken. "I would have if I could manage to pull it out of the wall."

"Alice," their mother said. "You're awful. Pass the peas to your father."

He was at the far end of the table, reading the paper, several glasses of whiskey into the evening. He had strolled in from the bar down the corner a half hour earlier, looking like he wanted a fight. But now he seemed more likely to pass out in his potatoes.

Alice gave him the peas without even looking at him. She went on, "Trudy suspects Adam only asked her because he knows he'll have to ship out soon. Sounds sort of unromantic if you ask me."

"I don't think so," Mary said. "A proposal's a proposal."

"Maybe if Henry had been drafted, he would have asked you by now."

"Alice!"

"Well — when do you think he's going to ask?" Alice said. "It's been a year. What's the holdup?"

She wondered if perhaps he was one of those wealthy cads who thought he could just string a girl along forever, though Henry didn't seem like the type.

"Honestly, Alice, the things you say!" Mary looked exasperated, but she began to laugh. "Why are you so excited to get rid of me, anyway?"

Alice thought, *Because the sooner you get married and start having babies, the sooner I'll be free to live whatever life I want.*

But she wouldn't say that — it would sound selfish. So she only responded, "I'm not!"

Suddenly there came a harsh voice from the end of the table. "Will you two stop yapping about it?"

Their father looked up from his paper, his eyes glassy. He wiped his nose with the back of his hand, cleared his throat. "Every night, your poor mother has to hear you scheming and planning and it makes me sick. You're living in a pathetic dreamworld."

Alice found him revolting. He didn't know what he was talking about, and it was wicked of him to pick on Mary of all people. Mary, who would never hurt a fly.

Alice thought she'd try to get him onto a different topic, and so she said, "Hey, Pop, what do you think about the Red Sox? Are they going to make it to the Series this year?" She had no clue about the Red Sox, they all knew that. But it was something to say and she felt the need to protect her sister.

"You shut up," he slurred, fully worked up now. "Mary, you used to be the good one. Now look at you. Ever since you met that man, you're a different girl. Too big for your britches. And for what? Someone like that — he's never going to marry a girl like you."

Though Alice had been thinking the same thing a moment earlier, she was livid. Of course he was going to marry her. Henry was going to save them both. Maybe that's what made their father so mad.

"My daughter turned down by a cripple," he said with a cruel laugh, and Alice imagined socking him clear across the jaw.

She looked at her mother, but she just sat there, silent. There was no telling what he might do to her when he got like this, or to any of them for that matter. Their mother had never once come to their defense, even when they were small.

"He will marry her," Alice said defiantly. "You don't know what you're talking about."

He rose from his chair, standing slowly, coming toward her. She vowed not to move, but at the last second, as Mary screeched, Alice got up and ran to the bedroom, with her sister close behind. He chased them up the stairs, grabbing hold of Mary's skirt for an instant before she managed to pull away. Alice slammed the door right in his terrible face and stood holding it closed until she heard him slink off.

"He's a fool," she told Mary, who was crying hard now.

"Oh, come sit by me." Her sister sat beside her on the bed, putting her head in Alice's lap. "It will all work out, you'll see," Alice said, stroking her brown hair.

She was trying to sound certain, but she couldn't sleep that night for wondering what would happen next. Three weeks later, she would know for sure. But by then Mary was gone.

Alice folded the towels one by one, filling a plastic laundry basket to its brim. She had hoped that coming up to Maine would help her stop thinking about her sister, but she realized now how foolish that had been. Maine was for quiet contemplation, Daniel had always said. Or, in her case, just plain stewing.

She carried the basket on her hip like a toddler, out through the house's screen porch and over to the cottage. She saw a cardinal swoop down from one of the pine trees and land on a bush by the grassy patch where they parked the cars, since there was no driveway. Daniel had fancied himself an amateur bird-watcher, and had always given them silly names. She imagined what he might have called this one: Miss Scarlet, maybe.

There was a ceramic plaque on the cottage door that read CÉAD MILE FÁILTE. "A hundred thousand welcomes." She and Daniel had gotten it on a trip to Dublin probably thirty-five years earlier. For some time, it had hung on the front door of their house in Canton, and then she tired of it, and so, like many other posessions with which she couldn't quite part, she brought it to Maine.

Alice unlocked the door and took in the familiar musty scent. She went to the bathroom linen closet, piling the towels one on top of the other.

So much of her life had been defined by the loss of her sister. Daniel said it was the reason for her drinking when the kids were small. For her insomnia, her moods. She told him she didn't know if all that was true — he had never known her before Mary's death, so how could he be so sure?

For years at a time, Alice could go along fine, not dwelling on it, until something came along again to open up the wound. This year it had been that story in *The Boston Globe.* Two years ago, Alice was sorting through a box that had once contained Patrick's ice skates and was now full of papers and photographs. At the very bottom, she found an envelope. Alice lifted the flap, and flipped through photos of her brothers in uniform; a few of a twenty-six-year-old Daniel on the porch in Maine, with baby Kathleen in his lap; and then a shot of two young women and one man, clad in long khaki shorts and button-down tops, their hair blowing wildly in the Newport breeze, all of them laughing gaily. On the back, in her sister's handwriting, were the words, *May 28, 1943. Me, Alice, and Henry.*

It had been taken six months to the day before Mary died, and just the sight of it had sent Alice into a tizzy. She tore the picture up and threw it in the trash, only to regret doing so an hour later.

There were always small reminders: she still felt a twinge every time she drove by the Liberty Mutual headquarters on Berkeley Street where Mary had worked; or at Easter, remembering the silly rabbit-shaped cake Mary used to bake each year. She often wondered who Mary might have become.

What sort of life would have unfurled from out of her youthful dreams, what sort of children she and Henry would have brought into the world. It was strange to think that Alice had turned into a mother of three, while her entirely maternal sister never had the chance to bear a single child.

Daniel had always tried to steer her away from the what-ifs, which he considered only wasteful, morbid thoughts. But now he too was gone. Since seeing that newspaper article so many months earlier, Alice was haunted by memories of her sister even more than usual. Maiden Mary, the newspaper had called her — anyone who was old enough to remember that night remembered her story.

The part they didn't know was that Alice was to blame. Sometimes she thought that carrying the knowledge of it around was a piece of her penance. Lately, as if God were emphasizing this, she had become painfully aware of the pairs of old ladies everywhere she went. In church pews and at the beauty parlor, and walking along the sidewalks of Boston, arm in arm. The men didn't last — that was something they never told you when you were young and desperately searching for one, thinking he'd make your life all that it was supposed to be. No, in the end, it was only women; in the end, just sisters. She had her friends, but that was different. Friends kept their distance after a certain age. She couldn't exactly invite Rita O'Shea over for a slumber party or call her at midnight with her worries.

If Mary had lived, they might be here in Maine together. If Mary had lived, Alice's whole life might have been different.

It was almost lunchtime. She thought she might as well stay in the cottage for a while and make herself a sandwich. She went to the kitchen — her old tiny summer kitchen, which she had complained about countless times over the years, yet so preferred to all the marble and stainless steel next door. She opened up a can of tuna, draining the water into the sink. She had cleaned out the fridge a week earlier and filled it with new condiments and pickles and seltzer and Pepsi and a dozen fresh eggs. In the freezer, there were Popsicles and several leftovers from her own kitchen back home, wrapped in tinfoil. On the counter, she had lined up a bag of onions and a stack of paper plates and cups. In the coming weeks, her children and grandchildren would come through, adding their own bits and pieces, so that by the end of the summer there would be four half-eaten boxes of cereal and several almost empty bags of chips in the cupboard; in the freezer, a lone frozen waffle and a gallon of ice cream from Brigham's with one bite left in the bottom of the drum. But the staples came from Alice.

She had once heard her grandson Christopher ask Kathleen how it happened that the cottage was always fully stocked. "Magic," Kathleen had said, and Alice had interrupted, "Actually, there's nothing magic about it, Chrissy. It's called your grandmother."

Now she pulled a small onion from the bag and a knife from the block on the counter, part of a set she had bought off the TV a couple winters ago. She began chopping.

She chopped in silence for a minute or so, saying a Hail Mary in her head as she went.

Outside the window, something darted across the lawn, catching her eye. Her chest tightened. Her hand locked tight around the knife. She knew exactly who was out there.

"Oh, no you don't," she said out loud.

She stormed outside, just in time to see the blasted baby rabbit eat a hunk out of one of her beautiful pink roses.

"No! Out! Out!" she said, stomping toward the creature like a maniac, waving the knife in the air. He perked up his ears, and looked straight at her. The nerve!

Alice rushed toward him, scrunching up her face, pointing the knife. A moment later, he darted under a hedge and into the woods.

"That's it," she yelled after him. "This means war!"

Her heart pounded, but she felt a bit silly now, standing alone in the yard with a steak knife, shouting at no one. She straightened up, smoothed her blouse, and went back inside to finish making lunch.

MAGGIE

Maggie had been standing in front of Gabe's building like a pathetic crazy person for twenty minutes. A cab came by with its light on and she hailed it, beginning to cry softly, admitting defeat. She told the driver her address and almost said, "I'm pregnant," as a way of explaining her tears, but that seemed a bit much.

She wanted to believe that she was overreacting. She didn't want the problem to be Gabe. Or, if it was Gabe, she wanted him to do something so big she couldn't let it go by — not just lying about being out with friends or buying drugs, but lying about another woman. Not just grabbing her uncomfortably by the shoulders, but actually slapping her across the face.

She had been waiting and waiting, and now perhaps that thing had come. He didn't want her to move in, and didn't seem to care whether that meant they were over. She was pregnant with his child and she was alone.

What a dick. What a chronically avoidant, immature asshole. And what kind of freak was she that a tiny part of her was already regretting how she'd acted, wishing she had said, "Okay, fine, we won't live together," so that they could go to Maine tomorrow and fall in love again. They'd been trying to make this work for two years, even though it was sometimes hard.

As her mother had put it when Maggie called her crying after one of their fights: "I know you want to be married and settled, but give it up. You can't make chicken soup from chicken shit."

Kathleen was forever saying things like that, things that probably made some sense in theory, but were not in the least bit helpful when it came to actually living your life. She kept handwritten AA mantras on Post-it notes stuck to her fridge and printed on coffee mugs and tea towels all around her kitchen: *One Day at a Time. Live and Let Live. To Thine Own Self Be True.*

In her less charitable moments, Maggie thought that her mother had really just replaced one addiction with another: the pride and the self-righteousness of sobriety instead of the rush and release of alcoholism. But then she would remember moments from childhood: her mother passing out on the front lawn after a cousin's wedding; her parents, drunk on margaritas at the cottage in Maine, laughing and singing and then usually fighting until after midnight, letting Maggie stay up (or, more likely, forgetting about her), which thrilled her, and scared her too.

After Kathleen joined AA, she started doing a lot of yoga. She also began concocting herbal remedies — calendula and witch hazel for Chris's acne, ground-up nettle leaves and plum oil for Maggie's allergies. Never have two adolescents coveted Noxzema and Benadryl so much.

Kathleen gave Maggie a dream catcher as a sixteenth birthday gift, and it was all Maggie could do not to tell her how stupid and clichéd this was. The same year, her cousin Patty got a car for her birthday, and she didn't even have her permit yet. Maggie was jealous, and then immediately guilty — her mother might have gotten her a Camry, too, if she could afford it. Maggie made herself feel so lousy about the situation that she decided not to get her license that year. Sixteen years later, she still didn't know how to drive.

Now Kathleen was off in California. Maggie knew her mother had her reasons for leaving, but part of her felt like Kathleen had chosen Arlo — a man she hardly knew at the time — over her own children. It was the same feeling she had as a child when Kathleen would go on dates and leave them with Ann Marie. On those nights, Maggie would sit at the table with her cousins in Ann Marie's bright, open kitchen, wishing she belonged there.

When she got home from Gabe's apartment, she climbed the stairs to her fifth-floor walk-up, sobbing. From the fourth-floor landing, she heard a door above creak open and prayed it was not Mr. Fatelli, the lecherous old guy next door, who always smelled like soup and wanted her to come inside and have a look at his pet lovebirds, Sid and Nancy.

But then she heard Rhiannon's voice: "Maggie?" came the soft Scottish accent.

"Yes, it's me," she said, walking up the last flight, wishing she could get inside and be alone, despite the fact that she genuinely liked Rhiannon.

Her neighbor on the other side was a gorgeous girl from Glasgow. She was not yet thirty, but had already divorced the older American businessman who had brought her here. Now she worked as a hostess at a trendy restaurant in SoHo by night and attended graduate school at NYU three days a week. Rhiannon seemed like a free spirit, maybe because she was a foreigner, and therefore felt adventurous (or maybe it was the reverse — she was bold enough to come here because she was just the adventurous type). She was always going on a boat ride up the Hudson or biking through the Bronx or trying every pizza place in Staten Island in the course of a week. She lived in New York the way everyone imagined living there, but no one actually did.

A few months earlier, at Rhiannon's urging, Maggie and Gabe had gone to the restaurant where she worked for dinner. Rhiannon had worn a tiny tight dress in Lewinsky blue; her muscular arms and legs were everywhere as she led them to their table.

Afterward, she chatted with them for a bit, joking with Gabe about her name: "This is what happens when Fleetwood Mac fans mate," she said. "I'm thinking of starting a support group with my friend Gypsy."

"Seriously?" he responded, clearly captivated.

"No, not seriously," she said.

"Ah, you got me," he said, giving her a wink, which annoyed Maggie ever so slightly. She imagined for an instant how he behaved when she wasn't around.

Out in the street afterward, Gabe said, "She's pretty hot stuff."

"You're not really her type, sweetie," Maggie said. "She goes for rich, old geezers."

"I meant her attitude," he said. "She's spunky. She must get bored with a gig like that. Why does she do it?"

Rhiannon had told Maggie that she had gotten the restaurant job only because she needed dental work. Until then she had done fine without health coverage. Maggie herself wouldn't dare to live without insurance for a single day. That would no doubt be the day that a piano fell from a tenth-story window and landed on her head.

"Are you okay?" Rhiannon asked now, seeing Maggie's tears.

"Gabe and I had a fight," Maggie said.

Rhiannon nodded. "Why don't we pop downstairs for a drink?"

"I just want to go to bed," Maggie said. "I hope that doesn't sound rude."

Rhiannon laughed. "Yeah, goddamn your rudeness. You really need to get that in check. Seriously, though, I'm worried about you. Do you want to talk?"

Maggie shook her head. "Maybe later?"

Rhiannon was her first New York neighbor who had become something like a friend. The two of them weren't all that close, but they had had several long chats out in the hallway, and on the day Rhiannon's divorce was finalized, they'd gone for dinner at a new place on Orange Street, and toasted to freedom, though Maggie wondered whether Rhiannon actually saw it that way.

"I'll be here if you need me," Rhiannon said now.

"I appreciate it," Maggie said.

Inside the apartment, she left her packed suitcase by the door and crawled into bed. A pair of Gabe's corduroys hung over the arm

195

of a chair. His Yankees hat was on the coffee table.

Maggie cried until she fell asleep. She dreamed of her grandfather at the beach in Maine, dancing on the shore alone, in his old palm-tree-print bathing suit, little curls of white hair on his chest. He was laughing, carefree.

When she woke up, she thought first of him. In a lot of ways, he had been more of a dad to her than her own father ever had. It was her grandpa who used to make her giggle with his ridiculous jokes when some kid at school hurt her feelings; her grandpa who came over and shoveled their driveway after a snowstorm. At the cottage in Maine, he'd sing lullabies to the grandkids at bedtime, always in an exaggerated, melodramatic voice.

He had been the one to drive Maggie to college, with all of her belongings in the back of his Buick, all the way to Ohio. That road trip was one of her happiest memories: she got to talk to him in a way that she never had before, without her brother and cousins there vying for his attention.

After ten hours in the car, they stopped for dinner at some ramshackle place on the side of the road. Her grandfather drank a pint of Guinness, and told her that when he had first met Alice he'd been so startled by her beauty that he nearly ran off; every word out of his mouth was utter nonsense. He told her that the day her mother was born was the most amazing one of his life, and that he had left his wife and new baby sleeping in the hospital room and gone straight to morning Mass at St. Ignatius, where he put a hundred-dollar bill in the collection plate.

"Your grandma and I are so proud of you," he said. "We know you're going to be a very bright star, Maggie."

"Thank you."

"You're the first one in our family to go to a non-Catholic school, you know," he said, and she rolled her eyes because he had been mentioning this all summer. "You've broken our hearts, but that's fine."

"Grandpa!"

"Be sure not to give up on your faith, okay?" he said. "You're going to the sort of place where they're not too keen on religion. But remember where you came from."

The food arrived, and he said with a straight face, "Maggie, my dear, do you know why you shouldn't lend money to a leprechaun?"

She sighed. "Because they're always a little short."

He nodded approvingly. "Well, will you look at her! All right, how about this: Paddy told Murphy that his wife was driving him to drink. Murphy told Paddy he's a lucky bastard because his own wife makes him walk."

Maggie groaned but she couldn't stop him

197

from launching into a series of Irish jokes, delivered in a terribly unconvincing brogue, which lasted all the way through dessert.

Maggie was twenty-two when he passed away, and even now, ten years later, the thought of it was jarring. She recalled a line from a poem she had memorized in college: *No thing that ever flew, not the lark, not you, can die as others do.*

But he was gone, and maybe Gabe was gone as well. It was almost ten, and the sky outside had turned pure black. Maggie looked at her phone. No missed calls.

In twelve hours, they were supposed to be leaving for Maine. Should she still go? She wished she were the kind of person who could bury her head under the covers and order pizza from Fascati's every afternoon and ignore reality, without thinking obsessively about him, or showing up at his door like a lunatic.

Maybe they'd make up in a day, or a week's time, and carry on with their plan. But Gabe was rarely flexible like that, never kind after a battle. And anyway, once you allowed yourself to picture such a scenario, it couldn't happen. That was just the way life went.

She sat up in bed now, and looked around at her place, the whole apartment — minus the tiny bathroom — visible from where she was. Could she really raise a child in a tiny one-bedroom apartment in Brooklyn, alone?

She had thought that she was ready to be a mother. But maybe the whole idea was absurd. If it was really over, she wondered how long she could stay here, before the ghosts of them would be too strong to bear. This apartment had brought them together, and every bit of it reminded her of him.

Theirs was one of those meeting stories everybody loved. Friends often asked them to repeat it to strangers at parties, or told them it sounded like the plot of a movie. He had lived in her apartment before she did, and months after she moved in, his mail still flooded the box by the door. At that point, she hadn't published a single story. She kept a small stack of form rejection letters from literary magazines of varying quality, a few with handwritten words of encouragement at the bottom, which thrilled her when she read them, though hours later she'd feel mortified by her excitement over being turned down nicely. Meanwhile, dozens of envelopes from Simon & Schuster arrived at her new place, addressed to Gabe, and she wondered what they might contain — fat advance checks, or royalty statements, or invitations to have his book published in foreign countries around the globe. She never opened any of the letters, which she later reminded him when he accused her of having snooping in her DNA. It wasn't biological, she insisted. It was situational. A sensible woman could catch a man in only so many lies before she started to hunt for clues of betrayal. Snoop and ye shall find, he'd say dismissively. *Well, actually, yes,* she'd think. *In your case, yes.*

Anyway, she found the letters inspiring: Here was a New York writer who had not only secured a publisher, but was so above it all that he could just walk away without even leaving a forwarding address. In her imagination, he was reclusive, brooding, and brilliant. She felt lucky to have taken over his space. The thought of him helped her write, helped her keep going, and she'd joke about it to friends, how the literary power of her neighborhood's former tenants — Truman Capote, Walt Whitman, Carson McCullers, and Gabe Warner, whose book she could never locate at the library — acted as her muse.

When she sold her collection of short stories, she wanted to dedicate it to her mother, but didn't want her father to feel bad. She couldn't very well make it out to both of them. Considering they had not been comfortably in the same room since her fifth grade ballet recital, it seemed cruel to make them live together on the page for all eternity. At the last minute, she decided to dedicate it to him, a perfect stranger: *To Gabe Warner, whoever you are. Thanks for making a writer's life seem possible.* Her mother was pissed, but what could you do?

Gabe had heard about it through a friend who had an advance copy, and so he showed up at her book party looking like the stunning, cocky bastard he was, wearing a suede jacket with elbow patches and jeans, coming right up to her and saying in his clipped prep school voice, "Maggie Doyle, I presume."

It wasn't until later that night, when they were lying in her bedroom, which had once been his bedroom, that she realized what his book had been: a manual for do-it-yourself naked photos called *Tasteful Nudes for the At-Home Pro,* with tips on how to hide your belly fat and light a room, how to incorporate props, how to destroy the evidence if your relationship went south or you ever wanted to run for public office. Gabe had been approached to do it by a young editor friend, and he said yes, for a laugh. The book was never published, because naturally he hadn't ever gotten around to handing in his final draft. The unopened letters from Simon & Schuster, from which she had drawn so much inspiration, were demands to get the book in, or else he'd be sued for his advance money.

Gabe had left the apartment and New York to follow a girlfriend to Boulder. But by the time of Maggie's book party he was back in the city, newly dumped, living with Cunningham and working as a part-time stringer at the *Daily News.* During one of their first dates, he told her with pride about a computer file of stock images he kept for the occasions when they'd ask him to go shoot weather.

"You wouldn't believe how stupid photo editors are," he said. "I mean, all these requests to capture kids playing soccer on a sunny day, or snow falling on taxicabs, or — my absolute favorite — rainbows. They're basically asking me to use and reuse the same shit, right?"

(Shortly thereafter, he was fired for doing just that. Now he got by on the odd freelance gig and biweekly checks from his father. The handouts embarrassed Maggie, but Gabe seemed to accept them just fine.)

Even then, so early on, she had a nagging feeling that she ought to run. This guy wasn't an author, as she'd thought, but an overprivileged slacker photographer who had agreed to write a book about homemade porn. She told herself to stop being negative and look on the bright side. Perhaps he hadn't finished it because he knew how gross it was. And now she'd never have to explain it to her parents.

He taught her how to deal with all the weird nuances of her own apartment: how to flush the toilet so the handle wouldn't come loose, the correct way to screw in the antique glass light fixtures, his trick of slicing an orange and heating it up gently on the stove to kill the unpredictable mix of smells from the

Korean restaurant downstairs. Mr. Fatelli had been there for years (Rhiannon had come along shortly after Gabe moved out), and he was somewhat baffled when he saw Gabe hanging around the place again, eventually seeming to settle on the belief that the two of them had lived there together all along. For some reason, things like this made Maggie feel like they belonged.

And if Gabe was a slacker, at least he was smart — his new place was filled with books, piled high on every chair and in each corner, mixed in with Cunningham's ridiculously huge collection of eighties movies on VHS. On Saturday mornings they would sit and read on the couch, their bare feet touching, each of them occasionally pointing out a funny passage to the other.

Twice, Gabe had come over to trap and kill a mouse after midnight. He had put together her table and chairs from Ikea. On the morning of her thirty-second birthday, he woke her up with a homemade chocolate cake, a ring of glowing candles around the edge, like mothers always baked in movies set in the fifties. In his best moments, he seemed like someone who could take care of her. Though she was thirty when they met and in some ways had been caring for herself since she was a little girl, she found with some surprise that she wanted this, needed it.

Gabe had gone up to Boston with her for

Easter the previous spring. He and her brother, Chris, goofed around in a back pew, struggling to be quiet in that way you do when something seems all the more hilarious because you know you cannot laugh out loud. Her aunt Ann Marie had shot them a look, and Maggie caught her eye, making a face that said she too disapproved. But in fact, she felt joyful watching her brother and her boyfriend, side by side. She imagined them being close for years to come — golfing in Ogunquit each summer, grilling out in the yard between the cottage and her grandparents' place as their children ran this way and that, and fireflies zipped from tree to tree.

But she couldn't always rely on Gabe. Once, sent out to pick up her prescription when she had strep throat, he got distracted by a friend from work, went for drinks, and ended up telling her to get the medicine herself — he was all the way in Manhattan, but if she really wanted, he'd be happy to pay for the delivery. They argued like crazy, almost from the start. Sometimes Gabe lied, even when the truth would do: He'd go out drinking with Cunningham until two a.m. and say he was on a photo assignment. He'd have a boozy lunch with an old girlfriend, and only fess up after Maggie unearthed the hundred-dollar receipt in his wallet. He seemed to get off on tricking her, making her wonder whether she was really as controlling as he said, or if he just had some sort of mommy complex, or both.

There were moments when her stomach sank a bit, when she wondered what exactly he was made of, and whether it could really last through the long haul. Like the night, a few months into their relationship, when they went with the Goons to a wedding in Gabe's hometown in Connecticut. The wedding was an over-the-top affair, customary among Gabe's rich friends. But even so, Cunningham and Hayes were behaving like — well, like Cunningham and Hayes.

Cunningham was one thing: boorish and annoying, but at least he tried to make conversation. Hayes still lived with his parents. He had an entire wing of his childhood home to himself, complete with a housekeeper. Half of what he said took the form of the phrase "*Something* this, motherfucker." For example, when Gabe had asked him in the church before the ceremony started whether he had remembered to turn off his phone, Hayes replied, "Phone this, motherfucker."

Hayes could hardly hold down a job, and seemed to live only in memory.

"Remember when Gabe's car was stolen after college?" he said over dinner.

Cunningham snorted. "Yeah, poor Gabe. Insurance company took good care of you after you claimed the brand-new golf clubs in

205

the trunk and the — what was it now?"

"Two thousand CDs," Hayes said.

Cunningham pounded a fist on the table. "That's right. Two *thousand* CDs. Big trunk that must have been. He didn't have to work for a year and a half."

"I worked," Gabe said in a mock defensive tone.

"Oh sure, you worked at Mike's Deli nine hours a week 'cause those guys were the easiest way to score coke in town," Hayes said.

Gabe laughed uproariously. He didn't look at Maggie. She felt her whole body tighten. She knew Gabe drank too much. She was sensitive about it because of her parents' drinking, so she tried not to be a scold. But he had told her early on that like her, he had never touched drugs.

Hayes's date gave Maggie a worried glance. "Who wants more wine?" she said.

"Wine this, motherfucker," Hayes said, and he snorted with laughter.

Maggie pushed her chair away from the table and said she was heading up to their hotel room to bed, even though it was only nine thirty, and the cake hadn't even been cut. The Goons and their matching blond dates looked up with alarm. Gabe's big brown eyes pleaded with her not to make a scene.

He didn't come upstairs until four a.m., reeking of scotch and knocking the suitcase off the dresser. He pulled his shoes and pants and shirt off clumsily, and climbed into bed beside her, where she had been lying awake for hours, watching the red neon minutes click by on the alarm clock. She wanted his arms around her, an apology, but she knew she wouldn't get it, and it was no use fighting with him when he was drunk.

He switched on the TV — some stupid Adam Sandler movie at top volume. Her heart sped up, with the familiar mix of sadness and exhilaration that preceded a fight. She rolled over and faced him.

"Turn that down, please," she said coolly.

"It's not that loud," he said.

"I was sleeping."

"You made an ass of me tonight," he said. "Why'd you have to go and do that?"

"You never told me that you used to do cocaine," she said. "I was kind of in shock."

"I used to do a lot of stuff before I knew you," he said.

"Oh? Like what?"

"Don't worry about it."

"You said you'd never tried drugs," she said, feeling like a naïve child in an afterschool special.

"Well, I guess I lied. One more thing for you to hate about me."

His tone was so indifferent that she began to cry.

"Do you do it anymore?" she asked.

"Jesus Christ, Maggie, lay off," he said. Then he softened a bit. "I haven't done it in years."

"When was the last time?"

"God, I can't even remember," he said. "Come on. I love you. Why are you being like this?"

"And what was all that about the golf clubs and the CDs? Did you commit insurance fraud? I don't understand it, because obviously you didn't need the money."

"Damn it, Maggie, are you a fucking undercover cop, or what?" he yelled. "Didn't you ever do anything stupid or crazy when you were twenty-two years old?"

The answer, as they both knew, was no.

He switched the TV off and threw the clicker to the floor.

"I want you to go in the morning," he said. "I've had enough. I'll drop you off at the train first thing. I'll get a ride back."

They had been planning to stay two more nights, to visit his parents and older sister, but this was always how he punished her — pushing her away, telling her to go, because he knew she couldn't bear it.

Tears crept from the corners of her eyes and down to her lips.

"Fine," she said bitterly. And now came the regret, because he had told her he loved her, they had been so close to making up, but she kept pushing.

A moment later, he was asleep. She stayed awake until morning, thinking, thinking. Was it just the childhood imprint of watching her parents go at each other at the breakfast table or at one of her brother's soccer games — screaming, shouting, storming off, only to make up again a few hours later? Is that why she fought with Gabe the way she did? Had she really been drawn to a hard-drinking, short-tempered man, when these were the exact traits in her parents that scared her the most? Her mother said that alcoholics tended to seek one another out as a way to make themselves feel normal. Maybe that extended to their children as well.

Maggie thought, as she often did at times like this, about her cousin Patty. She had been raised by the even-keeled, forever happy Aunt Ann Marie and Uncle Pat, and she had easily fallen in love with and married Josh, her law school boyfriend who was sweet and kind. It really might be as simple as that — good model, happiness; bad model, despair.

Her shrink had said once that the right sort of relationship wouldn't require so much thought. It would just fit. Maggie had wanted to point out that if that were true — if love actually came easy and stayed that way — the woman would likely be out of a job.

The problem was that you couldn't divide a person up, pick and choose the parts you liked and the parts you didn't. There were parts of Gabe that made her love him so much that she wanted to hold on to him forever, even though there was no such thing. She could actually cry at the thought of him dying before she did, when they were both in their nineties.

He stirred around seven o'clock, and she reached for him, running her hand down his stomach, dipping her fingers under the elastic band of his boxer shorts.

"You awake?" she said, feeling desperate for him, when he lay right there beside her.

He grunted.

"I'm sorry," she said. "I shouldn't have been such a drama queen."

Gabe opened his eyes. He grinned. "Damn woman, you're Oscar-worthy."

With those words came the familiar flood of relief: the fight was over, and it hadn't ended them. She slid his boxers down and climbed on top of him, kissing his neck. He pulled off her T-shirt and licked her nipples in tiny perfect circles. They made love and afterward he ordered them eggs Benedict from room service, and made Maggie laugh with the story of how Cunningham's girl-friend, Shauna, had passed out drunk on an ice sculpture after Maggie went upstairs.

"So, can I stay?" she said, in a child's voice that she hated the sound of.

"Are you going to behave yourself?" he asked.

"Yes," she said.

"Good, because I hate being away from you."

"Me too."

Things were fine between them for a few months after that. Gabe took her for a surprise long weekend in Berlin, and they had an amazing time popping into galleries and cafés. They stayed in a five-star palace, which had been the setting for the Greta Garbo film *Grand Hotel.* (Maggie sent her grandmother a postcard to tell her so.) She was impressed with how easily Gabe spoke to the locals, how charmed everyone seemed by him. She felt proud to be the one he had chosen.

But then one Friday night back in New York he canceled their dinner plans abruptly because he said he was coming down with a cold. She asked him if she ought to come over and bring him some soup, but he was tired and said he didn't want to get her sick. He called her before ten and said he was going to bed. The next day, sensing that he had lied (he seemed perfectly healthy to her, and it wasn't the first time she'd heard him pretend to be sick), Maggie looked through the call log on his cell phone while he was out picking up lunch, and there they were: two calls from the previous night, around three and four a.m., to a random number she didn't recognize.

Feeling sick to her stomach, Maggie dialed the number from her own phone and heard a voice mail recording: "You've reached Stephanie. Leave a message."

When he came home with sandwiches from the deli, she asked him about the calls. He went into the bedroom without saying a word and slammed the door, locking it behind him. She sat on the couch, still as stone, waiting. He returned to the living room twenty minutes later and screamed at her for snooping, saying he had been out with guys from college and didn't always want her in tow. He needed his space, time away from her, if this could ever work.

"Whose number was that?" she said, shaking.

"One of the guys. You don't know him."

"Gabe, I called it," she said.

He hung his head. "Oh."

"So?"

"It's not what you think," he said, a phrase that never led anywhere good. "It's the number of a dealer, someone who sells coke. It wasn't for me, I swear. It was for these guys who were visiting."

"I heard a girl's voice," she said.

"It's a decoy. It always goes straight to that voice mail; you leave a message and they call you back," he said. Then he actually began to cry, which she had never seen him do before. "You have to believe me. I don't want to lose you over something stupid like this."

Somehow she ended up feeling relieved by his explanation. At least he hadn't cheated; at least he still loved her. It wasn't until a week or so later that she considered the fact that Gabe had the number of a cocaine dealer. She didn't know anything about cocaine, but she knew enough to realize that there was a difference between occasionally trying it at a party, say, and being the guy with the hookup.

She didn't want to leave him. She just wanted him to change, even as she recognized this as classic child-of-an-alcoholic behavior, even as she could hear her mother's voice in her head saying the only person you can ever truly change is yourself.

Still, Maggie wanted somehow to jolt him into action, to make him realize that certain parts of him needed transformation, or she'd be forced to go. She remembered nights when she was a little girl. Sometimes, long after dinner and homework and baths were through, they would hear her father's car pull into the driveway, and her mother would say with a broad smile: "Let's hide from Daddy."

Back then, this was Maggie's favorite game, one of those deliciously rare moments when the grown-ups entered the world of children. But as an adult, she often wondered what all that had been about and imagined that perhaps her mother did it to send her husband a warning: *If you keep coming home at any time you choose, smelling like liquor without a decent excuse, someday you will walk through that door and find your family gone.*

KATHLEEN

The ginger tea had steeped now and on the kitchen table were six large buckets of steamed organic waste, ready to be served. Kathleen got a kick out of imagining herself writing in to the BC alumni magazine: *Kathleen Kelleher lives in California and is considered the best worm chef on the West Coast. Her most popular dish consists of four hundred banana peels, hold the mold, and fifteen dozen eggshells, lightly toasted, with a soupçon of decomposing apple core.*

Later, they would feed the newly hatched worms the first meal of their lives. She had once told Maggie that doing this felt somehow profound. You wanted to welcome them into the world properly. Maggie found all of it revolting. Kathleen understood — hers was not a glamorous way of life, and okay, yes, she could see how it might seem kind of goofy. But she couldn't help but get caught up in it. Arlo's passion was contagious.

The worms across the barn from the newborns had filled their containers with droppings now. This afternoon she would have to coax them into the corners of their boxes with sweet rose petals, while Arlo scooped up the results. He would place the droppings in oversize garbage bags and then put the bags in the back of his pickup. Tomorrow they would transport several loads to the edge of the property, where Arlo had set up a makeshift bottling assembly line. They paid high school kids ten dollars an hour to do that part.

When she heard his truck in the driveway, Kathleen strained the tea through a paper towel into two Boston Red Sox mugs and walked toward the back door.

He crossed the stone path and climbed up the steps, holding a bouquet of calla lilies wrapped in brown paper.

"Good morning, my love," he said, opening the screen door and stepping inside. The dogs clamored in behind him.

"Trade you," she said. She took the flowers from Arlo and handed him a mug. "These are gorgeous."

"Aren't they? One of the moms at this Girl Scout event told me she had a flower shop in town. She's been using our poop tea on all the merchandise and it's lived twice as long as normal. So I stopped in to the shop — amazing colors, Kath. You would have loved it."

He was all fired up from his lecture. She grinned.

Seeing her work, he smiled too. "You're amazing. You did all this just this morning?"

Arlo was the sort of person who went out of his way to be kind — unlike her family members, who acted as though giving a compliment would cost them too much. And she and Arlo valued the same things. That was important. They both believed in homeopathy and in living a chemical-free life; they both believed in protecting the earth. To most people back home, this was all just a little too far out. But Arlo was on the same page, or perhaps even a chapter or two ahead of her, when it came to such ideas.

On their first date, even though it wasn't technically advisable, they drove to his place after going for coffee. They watched the news and then had sex on Arlo's sofa, under a framed *Steal Your Face* poster. In the morning, he fed her strawberries from his garden. Afterward, despite the poster, Kathleen called Maggie to say that she might be falling in love.

Before Arlo, she had dated and slept with several of the men she met at AA. Which was funny, considering she had been with Paul for more than a decade when they divorced, and couldn't remember a time when they'd had sex sober. In Boston, a couple of the guys were brand-new to the program and therefore

217

forbidden, but she had done it anyway. One was there on a court order, recently released after three months in prison for a drunken bar fight that left his opponent unconscious. Another was only twenty, the same age as Maggie at the time. Every now and then it all struck Kathleen as wrong, but in the heat of the moment she mostly figured that they were all addicts confronting those demons head-on, and so they deserved a bit of a pass for seeking out pleasure that wasn't somehow related to booze. (For the same reason, she went through phases of allowing herself to eat whatever she liked — a bag of Chips Ahoy! cookies for dinner, two cinnamon crullers from Dunkin' Donuts as an afternoon snack.)

Arlo stroked her hair now and said, "We've gotta get to work out in the barn soon."

"Yes."

"But maybe a little disco nap first? I'm beat."

"You go ahead up, honey."

She took the mug back from him and put both cups down on the table.

"Don't let me sleep longer than fifteen minutes, okay?" he said.

She agreed, kissing him on the cheek before he made his way upstairs. The familiar sound of his feet on the creaking floorboards warmed her.

She sat down at the table. Mabel came over,

resting her snout on Kathleen's thigh.

"Hello, angel," she said.

A year earlier, the dog had had a tumor in her leg. Mabel was thirteen then. The vet had assumed they would put her down, but Kathleen insisted on surgery. The cost was five thousand dollars, which objectively she could admit was a lot. But it seemed like nothing set against another good year with Mabel.

"Merry Christmas," Arlo had said when he wrote the check, even though it was only September.

The phone rang.

Kathleen hoped it was the school superintendent from Keystone finally calling back. She momentarily ran over her usual spiel: *Sixty percent of the waste in our nation's landfills is food waste, which never should have gone there in the first place. We feed our worms on such waste — fruit peels, eggshells, grass and yard clippings. Most of our food comes from the cafeterias of six school systems in the area, and we'd love to make yours number seven.*

But when she answered, it was her sister, Clare, at the other end of the line.

"Did you guys know you're in the current issue of *Organic Living* magazine?" she said.

"You read *Organic Living?*" Kathleen asked.

"Joe picked it up at the doctor's office. He smuggled the copy out in his shorts!"

Kathleen smiled.

"Why didn't you tell us? Joe's taping the article in the store window right now."

Clare sounded happy. In her former job, Kathleen had always thought of her when she advised awkward adolescents that life would get better. For Clare, this had proven true. She had always felt somewhat removed from their relatives, Kathleen thought. They treated her like she was a snob for being inquisitive and bookish. (Even Kathleen herself was guilty of it. She didn't come around to seeing the beauty of her sister until much later. She realized that maybe she had been jealous of Clare when they were younger, because Clare was the smart one, the one who really didn't care what anyone else thought. Kathleen wasn't brave like that until she hit middle age.) Clare and her husband, Joe, were both the brains of non-brainy families. Their business, selling Catholic paraphernalia to priests and grandmothers, was a strange fit for a couple of liberal intellectuals who lived in Jamaica Plain. But they made a killing.

"How's Ryan?" Kathleen asked now.

"He's great. He got a second callback for *Kiss Me Kate* at Wheelock Family Theatre. The rehearsals are in August, so if he gets it, it will completely mess up our plans for Maine."

"Don't tell Ann Marie. She'll accuse you of elder abuse for abandoning Alice there."

"Oh please. Those two should just run off together and make it official already," Clare said. "That was mean of me. Joe's a bad influence. I'm sure we'll go for at least a week. Maybe more, depending. You and Arlo should join us."

"I don't think we can get away," Kathleen said, and though they both knew there was a lot more to it than that, neither of them elaborated.

"Well, if you change your mind, let me know. We won't pull up the drawbridge for our allotted month the way the Perfects do."

They talked about work and about Alice and an old schoolmate of theirs who had gotten married for the seventh time last month.

Then Clare said, "Which reminds me! Ryan told me this funny idea he had for a musical. It would be about different couples at their weddings, and then it would follow them into their marriages. The idea being that the wedding a couple has will predict what their marriage will be like. I think he's a genius! I know I'm biased. But he's on to something, right? Think about our three weddings — yours, mine, and Pat's."

Patrick and Ann Marie's had been an over-the-top affair at the Ritz-Carlton in Boston, exactly what one might expect from a couple of show-offs like them, pretending at the wealth they wanted so badly. Ann Marie's dress was pure white lace; the flower girls

221

wore pink tutus. All of their parents' friends were in attendance, the average guest's age hovering somewhere around fifty-three. But as far as Clare noticed, Pat and Ann Marie never exchanged a single tender gesture: no hand-holding as they came off the dance floor, or kissing, unless someone did the hideous fork ding, in which case they'd pucker for the cameras like a couple of hams.

Kathleen and Paul's wedding was emblematic of their shitty relationship, too, Clare said. They kissed passionately in the church, a fact that irked Alice to no end. They danced like crazy, bodies rubbing up against each other as if no one else were in the room. By ten thirty, they were both drunk. Two friends of Paul's got into a fistfight in the men's room. Kathleen tried to break them apart and ended up with blood on her dress. Afterward, she sobbed unabashedly at the head table, and when Clare came to check on her, she grabbed Clare's wrist and said, "In case you had any money riding on it, I'm pregnant."

They found this amusing now, proof positive, Kathleen thought, that almost anything could be funny given enough distance, time, and therapy. It grated on her, though, the way that no Kelleher could take a relationship seriously if it wasn't a marriage. She had been with Arlo for almost as long as she was married to Paul, but her family, even Clare, still thought of Paul as the primary partner of her life. Another lesson for Maggie: The most important choice you can make is the person you reproduce with. You'll be stuck with him forever, even when you haven't spoken in twenty years.

Clare and Joe had been married by a friend of theirs in a garden outside Harvard Square, with just Kathleen and Maggie and a few friends as witnesses, and then everyone had gone for a big dinner at Casablanca, with chocolate ganache cake for dessert. Neither of them wanted a honeymoon. They only wanted to spend a week together in their apartment, watching movies and cooking big dinners, which they ate in bed, spread out over old issues of *The New Yorker.* They spent years of Saturdays in that apartment in the same way, drinking coffee all morning, peaceful, satisfied.

Clare had gotten pregnant almost as an afterthought right around their sixth anniversary, the summer Joe's dad died. They named their only son Ryan after his paternal grandfather. Ryan was a hoot from the time he was a toddler. He sang and danced — Clare often said proudly that he tapped before he crawled.

Joe had wanted a boy's boy like Chris or Little Daniel. The whole theater thing had never been part of his plan. Still, he was a trouper about it. He even played the sound tracks to *Finian's Rainbow* and *Brigadoon* in the store, proclaiming them "almost like the Chieftains if you shove cotton balls in your ears and don't think about it too much."

Kathleen adored her brother-in-law, partly because of how much he disliked Alice. For years, he had gritted his teeth like most of them did every time she said something degrading about Clare. Then one Saturday, he wasn't there at a family dinner. Clare told Kathleen he had been ranting about Alice that morning and she was afraid he might blow. From then on he was required to be around Alice only on important holidays, when absences were inexcusable.

Clare was a good girl by nature, and inclined to suffer in silence forever. But now, because of Joe, when Alice invited them places, they were more likely to claim they were busy than not. Served her mother right, Kathleen thought. For most people, interactions with Alice were like a goddamn hostage situation, but hardly anyone ever said, "No more."

Kathleen told Clare to tell Ryan she loved his play idea.

"He's driving over to the shop now," Clare said. "I wish he was here so you could say hi. He misses you!"

Kathleen knew what this really meant: Clare missed her. She missed her sister too.

"I can't believe Ryan can drive," Kathleen said. "God, that makes me feel old. When I moved away he was in third grade."

"Tell me about it. It totally terrifies me. How did you cope when your kids started? I'm so scared he'll drive drunk, or get in the car with someone else who's been drinking."

They had all driven drunk in the past, some of them more than others. Their kids were probably far less inclined to do so. Well, Ryan, at least.

"The thought of Chris out on the open road still terrifies me, and he's been driving for twelve years," Kathleen said. "Maggie never learned to drive for some reason."

"Oh, right," Clare said. "Do you think that might have to do with hearing so many stories about the accident? I remember being freaked out to drive because of that."

They always referred to it that way, just two words, which they all understood: *the accident.* Patrick and Alice refused to talk about it, but Alice still had the faint scar running down her face. You could see it if you knew where to look.

It happened the winter Kathleen was eleven years old. Clare was nine then, and Patrick only seven.

It had been snowing on and off for days, and all you could hear from inside the house was the crunching sound of tire chains against the road. Alice hated the noise; she said it made her teeth hurt. She hated having them underfoot all day too, but it was too cold out to play in the yard.

"Can't you give me some peace?" she'd say, whenever any of them asked for anything.

At bedtime, Kathleen would whisper to her father that she didn't want to be alone with Alice, but he would only say, "Be my helper when I'm gone, okay? And know that your mother loves you."

Alice wasn't always this way. On the nights when she and Daniel went on dates, she would let them eat ice cream before their grandmother arrived to feed them dinner, and give Kathleen permission to brush her silky dark hair. When they had parties, Kathleen and Clare would get paid a dollar each to ferry the coats upstairs to their parents' bedroom, and they'd be allowed to stay up until ten, giddily running highballs and Canadian Clubs out to guests in the living room from the bar in the kitchen.

On those nights, Alice laughed more.

She seemed happiest of all during summers in Maine, surrounded by their cousins and aunts and uncles. There, she ran along the beach in her bathing suit, her long legs glistening with oil. Sometimes she would get right down on the cottage floor with them and play blocks or dolls.

But at other times, Alice grew cold and unkind. Kathleen was terrified of her mother's outbursts, her short temper that seemed

226

to spring from nowhere.

They were in the kitchen that afternoon — Kathleen was doing her homework at the table, Clare was running circles around the room, screaming at the top of her lungs.

Sternly, Alice told her to stop.

She had said she had a headache earlier, going up to her room to rest as she often did before their father got home from work. Some days, she drank whiskey. She thought it made her calm, but in fact it turned her angry, sad. Kathleen could smell it on her breath when Alice picked her up from school. She knew enough to be quiet.

It was three o'clock. Alice was unloading groceries. She had let them sit out all morning, so that the milk dripped with condensation, and the lettuce had begun to droop.

Clare kept running, playing Cowboys and Indians all by herself, pushing her palm repeatedly against her lips while she let out a steady stream of sound.

Alice shouted at her to hush up, or else. She had a fierce look in her eye, and Kathleen feared it. She willed her sister to stop. After another minute, her heart racing, Kathleen said, "Clare, come sit with me."

Clare went right on yelling.

"Be quiet, goddamn it!" Alice yelled, so loud and harsh that Clare began to cry.

Patrick darted toward her with arms outstretched, to comfort her, and tripped over one of the grocery bags. He fell to the floor, hitting his head on a glass apple juice bottle, which broke in two.

A thick bloody inch opened up on his forehead.

Kathleen covered her eyes and shouted, "Oh no!"

"Jesus," Alice said. She went to him, pulling a tea towel from the counter. She pressed it to his forehead, but the blood soaked through and onto her blouse. "Sweetheart!" she said. "Did you hurt yourself?"

Kathleen spoke softly, scared of what her mother might do, despite her measured tone. "Should I call the ambulance?"

"Don't be so dramatic, he's fine," Alice said.

Patrick moaned.

"Mama," Kathleen said. "Shouldn't we take him to the doctor?"

"He needs a bandage and a cookie, that's all," Alice said. "And I need a drink. Isn't that right, sport?"

Patrick didn't answer.

A half hour passed. The bleeding wouldn't stop. Their brother sat in Alice's lap, crying. She held the cloth to his head, and Kathleen and Clare both cried too.

"Quit that, girls, you'll upset him," Alice said.

But after a few more minutes, she seemed to wilt. "He's still bleeding. Oh God, I can't handle this."

Alice tried to call their father at the office, but his secretary said he had stepped out.

"Typical," she said. She seemed weary, and more angry even than usual. "I guess I'll have to take all of you," she said, picking Patrick up. "Into the car. Now."

She didn't tell them to put on their coats, so they climbed into the backseat without a word, wearing only sweaters and dungarees. It was frigid in there — they could see their breath. Clare tried to catch hers in her hand.

The snow fell heavily outside. Kathleen and Clare held Patrick tight between them. He kept the towel pressed against his head with his fingers.

In the front, Alice began to cry softly. "I can't do this," she kept saying. "I cannot."

Patrick raised his little voice. "I'm okay, Mommy. Don't cry."

She pulled the car out of the driveway. The snow came down in sheets. She switched the windshield wipers to high.

The chains on the tires grated against the street. Kathleen willed the sound to vanish. She recited the Lord's Prayer in her head. She counted backward from one hundred, whispering the numbers softly, though somehow Alice heard her and jolted her head backward. "Stop. That," she hissed.

Alice drove straight, crying loudly now. There were few cars on the road. She sped up. Kathleen watched the houses whiz by and held her brother tighter. They seemed to be going too fast. She wanted to tell her mother not to cry because she was scaring Patrick. Kathleen wished her father were there, that he might find them somehow.

They were moving along the road, same as ever, when suddenly it felt as though something had lifted them up. The car swerved to the side of the street, sailing, sailing across wet grass until it slammed into a tree. The impact hit Kathleen's body and went straight through. Patrick flew into the front seat, landing with a thud against the dashboard before falling backward. Kathleen and Clare hit the backs of the front seats, and Alice's head cracked the windshield.

There was silence for a moment, before Alice turned to them, her face covered in blood.

"Oh, my babies," she said, hysterical. "Are you all right? Is everyone still here?"

In the end, they were lucky. The doctor said God had been watching. Patrick was hurt the worst: he lay unconscious for several hours in a hospital bed, and when he woke up he had two broken arms and a shattered jaw. Kathleen got a slight concussion and lost two grown-up teeth, resulting in a painful string of root canals later that year. Clare somehow made it through with only bruises and scrapes, and Alice broke her wrist and sliced her face wide open. They used their savings for her to visit the best surgeon in Boston, but still she needed thirty stitches, some of them inside the skin. For months, she wore a bandage wrapped around her head and covered it with a navy blue turban, which made her look like Norma Desmond. She rubbed vitamin E on the scar every morning and night. Within a year, it had all but vanished.

They told neighbors and relatives that Alice had been in such a rush to get Patrick to the hospital that she'd driven too fast on a stormy day and lost control of the car.

But the night after the accident, Kathleen crept from her bed late and followed the sound of her parents fighting. She stood outside their bedroom door.

"Goddamn it, Alice, you could have killed them all."

"I know it, I know."

"You were drunk," he said. "What have I told you about drinking when I'm not here?"

"But you're never here!" she yelled bitterly. "I'm alone with them all day long."

"I go to the insurance company every day, not because it's so damn fun, but because it's my job," he said. "I have to do it for this family. You're their mother! That's your job. I can't be here to watch you every minute."

She sobbed.

"I told you I couldn't do it years ago," she said.

"That's nonsense. You're a wonderful mother," he said, his voice a bit softer now.

"Oh yes, clearly."

"Listen to me, Alice. I love you. I want to stand by you. But the drinking has to stop. I mean it. Cold turkey. I don't care how you do it, but you're going to do it. If you don't, I'll take those kids and I will leave. Do you understand me?"

Kathleen didn't hear any response, but in the morning when she woke up, her father was standing at the sink, pouring the liquor from every last bottle in the kitchen down the drain. She never saw her mother take another drink until after the day he died.

ANN MARIE

Around seven o'clock, Pat came into the kitchen in a pair of khaki pants and a polo shirt. He was looking down at his cell phone, typing away.

"Good morning," he said, kissing her on the cheek without glancing up from the phone. "Were you awake at the crack of dawn preparing for dollhouse-palooza?"

"Yup. Couldn't sleep. So much to do."

"You could take a day off, you know," he said.

"That lamb we had on Friday is in the fridge, thawing out," she said. "There's still mint jelly left too. And I'll make you some potatoes before I go, just in case."

He frowned. "In case you decide to leave me for a man who makes subway tiles for Barbie dolls?"

"In case you get hungry."

"I can fend for myself," he said, though they both knew he hadn't set foot in a grocery store in years, or prepared a meal, possibly ever.

"I don't mind. I wrote out directions for you on how to heat the lamb up. They're on the fridge, under the Celtics magnet."

"Thanks," he said.

"I spoke to your mom," she said. "She wanted me to remind you about the gutters."

"I'm on it," he said. "I called Mort up at the market and got a referral. I thought I already told her that. And the railing on the cottage porch is loose too. Did she mention it?"

"Actually, she said her priest is going to fix it."

"Her priest?"

"You know, Father Donnelly. I think he's sweet on her."

"Well, that's disturbing."

"Oh, not like that," Ann Marie said with a laugh. "He's a nice young man, that's all."

"How did she sound otherwise?" Pat asked.

"A bit crabby. She said she doesn't need any help, and I shouldn't bother troubling myself to come out there in the middle of June after Maggie leaves. I didn't have the energy to fight her on it. I'm still going to go, though."

"You're an angel," he said.

"You know you have your doctor's appointment tomorrow, right?"

"Yes, ma'am," Pat said.

234

He was so cheerful this morning that she felt sorry for what she was about to say.

"Honey, we need to send Little Daniel's check before I leave," she said gently.

Usually they sent it by the last of the month, like clockwork. But somehow, in the whirlwind of her June plans changing, she had forgotten to remind Pat. He was a disciplined man, with a memory so sharp he could tell you what he had for breakfast on his first day of kindergarten. But he never seemed to remember this. She imagined that he put it from his head quite consciously, allowing himself to think about it for only that one minute a month when he signed the check and handed it over to her to be addressed and mailed.

Pat was disappointed, she understood that. Ann Marie told him to pray on it, to have faith that it would all work out. He was angry that he'd spent more than two hundred grand for their son's education, and still, they were sending him money. Ann Marie didn't see what was so wrong with it — she knew women at the club who had bought houses for their kids. Pat said no one had paid his way. He had figured it out, and he expected his children to do the same.

She had to bite her tongue on that one. Ann Marie had spent every weekend and summer of her teenage years bagging groceries at Angelo's. Had any of the Kellehers ever had so much as an after-school job? How many times had she heard Kathleen complain that Pat was the only one whose education was taken seriously by their parents, meaning that Alice and Daniel paid for it in full? Yet it had never dawned on Kathleen that some people, including Ann Marie, paid their own tuition, waitressing all the way through college.

She had always warned Pat to be more conservative when it came to giving the kids money, but he had lavished gifts and cash upon them anyway. It seemed that now, right when Little Daniel really needed them, was not the time to draw the line in the sand.

Despite Pat's protestations, they had been mailing the checks for five months, ever since Little Daniel lost his most recent job. It wasn't the first time they had helped him out, but it was the first time he'd been let go for such a shameful reason. When Ann Marie thought about it, and about what might come next, she felt tired.

It hadn't helped that it happened only a couple of weeks after Fiona told them her news. Why did bad things always occur in multiples like that? The combination made Ann Marie question what she had always known about herself — that she was a good mother, that theirs was a traditional family.

Little Daniel had graduated top of his class from business school; he was terribly bright, and charming. But he'd had lousy luck when it came to work. His first boss, at a boutique investment firm, just plain had it out for the kid: he had dared to call Daniel arrogant, saying he wasn't deferential enough, when the boss himself was Daniel's exact age.

At the next place, a huge company in downtown Boston, they didn't challenge him. They gave Daniel paper to push around, and — no wonder — he got bored. So he started taking long lunches (he said all the executives did the same). He came in late. At his one-year evaluation, they told him it wasn't working out.

"What's wrong with him?" Pat had said that time, too testily for Ann Marie's liking.

"Nothing! He's off the charts smart, Patrick, like you. He was too good for that job."

Pat pulled some strings with Ronald Allan at the club and found their son a good, high-paying position at another big firm. It seemed like he was really working hard this time, but then, without warning, they laid him off and told him to be out in two weeks.

"This is outrageous!" Pat had fumed, uncharacteristically worked up. "I'm calling Ron and I'll give him a piece of my mind. And possibly a lawsuit."

He went into his home office and slammed the door. When he came out twenty minutes later, his face looked pale.

"Well?" Ann Marie said.

"Apparently they did him a favor, laying

him off like that."

"What do you mean?"

"There were complaints from some of the secretaries about certain behaviors."

Ann Marie pictured a gaggle of lazy girls in tweed, refusing to fetch coffee or answer the telephone, citing women's lib.

She didn't ask her husband to elaborate, might have preferred it if he did not, but Pat went on, "They found some very disturbing pornography on his computer. Bondage stuff, I guess."

Ann Marie was aghast. "These secretaries just claim he was the one who put it on the computer? It could have been anyone who did that."

"They found out because they do his expenses."

"And?"

"He charged it all to his corporate credit card. Two thousand dollars' worth."

"Oh my God."

She wondered if this had happened in other offices. She thought of poor Regina, who was so proud of the diamond on her finger, and cringed at the thought of her son — that all-American boy! — asking to tie her to the bedpost. And she thought of Fiona, too, the two affronts wrapped around each other. Her son was a pervert and her daughter was a lesbian.

It's no one's fault. It was in vogue these days to say that whenever something terrible happened. But everything unpleasant was someone's fault. What had she done to them?

"He's made a goddamn fool out of me," Pat said. "I'll probably be the laughingstock of the club now."

At that moment, a rush of estrogen, or maternal instinct, or who knew what, flooded her head and her heart, and all she wanted to do was protect that boy as best she could. Her only son.

"Oh, honestly, who cares," she said. "Ron Allan has worse skeletons in his closet than some dirty movies."

She called Little Daniel and told him to come over. He cried on the living room sofa and apologized for embarrassing them. He said he hadn't realized that he'd used his corporate card until it was too late. (That made sense to her, though she had hoped he would deny the entire thing.) He went to sleep in his childhood bedroom, her strong, tall, handsome son, who everyone still called Little Daniel, though he had towered over Big Daniel by the end.

In bed that night, Ann Marie ran her fingers over the carved wood of the headboard they had found in a shop in Killarney. They had had it shipped all the way from Ireland. Pat was in bed with her since Daniel was home, and he was snoring. She didn't know how her husband could sleep at a time like this.

Eventually, she went downstairs to her

crafts room and stared at her dollhouse for a long while, deciding that the armoire in the living room would look better in the entryway. She picked it up and moved it, then carefully wiped down the sides with a Kleenex to get rid of any fingerprints. She thought of Fiona as a child. She had never liked dresses, not the way Patty did. Was that a sign? In high school, she hung around with a boy, David Martin. She always said they were only friends, and raised hell when Ann Marie wouldn't allow them in her room together with the door closed. Their senior year, when she asked to go camping with David alone and Ann Marie said it was inappropriate, Fiona had said, "Jesus, Mom, he's clearly gay." It had never once dawned on her that Fiona might be too.

And what about her son? Ann Marie recalled a time when he was in high school, and she was in his room changing the sheets. Under the pillowcase, she found a copy of *Penthouse* magazine. Her eyes filled up with tears as she flipped through the pages — all those young, empty-eyed women with their legs spread, their mouths hanging open. He had walked in on her, catching her off guard, and she had shoved the magazine back under the pillow, as if he were the parent and she the guilty child. Ann Marie turned red and asked him how school was. Was that the moment? Could she have said or done something then? She should have told Pat, but even that seemed mortifying, and she reasoned that all teenage boys did a bit of exploring, probably.

At least she still had Patty. Suddenly, she hoped her older daughter might announce soon that she was pregnant again, even though she knew Patty and Josh planned to stop at three.

The following morning, she made Little Daniel pancakes stuffed with walnuts and chocolate chips.

"I'm not helping him," Pat said after he left.

She didn't have to speak; she just stared at him in disbelief.

Finally, Pat said, "Fine. But this is the last time."

That afternoon, she bought a two-foot-tall antique carriage house on eBay for five hundred dollars. It was covered in silk roses and vines and matched the color of her doll-house perfectly. She imagined escaping there, pressing her face up against the real glass windows and looking out on a rainstorm, safe inside.

At Ann Marie's urging, her son had softened the story when he told his fiancée what happened. As far as Regina knew, he had lost his job because the company was downsizing and had to cut the staff by a third, that was all.

They hadn't told the girls, or anyone, what really happened. (They hadn't told anyone about Fiona either, though she had said, "I would like to come out to the rest of the family in my own time." Ann Marie hoped that meant never.)

When Pat got on the phone with his mother or his sister Clare, he boasted like crazy, said Little Daniel was bringing in a salary in the high six figures and making them proud. She appreciated her husband's desire to shield their son from the Kelleher gossip mill, and she went along with it, even when that meant she had to lie right to Alice's face.

Pat reached into his wallet now and pulled out his checkbook. He made out a check for five thousand dollars and signed his name, ripping the page off with more intensity than seemed necessary. He handed it to her, and Ann Marie had the envelope waiting. She quickly placed the check inside and sealed it.

"Now," she said. "Let's get you some breakfast."

"I'll just have toast," he said.

"I have some of that yummy Irish soda bread from my mother's friend Sharon," she said. "Want that?"

He shrugged. "Sure."

"It's going to be a gorgeous day," she said. "It's supposed to get up to seventy-seven degrees this afternoon."

"That's good."

"Your mom said Maggie's heading north

sometime in the next few days," Ann Marie went on. "Kathleen wouldn't tell Alice exactly when. Typical. It's really a shame she doesn't go along too. But let us not forget how busy she is on *the farm*."

Pat chuckled. "You can't expect her to leave Farmer Arlo alone with all those animals to take care of," he said. "Another Woodstock might pop up out there without my sensible big sister around to stop it."

Ann Marie rolled her eyes. "Right. A billion worms and a hippie drug addict win out over her own mother and daughter. That makes good sense."

"A friend of the devil is a friend of Kath's," he said.

She frowned. "What does that mean?"

"It's from a song. Never mind." Pat paused, and then he said, "Poor Maggie."

"I know! But what's wrong with your sister? Doesn't she miss her kids, all the way out there in California? Honestly, Patrick, it hurts me to even think it, but I don't think she does."

Pat didn't have much of a relationship with his oldest sister, not anymore. When they were all young and Kathleen was still married, they were close. They spent almost every Saturday together. Twenty years had gone by, and Kathleen still blamed Pat for covering for her cheating ex-husband, even though he had done it to protect her. If she only knew how many times Pat had sat that guy down and told him to end his relationship with the other woman, to think about his family. Pat had genuinely believed he could talk sense into Paul, and maybe he might have eventually. They hadn't known about Paul's money problems until it was too late, but it wasn't their fault that Kathleen had been clueless about her own bank account.

Ann Marie thought Pat had much stronger grounds on which to be furious. With their mother well into her seventies, Kathleen had squandered their father's hard-earned money and up and moved across the country, leaving Alice in their care. Even back when Kathleen was religious, she was nothing but a Cafeteria Catholic. Maybe this was why she felt no obligation to her family, not one shred of guilt.

Pat's other sister, Clare, wasn't much better, and she lived only a few miles away in Jamaica Plain. Her husband, Joe, couldn't stand Alice, and Clare had sided with him. She visited her mother once a month or so, and then Ann Marie would have to listen to Alice gush about the fact that Clare had brought her the most beautiful roses, or a bottle of cabernet with the fifty-dollar price tag still on, as if these petty gestures made up for the past four weeks of neglect.

Clare was always telling Ann Marie that she wished she could do more. She was the sort of person who spent so much time telling you how busy she was that the complaint in itself seemed like a full-time job. *Try having three children,* Ann Marie wanted to say. Clare had a cleaning lady who came in once a week, and when Ryan was small she had employed a nanny. Ann Marie would never dream of paying someone else to do her job. Not because they couldn't afford it, but because no one could ever care for your children or your home as well as you could, she was certain of that.

Most of the time, the work of caring for Alice was left to Ann Marie, even though she had her own mother to think about. She had lost her father at twenty-seven and gotten none of the sympathy that the Kellehers seemed to want for their loss, even though they were all in their forties when Big Daniel died. Ann Marie herself was hit hard by it. He was such a good man, so kind to her and to everyone. He had been the one who kept them all together. But it was clear that her in-laws expected her not to react, even as she made the arrangements for the funeral by herself.

What bothered Ann Marie most about the Kellehers was the way they all leaned on her, yet never quite let her in, or even said thank you. She was certain that her sisters-in-law, to whom she felt superior in many ways, to be honest, still thought of her as the poor white-trash girl who had conned their brother into marriage.

Pat sympathized, but really this was a woman thing. Though Alice was an ally, sort of, Clare and Kathleen were mostly unkind to her, as if Ann Marie were just a guilt-inducing reminder of how little they did for Alice, for the family overall. On holidays, Clare would bring one side dish — *one!* — and spend the entire evening griping about how hard it had been to make it, until everyone at the table praised her bland sweet potatoes or her runny green bean casserole.

Kathleen came empty-handed. According to her, this was because she had to travel. (Did travel preclude a person from picking up a bottle of wine or a box of crackers and some cheese?) Before she moved to California, she would bring her two huge slobbering German shepherds along on Christmas. Ann Marie would be forced to let the dogs stay in her kitchen, where they had once been caught licking the leftover roast.

Those dogs were ancient now. Alice had told her that a year ago, Kathleen paid something like ten thousand dollars to give one of them chemotherapy. Ann Marie had never heard of such a waste of money in her life. She had cousins in Southie who would have been put to sleep for less.

Now when Kathleen came home for the holidays, she often tried to educate Ann

Marie's children on the Gospel According to Her. A few months after Patty's first baby was born, he cried at dinner, and she rose to take him into the bedroom and feed him, as Ann Marie had instructed.

"Nurse Foster right here at the table," Kathleen had said. "It's perfectly natural, honey. Don't go lurking in the shadows. Don't be one of those women pumping in the handicap stall at the Olive Garden."

Maggie nearly spat out her wine. "Really, Mom? The handicap stall at Olive Garden?"

Ann Marie responded softly, mortified, "I think Patty feels, as I do, that some people are made uncomfortable when they see a woman's bare breast. And so it's really better for everyone, including the baby, to find a nice solitary spot."

"That's bullshit," Kathleen said.

If this were her own sister, or if she were a different sort of woman, perhaps Ann Marie might have pointed out that Kathleen had bottle-fed both her kids from the time they were three months old. Instead, she swallowed her reply.

"I hardly think this is appropriate dinner conversation," Alice had said, silencing them. Patty went into the bedroom and shut the door.

There was a long pause. A few years earlier, Daniel Senior would have been there to make a joke, lighten the mood. Ann Marie assumed they were all thinking as much.

Finally Clare said, "Could someone pass the milk?" and they laughed.

Three solid hours of storytelling followed, as if for Daniel's sake.

The Kellehers allegedly hated one another, but when they got together and things were good, they stayed up all night, laughing and talking. More so when Daniel was alive, but still now from time to time.

Even after thirty-three years of marriage, Ann Marie sat at every family dinner and listened to them tell the same stories, over and over. She had never met a family so tied up in their own mythology.

What drove her around the bend most was when Alice would mention Sherry Burke, then put her hand on Ann Marie's and say proudly, by way of explanation, as if Ann Marie didn't know, "Patrick used to date her. She was the daughter of the mayor of Cambridge. A beautiful girl. She's a senator now!"

"A state senator," Ann Marie would correct her.

Her husband had dated Sherry Burke in high school, for goodness' sake.

Sitting there on those nights as they drank countless beers and bottles of wine (the next morning she would be the one to pick up all the glasses and load the dishwasher and wipe down the surfaces), she sometimes dreamed of screaming at them: "If you tell that goddamn story one more time, I will tie up the lot of you and duct tape your big mouths shut."

She meant the kids also — the nieces and nephews and even her own three, who were true Kellehers in their way. After letting the thought linger in her head a moment, she'd be overcome with guilt and do something ridiculous, like decide that she should go into the kitchen and whip up some brownies from scratch, then serve them warm with ice cream on top.

On the way to the dollhouse show, she called Patty from the car. There was no answer on the cell or at home, so she tried the office number.

"What's up, Mom?" Patty answered, sounding flustered.

"It's a Sunday. What are you doing there?" Ann Marie asked.

"I'm swamped."

"Where are the kids?"

"I think they went to a sports bar to watch the Sox game."

"What?"

"They're home with Josh."

"Oh. Are they doing okay?"

"You saw them two days ago," Patty said with a laugh.

"I know," Ann Marie said. "Maisy's coming over after school tomorrow for our special tea party, right? The teacher knows I'm picking her up?"

"Yes. Hey, Mom, I've got a brief I need to file first thing tomorrow, and I've barely made a dent. Can I call you later?"

"Sure, honey," Ann Marie said.

They hung up. Ann Marie felt a bit sad, but couldn't say why.

Turning onto Sycamore behind two twenty-somethings in a yellow convertible, she wondered whether Patty knew about Fiona. They had never been particularly close. Patty had always liked her cousin Maggie better. Ann Marie had once washed her mouth out with soap when she came across the child taunting her younger sister: "You're not really my sister, Maggie is." Fiona was crying her eyes out, but Patty kept on going.

Recently, Patty had remarked that she was shocked by how cruel her children could be.

"Sometimes they're like animals," she had said. "I want to lock myself in the bathroom and hide. How did you survive?"

Ann Marie waited in a short line of cars to turn onto the expressway. She glanced at the clock, even though she knew she was right on time.

Patty and Fiona seemed to start talking more after they moved out of the house, just as Ann Marie and her own sisters had. At Ann Marie's urging, her daughters began writing letters to each other from college.

250

(She had sent them the cutest stationery sets and plenty of stamps.) They chatted easily and went out for lunch when they were home for the summer. But then Fiona left for Namibia. Had she been running away? Was that what it was all about? Ann Marie didn't know anyone with a gay child. Who could she ask?

She hadn't spoken to Fiona about it since that first night at dinner. When she wrote to her daughter, she reported on the latest family gossip and the weather and her dollhouse. She could feel herself almost begging Fiona not to bring it up. Fiona, in turn, wrote about her work with children, the beautiful sunset over her village. Ann Marie felt relieved. She had long wanted Fiona to come home, but now, to her great shame, she almost wished she could freeze time: Fiona, caring, generous, far away, like she had always been. Not here, bringing a girlfriend over for Sunday dinner, adopting an African baby and carrying him around Newton in a sling while everyone whispered and stared.

Pat had said that it felt almost like a death: He was mourning the fact that Fiona would never have a wedding, never meet that charming do-gooder husband they had imagined for her, never have kids. Most painful of all, she could not possibly be a true, accepted Catholic now. If such places did exist, she would not go to Heaven with the rest of them.

Somehow Ann Marie had managed to raise three children who turned their backs on Catholicism in all sorts of ways. She had taught their CCD classes and taken them to church every Sunday. Pat was a eucharistic minister. She had forced Little Daniel to be an altar boy, and enrolled the girls in the choir. She had done all she could, and for what?

Patty had married a Jewish man, which was fine. Times had changed; Ann Marie still had to remind herself of that once in a while. She had held out hope for some time that Josh would convert. When he didn't, she dealt with it. But the fact that they had chosen not to baptize the grandchildren was like a slap in the face.

For a long time, Ann Marie thought her younger daughter was the one true Catholic among them. Fiona was prone to strep as a child, and once, after several rounds of antibiotics failed to keep it away for long, they took her to get the blessing of Saint Blase, patron saint of throat ailments, as a last resort. The blessing seemed to cure her, which generated Fiona's lifelong fascination with the saints. She had always been such a good girl. She worked in the service of the poor. But somewhere along the way Ann Marie must have failed her. She didn't understand how it could have happened.

She was terrified at the thought of her

mother or Alice finding out about Fiona. Or even Kathleen — wouldn't this development just make her year?

Women like Kathleen who focused so much on what motherhood had cost them rubbed her entirely the wrong way. She had always thought the whole movement toward "me time" and all that was a bunch of selfish garbage. But now she wondered what exactly she had gained by being selfless. She had gladly been everyone's chauffeur and cook and maid and advisor. Her children were a mess, even so. But each time she decided that she was done, that from now on she'd be carving out time for herself, something always came up: Alice wanted a ride to the eye doctor, or Patty desperately needed a sitter so she could stay late at the office. Was Ann Marie going to refuse them?

She turned off the highway at exit 10 and pulled onto a smaller road. After a few minutes she saw the yellow banner hanging on a plain building up ahead: *Wellbright Miniatures Fair.* She looked down at the seat beside her, where her photos sat in a plain white envelope: the dollhouse from the front, side, and back to show off the Victorian trim, and a shot of each room close up, which looked quite a lot like pages from *Better Homes and Gardens.*

Might she actually win? She'd never say as

much to anyone, but she thought she had a chance.

Ann Marie got so excited that she rolled her eyes at herself. She pushed all the nonsense out of her head and pulled into the parking lot.

ALICE

Alice put her paper plate in the trash and the tuna bowl in the sink. She filled the bowl with soap and hot water, letting it sit a minute before rinsing it out.

She and Patrick and Ann Marie had driven up to Maine four weeks earlier, at the beginning of May. Pat pulled the boards off the windows and mowed the lawn and fixed the smoke detectors, which were beeping from the far corners of the house in a whiny little chorus. Alice and Ann Marie moved efficiently through first the cottage and then the house, removing the sheets that covered the couches and chairs; unrolling the carpets; plugging the lamps back in; washing down every dusty surface; and vacuuming up the countless dead flies and yellow jackets that somehow managed to find their way inside but could never seem to get out.

There had been an elaborate spiderweb in the cottage shower. It stretched from wall to wall, probably three feet across. As she sliced through it with the broom and then turned the water on full blast, Alice had felt almost bad for the creatures that had spun it. They had had this tiny kingdom all to themselves for months, and then *poof,* it was gone.

She spent the rest of May alone, except for Ann Marie and Pat's weekend visits. She continued preparing the house and the cottage for the kids, but also clearing things away. As soon as she had signed the papers to give over the property when she died, she realized that it might not be so long. She threw out bags of old sheets and bathing suits and tattered flip-flops that had somehow ended up in the loft. She pulled blankets and clothes from the bedroom dresser drawers and closet. She gathered what seemed like hundreds of shells and pieces of sea glass and the odd sand dollar or starfish, and put them all back on the beach one night at dusk. She gave Daniel's collection of thrillers and political biographies to the Ogunquit library, their spines stained white by the sun that streamed through the bedroom window. She boxed up glasses and plates from the big house, but she had to be careful not to remove too much from the cottage too soon. She didn't want the children asking questions.

Kathleen's daughter, Maggie, would be the first family member of the season to arrive, with her photographer boyfriend, Gabe.

Maggie was the artist of the family. Sometimes Alice thought Maggie was what she herself might have become if only she had been born a generation or two later. Timing was everything when it came to being a woman — the moment you entered the world could seal your fate. Maggie got straight A's at Kenyon College. At thirty, she had published a book of short stories about love gone awry.

"Wasn't it marvelous?" Kathleen kept saying.

Alice did think the writing was quite polished. She even bragged about it to the librarians at her local branch. But how could she read a work of fiction by her own granddaughter without hunting for glimpses of herself, of Kathleen, and their marriages? Kathleen said Maggie was now at work on a novel. Would she come this summer, wanting to collect stories like a vulture? It always felt that way when she asked questions, as if Alice should be chronicled, each heartache and human connection and childhood memory an artifact in a museum exhibit, to be tagged and displayed, a life lived and finished, ready to be studied.

Then again, Gabe, the boyfriend, was one of the few summer guests Alice was actually looking forward to hosting. She was even willing to overlook the fact that he and Maggie shared a bed in the cottage. (Ann Marie's kids had the manners and good sense to sleep

257

in separate rooms if they weren't married yet, but she knew she couldn't expect that from Kathleen's.)

In the past, when Maggie brought her pampered college friends to Maine, they acted as though Alice were running a bed-and-breakfast, the innkeeper next door. They didn't bother to invite her to join them, and when Maggie stopped by in the mornings, presumably to do her familial duty, Alice would quickly create a story about all she had to do that day, to keep from looking pathetic.

But Gabe! Last summer, he told jokes and thanked her again and again for inviting him, and sang old songs with her late into the night. He reminded her of different times, when her brothers and Daniel's would come up to the cottage for long weekends, singing and drinking, everyone merry.

And if she was really being honest, she liked him most of all because one night after dinner, while Maggie was in the bathroom and the two of them — Alice and Gabe — had each had about a bottle of cabernet, Gabe took Alice's hand and said, "You're beautiful, you know that? I mean, one of the most stunning women I've ever seen. I want to photograph you."

He was flirting with her! No one had flirted with her in years. Her pulse sped up, and she felt a certain degree of regret when she heard the toilet flushing in the other room. She let him take her picture the next afternoon while Maggie was on the beach. He sent her the finished copy, and Alice cried to see how wrinkly she looked, how goddamn *old.* When he had snapped her in the bright sun, she had felt eighteen again.

Life had been so dreary the past several months. She hoped Gabe might put a spring in her step.

He was a charmer, but still Alice had her doubts about the relationship: generally speaking, Maggie had her mother's bad taste in men. Kathleen had said once that Maggie was intent on settling down, but Gabe certainly didn't seem like the marrying type. Kathleen had told Alice that he drank too much, though Kathleen thought everyone drank too much. She had also reported that he and Maggie fought all the time. "He reminds me a lot of Paul," Kathleen had said, her ex-husband's name a kind of shorthand for everything that was wrong with men.

Maggie and Gabe would be here any day now, Kathleen said.

"Well, when exactly will they turn up?" Alice had asked her daughter over the phone a few days earlier.

"I think it depends on Gabe's work schedule. Don't sweat it, Mom," Kathleen said, in that faux-calm tone that could make Alice's blood pressure soar twenty points. "They'll get there when they get there."

"I'd like some advance warning so I can get the cottage ready is all," Alice said.

"Then call Maggie's cell and tell her that," Kathleen said.

"She's your daughter," Alice said.

"Yeah, well, she's your granddaughter."

"Oh Jesus, Kathleen, forget it," Alice said.

"It's forgotten," Kathleen replied tersely.

And that was that. Typical.

The previous winter, after one of her many therapeutic retreats, Kathleen had returned home to Massachusetts for Christmas to tell Alice that she had tried hypnosis and had recalled painful memories from her childhood: Alice making her stay inside the cottage while the other kids played on the beach, because she had been sneaking cookies and had gotten too fat for her bathing suit. Alice leaving her behind at a carnival when she was eight to teach her a lesson after she had thrown a tantrum, coming back to get her hours later, her face streaked with dirt and tears.

"You were emotionally and verbally abusive to me," Kathleen had said.

Alice wanted to slap her, the way her own father would have if spoken to like that.

"Shut the hell up," she said finally.

"See? You're doing it now. Why can't you ever apologize for what you did, so we can move forward?"

"I have nothing to be sorry for," Alice said. "You're the one who should be sorry, Kathleen. You should be thanking me for all I've done, not tearing me apart for your own problems."

She had always been strict with her girls, but what was the alternative? Look at the sort of mothers they had become, in an effort to be soft, to be supportive, and, in Kathleen's case, to turn her daughter into her best friend. It was pathetic.

The problem with her children and grandchildren was simply that they wanted too terribly to be *happy.* They were always in search of it, trying to better themselves, improve upon their current situation so that they might feel no pain. They thought every problem on earth could be solved by turning inward.

Alice knew where this came from. It was perhaps her greatest failing as a mother that all of these children — her own, and her children's children, and probably the great-grandchildren, too — were godless. Patrick and Ann Marie were the only ones who even went to Mass. Little Daniel had been an altar boy, and his sisters had sung in the choir, but now none of them seemed to have any involvement at all. Clare said she was still a Catholic in her heart and so was Joe, but they couldn't stand by and be part of the Church after what had happened in Boston these past

261

few years. Alice thought this was just an excuse to sleep in on Sundays, nothing more. They certainly didn't stop selling those Catholic artifacts of theirs, so how offended were they, really? The "priest scandal," as Clare insisted on calling it, was merely a case of a few bad apples. Everyone knew that.

"How can you believe, when the world is such a horrible place?" Kathleen had asked her once, and that was when she realized that she had somehow failed to teach them about the true meaning of faith.

She felt that the Catholic Church had made a horrendous mistake with Vatican II in the sixties. They had tried to make religion palatable, doing away with Latin Mass and head coverings and no meat on Fridays. Her grandchildren had grown up calling priests by their first names, as if they were waiters — Father Jim and Father Bob, and so on. It turned her stomach. The Church had taken the fear and the awe out of the whole equation, so that now her children and grandchildren and millions of others like them felt not even a hint of guilt for going out for breakfast on Sunday mornings instead of to church.

Kathleen called herself spiritual, one of those New Age words that Alice could never quite take seriously. Kathleen had picked it up, along with a whole host of other annoying and ridiculous beliefs, at Alcoholics

Anonymous sometime in the late eighties, right after her divorce.

Daniel had made it far too easy for Kathleen to end her marriage. He had advised her to leave Paul as soon as she told them he had cheated. Daniel gave her eight thousand dollars and told her she and the kids could come live with them. When Kathleen said no to that offer, he came up with the plan that she should live in the cottage rent-free for as long as she wanted. No matter that Alice had been planning to have contractors come in and fix the warped floors that spring. No matter that he hadn't even consulted her, for surely she would have insisted that Kathleen get a job, get herself together. It couldn't be good for her to be cooped up in the cottage with the children and her depressive thoughts for months on end.

If Daniel had stayed out of it, Kathleen might have found a way to forgive Paul and move forward. Paul Doyle was an excellent son-in-law: he adored Alice. Maybe that's what bothered Kathleen most about him. He made a decent father and a good provider, and he was a hell of a lot more fun than the AA guys Kathleen brought around later.

The drinking was something else her daughter blamed her for, the most preposterous of all her allegations over the years. Kathleen had become an alcoholic, she said, because of what she had internalized from watching Alice drink.

This made Alice laugh. From the time Kathleen was eleven years old until the day Daniel died thirty-three years later, Alice hadn't had a single sip of alcohol, even in the moments when she wanted one so badly she could have burst, when she felt herself coming undone and thought perhaps it would be worth it to lose Daniel and the kids just for one measly sip of whiskey. In fact, it was quite possible that she had made it through her first decade of motherhood without killing them all thanks only to Canadian Club.

After a church trip to County Kerry when the children were young, Daniel became obsessed with the idea of ancestry and getting back in touch with their roots. Neither his parents nor Alice's had ever been attached to Ireland — her mother had once said that her own mother died trying to flee the place, so she didn't see much purpose in ever going back. But sometime in the mid-fifties, couples they knew from St. Agnes and the children's school began making noise about returning to the homeland. And so the parish organized a trip, and they all flew to Shannon and helped build a Catholic orphanage and toured the lush countryside in a rented bus. They photographed ruins and streets that were overrun with sheep. They ate boiled dinners and sang old songs in damp, dark pubs.

When they arrived back in Boston, Daniel bought a book of Irish names and meanings, and cracked it open over dinner.

"We are Kellehers," he said proudly. "And that means — hold on here — wait a minute, I know you're all on the edge of your seats."

He flipped to the page, pretending to consult it with amazement until Alice said, "Oh Jesus, get on with it."

"Kelleher," he read, "is the Anglicized form of the Gaelic Ó Céileachair, 'son of Céileachair,' a personal name meaning 'companion dear,' i.e., 'lover of company.' Hey, does that sound like your dad or what?"

"Do more!" Clare shouted, for she too was excited by ghosts of the past. "Do Mom's maiden name," she said. "Do Brennan."

Daniel tapped her on the head with the book. "One step ahead of you, little lady. I've got it right here. Brennan!" he said loudly, then, reading it over, "One of Ireland's most common surnames, Brennan derives from one of three Irish personal names: Ó Braonáin, from *braon,* probably meaning 'sorrow,' and Mac Branáin and Ó Branáin, both from *bran,* meaning 'raven.' "

"So Mom is a sorrowful raven?" Clare asked. "A sad bird?"

Daniel smiled. "Precisely," he said. "Mom is my lovely sad bird. What do you think of that, sad bird?"

Alice hated him in that moment. She looked

265

at her three children sitting there, staring and demanding more — more food from the icebox, more time, more love — as if they owned her. She added an extra dash of whiskey to her drink and took a long sip.

"It's time for your baths," she said, to a chorus of groans that made Daniel chuckle.

"You head upstairs," she told the kids. "I will be there in a minute."

She went out to the back porch, glass in hand. She drank down what remained, hoping to soothe her nerves. It wasn't working tonight. Alice sat on the top step and put her fist in her mouth, biting down so hard that a few minutes later, when she bent to shampoo Clare's hair in the bathroom, her daughter balked and said, "Mommy, your fingers are bleeding."

Alice wiped them on a pink bath towel hanging from the doorknob.

"Be quiet and close your eyes," she said harshly.

She thought of how she had never really liked children, though her friends always said positively everyone fell in love with their own once they had them. She felt as though her body was full of something bigger than itself, pushing against every inch of her, trying to get out. She wanted to say that she was here by some strange accident, that in reality she should be in a Paris apartment right now, painting in solitude.

She wanted to scream, but instead she inhaled deeply and said a quick prayer.

She tried to lighten her voice: "That's it, darling. You don't want the soap to get in, now do you?"

MAGGIE

Maggie got out of bed and went to the cupboard. It was almost ten thirty at night. She'd probably be up until dawn now.

She looked at her cell phone and checked her e-mail, but Gabe had made no contact. It had been eight hours since she left his door. Maggie wished he were here.

She also wished that she had been born the sort of person who lost her appetite when in crisis. She pulled a box of macaroni and cheese from the top shelf and set a pot of water on the stove to boil.

You're eating for two, she thought, to make herself feel better, though this made her want to start crying all over again. She went and sat down on the couch, turned on the television. *Grease* was on. It seemed like *Grease* was always on. Did *Grease* have its own channel?

Maggie realized that it might really be over. Preposterous how many times she had said that to herself, a sign that it *should* be over, probably. But the thought of that made her feel ill; each of them going on, living a full life without the other. Or staying together, but without this child. What if that was his final answer: Work on the relationship, but no baby? She couldn't imagine what she'd do.

In college, she had taken the bus to Toledo with a roommate who needed an abortion. Monica Randolph was only nineteen and she had gotten pregnant after an ill-advised drunken hookup with a friend.

She told Maggie this in a whisper after they had turned out the lights one night. In the darkness, Maggie couldn't make out the girl's face, and she was reminded of confession — stepping into the booth, telling your deepest sins to a priest who was usually a stranger to you. *Bless me, Father, for I have sinned.* The act of it had frightened her as a young girl.

At her first penance at age seven, Maggie had grown so terrified that she blanked on her prepared list of sins (she stole some of Chris's Halloween candy, she talked back to her mother). And so she defaulted to reciting the Ten Commandments, assuming she must have violated most of those: "I coveted my neighbor's possessions," she said slowly to the priest, who was no doubt bored out of his skull at hearing the deepest sins of fifty second-graders in one night. "I didn't honor my mother and father. I committed adultery."

On the other side of the screen, Father Nick

jumped up in his seat. "You *what?*"

Now in her dorm room, which seemed a million miles from there, Maggie switched on the light and said, "Oh, Monica, I'm so sorry. What do you want to do?"

Monica was lying under a floral bedspread in a *She-Ra: Princess of Power* T-shirt and a pair of cotton underpants. She looked about ten years old.

"Well, I can't keep it," she said.

"No," Maggie agreed.

"I made an appointment at a clinic in Toledo for Saturday," Monica said. "I was wondering if you would come with me."

Maggie said she would.

"And please don't mention it to anyone," Monica said.

"Of course."

She didn't think much about the thing itself, only that she and Monica weren't really all that close. Monica was on the soccer team and had plenty of friends. But maybe, Maggie reasoned, she had asked her precisely because they weren't so invested in each other.

On the ride to Toledo, they ate fast food. They talked about the latest gossip from their dorm, and about their families back home. It was at this point that Monica said, "I hope you don't think I'm going to Hell or something."

Maggie was confused. "For what?"

Monica pointed awkwardly at her stomach, then gestured around to the rest of the bus. "You're Catholic, right?"

Non-Catholics Maggie had met at Kenyon seemed to think that all Catholics spent 90 percent of their time decrying abortion, when in fact no one in her family had ever so much as mentioned the word. She assumed her grandparents and Aunt Ann Marie and Uncle Pat were staunchly pro-life. She wondered then what her mother thought of it — Kathleen was progressive for a Kelleher, but even she had retained some of her childhood beliefs, and it sometimes surprised Maggie to find out which ones lingered on.

"I think you're doing the best thing," Maggie said.

"Maybe I should wait and think it over some more," Monica said. Then, "Well, no. It's not going to be that bad, right?"

"Right," Maggie said. "I'll be with you. Don't worry."

"It's not like we're going to put a crib in our dorm room," Monica said.

"Only maybe as a place to store beer bottles," Maggie said, trying to sound light.

"I'm so glad you're here," Monica said. "You're really good at taking care of people; I've noticed that about you."

"Thanks," Maggie said.

They lived together for another six months, but they never discussed Monica's abortion except once, during a weeklong pro-choice demonstration, when people hung hundreds of coat hangers from the trees in the freshman quad, with personal stories attached.

"I can't bear to look at them," Monica said. "I know what they're trying to say, but it's just too raw."

The following year she moved off campus. They never really talked again.

A few minutes earlier, Maggie had feared that she'd be up all night. Now she sat on the couch while John Travolta sang "Grease Lighting" in the background, and felt as though she hadn't slept in days. She got back into bed. Was this a pregnancy thing or a depression thing? Possibly both.

Before she drifted off to sleep, she thought of how, if life had turned out differently, Monica would have a thirteen-year-old child today, instead of living with her boyfriend and four cocker spaniels in San Francisco, performing in a bluegrass band, as Maggie had read about her in the alumni magazine.

She wondered if she had given the girl the right advice, but back then at Kenyon, an abortion had seemed like a reasonable step for dealing with an unfortunate situation.

Now that she herself was in the same position, it seemed less obvious. She was older, that was part of it. She wasn't some college kid who couldn't afford a child, couldn't somehow figure it out. But she also wasn't ready, the way she thought a mother ought to be: married, stable, living in more than two rooms.

You're Catholic, right? Monica had asked all those years ago, and Maggie had shrugged the comment off. But maybe that was part of it too. She wasn't religious in any formal way, but she still felt Catholicism coming through her pores so many years later. She still wanted terribly to be good, even if no one was watching. Out of habit, she prayed to Saint Anthony when she lost something, or said a Hail Mary whenever she heard an ambulance siren outside her apartment window. She didn't go to church on Ash Wednesday anymore, but when she saw ashes on the foreheads of strangers in the street, she would realize with a start that Lent was coming and decide to give something up, just for the heck of it. No sugar, gossip, or snooping for forty days.

Maggie had been baptized as an infant, and she had made her First Communion. There were presents, mostly of a religious nature, and a few checks and twenty-dollar bills as well. There was a chocolate cake with rich buttercream frosting and pink sugar flowers in the shape of a cross. It was one of those nights when all the adults — her parents, Aunt Clare (not yet married then), Uncle Patrick and Aunt Ann Marie, and all the neighbors — got drunk and sang Irish songs,

273

almost forgetting that the children existed, so that she and her cousin Patty got to stay up until midnight eating cake and honeyed ham with their fingers, playing Barbies on the sunporch.

As a kid, Maggie had been forced to go to church most Sundays, but after the divorce, after AA and an all-out war on tradition on her mother's part, they never went anymore, except maybe on Christmas and Easter with her grandparents. The Catholic Church, like the family itself, was a strange blend of resentments and confusion and contradictions and love and comfort to her, even now. She was an atheist, and yet the one or two times a year she went to Mass, a familiar song would begin to play and she would find herself singing, caught up in its beauty: *Lamb of God, you take away the sins of the world, Have mercy on us, grant us peace.*

The previous Christmas, her cousin Patty's kids had brought the gifts up to the altar, the crystal goblet of wine shaking in poor Foster's hands. Maggie had a vague memory of being in that exact position at her great-grandmother's funeral, the feeling of all eyes on you, and what sort of terrible fate might befall you if you spilled Jesus' blood on your good white shoes.

When the priest blessed the bread and wine, half the congregants genuflected, including Kathleen and Maggie and the other

Kellehers. The rest of them stood, and Alice whispered in a superior tone, "Those people don't go to church."

The family knew her to be lapsed, but that night Maggie had felt moved to take Communion, and so she followed her cousins to the altar, remembering precisely how to cup her hands, removing the host from the palm of the right with the fingers of the left, instinctively performing the sign of the cross before she headed back to her seat, and then feeling a bit silly about it. She could only imagine what Ann Marie must be thinking.

Later, she remembered why she had stopped taking Communion in the first place — when she was twelve, she had asked her mother why she didn't rise for Communion like everyone else, and Kathleen had explained that divorcées were forbidden from doing so. After that, Maggie had stayed seated next to her mother in the pew on holidays, in a defiant show of solidarity.

It was pouring when she woke up around seven the next morning. Rain came through the window screens and puddled under the radiators. Somewhere outside, something was burning — tires, maybe. The smell made her stomach turn.

"Great," Maggie said out loud.

She looked instinctively at her cell phone. He still hadn't called. But there was a missed call from the house in Maine. Her grandmother hadn't left a message, never did. When Alice and Daniel had gotten their first answering machine, sometime in the eighties, Daniel recorded the outgoing message, saying, "You've reached the Kellehers. Please leave your name, address, and phone number at the tone."

Everyone made fun of him, and he changed it to a simpler greeting, which was even funnier, because after he said, in his most professional voice, "You've reached Daniel and Alice; please leave a message," there was the fainter sound of him saying nervously, "Was that good? Okay," before the beep sounded. Alice had never changed the message, and it was sad and somewhat sweet to hear his voice whenever Maggie called her grandmother all these years after his death.

She closed the windows. Outside, people in suits rushed toward the High Street subway stop, a sea of black umbrellas. It was a Monday, and all of New York was heading into work, everyone but her.

Maggie went to the kitchen for a glass of water. She felt dried out, husklike, from all the crying. And then, like a shove from behind, she saw it: the burner she had lit the night before for her macaroni, still on. The pot of water she had set there was now empty and burning all along the bottom. Black metal flakes dusted the stovetop. That smell, the tires.

Childishly, she let herself imagine him receiving the news: *"She died in a fire a few hours after leaving your place, Gabe. She was carrying your baby."* He'd crumble to the ground, screaming, *"No, no!"* He'd never love again.

She took a pot holder from a hook on the wall and put the pan in the sink to cool off. She pushed the just-closed windows open and let the rain come in.

Smoke detector needs batteries, she thought. *Brain needs transplant.*

She retrieved *The New York Times* from its spot on her doormat and slipped it out of its blue plastic wrapping. Maggie sat on the couch and glanced at the front page: the CIA had sent an innocent man to Morocco to be tortured; a thirteen-year-old girl in Brownsville had been killed the night before, the victim of a stray gang member's bullet, while she was eating cake on the front stoop, celebrating her mother's college graduation.

What right did Maggie have to feel like shit about her own life when people were being extradited by the government for no good reason, and a child innocently eating cake in a party dress could be killed only a few miles from here? But still, she felt sorry for herself. She had just (*narrowly? No, not really*) escaped death. She missed Gabe. Right now she should be waking up in his bed, going to the market on East Eighth Street for snacks they could take along on the ride. She should be walking through the rain in her vacation bubble, impervious to weather and gang violence and bad hair, umbrella be damned.

She knew it was wrong to think one's own problems were the most dire in the world, but that didn't stop her from feeling like it anyway. She was pregnant and alone. She wasn't sure she could do this.

Her phone rang. She reached for it, but it was just her friend Allegra. Maggie let it ring through.

The last time she and Gabe had had a big fight, Allegra had told her to leave him.

"Come on," she had said. "You can't tell me that deep down this really feels right, can you? I went through the same shit with Mike. And believe me, now with Jeff, it's like — when it's right, it's right."

Maggie hated when people said that, as if ultimate rightness between two human beings were as easy to recognize as a plastic thermometer popping up from out of a turkey's bottom: perfect temperature achieved, you have now completed your mission, go forth and live in bliss. She was slightly suspicious that such certainty happened only to fairly simple people, nonthinkers.

Allegra was the last person she wanted to speak to right now.

Her stomach felt as though it were expanding outward, moving up toward her chest. She went into the bathroom and threw up.

Between the hours of eight and ten, Maggie took a shower, paid her cell phone and cable bills online, and scrubbed her already clean kitchen cabinets, all in the interest of keeping her hands in constant motion so she wouldn't call Gabe. There was only one thing she could say to get his attention now, before he had had a chance to cool off, and she needed to be sure of him before she broke the news, if they stood any chance at all.

She checked her e-mail. He should be on the way to his morning photo shoot by now. In fact, he probably hadn't even gone. There was nothing from him, only a short note from her brother (*Hey, isn't Mother's Day coming up? Are we doing something, or . . .* Mother's Day had been two weeks earlier. She had sent nice flowers with both their names on the card, and now she wrote Chris back to tell him so.) There was a message from her boss, Mindy, with the subject line ASSIGN-MENTS FOR THIS WEEK.

Maggie signed out. She wished she hadn't cleaned her apartment so thoroughly in advance of the trip to Maine, so that she might have some dishes to wash, or a bathroom floor that needed scouring. She kept her place spotless. Her shrink had once asked whether she thought this was a reaction to her mother's choices, and Maggie laughed, because what behavior on earth wasn't a re-action to some mother's choice?

Even after her parents' divorce, after her mother got sober, Kathleen still could never manage to vacuum the carpets or take out the trash like all other mothers seemed to be able to do. Dishes lay grimy in the sink and on the countertop for days. A thick layer of dust and dog hair covered the bookshelves and tables and windowsills. Piles of magazines and cardboard boxes that Kathleen intended to recycle someday were stacked in the back hall. She was forever writing down phone numbers on scraps of paper and then losing them hours later. She kept doing this, even after Maggie bought her one of those white-boards you could attach to the refrigerator door with magnets.

The farmhouse in California was even messier than the home Maggie had grown up in, with fruit flies buzzing all around the kitchen, landing in your tea or your breakfast cereal. Kathleen never changed the sheets in the guest room. Maggie might go there and not return for nine months, but the sheets would stay put. She didn't enjoy visiting, especially with Gabe, who had never hidden his feelings about the place. And she won-dered about Arlo — had he too lived in his own filth for years, so that the situation seemed completely normal?

■ ■ ■ ■

Maggie dialed her shrink's number at ten o'clock, the exact time she knew Dr. Rosen got to the office. She was always saying that Maggie should feel free to call and talk between sessions if she needed to, but Maggie had never thought of taking her up on the offer until now. It seemed like an option for suicide cases and manic-depressives, not women like her, suffering from a mix of romantic turmoil and white-girl blues.

Now she said, "Hi, it's Maggie Doyle. Do you have a minute?"

She told Dr. Rosen about Gabe, their fight. She did not mention the baby.

"We were supposed to be heading to Maine today, and I'm feeling sort of adrift."

"Have you thought of going by yourself?"

"I don't know," Maggie said. "I took the days off from work, and I really need to focus on writing my book. And maybe it would be good for me. But then I think about the spotty cell phone service and having no one around but my grandmother."

The cottage was an isolated place, which could be cozy or smothering, depending. She had experienced it both ways over the years. She wished her mother could come along. It struck her then, as it often did, that Kathleen was no longer in Boston. She had moved across the country, and though Maggie still saw her almost as often as she had when they were both on the East Coast, there was something sad and lonely about this. She couldn't just run home to her mom, a three-hour train ride away, even if she wanted to.

"It might feel really good to go alone," Rosen went on. "Empowering! Time to work on your book, a change of scenery."

"We were going to take Gabe's car, and I don't know how to drive, so —"

"Take a bus, gosh," Rosen said. "At least think about it. Time off from Gabe seems advisable."

Maggie's heart sank. She tried to think of some way of mentioning the other part, without actually saying the words.

"You can always call me again if you need to," Dr. Rosen said, apparently her way of ending the call. The woman who had taught Maggie about boundaries had a hyperawareness of them herself: she knew all about Maggie, while Maggie couldn't ask her a simple personal question. "Where are you going on vacation?" was met with an uncomfortable smile and a reassuring, "Don't worry, we'll pick right up again the week after next," as if Maggie had intended to trail her to the Berkshires and have a breakdown, when she had only been making conversation.

Maggie resented her for a split second, then resented herself for being completely incapable of having a fully functional and honest relationship with anyone, including a paid mental health professional.

"Thanks for everything," she said politely.

They hung up. She glanced over at her suitcase, still packed. Maybe she should go alone. It might be good for her. If only Alice weren't such a wild card, her behavior fluctuating from amiable to nightmarish in a flash.

Maggie had an embarrassing desire for Alice's affection, which made her act strangely around her. She actually drank more in Alice's presence in an attempt to win her grandmother's approval. Dr. Rosen had had a field day with that one. Still, her real allegiance was always to Kathleen, and when she thought of what Alice had put her mother through, she almost wanted to break all ties with her grandmother.

It wasn't just Kathleen — they had all been the recipients of Alice's wrath at one time or another. She was strange: effervescent and charming, her presence taking up so much space. Yet she sometimes slipped into venomous moods without warning. Alice could say the cruelest thing, a comment you would carry with you for the rest of your life, and then a minute later, she'd be smiling, wondering why on earth you had to be so sensitive. A week before Maggie's prom, she had been over at her grandparents' house for dinner, and Alice and Daniel had her laughing all night, as they danced across the living room, teaching her the Charleston and the two-step. She had loved them deeply in that moment, vowed to visit more often. But then, on prom night, in front of her date and his parents, Alice had said, "Oh, Maggie, you couldn't have laid off the ice cream for this? Darling, you are positively fat!"

Maggie knew her grandmother's aversion to her branch of the family had to do with jealousy over how much her grandfather had loved them, especially Kathleen. Which was strange, really. Wouldn't you want your husband to be devoted to his children and grandchildren? But that wasn't the way Alice worked.

Right after her grandfather died, Maggie had made a real effort to call Alice two or three times a week. (She hid this fact from her mother, who had vowed never to speak to Alice again after what happened at the funeral.) But Alice didn't want to talk. She always cut the call short, saying, "Shouldn't you be working on your writing instead of jabbering on the phone with me?" or citing long-distance charges as if it were 1952. Maggie didn't call much anymore. She occasionally thought to write a long letter, but she could never think of what to say. Alice didn't call her very often either, and when she did, it was usually with some odd request. Would Maggie please go to St. Patrick's Cathedral and light a candle for her cousin Ryan, who had an audition coming up, or for Fiona, who was serving the Lord through her Peace Corps work so far away? Maggie would always say yes, intending to follow through, but then she would forget, or reason her way out of it — the cathedral was all the way uptown, and did the God she didn't believe in really care that much more about a five-dollar candle, lit among tourists drinking Starbucks coffee in the pews, than he did about a solemn prayer delivered in the diminutive chapel on Cranberry Street, right by her apartment?

Maggie always thought that family gatherings would be fun, great, loving times, but usually they were either boring or tense. The truly enjoyable get-togethers had gotten fewer and farther between since her grandfather died, but the memory of them kept the Kellehers coming back together, trying to re-create the magic. She knew all this, and yet she still craved it.

She especially missed childhood summers when the whole family would go up to Maine together. Alice was the hostess in those days, organizing group dinners and long car rides to new beaches, or instructing her husband to take all the grandkids out digging for clams in Kittery at low tide. They piled into his old Buick. At the shore, they stood in shallow water for hours, thrusting their rakes and their bare feet down deep into the oozing sand, screaming with delight and fear when they hit a clamshell. They filled buckets with the creatures, and by the time the sun set, Daniel would say, "Okay, let's bring these fellas home so Grandma can cook them up." Then Maggie and Fiona and Patty would yell out "No!" and the boys would yell "Yes!" while their grandfather stood there laughing. They always returned to the cottage without a single clam.

Every year since her uncle Patrick had created the cottage schedule, Maggie had gone to Cape Neddick for a few days in June, usually with Allegra or a couple of friends from high school, but it wasn't the same. Her grandmother rarely invited them over or seemed to want to spend time together. She acted like she was entirely too busy, though doing what, Maggie could never be sure. Besides the awkward hello and good-bye, and one or two rushed dinners, she hardly ever spoke to Alice on those trips. Alice seemed content to be shut up alone in the house next door.

But when she brought Gabe to Maine the previous summer, her grandmother suddenly brightened. The fun they had reminded Maggie of the old days. Alice played the piano in the cottage after dinner one night, and Gabe sang along, belting out show tunes, unbearably off-key. Maggie was shocked and touched that he knew the words. He asked Alice about her favorite books, her funniest memories of Maggie as a kid.

"You're amazing," he told her over and over, to Maggie's slight agitation, for she had told Gabe of Alice's unkindness toward her mother, and she almost wished his affections would be harder for Alice to win.

In a night, he somehow pulled from Alice what Maggie was always aiming for — real conversation, tales of the past that would die with her unless she told them now. Alice was in the middle of some story about babysitting for Maggie and Chris when they were kids, and how they had hidden from her at the zoo as a prank, throwing Chris's baseball cap into the monkey cage. Gabe laughed, and Maggie did, too, though she was positive the story was made up.

She asked then, "So, Grandma, what was your childhood like? Tell us about that."

Alice's eyes changed quickly. "I was talking about something else," she said. "You interrupted me. Anyway, I should be getting on with my evening. I'll see you kids tomorrow."

That night in bed, Maggie said, "What did I tell you? The woman hates my guts."

"You know, she really does seem to," Gabe said with a smile. Then he wrapped her up in his arms and said, "But I love your guts. I think you have the sexiest guts on the planet."

"Honestly, though," Maggie said. "I wish she liked me half as much as she likes you."

"You two are family, it's different," he said. "I don't understand why you need her approval so badly. You're nothing alike."

Now she tried to imagine what she and Alice would say to each other if they were forced to spend two weeks together. She couldn't quite picture it, but she wanted to. She thought of Alice, alone up at the beach house. She was slipping a bit mentally, maybe; she seemed confused sometimes. Kathleen always said Alice was as healthy as a horse, but how many good summers did she have left?

Maggie thought of the cottage itself, and how much she loved the place. Dr. Rosen was right — how hard was it to take a bus? The ocean would restore her. And if she was having a miserable time, she could always turn around and come home.

She would go alone.

But she'd give it a day, in case Gabe changed his mind and decided to come too.

Around noon, Maggie dialed the number of her grandparents' house in Maine. Alice answered after four rings, sounding sort of tipsy. Maggie had never seen her grandmother drink until after her grandfather died. But since then, it was rare to see Alice without a glass in her hand, even at this time of day.

"Grandma, it's Maggie," she said.

"Hold on, let me stick a thingamajig into my book to save the page," Alice said. She came back onto the line a moment later. "How are you, darling?"

"Good. You?"

"Marvelous. I called you earlier."

"I know, that's why I'm calling."

"How on earth do you know? I didn't leave a message." Her words were soaked in suspicion, as if Maggie were either lying or working for the CIA.

"What's going on there?" Maggie asked.

"I just put a chicken into the oven for dinner later, and now I'm sitting here on the porch with my feet up. They have been absolutely killing me. Circulation, I guess. Have you seen the new adaptation of *David Copperfield* on PBS? I think you'd really like it. They're airing it in five parts this week. I watched the second part last night. A woman from church told me about it, and there's that actress with the enormous eyes, oh, what's her name, what's her name? Ann Marie would know it, I'll have to ask her. She was in *Bleak House* also. Anyway, when are you coming?"

The way Alice rambled made Maggie wonder how long it had been since she had spoken to anyone. Sometimes Maggie would picture what an average day might look like for Alice, and the thought of her grandmother's lonesomeness was like a punch in the gut. She felt happy about her decision to visit.

"I'll be there tomorrow. So maybe we can watch the rest of the show together."

"Okay, well, tell Gabe I've got a new book of sheet music from the library — *Broadway: The Patriot Songs.*"

"Actually, it's just going to be me," Maggie said.

Perhaps Alice hadn't heard her, because she only responded, "I need to get to the Shop 'n Save before they run out of the good muffins that he likes. And they've got hamburger meat on sale, so we can do burgers on the grill tomorrow night if you want. Or I could do a meatloaf. Let's do that, because it might rain."

Maggie wished she didn't feel envious of the fact that Alice clearly wanted to see Gabe more than she wanted to see her. Maybe she should have said, *We broke up,* or *Grandma, he's an asshole.*

Instead, all she said was "Sounds good."

"Well, this must be costing you a fortune," Alice said. "A long-distance call on a cellular phone? We'd better wrap it up."

"There's no such thing as a long-distance call from a cell phone," Maggie said.

"What?"

"Nothing. Love you."

It felt sort of unnatural, saying *I love you* to Alice. But it was just as strange not to say it, so Maggie did.

As soon as they hung up, Maggie looked at her phone, in case she had somehow missed a call from Gabe.

Her fear began to swell but she pushed it down. She knew she was pregnant, but at certain moments it was still easy enough to believe that nothing was happening. Perhaps this was how those women who delivered full-term babies into McDonald's toilets started out.

She watched TV. An hour later, in the middle of a *Golden Girls* episode, her heart began to thump out of nowhere. She tried to take deep breaths. When she looked down at her calves, they were covered in red splotches.

Maggie put her head between her legs — wasn't that something people did?

It didn't seem to help. A moment later, she sat up straight and called her mother. She couldn't keep the secret any longer. This child was literally making her sick. (Could you possibly be allergic to your own fetus? No, that was ridiculous.) Kathleen would know what to do.

Maggie spoke to her mother at least once a day, but now that there was actually something important to say, she feared it.

291

It would never have dawned on her to call her father, even though he was in the same time zone. She talked to him every couple of weeks, but only about the most banal topics: how the Red Sox were faring, what he thought of the latest season of *Law & Order,* whether her super had properly installed the carbon monoxide detector. He had married his longtime girlfriend, Irene, the previous year and asked Chris to be his best man. Maggie had felt so sad for her younger brother that this well-meaning but emotionally tone-deaf man was his one and only father, though of course he was her only father too. He and Irene were heavy drinkers, just as he and Kathleen had once been — they were fun and boisterous much of the time, but the flip side was that they had loud, drunken arguments in front of other people, and did God only knows what when no one was looking. Maggie prayed her father had had the good sense to get a vasectomy.

After Maggie dialed her number, Kathleen answered the phone sounding muffled.

"We're out in the barn up to our elbows in shit," she said happily. "You okay?"

"I'm freaking out," Maggie said. "I really need to talk."

"Okay," Kathleen said. "Let me go into the yard. Hold on."

There were a few banging sounds and her mother said, "Oh Jesus, can we get rid of

292

some of this?"

Then Kathleen came back clearer. "What's wrong?"

"I have these red splotches all over my legs, and I can't breathe too well."

"Like big clusters of splotches or more like bug bites?"

"Clusters."

"Are they red or brown?"

"Red."

"Sounds like hives," Kathleen said calmly. "You never get those."

"I know. I'm freaking out. I can't breathe."

"Calm down. I think you might be having a panic attack. You need to take some Saint-John's-wort. And nettle is a great herbal antihistamine. Same as I gave you for your pollen allergy. And take some deep breaths, sweetheart. That's the most important part."

"I don't have that stuff," Maggie said.

"Yes, you do. I left a bunch of things under your sink last time I was in town."

Maggie had thrown it all out after a bottle of sandalwood oil leaked onto everything else, leaving a sickly sweet odor behind in her bathroom for weeks.

"Would a Benadryl work?" she asked now, looking in the medicine cabinet to see what she had.

"Sure," Kathleen said. "But get that other stuff I mentioned too. So, what happened? What has you so freaked out?"

"I have to tell you something pretty huge," Maggie said. "But first, Gabe and I had a big fight. He told me he doesn't want to live together. I think we may have broken up for real."

"Oh, honey, I'm sorry. Listen, it's for the best." Kathleen spoke quickly, barely pausing between words, as if she were speed-reading from some script on helping the broken-hearted. "I know it doesn't seem that way now, but trust me. The universe works in mysterious ways."

Maggie felt sick at this casual comment. She still wanted him to be right for her, wanted Kathleen to say something else, though she knew her mother had never liked Gabe.

Despite her mother's complaints about Alice, they were shockingly similar in certain ways. They both prided themselves on telling the absolute truth as they saw it, even if it hurt.

"What did you want to tell me?" Kathleen asked.

Maggie leaned against the counter. She couldn't shake the feeling that Kathleen was rushing to get her off the phone. Why had she assumed that it would be smart to tell her mother? Kathleen would likely go ballistic when she heard the news, telling Maggie that she had ruined her life. She wasn't going to start sterilizing bottles and knitting booties anytime soon.

"I wanted to tell you that I'm going to Maine anyway, without him."

"Interesting," Kathleen said. "Why?"

"I don't know, I thought it might be good for me, and I've taken the time off work."

"Run straight into the nurturing bosom of your grandmother," Kathleen said.

"Yeah, right," Maggie said. "Well, I would go see my mother but she's up to her elbows in shit."

"You know there's always room for you here," Kathleen said, but she didn't press the matter.

"I miss you," Maggie said.

"I miss you too. You're about the only thing I miss from back there. How are the hives?"

Maggie looked down. "On one side they're gone, and on the other side they're fading. That was fast."

"Hives are weird like that."

"How are you able to diagnose over the phone?" Maggie asked. "Who taught you?"

"No one taught me, I'm just a mother," Kathleen said. "You'll be the same way some-day."

That was Maggie's chance to tell her, but her mouth felt dry; she couldn't form the words.

"Go lie down for a bit, and then maybe take a long walk on the Promenade," Kathleen said. "Be very kind to yourself, okay? Call me anytime today if you need to. And let me know once you get to Maine tomorrow."

"I will."

"And give my best to Malice."

"Mom —"

"Sorry. Alice."

That afternoon, Maggie was lying on the couch when she heard a commotion in the hallway. She pictured Gabe climbing the steps, suitcase in hand. She got up quickly and looked through the peephole.

Her neighbor Rhiannon was lugging a bookcase up the stairs. She looked amazing in her grubby T-shirt and shorts. She probably hadn't even showered. Her toned upper arms were straight out of a magazine photograph. Maggie made a mental note about bicep exercises.

Despite her desire to get back into bed, she poked her head out.

"Need some help?"

"Can you get the door?" Rhiannon asked. "It's unlocked."

Maggie left her own door ajar and pushed Rhiannon's forward. The apartment was laid out exactly like her own, but instead of hand-me-down china from her aunt Clare and the stained sofa and love seat on long-term loan from her mother, here there were beautiful grown-up pieces of furniture and a row of elegant handblown glass vases on the windowsill. Lined up on the bathroom sink and tub were various containers in different shapes and sizes: a purple pot of lemon-scented cream, a slim vial of coconut oil, honey-almond sugar scrub packed in a mason jar, and eye pads infused with coffee-bean extract. There were lotions made specifically for knees, hands, cuticles, feet, throat, eyelids. Maggie wondered how many of them Rhiannon actually used, and whether they could possibly play any role in her beauty, which seemed predetermined, unchangeable.

At the moment, Maggie's shower contained half a bar of soap with a hair stuck to it, whichever shampoo had been on sale at Duane Reade, and the matching conditioner, with the lid popped off so she could shove her fingers inside and scoop out the last remaining drop, instead of walking four blocks to the drugstore to buy more.

"I found this on the street. Isn't it gorgeous?" Rhiannon said, shoving the weathered wooden bookcase against the wall of her little foyer, where it suddenly looked as if it had always resided. "It was about to get ruined by the rain."

"It's great," Maggie said.

"How about a cup of tea?" Rhiannon asked.

Maggie smiled. "No thanks."

"A whiskey?"

"Ha, no. Okay, I'll take an herbal tea."

Rhiannon went to the kitchen and said over

her shoulder, "Any developments on the Gabe front?"

Maggie had told her the story months ago — that they were in love, but they could never seem to stop arguing; that Gabe had a tendency to lie. Rhiannon was less judgmental than most of Maggie's friends, perhaps because of what she herself had been through.

"No word from him," Maggie said.

"What happened?"

"He said he doesn't want to move in together after all."

Rhiannon popped her head out of the kitchen. "He *what?*"

Maggie nodded. Suddenly, she began to ramble, her words growing faster as she went, gaining momentum: "Yes. And we were supposed to be going to Maine today, but now I have to go by myself tomorrow and I'm scared of what that's going to be like, because my sort of crazy grandmother will be there, and he hasn't called me and I am obsessively checking my cell, because I need this to work out."

She felt herself unable to stop talking. She realized she was finally going to say it, and to someone she hardly knew: "I need him to come around. Because I love him. I really do. And there's another thing." *Oh God, here she went.* "I'm pregnant."

Rhiannon guided her to the couch and they both sat. Hives crept down Maggie's arms —

red, itchy, puffed-up welts that hadn't been there three seconds earlier but looked as though they would stay forever. Was this physical assault on her extremities really necessary, on top of everything else?

"Why do you say that?" Rhiannon asked. "Is your period late?"

"It's more than that. I already took a home test."

"Those can be wrong," Rhiannon said hopefully.

"And I went to the doctor for a blood test."

"Oh. Well, what does Gabe say?" She paused, taking in Maggie's expression. Then she said, "He doesn't know."

"I was waiting for the right time to tell him. I thought once we went up to the beach in Maine it would be easier, and — it's a long story . . ." she trailed off, putting her head in her hands.

Then she began to laugh. "I can't believe I told you that. I haven't told anyone."

Rhiannon squeezed her hand, and said, "I'm glad you told me. We'll figure this out, don't worry."

Maggie wished it were Kathleen sitting there. But maybe your family could never give you the perfect response, the kindest reply. Maybe their vision of you was too tied up in their hopes and fears for them to ever really see you as just *you*. Perhaps that's why her mother had gone so far away in the end

— to be seen clearly, to scc others that way.

"I keep breaking out in hives," Maggie said.

"Those are the worst. I had them all through my divorce. Actually, I had them on my wedding day, too, which might have been a sign. You need Claritin. Hold on, I have some."

Rhiannon went into her bathroom, and then emerged with a little box in one hand and a bottle of pills in the other.

"I also have Valium," she said, shaking the bottle. "Want one?"

"I'm pretty sure Valium's a bad idea when you're knocked up," Maggie said.

"Shit, right. Good point. Sorry, I'm flummoxed. I want to help."

Maggie smiled. "You're sweet."

"Forget sweet. I owe you one."

"What for?"

"You really saved me the day of my divorce, Maggie. Do you even know that? If we hadn't gone to dinner that night, I don't know what would have happened to me. I don't have many friends here."

Rhiannon hadn't seemed desperate that evening. They had eaten a nice meal, had a glass of wine, laughed about their lives and their ridiculous dating histories. It was hard to imagine that Maggie had done anything extraordinary for her.

"So you're keeping it then?" Rhiannon asked.

Maggie felt a knot tighten up in her chest. All the times she had imagined being pregnant, she'd never envisioned having to answer that question. But the answer came fast: "Yes. Definitely."

Rhiannon nodded. "Good for you. Hey, do you want to borrow my Subaru to drive to Maine?"

"You have one?" Maggie asked.

"I never drive it," Rhiannon said. "I just keep it around in case I need a getaway car."

"That's okay," Maggie said. "I don't even have a driver's license. But it's no big deal. I'll take the bus. I can sleep, get some reading done."

Rhiannon looked thoughtful. "How long is the drive?"

"Five hours."

"That's nothing. I'll drive you there tomorrow and then turn back. I've got class on Wednesday afternoon."

"That's crazy."

"Not really. I've never seen New England. I love long car rides. And I haven't been anywhere in weeks. I'm starting to get stir-crazy."

Maggie raised an eyebrow.

"Also, I'm thinking you could use the company," Rhiannon said. "And, what could be more fun on a day off than a drive to the beach?"

"Really?" Maggie said. "That might be

great if you're sure you don't mind. This is one of those moments when it hits me how moronic I am for not knowing how to drive."

"Don't worry about that. This way it will be cheaper than if you had to rent a car anyway," Rhiannon said.

Maggie wondered if Rhiannon was picturing her as an impoverished young mother, saving pennies for the baby's formula. And was that perception so far from the truth? She was suddenly paralyzed by the thought of money: she made a mental note to inquire about freelance work, as much as she could manage in the next seven months, and to find more people who needed help with their online dating profiles. Maybe she could place an ad on Craigslist, even though the thought of being a single, pregnant matchmaker — the brains behind other people's awkward first dates — made her want to throw up.

"What do you say?" Rhiannon asked now.

"If you're sure it's not a pain," she said. "Why don't you sleep on it and we can decide tomorrow? I really don't mind taking the bus."

"No need," Rhiannon said. "Consider me your chauffeur."

KATHLEEN

Kathleen prepared the wooden box, laying down first a layer of damp leaves and then a layer of dirt. She began to pat the dirt so that it was even.

She thought of the advice she had given Maggie an hour earlier: nettle root, and Saint-John's-wort, and oh, did I mention getting rid of that horrendous Waspy jerk boyfriend once and for all? Not just waiting around, as she knew Maggie would, to see what *he* wanted? No, Kathleen hadn't said this last part. She knew Maggie didn't like it when she blurted out her opinions like that. Everything in due time, she told herself. Still, it was hard to watch your baby torture herself over an unworthy man. She had had to rush to get off the phone so she wouldn't say as much.

"Uh, Kath, I think you've beaten that dirt down enough," Arlo said.

She hadn't been paying attention. In her frustration, she had packed it too hard. She'd have to start over, and there were twenty-four boxes to go after this one.

"We need a goddamn intern," she said.

"Calm down. Maggie will be okay."

"This isn't about Maggie," she said, though she knew it was. Then she added, "Sorry. I'm not myself today."

He shrugged. "You can't help it if your family drives you nuts."

"Maggie doesn't drive me nuts," she said. "The rest of them, yes. But not Maggie."

She could not believe Gabe had broken up with her daughter the day before they were supposed to leave for vacation. Kathleen had never liked the kid. She wished Maggie would go somewhere fun with her girlfriends, or come out to California for a visit. But for some reason she wanted to go to Maine instead. It couldn't be good for her to be isolated up there with only Alice for company.

The whole idea made Kathleen nervous. She could picture her mother giving Maggie all the wrong advice (*He's great! You're fat! Drink more!*). That was the best-case scenario. Worst case, she'd be cruel, and hurt Maggie, who was already hurting enough.

Kathleen wished she could be there to help. But there was nothing on earth that could get her to Maine. She associated the place with Alice in every way. It made Kathleen remember what she wanted to forget.

When she reflected on her childhood, she

304

thought of how Alice had had three children in her twenties, right on the heels of her sister's gruesome death. No wonder she drank. Alice would never discuss the death, but Kathleen recognized her mother's response as a clear case of survivor guilt. Though why Alice had decided to have children when she did, Kathleen would never know. No doubt, they all would have been better off if she had waited.

Five years back, after her brother Michael died, Alice had gone into a deep depression. He was the last of her siblings. Her husband was gone and so were most of her friends, her family. Kathleen talked to Alice at length — a rare moment of connection between them — and convinced her to come along with her and Maggie to a yoga retreat in the Bahamas for New Year's.

Kathleen had long dreamed of going on one of these immersion trips. A friend at AA had told her they were a great way to see the Caribbean on the cheap. Kathleen thought the whole excursion might be a bit too hippie dippy, even for her, but she loved the serenity that yoga brought, and on these trips, her friend had told her, you got to lie on the beach and connect with your surroundings. Each day, there were mandatory classes and an afternoon lecture by a master swami. Kathleen read up on him and thought he was terribly impressive. He had developed the

Five Points of Yoga, the most important of which was "We become what we think."

Kathleen imagined the three of them — Maggie, Alice, and herself — side by side, three generations of women absorbing power and wisdom from one another. She realized it was a mistake from the moment they arrived. The swami asked to inspect their belongings. Kathleen had expressly told her mother that there was no caffeine or alcohol allowed, and Alice had said that was fine by her. But when he unzipped her suitcase, he found two Ziplocs full of tea bags, three bottles of red wine, a huge bottle of rum, and a blender. A blender!

"What were you thinking?" Kathleen demanded, mortified.

"I was thinking, what's the Bahamas without mixed drinks, that's mostly what I was thinking," Alice said, flashing a big flirty smile at the swami, who sort of smirked in response.

"Grandma!" Maggie said, sounding amused. "You're bad."

Alice refused to accompany them to the yoga and meditation classes, even though Kathleen had prepaid. Instead, she walked the beach alone for hours. When Kathleen said that she could have stayed in Massachusetts if she wanted to do that, Alice's venom came out: "I wish I had stayed," she snapped.

She got in trouble with the swami for smoking, and — done with flirtation now — shot him the deadliest look before saying, "Oh, honestly, we are *paying* to be here. Go ahead and send me to the principal's office."

Maggie chuckled at that. Apparently she too thought it was ridiculous.

That night Kathleen discovered Alice and Maggie out on the beach, sipping rum they had mixed with organic pineapple juice. They were giggling, and she felt furious at the idea of being the odd man out.

"I don't know why either of you even came," she said. "You're making a fool out of me in front of a man I very much respect."

Maggie got to her feet then. "Oh, Mom, please don't be upset."

"I'm fine," she said sharply. "I'm going to bed. There's a sunrise meditation in the morning, but I'll go ahead and assume you two will be too hungover to come along."

She stomped back toward the bungalows. Maggie didn't follow her. Kathleen felt stupid now. Perhaps she had overreacted. But she worried about Maggie and Alice spending time together. As far as Kathleen was concerned, her mother was like Hannibal Lecter: you'd be a fool to get too close, but sometimes her charm made it hard to resist. Kathleen herself still told Alice things she shouldn't from time to time, only to have them thrown back in her face.

When they got home from the Bahamas,

Kathleen called Alice and said, "You know, I brought you there to help you figure out a way to cope."

"I don't need help. What you people get from headshrinkers and gurus and meditation, I get from my faith," Alice responded. "I need to focus on going to Mass more, that's all."

"You already go every day," Kathleen had said.

"I go for all the Sundays you've missed in the last twenty years," Alice replied.

Well, she had walked right into that one.

At the end of every AA meeting, before coffee, they joined hands and said the Lord's Prayer: *Our father, who art in Heaven, hallowed be thy name . . .* The defiant teenager in Kathleen always rose up at that moment: these words, forever synonymous with the spicy air and somber music of the Catholic Church. They evoked countless Sunday mornings spent standing in a pew with her parents, brother, and sister; wearing a ridiculous hat on her head; glancing nervously at the Stations of the Cross, the crucifixion displayed so graphically on the walls. She didn't understand a word of the Latin Mass, though she had memorized the entire thing somewhere along the line. She stood there each week, waiting for the hour to pass, thinking of Hell and pancakes and high school boys.

Kathleen's days as a practicing Catholic were all based in fear. She spent most of her time searching for the loopholes. No sex before marriage, unless you really truly intended to get married. Absolutely no drinking during Lent, except out of state.

In recent years, she had come to detest the Church. She knew one of those grown men on the news in Boston, with his head lowered, telling the tale of how some priest had forced sex upon him when he was an altar boy. His name was Robert O'Neil. He had been in her class in grade school. Kathleen pictured him as he had been then — freckle-faced, dressed in corduroys and crocheted sweaters, a slight gap between his teeth. She seethed to think of the private hell the poor kid was in all along. Now, he said, he was ruined — estranged from his wife, afraid to let his own children so much as sit in his lap.

Alice's parish had shut its doors two years back, and she had mourned that church as if it were a loved one. Kathleen felt for her, imagining what it might be like to have to let go of the community that you felt was the most essential part of you. But what about the fact that her church and dozens of others like it were in financial trouble to begin with because the archdiocese of Boston could hardly afford all the legal bills associated with the accusations made against priests? She tried to engage her mother in a conversation about this, but Alice would not hear it. Though she lived to criticize pretty much everything else, she plain refused to see anything bad in the Catholic Church.

Until she was in her mid-twenties, Kathleen had always thought of her mother's religiosity as semi–trumped up, just another way in which Alice could pose and be dramatic. Did she really need to go to church *every day,* with that ridiculous white scarf covering her hair? Kathleen imagined she did it only to make her children feel guilty about their comparative lack of devotion.

But then one Easter, her uncle Timothy told her a story about the time he was home on leave from the war and bragged to Alice and the rest of their siblings about how Marlene Dietrich had performed for his squadron in Italy.

"I was the first to ship out," Uncle Tim said. "The other boys hadn't gone yet, but we knew they would soon. So I wanted to get them revved up. This was before Mary died," he added, a rare reference to the sister they had lost. "I was going on and on about what a looker Dietrich was. She was a good person, too, you know — a German, but she renounced Hitler. He had all her films banned. Anyway, there I was going on and on about how sexy she was, how much all the guys were falling all over one another imagining what they might do with five minutes alone with her. I'll admit, I got carried away. My brothers were egging me on. We were all crazy about Dietrich."

Kathleen tried to picture her bald old uncles as a posse of horny young guys.

"So then Alice said, 'What do you mean? What would you do?' and then Mary said, you know, 'They'd have their way with her.' "

He paused, took a sip of his drink. This was all that Kathleen had ever heard about her aunt. There were no pictures of her anywhere; no one ever told stories. She wanted more.

"All of a sudden," Tim continued, "Alice stormed out of the room crying."

"Why?"

"No one knew. I thought she'd like the story. She was always nuts about those old movie stars. Anyway, we ignored her. Typical drama queen Alice. But the next day she told me that she'd been up praying for me all night, for me and the rest of those souls in my squadron. She said we'd go to Hell for thoughts like that."

"How old was she?"

"Twenty or so? You see, she was always an innocent," Uncle Tim said. "A flirt, but a clueless one. She pretended she never wanted to get married, but I think that was just because all of that man and wife stuff scared her. You wouldn't think it to interact with her since she can be such a pain in the ass and she's always acting so fancy, but the truth is, she's never changed. Her whole life she's been asking God for help, and really expecting it to come. She's been to Mass every morning since me and my brothers shipped out, as far as I know. She actually wants to be good."

It dawned on Kathleen that the church was Alice's public forum, the place where she went and behaved herself, the place where others viewed her as she wished to be viewed. At St. Agnes over the years, Alice had organized the Sunday school classes and the canned food drives, the fund-raisers for the retired priests and the Christmas swap meet. No one there knew what kind of cruelty she was capable of at home. They all saw her as a saint.

She actually wants to be good.

Kathleen had thought of this at her father's funeral, as she watched Alice with her eyes fixed on the priest, as if his words might provide an explanation, an answer. She envied her mother that level of faith, especially at that moment.

They were in Maine when he told them he was dying. It was the last time Kathleen had been there, probably the last time she ever would. The whole family had gone up for Labor Day weekend, and everyone was getting along unusually well — no blowups or heated words or incidents of someone (usually Kathleen) storming out and checking into a motel. Ann Marie and Alice had made a big dinner of grilled steak, corn on the cob, potato salad, and tomatoes and cucumbers from the garden. Afterward, the kids stood out on the porch roasting marshmallows over the charcoal grill, like they had done when they were small.

Daniel put a hand on Kathleen's shoulder and said, "Take a walk with me?"

They headed toward the beach, and she looked back at the cottage, thinking that everything seemed perfect, at least for the moment. The sun had set, and there was her whole boisterous, bizarre family outside their favorite spot in the world. Patrick and Ann Marie and Clare and Joe were drinking beers and sitting in beach chairs, while the kids stood over the coals. Alice was in one of her moods. She buzzed around them, picking up stray napkins and paper plates in a huff, but no one paid her much attention.

"Are you doing okay with the drinking?" her father asked. He asked this at almost every family gathering, even though she had been sober for fifteen years.

"Yeah, thanks, Daddy." She wondered whether he ever asked Alice that same question, but figured the answer was no. For Alice, quitting drinking hadn't really been a choice. Kathleen knew she resented Daniel for it.

"I'm proud of you," he said.

They walked toward the shore, and when they reached the water, he slipped out of his Top-Siders, letting the waves pool around his feet.

"It's a beautiful night," he said, and before she could respond he added, "Sunshine, there's something I need you to know."

"Okay," she responded, thinking of other things — that it was nice to be up here, that there was nowhere else on earth where you could see so many stars.

"I'm dying," he said plainly. "I have cancer."

For a moment, she thought it was just one of his stupid jokes.

"That's not funny," she said, but when she looked into his eyes, she saw tears there for the first time she could remember.

Her heart sped up. "You're serious?"

"I found out on Tuesday," he said. "Well, the doctor sent me in for tests two weeks ago, and to be honest I had a feeling even then. But I hoped I was wrong. Anyway. Turns out I was correct, as usual."

He gave her a wink.

"Daddy," she said. "What type is it?"

"Pancreatic. Same as your uncle Jack had."

Her head was swimming. "How did this happen?"

"Well, remember I told you I was having some chest pains?"

"Yes."

"They started to get really bad. I'd wake up at night and the pain would be sort of all the way through to my back. Your mother thought I was having a heart attack every darn night. I thought, maybe, you know, heartburn. Anyway, Alice kept nagging me to go see Dr. Callo. He sent me in for an ultrasound, which I thought was excessive, but then he told me it was cancer. Then there was another test to determine what stage. And that's all she wrote."

She could tell he was trying to sound cheerful, as if a light tone might soften the blow of his words.

"Why didn't you tell me any of this?"

He shrugged. "I didn't want to worry you kids."

She could swear she heard her heart thump against her ribs. "What now?"

"Now we wait."

"What do you mean, we wait? Wait for what?"

"There's not much they can do for it, sweetheart. It's spread to my lungs. It's everywhere. There's almost no chance of recovery."

"Well, almost no chance is better than no chance," she said. "You can't just leave it. They're doing amazing stuff these days."

She was beginning to feel hysterical. He was usually the one to make sense of life for her.

315

He squeezed her shoulder. "Listen to me: I have given it a lot of thought. I don't want any of that — no hospitals, no tubes, no radiation microwave bull crap. I just want to keep going. I feel fine, really. This is what I want." He gestured back toward the cottage. "I want all of you together. I want to see your mother's smile as many more times as I possibly can."

"What does she say about all this?" Kathleen asked. "Why hasn't she tried to talk sense into you?"

"She has," he said. "Believe me, she's livid. But from now on, I want us to pretend nothing's happening, okay?"

"No, it's not okay. Are you saying there's no chemo, no surgery that will —"

"No. Radiation might help to shrink the tumor a bit, but not in any meaningful way. Surgery's not an option. I'm too far gone for that. Anyway, I never believed in surgery. My father used to say that once they cut you open, you're done for. I think there's some truth to it. Something about the air getting in."

She wondered whether he might have brain damage, if maybe this was one of those moments in life when the child was supposed to do the opposite of what her parent said. But then he continued: "Kathleen, if I thought there was even a shred of hope that all that junk would make me better, I'd do it in a

316

heartbeat. But the doctor made it very plain that it won't. I've known him forever. I asked him, 'Jim, if this were you — ,' and before I had even finished the sentence, he said, 'I would just try to enjoy the rest of my life to the fullest.' Fact is, if I'm lucky I could have another good year left."

With those words, Kathleen felt a black cloak wrap itself around her body, tight. She wanted to cry into his sweater as she had often done over the years when life got too hard, but she knew that she needed to be the strong one now.

"I understand if you don't want radiation," she said softly, remembering her sponsor, Eleanor, at the end — too weak and sick to walk, her hair falling out. "But there are natural approaches too. Homeopathic medicine has made big strides."

He grunted. "No thank you. I plan to start smoking cigars and eating raw hamburger rolled in salt like my mother used to. Steak tartare, that's called. I'll pass on the chanting and all that, kiddo."

She laughed, in spite of the situation. She had given him an Irish chant CD a few years back, and he had mocked it mercilessly every chance he had gotten since.

"Not chanting," she said. "There's real science behind it. I'll do some reading. At the very least, it might make you feel more comfortable."

Then she did start to cry, and the tears were fat and fast.

He hugged her close. "I'm going to tell your brother and sister now."

She nodded.

"There's one last thing," he said. "Kathleen, your mother has been through hell in her life, in all sorts of ways. I only ever wanted to make that better for her, not add to it. I'm worried about how she'll fare on her own. You, too, sweetheart. In my fantasy I picture the two of you helping each other through. That's how I'd like it, anyway."

It was typical of her father to be worried about Alice, even as he stood before Kathleen to say he was dying. She had a vision of the future without him in it and felt like she needed to sit down.

For as long as Kathleen could remember, he had wanted her to understand Alice. He had confided in Kathleen about the aunt she never knew who died young in a fire, a fact that Alice always blamed herself for. He had been angry when, in the throes of a teenage brawl with Alice, Kathleen had brought it up just to hurt her mother. She had felt terrible for doing it — still did, even all these years later. But she had never told anyone the story, not even Maggie or Clare.

"I'll look after her," Kathleen said weakly. "Even though all we have in common is loving you and being bad drunks."

He smiled, shook his head. "You
surprised."

That scared her. Already she had seen
much of Alice in herself — how small she fel.
on occasion; the way she was quick to judge
or to argue or to bully. (How many times had
Kathleen pushed Ann Marie to do her bidding? And she was proud of it, which was
even worse.) There were certain words she
was incapable of uttering without sounding
like her mother. Even the earthy, almost sour
smell of her skin when she woke each morning was like Alice's, no matter what soap or
lotion Kathleen applied before bed. And the
drinking. If they had more than that in common, she would rather not find out.

After he told her the news, Kathleen stayed
up late every night, doing research. None of
it made sense to her. When she read "Your
pancreas is about six inches long and looks
like a pear lying on its side," she was filled
with rage. This little nothing, this sideways
pear, would be enough to kill her father, who
was everything? It seemed impossible.

Her dining room table, already piled high
with magazines and newspapers and stray
socks and Lean Cuisine trays, was now
covered in computer printouts about cancer
and a dozen library books on natural remedies.

Over the phone, Kathleen cried to Maggie,

who was newly in New York and constantly worried that she ought to come home. Kathleen told her to stay put, though she secretly wished Maggie would return, and many weekends she did, always leaving the overage art dealer she was dating behind, thank the universe.

Kathleen wanted a drink more than she ever had in her life. She wondered if Alice felt this way too. She could remember the way one glass of wine would dull the edges, how two would make her cheeks grow warm, her thoughts turn rosier, more hopeful. But she also knew she was incapable of drinking just one or two glasses of wine, even though she was occasionally capable of convincing herself otherwise.

She began going to AA meetings twice a day.

Kathleen brought her father teas and herbs that she bought from a well-respected healer in Chinatown. She put a jar of polished runes on his nightstand — smooth green stones that she told him were for decoration, though in truth she had bought them because it was once believed that they could bring the dead back to life. She lit chakra candles at his bedside that were said to unblock points of stress in the body and allow for white blood cells to thrive. Every morning, as usual, she meditated for two solid hours, but now rather than concentrating on herself, she focused on her father's insides, communing with the cancer, willing it to shrink and vanish.

Her family, including Daniel, made fun of her, and she laughed, too, as if to say, *I know it's goofy, but indulge me.* She realized it was probably bullshit, but why not try? Sometimes she even believed that maybe it would work.

In early October, Alice showed up at Kathleen's house, a foil-wrapped package in her hands.

"What's that?" Kathleen asked, meeting her at the door, annoyed that Alice hadn't thought to call ahead. She was still in her pajamas and had been out in the back garden in the middle of her morning meditation.

"A coffee cake I got you at the Fruit Basket. Very moist. Delicious."

"A coffee cake you got me, or a coffee cake you and Daddy ate half of before you decided to bring it over here?"

"You've always liked cinnamon swirl."

"You didn't answer the question."

"You don't want it, fine. Truth is, you're putting on the pounds lately. Understandable given what's happened, but still, you have to watch yourself."

Kathleen took in a deep breath. She had only just begun trying to practice patience with her mother, and already she was failing.

They went into the kitchen and sat down. Immediately, Kathleen saw the room through

Alice's eyes. She had never been particularly tidy, but since her father got sick she had gotten worse. There were dishes stacked precariously a foot above the rim of the sink. She hadn't taken the trash out in a week, and the plastic bin was over flowing. When she realized that one of the dogs had peed on the linoleum floor earlier that morning, Kathleen had covered the yellow puddle with a paper towel, planning to deal with it after she'd had her coffee.

"Can I get you anything, Mom?" she asked.

"No, I'll only stay a minute. Your father needs me there."

"I'll be close behind you then," Kathleen said. "I was planning to come over soon."

Alice's eyes darted dramatically from wall to wall. Kathleen felt her insides tense up.

"This place is a disaster area," Alice blurted after a moment. "How do you stand it?"

"I manage," Kathleen said.

"You let people come in and see it this way?"

"Well, most people wait for an invitation rather than barging in with gently used coffee cake."

"Excuse me for not being Emily Post. My husband has cancer."

"Oh, really? I hadn't heard."

Alice sighed and straightened her posture and smiled, as if to say that she was gathering up the sort of strength one needs to talk to a lunatic.

"Actually, that's why I'm here."

"Okay," Kathleen said. "What is it?"

"Well, as you know, your father is being very stubborn about the radiation. I've been thinking about it a lot, and I am convinced that you are the only one who can talk him into it."

Kathleen smiled. "That's the same thing I thought about you, before I realized he was right."

She felt a certain tenderness for Alice then, and put her hand atop her mother's.

But Alice pulled away. "What makes you say that?"

"His cancer is too far gone, Mom. You know that. All that stuff would just make him miserable."

"So he thinks," Alice said. "But there's always something they can do. They tell him it's too far gone, but I see him every day and he's okay. He's still himself, Kathleen. I know it's not too late. I am begging you: convince him to do the radiation. If it doesn't work, what's the harm? At least we'll know he tried everything."

"I can't," Kathleen said. "I want to respect his wishes. Besides, I don't even think Dr. Callo would do it. All we can do now is hope for the best and try to make Dad happy."

She saw from the look in her mother's eyes that Alice had turned a corner, so quickly

323

that Kathleen wasn't even sure of the exact moment it had happened.

Alice got to her feet. "So you're telling me I'm supposed to sit here and watch him die? And never set foot in a goddamn hospital room? Just lie next to him in bed and say, 'Good night, darling. I hope you won't be dead when I wake up.' "

"I know it's hard," Kathleen said.

"This is you — your doing," Alice said hotly. "Your ridiculous herbs and all that. You've convinced him it's all he needs."

"That's not true!" Kathleen said, growing angry. "You're just looking for someone to blame, but this is no one's fault. And I won't have this energy thrown at me when we should all be focused on getting him stronger."

"Energy! Focus! The man needs drugs, Kathleen. He needs a doctor. If you don't at least try to talk to him about treatments, I'll never forgive you."

Kathleen shrugged her shoulders, feigning indifference. It was typical Alice insanity, which her mother would no doubt forget by tomorrow.

But after Alice walked out, Kathleen cried for a long, long time.

When she drove over to her parents' house later that afternoon and entered their bedroom, her father was asleep. Everything she'd brought over in the previous weeks — the

324

runes and the vitamins and the candles and the tea — was gone.

He began to deteriorate fast. His skin turned a sickly yellow, and eventually so did the whites in his blue eyes. He was queasy almost all the time, and couldn't keep down a bite of food. He shriveled as they watched, helpless. Daniel had always been a cheerful man, but now he grew melancholy for the first time Kathleen could remember. Everyone wanted to see him laughing again, maybe more for their own sanity than for him. To see him somber was nauseatingly odd, like a bone that's broken, poking through skin.

They all gathered around him and did what they could. They watched an obscene amount of the Three Stooges and Jackie Gleason on video. Her nephew Ryan sang Daniel's favorite old Dean Martin songs. Maggie mailed books of Irish riddles and jokes. Ann Marie made more soup than the average person consumes in a lifetime, and she was tender with Alice — bringing her gifts and taking her out to lunch every once in a while.

He was never alone. They gathered at Alice and Daniel's house, the house they had all grown up in, for dinner five or six nights a week. They sat around his bed. They looked through old photos from the cottage in Maine — one night, he said plaintively, "I'll never see it again" — and laughed at all his jokes.

They let him talk on and on as he told one of his meandering stories, when they would normally have said, "Dad, would you wrap it up? We don't have all day."

Kathleen wanted to soak up every second with him. Sometimes she wished the rest of them would go away. She thought that this was the worst part of grieving — the limbo phase when the person you love most is still there in front of you, but you know he won't be for long.

By the end, he was down to ninety-seven pounds.

He lived through Thanksgiving and Christmas, and then it became clear that there wasn't much time left. Just after the first of the year, as Kathleen looked out her kitchen window to see a light snow falling on the driveway, her phone rang. He was gone.

Patrick and Ann Marie hopped to it as usual, making all the arrangements. She took a rattled Alice to pick out a casket and called the caterers. He reached out to the lawyer to deal with the will.

He reached out to the lawyer the day their father died. Kathleen still thought of this with disgust: *What kind of person?*

Patrick was the one who called her with the news that Daniel had left almost everything — other than the house and the property in Maine and his pension and some savings for Alice — to her.

"He had three hundred thousand dollars, and he's giving it all to you," Pat said. "Clare and Joe get the Caddy. I get a watch of Grandpa's and Dad's two-year-old Pings."

"Pings?"

"Golf clubs. It's a lot of money, Kath. You and Dad, up to your old tricks right till the end," he said, as if they had been in cahoots. In truth, her father had never mentioned money, and she had never thought to ask.

Three hundred thousand dollars was five years' salary for Kathleen — more than enough to pay off her children's college tuition. But if her brother had thought she would take any joy in this, he was wrong. He and his wife had always cared so much about material possessions. Kathleen only wanted her father back.

After he died, she took a week off from work. She spent five days in bed, getting up only to pee and drink the occasional glass of water. She didn't check the mail or turn on the television or eat. She didn't want to talk to anyone, besides Maggie, who curled up in bed beside her, running a hand over her hair. They didn't say a word. Kathleen thanked the universe for her daughter, her creation, the only one in this damn family who understood her at all.

At the wake, Ann Marie wept hysterically, which made Kathleen insane.

327

"I want to slap her," she whispered to Maggie.

"Mom —" Maggie responded warningly, always the more grown-up of the two of them. But a moment later Ann Marie's sobs reached a new level, and even Maggie raised an eyebrow. She leaned close, putting her lips up against Kathleen's ear: "Do you think she's crying about Grandpa, or the Pings?"

A hundred people came to the funeral the next day, even though there was a foot of snow on the ground, and more was falling. Kathleen could hardly manage to change into her navy blue dress, the one Maggie had picked because it was the only thing she had that was close enough to black.

After the Mass, they went to Pat and Ann Marie's, the house clogged full of people, a stupid tradition. Kathleen didn't feel like talking to anyone. She hardly recognized most of them. They ate ham sandwiches and lasagna off plastic plates, standing up in the kitchen. Each stranger in their turn approached her and awkwardly said how sorry they were, what a good man he was.

They gathered in groups and drank and drank and drank, and laughed uproariously. Why did the Irish always insist on turning a funeral into a frat party? A while passed and she wondered how long she had to stay. She knew from experience that it would go on all night.

Kathleen had counseled teenagers through the deaths of their parents. Her life was blessed, relative to so many others. Yet in this moment, she did not care. She was well aware that she was acting like a child, but what did it matter? Her father was gone.

When Ann Marie put out dessert and coffee, Kathleen took an éclair and sat on the couch in the den with Ryan and some younger kids she didn't know, watching cartoons, pretending like she was monitoring the children's behavior, though in truth, if they had set her hair on fire she might not have noticed.

She watched the credits roll on an episode of something called *Ren & Stimpy*.

"Do you like *SpongeBob*?" Ryan was asking the other kids sweetly. "He's up next."

"Yes!" they shouted.

A little boy turned to Kathleen with a huge grin. "He lives in a pineapple under the sea," he said. At least that's what she thought he said.

"Oh my," she replied.

Kathleen envied them — so many years away from actually feeling the weight of anyone's death. They were here because someone had dragged them, unsure and unconcerned about whether this was a First Communion or a funeral or some old person's retirement party.

Through the doorway that led to the dining room, she saw Alice standing by the makeshift bar, pouring a glass of red wine, filling the glass to its brim. A moment later, she put it to her lips and swallowed nearly half.

Kathleen jumped a bit in her seat. She had not seen her mother drink since she was a child, and no sight could have surprised her more.

She got to her feet and walked out into the hall, looking one way and then the other, for Maggie or Clare. She didn't see either of them. She walked toward Alice.

"Mom? What are you doing?"

"I'm having a drink, what does it look like?"

She was drunk. Her lips and teeth were tinged dark blue. How much had she had? Kathleen had the urge to run and get her father.

"Maybe we should get you to bed," she said.

"To bed? It's six o'clock. I'm not some feeble old woman, Kathleen."

A few people gathered around the table glanced over at them now.

Kathleen said, in a hushed voice, "I didn't mean that, I'm —"

"What? You killed him, and now you want me dead, too, is that it?"

Kathleen took a step back.

"Not content to have just *most* of our money, you want it all," Alice said, and it took

330

everything in Kathleen not to hit her.

Instead she turned around and made her way through the crowd until she spotted Maggie and Christopher, and then she pulled them by the backs of their shirts as if they were children who had run into traffic. She yanked them toward the door and out to the car, and only then did she allow herself to speak.

"I will never talk to that woman again," she said.

"What did the bitch do now?" Christopher said.

Under other circumstances she might have worried about his language, even scolded him, but Kathleen was strangely grateful.

The next day, Alice called and left messages in an almost gossipy tone, as if the funeral had been the wedding of a distant cousin: "Call me back so we can discuss Mary Clancy's obvious face-lift," she said, and "I thought Ann Marie's deviled eggs tasted almost spoiled, didn't you?" That comment made it clear that she knew she had done wrong, but she made no mention of what she had said.

Kathleen went ten months without speaking to her, until they came to a truce brought on by the fact that, like it or not, they had to sit around Ann Marie's Thanksgiving table with the others.

But the resentment lingered on, even now.

331

A few months after the scene at her father's funeral, Kathleen met Arlo. The farm in California was his lifelong dream, and within weeks of meeting each other they were talking about it in earnest. By then, she had already vaguely decided that it was time to leave Massachusetts, where all the ghosts of her life remained. Maggie was settled in New York, and Chris was off at Trinity. There was nothing tying her to Boston anymore. The Kellehers thought she was nuts — "using Dad's money to fund a worm poop farm" sounded like the perfect punch line to one of their Kathleen jokes. *What stupid decision will she make next?*

She and Arlo had known each other for all of six months when they moved. Looking back on it now, Kathleen marveled at her willingness to take such a risk, but she might have jumped at any excuse to leave. Arlo had never been married. He had dated a woman named Flora for seven years, and she still called from time to time, to catch up and wish him well. They were that kind of people. Kathleen really wasn't, but she tried to let it wash over her. She had even gone to dinner with Flora and Arlo once, to a quiet candlelit place up the mountain, and listened almost contentedly as Flora told them about her pottery studio in Portland, her life spent dating Dead Heads ("Even now, no one else does it for me"), her years with Arlo ("We thought we were soul mates because our names were almost anagrams"). It was worth it when Kathleen heard Arlo describe their life. It sounded peaceful, fulfilled. And it was.

She knew that for her it was at least partially about being away from the Kellehers. For the first time in her life, her chaotic family was at a distance. She didn't have to be a part of all that anymore. Then again, she didn't get to be a part of all that anymore. She'd hear crazy stories about gossip and arguments and misunderstandings — from her kids, from Clare, and from Alice, now that the hatchet was more or less buried between them — and once in a while she would find with some surprise that part of her missed it, in spite of everything.

And there was guilt, the trademark emotion of the faith they were born into. When Kathleen promised her dad that she would take care of Alice, she had forgotten how impossible that would be. She knew that women in her position weren't supposed to roam so far. You were supposed to stick by your children and your aging parents, sacrificing your middle decades for their comfort, no matter what they had put you through. No matter what.

MAGGIE

Maggie and Rhiannon had arranged to drive to Maine on Tuesday morning. By the time she woke up, Gabe still hadn't called. Her sharp disappointment made her realize how much she had been hoping, believing, he might come around. She felt weighted down with gloom, but somehow managed to drag herself toward the shower so that she'd be on time. Politeness above all else, she thought. Where the hell had she learned to be like that? By watching her mother, she realized, and then doing the exact opposite of what she saw. Or possibly it came from her aunt Ann Marie.

Maggie made her way next door with a duffel bag slung over one shoulder, just half of what she had originally packed, since she'd be staying only a few days now.

She knocked, and Rhiannon appeared in a cotton sheath that ended at the midpoint of her thigh. ("Your knees should have a party and invite your skirt down," Maggie's grand-

334

father had said whenever she wore a dress he deemed too short.)

Maggie had never had a knack for clothing. Women in New York amazed her with their perfectly chiseled bodies; their ability to wear stiletto heels in rain, sleet, or snow; and their innate resolve around bread baskets. Given the choice, she'd prefer that everyone walk around in a potato sack to level the playing field a bit.

Her size-eight jeans had felt snug when she put them on this morning. Now they felt as tight as snake skin, and she had to remind herself that she was pregnant, after all (while sparing herself the knowledge that the size eights were tight long before she was pregnant).

They were on the road at nine fifteen, and had already stopped for rations by nine thirty. Rhiannon pumped the gas while Maggie went inside to pay and get breakfast.

"Something very sugary with nine hundred grams of fat," Rhiannon requested, surprising her.

"I like the way you think."

Maggie walked the aisles as an instrumental version of Journey's "Open Arms" played over the loudspeaker. Gabe had drunkenly belted out the song at the karaoke birthday party of one of his former co-workers a few weeks earlier.

She couldn't quite say where they were

now. Queens, maybe.

Her phone was in her pocket and set to vibrate. She pulled a bag of powdered mini doughnuts from a hook on a wall of processed desserts.

The man behind the counter wore a cross the size of a brick around his neck. She thought of the tiny silver crucifix she herself had worn as a child, the type her grandmother and Aunt Ann Marie still wore to this day. That sort of understated cross, always tucked into a sweater or blouse, said, "I love Jesus Christ." A cross like the one this man wore seemed to say, "I want you to *think* I love Jesus Christ."

"Nice day for driving," he said as he rang up her purchases. "Lucky you're not stuck in here."

She considered pointing to her head and saying, "Well, you're lucky you're not stuck in here."

Instead, she just smiled. "Have a good one," she said.

Back in the car, Maggie opened the bag of doughnuts and handed one to Rhiannon.

"Onward, driver," she said.

She was grateful to Rhiannon for the special treatment. But she couldn't help thinking she should be with Gabe right now, driving fast, laughing and singing along to the radio. She suddenly wondered what the hell she had been thinking. She sucked on her bottom lip to keep from crying, feeling like a stupid little girl.

"So," Rhiannon said cheerfully. "On a scale of one to ten, how much do you feel like killing yourself today?"

Maggie grinned. "No comment."

"I know how you feel," Rhiannon said. "I got pregnant when I was still married to Liam. I found out two days after the first time he shoved me. Which was also the day I knew I'd leave him. Though I probably knew long before that. I'm not actually the settling-down type, as it turns out."

Maggie hadn't heard any of this before.

"He shoved you?" she said now.

"Yeah, he used to like to push me around a bit."

She said it so casually. Were Gabe's crimes really anything compared to this?

"What did you do?" Maggie asked.

"I had an abortion. I never told him about it."

Maggie inhaled deeply. "Wow."

"Yeah. I was thinking about your situation after you left last night. You're brave. I'm glad you told me. I never told anyone. It seems like the logical people to tell would be a best friend, your mother, your husband. Well, clearly my husband was out. My best friend was someone I hadn't talked to in a year. And my mother and I have never once discussed

anything more consequential than tennis results."

Maggie didn't know how to reply. She knew
her relationship with her own mother
stretched way too far in the other direction.
Once, when she was an adolescent, away at
her father's place for the weekend, Kathleen
had not only read Maggie's diary, but actually made notes in the margins, such as *These
negative feelings about your body are very
common, but you must learn to see them as
side effects of our messed-up culture* and *This
jackass is simply not worth your crush. Reminds
me of someone I slept with in college, who
turned out to be gay.*

Twenty years of sobriety and a career in the
mental health field hadn't stopped Kathleen
from oversharing: Maggie was thirty-two and
still working on creating what her therapist
called "the generational boundaries." A few
times, Kathleen had come to New York unannounced and stayed in Maggie's cramped
apartment, sleeping in the bed with her, for
two, three weeks at a stretch. It drove Maggie
insane, but she never had the heart to tell
Kathleen to leave, or to check into a hotel
like normal parents would do. And when it
came time for her to go, they would both cry.

"I always wished there was a bit more
distance between my mother and me. She's
told me much more than I ever wanted to

know about her personal life," Maggie said, and instantly felt guilty for saying so. "Sometimes I'd give my left arm for the kind of mother who only talks tennis."

"Why haven't you told her about the baby yet?" Rhiannon asked.

"Her opinion can completely color my judgment, and I wanted to make up my own mind first. Does that make sense?"

Rhiannon nodded. "In a way, I envy the connection you have. Before I left home, I really tried to get my mother to talk," she said. "I tried to cut out the falseness between us and get her to fight with me about what she resented. Those dark things that happen in every family. But she wouldn't, or she couldn't."

Maggie wondered about the dark things, what that came down to in Rhiannon's life. She wanted to hear more, but Rhiannon said, in a different tone, suggesting she didn't want to go further: "Do you know anyone like that, or is this a Scottish trait?"

"My grandmother is the same way," Maggie said. "She never wants to talk to me about anything more meaningful than the fact that Bounty paper towels are on sale."

They drove on for a while without talking, NPR on in the background. Maggie thought about Gabe. She wondered whether she would ever wake up again with her head on his bare chest. She tried to imagine how she might go to any of their favorite places without him — the movie theater in Brooklyn Heights, which had only 150 seats and served egg creams, or the old Italian bakeries in Carroll Gardens where a black and white cookie the size of your head cost a dollar. She pictured herself pushing a stroller up Court Street in the cold, surrounded by strangers.

She turned to Rhiannon, and without thinking she asked, "Did you ever consider raising that baby alone?"

"Not for a second," Rhiannon said. "That's why I think you're so amazing."

"Or possibly insane," Maggie said.

"Will you go back to Gabe if he asks?"

"I don't know," Maggie said, though she was fairly sure she did. "I have a lot invested in him."

"For what it's worth, I know it's a tough situation, but I think you can do much better. Marriage would only make it worse, believe me. You think it will sort of fill in the lines, cover over the splotchy bits. But in fact it does the opposite."

"I know," Maggie said, though sometimes she had believed that if they got married, the rest would work itself out. All around New York City — on the subway, in the cafeteria at work — were wedding bands on the fingers of men her age, the men who hadn't been ready to commit back when she met Gabe, and had somehow gotten scooped up in the meantime, every last one of them a shiny reminder of what she didn't have.

She knew it was strange, how badly she wanted to be married, despite what she had seen. The urge seemed hardwired, so that each time she heard of something bad happening to an adult — a co-worker of her dad's got laid off, a friend of her mother's had emphysema — the first question out of her mouth was always, "Is he married?" As if that guaranteed safety, someone who would tenderly care for you forever, instead of resenting you for losing your job or smoking all those years when she had begged you to quit.

It wasn't a terribly liberated thought, but sometimes Maggie envied her grandmother and other women from her generation, for whom love and marriage and children seemed automatic, a given.

"Despite what he's put me through, I really do love him," she said now.

"Hmm." Rhiannon nodded her head. "Love's a bitch."

"I have this theory about how the things we love destroy us," Maggie said.

"Oh, I love theories like that. Go on," Rhiannon said.

As far as she had seen, Maggie explained, what made people and pleased them, and threatened to ultimately ruin them, was love.

Not romantic love necessarily, but the love of something, the thing that defined your life. Her mother was in love with booze. While other people might have a glass or two of wine with dinner because they liked it well enough, Kathleen loved the stuff, and so it destroyed her. Her uncle Patrick and aunt Ann Marie loved status, money, appearance — that would wreck them one day, if it hadn't already.

Maggie herself did not love liquor, though she feared its power over her anyway, knowing how alcoholism ran through her veins like blood. She didn't love money, either. If she had enough for a roof over her head and school loan payments, if she could find a way to afford to raise a child, that would be plenty.

Maggie's ruinous love had always been men. She fell for someone, and desperation overtook her. She wanted him all to herself, to build a cocoon around the two of them, to keep him safe, but more so, to keep him near. She lost interest in her work and friends, though she tried to pretend otherwise. In every other way, she was controlled, sensible. But men brought out some crazy part of her. Gabe wasn't the first. Before him there had been Martin, the fifty-two-year-old gallery owner who she had met during an informational interview in Manhattan her senior year of college. She had sent along some fiction samples with her résumé, and the first thing

Martin said to her was what she most wanted to hear: "You're no gallerist. You're a writer."

He was handsome, charming, knew all the most interesting people in the city. They had dinner that night in the West Village, at a dimly lit café that she was never able to find again. When they were leaving, his long fingers brushed her neck as he helped her into her coat. They went back to his apartment — surprisingly cramped for a man his age — and made love in his bed. He seemed to love her youth, running his hands over her thighs, her breasts, saying again and again that she had the smoothest skin he had ever touched. She thought his age — the slight wrinkles around his eyes when he smiled, the strength and assurance of his hands — suited her old soul much better than those shiny-faced college boys back at Kenyon.

After graduation, she moved into his place. He helped her get a job at a small literary journal run by a friend of his. The affair lasted a year. When it ended she felt empty and lonesome; she immediately met Chad Patterson, a kid from Wisconsin, two years her junior, who had come to New York to be an actor. He had been crashing on friends' futons, and she offered to put him up in her new studio, mostly because she hated sleeping alone. The arrangement had all the makings of a perfect disaster, and it fell apart quickly, though three months after their official breakup, he was still staying on the couch. She could bear to throw him out only after she returned home late one night to find him wrapped up in the long legs of some blonde he'd met at a callback for *Baby with the Bathwater.*

She had attempted to work on it in therapy, read every book on co-dependence, but nothing ever seemed to change her feelings about men. Her behavior was who she was, who she had been. How could anyone ever alter that? Sometimes her shrink made her feel that self-improvement was untenable: her family, and by association she herself, were drunks, sour grudge-holders, emotional cripples who needed so desperately to change. Other times she thought self-improvement made sense only for the immortal. Improving yourself for what exactly?

They had lunch at a rest stop in Massachusetts. Maggie was almost positive she had been there with her family dozens of times, though all Massachusetts rest stops looked identical when you didn't drive, so who knew? These places always had the same antiseptic smell, the same bored-looking employees, the same manicured parking lot and service station. They were ugly landmarks that seemed incongruous compared to New York City behind and Cape Neddick ahead.

They ate gigantic slices of pizza and

watched the people streaming in and out. Maggie thought of the baby inside her, though it was hard to imagine as an actual person. She had visited a website that pregnant mothers were gaga about, on which, each week, you got to see what kind of fruit or vegetable your child most closely resembled: *Your baby is a chickpea,* she had read two weeks earlier, and then just a few days ago, *Your baby is a walnut.*

They finished eating, and Maggie promptly threw up for the fourth time in two days. She wondered why they called it morning sickness if it could hit you at any hour.

Back in the car, Rhiannon asked, "Will it just be you and your grandmother in the house in Maine?"

"Yes," Maggie said. "Actually, each of us in a separate house, but on the same property."

"That sounds cozy."

Maggie grinned. "I know, right? We have a big Irish Catholic family, so I guess in theory we need a lot of room."

"I like that you call yourselves Irish. Why do Americans always want so badly to be from somewhere else?" Rhiannon asked.

Maybe she had a point. Maggie's grandparents and Aunt Ann Marie and Uncle Pat were particularly obsessed, but the whole Kelleher family was crazy about Ireland, including Maggie herself. The music, the history, the dancing, the sad stories from the past. Her mother had once been this way, too, but now she made fun of the rest of them for it.

They all wore claddagh rings instead of wedding bands. Ann Marie and Pat slept in a bed with a headboard that had the words HIMSELF and HERSELF carved in the soft wood above where they lay their respective heads, and a shamrock in between.

Her cousins Patty and Fiona had been forced to take step dancing lessons as kids. They competed at the Stonehill Irish Festival every summer. Patty wore her gillies around the cottage in Maine, laced halfway up her calves, an absurd bathing suit accompaniment that nonetheless made Maggie burn with jealousy.

Since she had grown up in the suburbs of Boston, Maggie's friends from childhood were all Irish, too, so that it wasn't until her first March in Ohio that she realized not everyone wore head-to-toe green and ate corned beef and cabbage on St. Patrick's Day.

Pat and Ann Marie and their kids made regular trips to Ireland — Patty always mailed Maggie Aero bars and other local candies, which had melted completely by the time they arrived in Massachusetts. On those visits, Uncle Pat had unearthed various distant cousins who lived in County Kerry. He gleefully showed them around Boston, letting them stay over in the guest room, sending them home with Red Sox jerseys and several pounds of Dunkin' Donuts coffee, which apparently they were crazy for.

She told Rhiannon this, and Rhiannon laughed.

"Are there eighty-seven cousins on each side?"

"My mom has something like forty cousins. There are a lot fewer in this generation. On my dad's side, we have ten," Maggie said. "But we were never all that close to them growing up. We'd see one another at christenings and on Easter, stuff like that. But my mom's side of the family was always the closest. Totally messed up, but close."

"And how many cousins on that side?" Rhiannon asked.

"Only four," Maggie said. "It always seemed like more, like a bigger family."

She still pictured them as their childhood selves. Ann Marie and Patrick's kids: Patty, Fiona, and Little Daniel (her mother often joked that these names had doomed them to sound like a trio of Irish peasants from birth). Clare and Joe's only child was named Ryan, after someone, though Maggie couldn't remember who.

Little Daniel, handsome even as a kid, was a charmer who always struck her as unnecessarily arrogant. He was cruel to his younger boy cousins when none of the adults were watching; later he became a young hotshot and now he was in finance or real estate, or some similarly incomprehensible line of work. At Thanksgiving he had given her his business card, which did nothing to shed light on the matter. Maggie really only understood jobs that could be described in a single word: *writer* or *doctor* or *teacher* made sense. *Vice president of debt capital markets and global currencies* did not.

Little Daniel's sister Fiona was boyish and quiet and unadorned, involved with all kinds of social causes, even in high school. Maggie wondered sometimes whether Fiona was actually happy, still off in the Peace Corps at age thirty. Kathleen thought Fiona might be gay and that she lived halfway around the world partly as a means of keeping that to herself, of never having to come out to the family or deal with their reaction. If that was true, Maggie wished she could write Fiona a letter and say, *You're my cousin and I love you! You're allowed to be a lesbian. No one's going to judge you.*

But Fiona's parents wouldn't want to know. For God's sake, they probably still thought Kathleen was going to Hell for getting a divorce.

Their sister Patty was older than Maggie by four months. The two of them were so similar that as kids they declared that they were the true sisters. (*Poor Fiona,* Maggie thought now, too late.) Patty and Maggie looked alike, with the same brown hair and freckles. They both played basketball and loved writing and chasing boys. As children they each wore one half of a heart-shaped best friends necklace and spent countless hours together after school, listening to music and eating cookie dough straight from the package when Ann Marie wasn't looking.

They hardly ever spoke anymore. Patty had this big grown-up life: a husband, three kids, a house in the suburbs. The two of them had always been compared to each other, and now Maggie compared them herself.

Last, there was her cousin Ryan — a teenage musical theater prodigy who was coming to stay with her for his NYU audition when she got back to town. (Maggie was crazy about that kid. Once, when he was only four or five, she had taken him to the movies. As soon as the opening credits rolled, he said he had to go to the bathroom. Maggie was nervous to let him go into the men's room alone, but he said he did it all the time, and it was the type that was designed for one person, so it wasn't like some pervert could get him. Still, she stood close by the door, waiting. After only thirty seconds or so, he began to sing, softly at first, but then at the top of his lungs: *Off we're gonna shuffle, shuffle off to Buffalo!* Maggie rapped on the door. People passing by giggled and stared.

She tried the handle, but Ryan had locked it. A crowd gathered. Sixteen minutes later, the child emerged. "There's a full-length mirror in there!" he said, beaming.)

Compared to the other boys in the family, Maggie's brother, Chris, seemed like a disaster. He'd never gotten a decent job after college. He was now working as a "marketing field rep," which meant that he stood outside the student union at BU, handing out fliers about new burger joints and sample sales to co-eds. He sometimes had a scary temper. Whenever he acted up, Kathleen would inevitably blame the uncles, Joe and Pat. Why hadn't they come around more and given the kid some male bonding time? Maggie would point out that they had sons of their own, and it wasn't like Chris was *fatherless*. But maybe her mother had a point.

Maggie thought of this now, imagined an old photograph of all six grandkids on the beach that sat on the piano in her grandparents' house in Canton. What would anyone think of how it had all turned out? She had told Rhiannon they were close, because in her head, that was the truth. But so much had changed.

When she saw the familiar WELCOME TO MAINE sign, she felt like she had arrived home. They stopped at Shop 'n Save on Route 1 for groceries. It had changed into a

Hannaford sometime in the mid-nineties, but the Kellehers still called it by its original name. Walking the familiar aisles made her feel simultaneously safe and lonesome.

On the drive to the cottage, she pointed out familiar spots — the lobster pound and the old-fashioned pharmacy and the Front Porch, where tourists went late at night to watch male Judy Garland impersonators singing their hearts out.

They passed Ruby's Market and Maggie thought of how much she had loved bringing Gabe there last summer. The two of them had eavesdropped on the couple who owned the place, as they railed on about their ungrateful grandchildren, who had dared to move away to the big city. (And by big city they meant Portland, thirty miles north.)

Soon enough, they reached the fork in the road, where the initials *A.H.* were carved into the trunk of a tree, along with an imperfect shamrock. Maggie told Rhiannon to go left.

"Here?" Rhiannon asked skeptically, as newcomers always did, for the opening looked like just a footpath into the woods. They turned onto Briarwood Road and the tires blew sand up off the ground, which gave the impression of a fine mist floating between the pine trees.

"It's so beautiful," Rhiannon said.

A few moments later they had arrived, and Maggie's stomach fluttered, as it always did when she caught sight of the cottage's weathered wooden shingles, the beach chairs stacked up beside the front door, and the ocean in the distance.

Alice's car wasn't there when they pulled in, but as they unloaded the groceries, Maggie heard someone barreling down the road.

"I think I know who that is," she said. "Brace yourself."

Alice turned in without signaling, and pulled up a few inches behind Rhiannon's Subaru, even though there was enough room in the grass for seven cars. When she got out, she bore a puzzled look.

"Maggie?" Alice said, staring at Rhiannon as if, without Gabe there, she couldn't be sure it was really her granddaughter standing before her.

"Grandma, this is my friend Rhiannon," she said. "Rhiannon, my grandmother Alice."

Rhiannon extended a hand.

Alice shook her head quickly back and forth, and Maggie realized that she probably should have prepared her for this. With all the insanity of the last two days, she hadn't even thought.

"I don't understand," Alice fumbled. "Where's Gabe?"

She looked past them into the car, as if perhaps they had tied him up in the backseat.

"He's not coming," Maggie said. Her eyes met Alice's and she saw that her grandmother was crushed. "We had a big fight. We sort of broke up. I tried to tell you when I called, but —"

"No, you didn't tell me," Alice said. "I would have remembered that. And I wouldn't have paid full price for the corn muffins he said he liked if I'd known. I don't want those in my house. What am I going to do with them?"

"I'm sorry," Maggie said, her face turning pink with embarrassment. "I can pay you back."

What the hell must Rhiannon be thinking? A granddaughter reimbursing her own grandmother for five dollars' worth of store-brand muffins?

Something in Alice seemed to change then, as if she was reasoning with herself. "Oh, don't be silly. You'll still come to dinner, I hope? I haven't made an entire meatloaf for nothing. Your friend can sleep in the guest room in the cottage; there are sheets on the beds."

"Oh, she's actually turning back tonight. She just came along for the ride," Maggie said.

"Back to New York? Tonight?" Alice said. "That's ludicrous. You'll at least stay for dinner, won't you, Diana?"

"It's Rhiannon," Maggie said.

"I'd love to," Rhiannon said. "Is there anything we can bring?"

"Not at all," Alice said sweetly, and Maggie wondered if her discomfort was apparent to Rhiannon, or if she was finding Alice altogether charming, as strangers often did.

Maggie started to speak, but Alice had already turned away and was walking toward the big house.

They made their way into the cottage.

"Your grandmother is gorgeous," Rhiannon said in the kitchen, starting to unpack the food.

"Thanks," Maggie said, like she always did when people commented on Alice's beauty. It was a strange, knee-jerk response. *Thank you for being surprised that a relative of mine is particularly good-looking, and by extension giving away what you think of my appearance.*

At Kenyon she had dated Christian Taylor, the son of two Cambridge intellectuals, for over a year. His parents had nothing much to say to her mother when they met, but at graduation, after they were introduced to Alice, Christian's mother pulled Maggie aside and said, "Your grandmother is stunning, very exotic looking. Does she have Egyptian blood?"

The Kellehers on Maggie's mother's side and the Doyles on her father's had migrated from County Kerry, Ireland, to Dorchester, Massachusetts, three generations earlier, and most offshoots of the clan had since made it no further than the suburbs of Boston.

"No Egyptian blood that we know of," Maggie had said.

Before they went next door, Maggie asked whether Rhiannon had a good heavy sweater for walking on the beach later. She wanted to show off the perfect stars, perhaps as a means of deflecting attention from whatever horror show Alice might pull at dinner.

Rhiannon said she hadn't brought anything bulky.

"That's okay," Maggie said. "The dresser in my grandparents' old bedroom is full of stuff. Take your pick. Just not the green old-man sweater in the bottom drawer. I get dibs on that one."

"Deal," Rhiannon said, walking toward the bedroom. A moment later she called out, "Oh, but the drawers are empty!"

Maggie walked toward her. Grains of sand clung to the soles of her feet. When she saw the drawers pulled out with only the familiar seashell-printed liner paper in the bottom, her stomach jolted with alarm. She walked to the closet, expecting to see the oversize pink bathrobe that Ann Marie had left there years earlier, and the stack of white knitted blankets made by her great-grandmother. But the closet stood bare.

Maggie thought of her grandfather's green

sweater, which he had given her on an early-morning walk to Ruby's Market when she was in middle school. She remembered being mortified wearing it all the way up Briarwood Road, and she shoved it in a drawer in the cottage as soon as they arrived home. But it had become her tradition to pull it out on arrival each summer, and wear it every morning while she drank her coffee. Ridiculously, the thought of someone else — one of her cousins, or worse, a friend of theirs — taking it made her want to cry.

"We were looking for a sweater in the bedroom in the cottage, and the drawers were all empty," she said to Alice shortly after they'd arrived for dinner.

The three of them stood awkwardly in the kitchen while the meatloaf cooled on the counter. The potato salad was covered in foil and sitting in a sweaty bowl. Maggie hoped it hadn't been decomposing in the freezer since the previous summer. With Alice you never knew.

"I can lend you a cardigan, but it might be snug," Alice said.

"Thanks, but no, I just meant — well, where did everything go?"

"I got rid of some stuff in the cottage," Alice said. "It was getting too cluttered over there."

"Do you remember if there was a green

sweater of Grandpa's?" Maggie asked.

"I don't remember what I had for breakfast, darling," Alice said, her voice a false saccharine sound. "Honestly, I only cleared out a few things from the cottage and my house too."

"Okay," Maggie said. "Well, if you see that green sweater —"

"Let's eat," Alice said. "Out on the porch, maybe?"

She had already set the table there, and so they carried the serving dishes out past the screen door and sat down. Besides the meatloaf and potato salad, there was a dish of bright red tomato slices from Alice's garden, sprinkled with salt and freshly ground pepper. She had also cut up a banana and placed the slices in a teacup along with ten or fifteen blueberries, showing her old-lady colors in a way that, to Maggie's surprise, made her feel a bit sad.

Rhiannon placed her napkin in her lap and sat up extra straight. So Alice had intimidated her after all.

"Eat! Eat!" Alice said. "Come on, serve yourselves, we're all friends here."

Rhiannon took a spoonful of the potatoes, a few blueberries and tomato slices, and a big hunk of meatloaf — at least a quarter of what Alice had prepared. It was a normal-size portion by normal-person standards, but Maggie knew Alice was probably appalled. In solidarity, she cut herself an equally big piece of meat and took a bite, avoiding her grandmother's gaze.

Alice sipped her wine, then put the glass down and cut herself a sliver of meatloaf.

"I thought we might get a second meal out of this later in the week, but c'est la vie," she said. "Haven't you girls been eating?"

"We've done nothing but eat since we got on the road this morning," Rhiannon said.

Alice nodded vigorously.

"Gosh, Shannon, you must have a hollow leg."

"It's Rhiannon," Maggie said.

Alice ignored her.

"How on earth did you two meet anyway?" she asked, with the same fake smile she'd had out by the car earlier.

"We live next door to each other," Rhiannon said.

"Oh, I see. Where are you from, dear? You have the prettiest accent. Almost Irish sounding, isn't it?"

"I'm from Scotland," Rhiannon said.

"Marvelous! My husband was there on business once — he brought me back a scarf. Itchy as hell, but it was gorgeous. Now, sweetheart" — She looked at Maggie and paused for dramatic effect — "I'm dying to know — what happened with Gabe?"

(Apparently, that's all there was to say, as far as Scotland was concerned. Thousands of years of history and culture boiled down to one itchy scarf.)

No matter what else existed between them, there would always be that generational divide that stopped her from telling the full truth: you weren't going to tell your grandmother that your boyfriend was a possible cokehead, that you'd skipped your pill and gotten pregnant, and so you spoke in a kind of shorthand. Perhaps Alice did the same, for reasons of her own.

"I caught him in a pretty major lie," Maggie said.

"That doesn't sound like Gabe," Alice said.

"Actually it does," Maggie said.

"Oh," Alice said, smiling. "He always seemed so charming. I guess it's the charming ones you have to look out for, though. Well, that's — Maggie, I'm sorry. Have you spoken to your mother lately?"

"Yes, we talked yesterday," Maggie said. "Why?"

"I just wondered if she knew about you and Gabe. She hadn't told me."

Suddenly Alice switched gears. "I told Patrick that I want to get the gutters on the cottage all cleared out sometime this week," she said. "The one Mexican in all of Maine is coming to take care of it. Mort recommended him, and he's cheap, of course, so —"

"Grandma, don't talk that way," Maggie said.

"What? He's illegal. He's happy for the work," Alice said. "All they eat is rice and beans anyhow; how much money do they need?"

Maggie clenched with embarrassment, though Rhiannon chuckled.

"Okay," Maggie said. "Whatever, that's fine."

"This place is incredible," Rhiannon said. "Such a beautiful spot."

The house was gorgeous, but it never seemed to fit Maggie's grandparents. It looked like something you'd see in a design magazine: sprawling open rooms, each on a different level, with staircases connecting them all. The kitchen was all stainless steel, and the bathroom fixtures were ridiculously modern. If you came upon it by mistake, you'd expect to find a pair of Swedish super-models living inside, hosting lavish parties attended by rap moguls and starlets.

"Thank you," Alice said. She lowered her voice as if she were about to tell the juiciest of secrets. "Rhiannon, your skin is absolutely gorgeous."

"Thanks. My ex-husband used to say —"

Alice sputtered. "Your ex-husband? You had a husband?"

Maggie couldn't tell if this was some re-action to divorce in general, or to Rhiannon in particular. Possibly her age.

"Yes. If you can believe it," Rhiannon said with a laugh.

"Well, don't worry. A girl as pretty as you. You'll have the boys banging down your door again soon, no doubt."

Maggie took note of the fact that her grandmother had offered her no such assurance.

"Did Maggie tell you her mother is divorced also?" Alice said, as if Rhiannon and Kathleen had some rare and jolly hobby in common — a pair of rowboat enthusiasts, championship jugglers. "Now, there's a girl who was not suited to it, looks-wise. She put on weight after all that, didn't she, Maggie?"

Maggie felt like any answer she could give would be a betrayal of her mother, so she just took a bite of potatoes in response. She was desperate to change the subject.

Alice reached for the wine bottle and poured herself a second glass.

"Anyone else?" she asked. "Maggie, you haven't touched yours. Don't you like it? Would you prefer a white? I have one open."

"No, I'm fine," she said.

Alice frowned. "Are you on the wagon?"

"No. I'm a bit hungover, actually," Maggie lied, since this was the only acceptable reason for not drinking among the drinking members of the Kelleher family.

Alice filled Rhiannon's glass and her own,

emptying the bottle.

"I will be too tomorrow, if I'm not careful. Don't tell your mom," she said, "or she'll drag me off to rehab with that whoosie what's-her-name actress."

"The meatloaf is delicious, Grandma," Maggie said. Neutral ground.

"It is, so moist," Rhiannon said.

"It's just one part ketchup and one part Worcestershire that does it," Alice said with a pleased grin. Then she slapped her palms against the table.

"Drat, I forgot the rolls!" she said, getting up and rushing toward the kitchen.

Maggie looked at Rhiannon.

"What did I tell you?" she whispered.

"What a character," Rhiannon said.

Alice returned with a basket of rolls in one hand and a fresh bottle of red wine in the other.

"They're only burned a smidge on the bottom," she said. "Still perfectly good."

Rhiannon and Alice drained the second bottle of wine while Maggie led them in conversation about the most benign topics she could think of — the scaffolding she had noticed outside the church her grandmother attended each morning, movies they had all seen or wanted to see, the weather forecast for the week.

Alice opened a third bottle after they had cleared their plates. Maggie pushed her glass away, still full. Rhiannon's glass was full too. Alice filled only her own and took a long sip.

"Maggie mentioned you're a fellow book lover," Rhiannon was saying. "Are you reading anything good?"

Alice smacked her lips together. "Yes! The most marvelous biography of Vincent van Gogh. Fascinating, absolutely fascinating."

"How interesting," Rhiannon said. "There's an amazing collection of his work in Amsterdam. A whole museum dedicated to him."

Alice nodded, as if she was well aware of this fact. "You know, there's an art museum a mile from here, by Perkins Cove," she said.

Maggie had been there once or twice as a kid. The Van Gogh Museum it was not. But she felt protective of Alice just then, and so she said, "It's really lovely. It overlooks the ocean."

"There used to be an artists' colony there," Alice said.

"Really?" Maggie had never heard that before.

"Yes," Alice said. "They were at their height when we built this place."

"Did you like the artists, or did you find them annoying?" Rhiannon asked.

Alice scoffed. "Annoying? No. We knew them well. I used to be a painter myself."

"You did?" Maggie asked.

"Yes, you knew that."

"No, I didn't."

"You did, Maggie."

Maggie was sure she had never heard this before. She made a mental note to ask her mother about it.

"Why did you stop?" Rhiannon asked.

Alice threw up her hands. "Who has the time? Between this and that."

Between *what* and *what?* Maggie thought. Cocktail hour and *Masterpiece Theatre?*

"You should get back into it," Maggie said. "I'm sure there are some great classes in Boston. It could be a fun thing to try this winter."

"Please, I'm too old for that," Alice said.

"You're not too old for anything," Maggie said.

She wished Daniel were there, and said so out loud. "I'm sure Grandpa would love to see you painting again."

"Oh, hush," Alice said sternly.

"Did he not like the fact that you painted?" Rhiannon asked. She had obviously thought it was a harmless question, but Maggie braced herself.

"My husband never said a harsh word to anyone, least of all me," Alice said. "If I wanted to paint, he thought painting was just fine."

"Oh, I didn't mean —"

"I don't want to talk about him," Alice said. "Enough."

"But why?" Maggie asked. "Don't you

think it could be good for us to talk about him? We both loved him so much."

"I was his wife," Alice said sharply. "You don't get to say that you loved him like I did."

"I didn't mean that," Maggie said, trying to ignore the sting of it, and too embarrassed to look toward Rhiannon. "I'm sure no one loved him as much as you. But that's the thing: you never talk about him."

"What exactly do you want to know?"

"Anything! How did he propose? Where did you go on your first date? I don't even know how you met!"

"How we met?" Alice said, aghast, as though Maggie had asked about their favorite sexual positions.

"Yes, how did you meet Grandpa? I've never heard the story."

"That's because there is no story," Alice said.

"There has to be a story."

"There's no story," Alice said firmly. "My brother Timmy introduced us, and that's all."

"And what did you think of him? Was it love at first sight?"

"Maybe it's a bit too hard right now, Maggie," Rhiannon said.

Though Maggie knew it was childish, she felt slightly betrayed. "But even if it is," she said to her grandmother, "don't you ever just want to get it out there?"

Alice's eyes widened. She looked at Rhiannon. "I hardly think that's appropriate dinner table conversation," said the woman who had probably imbibed a bottle and a half of wine over dinner, and brought up the cheap Mexican handyman and Kathleen's postdivorce weight gain in the first ten minutes.

"Are you gals about full?" Alice said. "Because I'm tuckered out."

It was exactly the way she had shut down the previous summer when Gabe was there. Maybe there would always be this wall with Alice, no matter how badly Maggie wished things might change, no matter how many times she forgot for a moment that their family wasn't what she wanted it to be.

Rhiannon stood and began piling the dishes.

"I'll get those later," Alice said.

"It's the least I can do," Rhiannon said. She stacked the plates and side platters into one neat load.

Alice and Maggie followed her silently into the kitchen.

The wax-paper bag of corn muffins Alice had bought for Gabe sat on the counter. Maggie missed him for an instant, a sharp pain in her chest.

"Should I take these?" she asked.

"No, don't bother. Leave them," Alice said. "They'll go stale, but maybe I won't notice if I toast them."

■ ■ ■

They were full from dinner and it had started to spit rain, so Maggie and Rhiannon decided not to walk on the beach after all. Still, Maggie didn't want her to go. She was thinking in a panicked way about her grandmother and her mother. They were both selfish and stubborn, but as parents they had each been tempered by a good, kind man — Daniel, in both cases. She herself would have no such balance if she brought a child into the world. Not unless Gabe came back.

"Why don't you come to the cottage for a cup of tea before you get on the road?" she said. Maybe simply having another body in the room would calm her down.

"That sounds good," Rhiannon said. "I think your grandmother got me a bit smashed." She shook her head. "That's a sentence I've never said before."

They stood at the kitchen window. Maggie could see Alice across the way on her porch, talking on the phone. Who was she talking to? Probably Ann Marie.

"Maybe I shouldn't have come," Maggie said. "It's going to be so lonely after you're gone. And my grandmother — I'm not sure I can take her."

"She's not that bad," Rhiannon said.

"Maybe I should call Gabe."

"Do you really think that's a good idea?" Rhiannon asked.

"No. Yes? I don't know. I can't believe I haven't heard from him."

"If I tell you something, do you promise to take it in the spirit in which it's intended?" Rhiannon asked.

"Sure," Maggie said.

"Remember when you and Gabe came to my restaurant for dinner?"

Maggie nodded, feeling her heart sink.

"Well, when you were in the bathroom, he put his hand on my ass. I think he tried to kiss me. I don't know. He was drunk. I wasn't going to say anything, but — well, I see you holding out hope and it scares me, Maggie. He's not a good guy. And you're wonderful."

With that, finally, she knew for sure what she had been trying not to know for days: it was only her in this; he wasn't going to be there to raise a child.

Maggie felt foolish about how much time she had spent with Rhiannon, talking about Gabe, without knowing that the two of them shared a secret of their own. Naturally Gabe wanted Rhiannon — what guy wouldn't? Her body tensed up. She wished she had never introduced them.

"I'm going to bed," Maggie said. "You probably shouldn't drive. You can sleep in the big room. Okay?"

Rhiannon seemed taken aback by her

abruptness, but she just said, "Yeah, okay. I'll leave first thing in the morning."

Maggie turned toward the bathroom to wash her face.

"I'm sorry," Rhiannon said. "Maybe I should have kept my mouth shut."

"Maybe," Maggie said. She closed the door behind her, feeling guilty. She was never mean like that, not to anyone, let alone a friend. She started to cry.

Maggie couldn't sleep. After she heard Rhiannon go to bed, she paced the living room, paying attention to each creak of the floorboards as she stared at her cell phone screen and searched for a signal.

Finally, in the corner by the kitchen, she got two bars. She dialed the number, her heart racing as she listened to the phone ring. For a second, she thought he was going to let it go to voice mail, but then he picked up.

She heard people laughing in the background, the sound of women's voices.

"Mags?" Gabe said. "Hello?"

It was so bitter and sad, looking for safety in the person least likely to give it to you. Like drinking salt water, she thought. The house felt eerily quiet.

"Hi," she said.

"Hold on, I can't hear you — let me go outside for a sec," he said, and then there was a lot of muffling and yelling and laughing before the noise faded.

"How are you?" he asked. His voice was faint; she could hardly make it out. She crouched down lower, searching for a signal.

"Fine," she said. "Listen. There's something I have to tell you."

"Hello? Are you calling from your apartment? You're all fuzzy."

"No. I'm up in Maine."

She tried to sound unafraid, wanting him to be shocked by her, maybe.

"What?" he said. "I can't really hear you."

"I'm in Maine."

"Oh yeah? By yourself?" he asked.

"No," she said. She didn't think she could mention Rhiannon's name without crying again. "My brother and some friends are driving up now."

"Oh hey, fun," he said. "Tell Chris I say hi."

"How's New York?" she asked. And then — as furious as she felt, she couldn't help it — "I miss you."

"I'm in East Hampton, actually," he said. "Missing you too."

Her stomach flipped, and suddenly her sadness turned to anger, the two feelings so much aligned when it came to him.

"Why?" she said.

"Why do I miss you?" he said.

"Why are you in the Hamptons?"

"Some girl Hayes knows from college, her

parents have this sweet beach place and he was going anyway with a bunch of people, and I don't have any work for the next two weeks, because, well, you know, so I figured I'd hang here."

All that she had imagined fell away, set against those words. He was not curled up on his couch, waiting for her to come home. Had she stayed in Brooklyn, waiting around, he wouldn't have shown up at her door tomorrow or the next day or the next.

"It's gorgeous here," he said. "We're actually about to take a nighttime sail."

He sounded like he was having the time of his life.

"What did you need to tell me?" Gabe asked.

"Forget it," Maggie said. "I should go; I think I hear Chris's car outside."

"Okay," he said. "Listen, I'm sorry for how things went the other day. But it seems like cooling off for a while is probably smart, right?"

"Good-bye, Gabe," she said.

She hung up, feeling wholly unsatisfied. She resisted the urge to call him back. Instead, she sat down at the table and switched on her computer. Her uncle Pat had had the cottage wired for Internet the previous summer, even though there was still no TV or phone.

She started typing an e-mail, and when she finished she didn't even bother to read it over. She just hit SEND.

Gabe,
There are two things I want to say that for some reason I could not get out over the phone just now. First, that I think I've finally realized how bad you are for me. I'm grateful to you for really hitting me over the head with it this time. Clearly I needed that. Second (and I admit this bit of news is complicated by my first point), I am having a baby. Mostly when I imagine it, this child is only mine. But I know that technically he or she is yours too. You deserve to know, so I'm telling you. I don't think you deserve much more than that. Please leave me alone for now. I'll be in touch when I'm ready.

After dinner, Alice went out to the screen porch and called Ann Marie.

"Your niece arrived today, and not with Gabe," she said.

"Oh?" Ann Marie said, sounding distracted, not seeming to care.

"Instead she brought a woman," Alice said.

"What do you mean, a woman?" Ann Marie asked.

"A woman who lives next door to her," Alice whispered, as if Daniel were sitting there and liable to scold her for gossiping with their bigmouthed daughter-in-law.

"You mean, like a date?" Ann Marie said. "Hold on, Mom. Pat, honey, can't you watch this in the other room?"

It hadn't even dawned on Alice that Maggie and Whatever-Her-Name-Was might be together in *that* way. No, she was positive they weren't. Then again, Alice had always been clueless about such things. She had once remarked to Daniel that it was nice how many pairs of brothers you saw walking around Ogunquit, arm in arm, and he had laughed like a hyena.

Now she replied, "I'm not sure what sort of relationship it is, to be honest. Just strange, that much I know. Maggie has the girl drive her here and tells me she's leaving tonight. Well, I can see quite clearly that she hasn't left. I'm not blind."

"That's odd."

"Kathleen made such a mess of that child. I wish there was something I could have done to fix her. Now it's probably too late."

She was fuming from their dinner conversation, but she didn't feel like getting into the specifics with Ann Marie.

"You're always taking too much upon yourself," Ann Marie said. "There's nothing you can do. Lately I'm starting to think that children just become who they become."

"Well, I thank God every day that your three turned out the way they did," Alice said.

"Our three have their moments," Ann Marie said.

It was precisely this sort of comment that made her so dear, because really her children were angels. They had probably turned out so well because of Ann Marie's refusal to make excuses for bad behavior, as Alice's own two daughters were prone to doing for their kids. Alice had sent Christopher and Maggie a twenty-dollar check on every one of their birthdays since they were babies, and had either of them ever bothered to write a thank-you note?

Little Daniel always mailed a card on Alice's birthday and even sent her flowers on Mother's Day. He was a handsome devil, a darling boy. He was quick as a whip, like his father, and engaged to a sweet young beauty, a Catholic, thank God. She was Italian, not Irish, but what could you do?

Patrick and Ann Marie's daughter Fiona was a saint. Alice often thought that if Fiona had been around in her day, she would have been one of the girls who chose to become a nun. Perhaps she still would. As a child, Alice had loathed the nuns. They rapped her knuckles, and made her write with her right hand, her left hand tied to the back of her chair, though it was perfectly clear she was a lefty.

Even so, to have a granddaughter in the sisterhood would be a real point of pride at Legion of Mary meetings. Mary Daley's son was only a deacon and she got so much attention for it, you'd think he was the pope.

Patty, Ann Marie and Patrick's middle child, had gone to law school and was now working long hours, despite the fact that she had three small children. She had married a Jew, which had just about killed Ann Marie. She never said so, but Alice could feel it.

Still, Ann Marie and Pat's three kids would

always be her favorites, especially Little Daniel.

She found Maggie to be the most difficult of all the grandchildren. When the girl let her guard down and had a few drinks, she could really be a hoot. She had a good sense of humor, like Daniel's. But there was a sort of forced quality about her most of the time, a formality that rubbed Alice the wrong way. Maggie was obsessed with getting to the bottom of every conflict, thanks most likely to the fact that Kathleen had shoved her onto a therapist's couch as soon as she was in middle school. After Daniel died, when Alice didn't want to think of him or Kathleen at all, there was Maggie, calling her every other day like clockwork. Alice tried to ask God for patience, to tell herself that her granddaughter meant well, but she felt annoyed even so.

Daniel had loved the stuffing out of that child, same as he had with Kathleen.

Once, when Maggie was six or seven, Alice had gotten up for a glass of water and found her crying in the cottage kitchen in the middle of the night.

"What happened?" Alice asked.

"I heard a scary noise," Maggie said. "It woke me up."

"Did you tell your parents?" Alice looked in vain toward their bedroom.

"They're asleep," Maggie said. She kept

right on crying.

"Did you think it was a ghost?" Alice asked. She meant it as a joke, but Maggie's face turned deadly serious.

"Oh, Grandma, I wish I could see a ghost," she said. "Then death wouldn't be so scary. Seeing a ghost would mean we get to keep on living. Well, sort of. Right?"

Alice was startled. What kind of child said a thing like that?

"Get back to sleep now," she said sternly. "You're fine. You only heard the wind off the dunes."

When she got into bed beside Daniel a few moments later, having forgotten all about her glass of water, Alice felt so rattled she had to shake him awake to tell him the story.

Daniel just chuckled groggily. "What a clever munchkin that one is," he said, before immediately falling back to sleep.

After she hung up the phone, Alice walked to the kitchen. She poured herself a glass of wine, and then she set to washing the dishes.

Maybe she ought to be kinder to Maggie. After all, she was going through a breakup. She seemed a bit out of sorts. But why the hell did she have to bring that friend here with no notice at all? Why had she said those things about Daniel right in front of that Scottish girl?

Alice saw her grandchildren as extensions

of their parents, so that Ryan's ambition and disappointment had her praying for Clare, and Chris's roughness made her light candles for Kathleen. But she also blamed her daughters for how their children had turned out. How could she not? Kathleen had no sense of propriety whatsoever, and so her child saw nothing wrong with coming to Alice's dinner table and asking her about her life's most devastating moments.

Maggie had said that Daniel would want to see her painting again. That alone made Alice want to slap her across the face. What did she know about any of that? Daniel was a wonderful man, and she had loved him dearly. But he had never been interested in seeing her become anything besides another mother, another proper housewife. He had insisted that she stop drinking because of it; he had consulted their daughter about his cancer treatment rather than worry Alice's pretty little head.

Don't you think it could be good for us to talk about him? her granddaughter had asked preposterously, and in front of a complete stranger. Alice assumed she wanted to know only for the sake of that goddamn book she was writing. She wasn't about to bare her soul to fulfill Maggie's literary aspirations. The story of how she met Daniel, of how she lost her sister, would remain hers alone. It wasn't anyone else's business. But now Maggie had her thinking about all of it, and she hated to think about it.

Alice walked back out to the porch for a cigarette. In the distance, the waves were crashing against the rocks. This had been Daniel's favorite time of night, sitting out here with a cup of peppermint tea, listening to the surf before bed. She missed him — there was a pit in her heart where he had once resided.

A short while later, she went to the bathroom and switched on the radio to have a bit of noise. She changed into a cotton night-gown and removed her teeth, brushing them gently before she placed them in a glass of cold water on the edge of the sink. The dentures were a new acquisition this year. She was happy at least that Daniel hadn't lived long enough to see them.

Alice pulled back her hair and washed her face with cold cream. Her skin had gotten so terribly dry as she aged. It was as thin as tissue paper now, and could tear from the slightest bump. She dipped her fingers into a tub of Eucerin, as she did each night, rubbing the jelly into her cracked legs and pulling a pair of stretchy black pants over the top to seal in the moisture. Tomorrow she was having lunch with Father Donnelly. Maybe that would cheer her up.

She shut off the radio and got into her bed, which was far too big for only her. The memories plunged forth and she had to leave the light on, as if she were her own timid child.

The Holy Cross–Boston College football game at Fenway Park fell on November 28, 1942, two days after Thanksgiving. Alice's brothers Timmy and Paul and so many of their friends were home on leave for two weeks, and they were giddy, running around town in their uniforms, making the girls swoon. Her other brothers hadn't come home: Jack was on the USS *Augusta,* somewhere off the coast of North Africa. Michael, only fifteen, was fighting in the Pacific. He was technically too young, but he had snuck into the military, afraid to miss out on the excitement.

With two of the four boys home and their mother a nervous wreck, convinced that all of them might be dead by Christmas, that Thanksgiving was a feast unlike any they had ever had — their mother cooked a turkey and gravy, buttery mashed potatoes and au gratins, too, and Mary baked apple pie and peach cobbler. By the time Saturday came, they were still stuffed.

The boys all hoped to go to Boston College once the war was over. They had been rooting for the Eagles since they were kids. This year, BC was undefeated, and winning this game would mean a trip to the Sugar Bowl.

380

But in an upset that sent her brothers into a tizzy (no doubt they'd lost plenty gambling on the game), Holy Cross won, fifty-five to twelve.

Alice didn't give a fig about any of this; she hadn't even gone to the game with the boys. But she had been preparing to meet Daniel Kelleher at the Cocoanut Grove later that night since right after breakfast. Mary wasn't coming. She was supposed to, but at the last minute her Henry got tickets for a show at the Shubert, and she pulled out.

"You're making me go alone?" Alice had moaned that morning in the bathroom as they washed their faces.

"You won't be alone, you'll have the boys there."

"Mary, you'd better come meet us after the show."

"We'll see what Henry wants."

"What Henry wants! Always what Henry wants!" Alice walked into the hallway and slammed the door.

"Oh, honestly!" came Mary's voice from the other side.

She left the house a short while later. "Good luck tonight," she said, pinching Alice's cheek.

Alice spent the afternoon primping on her own, which was nowhere near as fun as doing it with someone else. But by the time she was ready, she felt like a million bucks. The silver silk dress she had picked out fell perfectly over her hips, pooling on the floor and covering the scuffed toes of her shoes. The dress belonged to Mary and was too big for Alice on its own — she had tied a blue ribbon tightly around her waist to give it some shape. She was wearing Mary's favorite gray suede gloves, lined with mink, and her mink coat too. The coat had been a present from Henry, but Mary hardly ever put it on. *Finders keepers,* Alice thought. It was wintertime. Someone ought to be getting some wear out of it.

She herself didn't have a single dress nice enough to wear to the Cocoanut Grove. Everyone would be in formal evening attire, and she wasn't about to try to dress up a convertible suit with pearls, as her mother had suggested. But her brothers had invited her to come. A shipmate of Tim's had an older brother named Daniel who'd gone to Holy Cross and was now home on leave from the Pacific for a week. Timmy had gotten it into his head that this older brother ought to marry one of his sisters.

For months he had been writing Alice about how wonderful Daniel was, even though he wasn't a Boston College grad. He was sweet and funny and smart as heck, Timmy said. He had been born smack in the middle of ten kids and had the patience of a saint. (*Perfect for a pain in the neck like you, ha-ha!* he had written.)

Alice wrote back: *If you like the man so much, why don't you marry him?*

Ha. Ha, Timmy responded. *Just come out with us to the BC game at the end of the month, and afterward we'll go somewhere special for dancing.*

Having no intention of meeting a date in the freezing cold and wind of a football game, she had arranged to get together with the boys afterward at the Cocoanut Grove. Really, she had agreed to the setup only because she wanted an excuse to go.

Alice had been there twice before, once to see Joe Frisco perform, and the other time, Helen Morgan. She loved the place — the long oval bar beside the stage, the wide dance floor surrounded by tables covered in white linen cloths. The room was lined with palm trees and dripping with lights. In summertime, the roof could be rolled back for dancing under the stars.

She arrived at seven thirty, right on time, gliding through the revolving door, feeling like a movie star. She wore a bright red lipstick that her aunt Rose had sent from New York the previous Christmas. She had styled her hair in a soft wave, like Veronica Lake in *Sullivan's Travels.*

Inside the club, hundreds of people stood shoulder to shoulder: handsome men in uniform by the dozens, glamorous women in their finest gowns. Every corner was full, every table taken up. Alice scanned the room for her brothers, pushing through the crowd. She looked out over the packed dance floor, but she didn't see them anywhere. She lingered over small talk with the redheaded coat-check girl for far too long, just to have something to do: *Yes, it was a chilly one out there. Pity about Boston College, and did Alice know that the entire team was meant to be there tonight for their victory party, but had canceled, and it was a shame, really, because the redhead had been pining after the BC fullback for positively ages.*

When she went back toward the dance floor, the boys still hadn't arrived. And so she stood alone by the bar, feeling like an absolute fool and vowing to murder her brothers as soon as they showed their faces. She held Mary's gloves in one hand, swinging them back and forth a few times, before realizing that she looked like a nervous Nellie. She set them down on the oak bar, running her fingers over the suede, counting the minutes.

It was ten to eight when they finally rolled in, drunk as skunks and towed by a couple of strangers. Alice's brothers were big, dark, strapping men. The pair behind them looked like scarecrows in comparison — rather short and spindly, with hair the color of red-tinged straw. They barely filled out their uniforms.

"There she is!" her brother Paul hollered, far too loud. Even in the din, a few people turned to stare.

"You're late," she hissed, when the boys got close enough. "I've been waiting here forever."

"Oh, now, don't be dramatic," Paul said. "We're only a few minutes behind schedule, and believe me, you wouldn't have wanted to see us before we had a drink. Tim was in tears!" He laughed raucously, and the other boys joined him.

It hit her then, as it sometimes did, that her brothers had already been to war and would soon have to return, like so many other young men in the room. There was news all the time of boys you had grown up with, dead and gone. Yet they still got upset over football games, and dressed up to go dancing. Life didn't stop for anything.

One of the scarecrows extended a hand. "Daniel Kelleher," he said. "Pleased to make your acquaintance."

Is he handsome? she had asked her brother Timmy at Thanksgiving dinner, and he had scoffed before saying, *He looks like Clark Gable, okay?*

She realized now that her brother had been joking.

"Can I get you a drink?" the scarecrow asked. Alice requested a gin and tonic with lime.

He made his way up to the bar and she grabbed Timmy's sleeve.

"How could you?" she hissed.

"What are you talking about?" he said.

"He's a dud!"

"Quit being such a snob. Give him a chance, will ya?"

Daniel returned a few minutes later with a glass of clear liquid on ice.

"They were fresh out of limes," he said. "Or should that be 'out of fresh limes'?"

Alice hated him at once. She took the glass from his hand and turned toward the others to let all of them — especially Daniel — know that she wasn't interested.

"These boys of ours are a bunch of real sore losers, Alice," Daniel said with a laugh. She narrowed her eyes. He meant his own brother, too, but she certainly didn't appreciate his referring to her brothers that way.

"Never underestimate the power of the Crusaders," he went on, beaming. "Fifty-five to twelve, how does that feel, fellas? I bet it smarts, huh?"

"There's such a thing as an ungraceful winner, too, you know," Alice said. She gulped down the gin.

"Uh-oh," Timmy said. "Pay her no attention, Daniel. She's just sore with us."

"No, no, she's right," Daniel said with a grin. "Very ungentlemanly of me."

"Well, I owe you a drink, I guess," Timmy said.

"You owe me more than that, but we can discuss it when your sister's not around," Daniel chuckled.

Alice emptied her glass. "Timothy, another G and T," she said. "You certainly owe me a drink too."

Timmy went to the bar and the other boys started talking about football.

Daniel turned to her. "So, your brothers tell me you work in a law firm. That must be exciting."

"Not really."

"Aww, come on. I think if it were my job I'd want to read all the files for the juicy scandals. Who's suing who and all that."

She cocked her head. She had never thought of that. It wasn't a half-bad idea.

"I'm saving up to go to Paris when the war is over," she said, which was almost the truth. "I'm going to be a painter someday. Well, at least I want to."

"It's good to have a daydream," he said. "That's what my mother always told us."

She wanted to tell him this wasn't a stupid *daydream*, that someone had paid her for her work, but he kept talking: "I've been working as a trainer in the gun mount on my ship for six months. It gets dull sometimes, you know? Before that, I worked as a junior executive at an insurance company, and yes, it was as bor-

387

ing as it sounds. I'll have to go back to it someday. But I want to hit like Ted Williams. That's what I fantasize about to get me through. I'm always getting in trouble on the ship for my ghost batting." He assumed the batter's position and swung an imaginary bat, right there in the middle of the club. "Say, did you hear about Ted Williams's brother? He's a drifter type, I guess, no good. Anyway, poor Ted buys a big brand-new house, fills it up with nice furnishings. And this brother of his comes to the house one day, backs a truck up to the front door, and steals all the furniture. He even took the washing machine! He sold every last thing."

Alice stared blankly. She wanted to go home.

"Gosh, I'm sorry," he said. "I talk a lot when I'm nervous. May I say, you look beautiful." He twisted his fingers around the cuffs of his sleeves. "Your brother said you were a looker, but, wow. How he ever saw fit to set a guy like me up with a girl like you, I'll never know."

My sentiments exactly, she thought, though she smiled back.

When Timmy returned, she drank the second glass of gin down quickly, and then another. She began to feel warm and light, swaying in place to the music. She hadn't had much to eat that day — she never did before a date — and she thought a bit tipsily that this Daniel wasn't really the sort of guy you needed to starve yourself for, but maybe he wasn't so bad.

He asked her to dance. It was a fast one, "Don't Sit Under the Apple Tree," even better than the Glenn Miller version on the radio. She was pleasantly surprised to find that Daniel wasn't as clumsy as she might have imagined. He dipped her back and his big palm felt hot against her spine. He spun her and spun her until she began to feel dizzy. After a while, Alice grabbed his arm and said, "I need to sit down."

He took her hand and led her off the floor. Her brothers were gone by then, off to the movies to forget the pain of what they had seen at Fenway Park. Alice couldn't believe they would just up and leave her like that, but leave they had.

There were no empty seats at the bar. Daniel approached a bunch of men in air force uniforms clustered around the taps. He put a hand on one man's arm.

"Hey, pal, do you mind giving up your seat to the lady?"

The young man jumped to his feet — he was tall, with jet-black hair and broad shoulders. She wished for a minute that Daniel Kelleher could somehow figure out a way to look like him.

"My pleasure," he said as he stood up, and Alice wanted to grab him and say that she wasn't with this guy, not really. She imagined how years later, they'd tell their friends the story of how they'd met while she was on some dreadful fix-up courtesy of her stupid brother, and then her real true love came along and offered up his chair.

But a moment later, the man was pulled off into the crowd.

"Can I get you anything?" Daniel asked. "Another drink? A glass of water?"

She knew she ought to go for the water, or see if he'd like to sit down to dinner so she could get some food in her stomach, but Alice just said, "Another gin sounds swell."

It was then, as he leaned forward to get the bartender's attention, that Alice spotted her sister chatting with a beautifully dressed older woman. Mary's cheeks were flushed, and she wore an emerald green gown that Alice had never seen before. Had she been wearing it under her coat when she left the house that morning? Or had Henry given it to her today?

Mary was laughing at something the woman had said. Alice thought her sister looked like a member of high society, no different from her companion. The sight made her feel uneasy. A moment later, Mary looked up and their eyes met. She kissed the woman on the cheek, gesturing toward Alice. They parted ways, and Mary began moving through the crowd as the band switched gears and started to play a soft, slow song, one of Alice's favorites, "Moonlight Serenade."

Halfway to where she stood, Mary pulled someone up from a table full of elegant men and women in fine attire: Henry. She whispered in his ear and he rose to his feet. They walked slowly toward the bar.

"There you are!" Mary said when she reached her side. She embraced Alice, and Daniel looked up in surprise. "I've been looking all over for you. Where are the boys?"

"They went to the movies," Alice said. "What are you doing here?"

"You told me to come. And it turned out some of Henry's friends were here already. With a table, as luck would have it." She looked toward Daniel expectantly.

"This is Timmy's friend," Alice said.

"Daniel Kelleher," Daniel said, extending his arm and shaking Henry's hand vigorously, like he was hammering a nail. "Pleased to meet you, uh —"

"Henry," Henry said. "And this is Mary, of course."

"My sister," Alice said quickly.

"I've heard of you," Mary said, without a hint of her old shyness.

"All good, I hope," Daniel replied.

"Oh yes." She turned to Alice and smiled. "Nice dress."

"I know it's yours, I —"

"No, really, it looks lovely on you," Mary said. "Have it."

The plain statement made Alice's blood run hard and fast. How dare her sister speak to her that way, as if she were above her now? She tried to remember the Philippians — humility before all else.

Henry and Daniel leaned into a swarm of men trying to place their orders at the bar.

"I'm having a heck of a time of it," Daniel said, and Henry simply signaled to a bartender in a tuxedo and said, "Charles, can you help us out?"

"Absolutely, Mr. Winslow," he said.

Daniel turned pink.

"How's it going?" Mary asked Alice when they were alone.

Alice took a deep breath, trying to move past her bitter feelings.

"The date is clearly a flop," she said with a conciliatory smile. "Thanks, boys."

Mary lowered her voice and looked over her shoulder, making sure Daniel couldn't hear. "He doesn't seem so bad. You're too hung up on looks."

"So you admit he's ugly."

Mary smiled. "Shh! No! A bit dishwatery, maybe."

"I'm not exactly in the market for dishwater."

"Fair enough." Mary smiled. "It's true you two make a bit of an odd couple."

"I told him I wanted to be an artist and he laughed."

"What!"

"More or less. He's probably right. It probably won't ever happen."

Mary shook her head. "Did you tell him you've sold a painting?"

"Oh, don't be silly," Alice said, though she was grateful to her sister for thinking that just then.

"You look dynamite in that dress, by the way," Mary said. "Better than I ever did."

"Hush," Alice said.

The men returned with the drinks, and Mary and Daniel started a conversation about the navy, specifically about Timmy's lifelong obsession with playing pranks. According to Daniel, their brother had gotten socked in the face for shaving off a shipmate's left eyebrow when the fella was passed out drunk.

"Why not both eyebrows?" Mary asked.

As Daniel began to respond, Henry gently grabbed Alice's wrist to get her attention.

"Can I tell you a secret, kiddo?" he whispered into her ear.

"Sure," she said.

"I'm a bit intoxicated," he said.

"Me too," she said. "Great secret."

"No, no, that's not it. The secret is that I'm going to ask your sister to marry me tomorrow at the beach. I've got the ring right here." He tapped his breast pocket and gave her a wink. "Picked it up this afternoon before I met her at the theater. You're the only person who knows other than my sister. My father wants me to head up a branch of the company down in New York for a year or two, so we'll likely be moving there after the wedding."

Alice forced out a smile and said that it was wonderful news. This was what she had wanted. But she felt herself filling up with anger — why should Mary have a love, a real love, and not her? Why should Mary be the one to go free and be a wealthy woman, living as she pleased, meeting all sorts of fascinating people? Alice had thought Henry would bring good fortune to them both, but perhaps that had been naïve. Here she was with the dud to end all duds, and there was Mary, living like Isabella Stewart Gardner herself, off to New York for a new adventure.

Alice knew her rage and her stubbornness often burst from nowhere, but knowing didn't change it. A daydream, that's what Daniel had said about her life. Maybe he was right. Alice felt like a fool.

"I'm going to ask your dad for his permission in the morning while you and Mary are at church, which I'm not terribly excited about," Henry went on. "If you could try to keep her out a half hour longer than usual or so. Maybe go for breakfast."

"Absolutely," she said briskly. Then she turned to the others and said, "I have to go home now."

"What? No! You two should come down-stairs and have a round with us," Mary said. "It's not that late."

"Sure!" Daniel said.

"No thank you," Alice said.

"Oh, come on," Mary said. "Let us buy you a drink."

"You're acting a bit big for your britches," Alice hissed at her sister, echoing their father's words of a few weeks earlier.

Mary frowned. "Am I?"

With that, Alice felt guilty. What had her sister done to her, really?

"Let's go downstairs," Mary said.

Down below was the Melody Lounge, a dim bar with booths along the wall, where Alice had allowed Martin McDonough to kiss her right out in the open one night over the summer, considering it her patriotic duty, since he would be heading to Germany the following day, though after a moment she had told him to stop.

Alice looked toward the table where Henry had been sitting. Naturally, her sister wouldn't deign to introduce her to their sophisticated friends. She saw that once Mary was formally a part of that world, Alice herself would be invisible to her. New York was hours away. Why hadn't Mary told her?

"I really can't," she said. "I'm going home now."

"Oh, Alice!" Mary said.

Alice ignored her. She turned to Daniel. "Please get my coat."

He looked crestfallen, but he did as she said.

She stood there with Mary and Henry in silence until he came back. Alice burned with embarrassment when Mary caught sight of her own mink hanging on Daniel's arm, though neither of them said a word about it.

Alice put the coat on. "See you," she said to them. She moved toward the exit without waiting for a reply. The crowd had grown even thicker now. Every table on the dine-and-dance floor was filled, and people stood in any empty corner or patch of space. It was near impossible to move. Daniel followed close behind, careful not to lose her in the throng.

"You should be nicer to your sister," he said loudly, trying to be heard above the hubbub of voices and music and clinking glasses.

"You don't know the first thing about it," she said, pushing past a group of men in heated conversation.

"No, you're right. I don't," he said. "Slow down, I'll walk you."

"Walk me? I'm all the way in Dorchester," she said, still moving. "And anyway, I live with my parents and I'm a good girl, so forget whatever it is you had in mind."

She knew he had nothing of the sort in mind, but she was spoiling for a fight.

She went through the revolving door and he followed. Outside, the air was frigid. Alice pulled the fur coat tight around her waist.

"I meant I'd walk you to a taxi," he said. "You're bound and determined not to like me, aren't you, Alice Brennan?"

She grinned with closed lips.

"It was a pleasure meeting you," he said. "I'm sorry for — well, I'm not quite sure what. I guess another date is out of the question."

"That's right," she said. Then, a little quieter, "Sorry for spoiling your evening."

"You didn't spoil anything," he said. "The night's still young. Who knows? Maybe I'll go back in there and find myself a pretty girl to dance with."

"You ought to," she said.

He smiled goofily. "Shoot, I hoped that would make you jealous."

Daniel raised his arm to hail a taxi for her. She looked at him and thought that she would probably never see him again and she didn't much care. She was eager to get home. But just as a cab pulled to the curb, Alice saw Mary coming out of the club.

Daniel didn't notice. He had opened the back door of the taxi and now stood there awkwardly, with his hand on the car's roof.

"You take this one," she said quickly. She didn't need him hanging about while she and Mary argued. "I'll get the next one that comes along."

"No, I insist," he said.

"Really, look, there's another pulling up now, and it's going in my direction."

"You sure?" he asked.

Alice nodded. They said good night. She let him kiss her on the cheek. Then she watched him climb into the cab and ride off down Piedmont Street.

Mary was approaching. Alice held her breath.

"What got into you back there?" Mary asked when she reached her side. "Why did you run off like that?"

Alice just looked at her, without saying a word.

"Let's take a walk," Mary said. "I need to talk to you."

"I'm tired," Alice said stubbornly. "I want to go home."

"I'll come with you then," Mary said.

"What about Henry? You're going to just leave him inside?"

"We're here with other friends; he'll be fine," Mary said. "And anyway we're going to the beach tomorrow for some reason, even though it's freezing out. It's where we had our first kiss."

Alice realized then why he had chosen to propose there. And while every bit of her said that she ought to be excited for Mary, she just felt numb.

"Oh yes, your other friends," Alice said. "I hope they didn't catch a glimpse of you talking to the likes of me."

"Is that what this is about?" Mary said. "For heaven's sake, Alice, I'm terrified of those people. Most of them wouldn't save me from drowning if it meant their trousers might get damp."

Alice's heart stung, to think of her sister that way.

"You can't leave," Mary said. "Something's happened. I need to talk to you."

"What is it?" Alice asked.

"Henry is moving to New York. He just told me tonight — well, someone let the cat out of the bag at dinner. He looked really peeved and said we'd discuss it tomorrow. Alice, I am so afraid that he's taking me to the beach to end it. I had this vision of you and me tonight, turning into those horrible old spinsters who live at home forever."

She hadn't seemed worried inside the club, but Mary had always been good at painting a rosy picture in mixed company.

Alice's chest tightened. In the morning, Mary's bad dream would show itself to be a misunderstanding. Mary would get everything Alice herself had wished for. *Those horrible old spinsters,* she had said. Was that to be Alice's fate?

She might have put her sister at ease, whispered that tomorrow Mary would get what she wanted most. But instead Alice said, "You shouldn't have gone to bed with him."

The words were a sweet release as they came out of her mouth, but she instantly felt bad once she'd said them.

Mary looked taken aback. She bit her lip and stood there in silence until Alice let out an involuntary shiver.

"You must be cold," Mary said. She reached into her purse, "Here, take my mittens."

"I have some," Alice snapped. It was then that she realized she had left Mary's suede gloves sitting on the bar. "Damn it to hell," she said, before she had time to think. "I forgot them inside."

"Which ones?" Mary said, in a tone that implied she already knew.

"The gray suede."

"Oh, Alice, they're my favorite — you know that. I saved up to buy them."

Alice knew she ought to feel guilty, but she didn't.

"Go get them, please," Mary said.

"I'm not going back into that crowd," Alice said.

"Quit being willful, and go get them, and I'll hail us a cab."

"No."

"Alice!"

"Why do you care so much? You know Henry will buy you a new pair."

"Why must you always be so pigheaded?"

"I'm not! My head hurts. And you're the one who wants the silly gloves so bad."

Mary blinked. "Fine then. You hail us a cab, and I'll get them."

She didn't respond.

Mary turned around with a sigh and went back into the club.

Alice stood there, still as stone. She lit a cigarette and smoked it down to the bottom.

After a few minutes, a taxi ambled down the block, and she waved it over, climbing into the backseat. She thought of leaving Mary behind, but at the last second she said, "I'm waiting for my sister, she'll just be a minute."

She pulled a compact from her purse and stared into the mirror. Her makeup seemed to have drooped. She looked ten years older than she had when the evening began.

Mary was taking ages. Alice imagined her inside, saying her long good-byes, as if she weren't going to see Henry again tomorrow.

The driver shifted impatiently in his seat. Alice started to feel a bit embarrassed. *Hurry up,* she thought.

Still looking in the mirror, she heard a ruckus out by the doors, voices booming, the sort of noise that could mean only true joy or terror. She felt jealous of whoever they were for a moment, but then there came the sound of breaking glass and the wail of the fire alarm.

The driver yelled, "Jesus Christ! We gotta get outta here, lady."

Alice looked up, confused. Smoke poured through the windows of the club. People were shoving one another to get out at the revolving door, its panes shattering in the fray. They streamed out to the sidewalk, all of them yelling, crying.

Without thinking, she jumped out of the cab, unable to breathe. The driver sped off.

She scanned the sidewalk, praying that Mary had already come out.

Seconds seemed like hours, as she stood there. She felt cemented to the ground, unable to move. Sirens roared and then firemen pushed past Alice, trying to get inside.

"You've got to scram, honey," one of them said. "You're going to get hurt."

"My sister's in there!" she said, frantic. "You have to help her."

"Just go on home," he said. "Tell your parents. Your sister will be okay. Just go home."

Alice watched them move toward the doors at the edges of the building, but they did not go in. They pushed and pushed until one firefighter screamed over his shoulder to a few others, who were unwinding a hose from the truck: "Christ, we can't get in. They're screaming bloody murder in there. The doors must be locked from inside."

"Break 'em down," someone yelled.

They took axes to the doors, but it was no use.

"There's not enough time!" the first guy shouted.

Alice felt like she might pass out. She wanted to run inside and grab Mary's hand, but the front entrance was already clogged with people, lying one atop another like fallen dominoes, some of them screaming for help in agonizing tones, some of them already trampled and dying. She was terrified, too afraid to be brave.

The firemen broke in through the windows as best they could, and a few people managed to get out that way. She watched them, her stomach a jumble of nerves. She prayed as she searched the faces for Mary's.

The sidewalk, which had been quiet and near empty a few minutes earlier, was now swarming with chaos. Those who managed to get out screamed in horror for their loved ones still inside. Sailors and soldiers, all home on leave for Thanksgiving, just out having themselves a night, were suddenly thrown into rescue duty. They had escaped death in combat overseas, but now they were carrying people out like mad, running back into the fire five times, some of them never reemerging on the sixth.

"We can't get to them all," yelled a young boy with a heavy older woman in his arms.

Another moaned, "Oh Jesus, Jesus. When I

went to pull her out, her arm came right off in my hands."

Alice shouted at them: "You have to get a girl named Mary. Please! She's wearing a green dress. Please!"

Flames burst through the roof of the club, and a huge crowd gathered in the street, seeming to come from all corners of the city, blocking the path of the fire trucks, until soldiers formed a human chain and pushed the throngs down Shawmut Avenue.

It had all happened so fast. Alice ran toward Broadway, thinking that perhaps she could find her brothers at the cinema. They'd be able to save Mary, she knew it. Before she could turn the corner, she saw a handful of people inside the club who had managed to break the small windowpanes along Piedmont Street, but had gotten stuck in the windows' metal bars, their heads out, halfway to safety, their bodies burning as they screamed. A priest stood before them on the sidewalk, reading them their last rites.

Alice looked on and screamed her sister's name. She could not move.

Injured people lay on the sidewalk and on the floor of the garage next door to the club, waiting for help. After a while, ambulances roared, rolling in from Lynn, Newton, Brookline, and the Charlestown Navy Yard, but there still weren't enough of them. Taxicabs drove the overflow.

A newspaper delivery truck was allowed to come through, and Alice watched as the two men inside began to carelessly toss folks into the back. She raised her voice to protest before realizing that all of them were dead.

Alice vomited into a sewer grate. Her head throbbed. She felt like she might faint. She leaned forward a bit, losing her balance. A young guy in uniform came up to her, taking her by the elbows.

"Miss," he said. "Are you all right? Miss, we've got to get you home."

She did not remember getting on the streetcar, or walking up the block to her parents' house. But she found herself on the front porch, the stillness of the neighborhood impossible to comprehend after what she had just seen. Then she was turning the doorknob and stepping inside, removed from her body as if in a dream.

They were all sitting in the den. Their faces lit up when she walked through the door.

"You're alive!" her mother said, excited to see Alice in a way she never had been before. "There's a horrible fire at the Cocoanut Grove. We heard about it on the radio. Oh Lord, thank you."

The boys jumped to their feet and held her close, and even her father hugged her. Alice felt so loved for an instant, before she remembered: "Mary was inside."

"What do you mean?" Timmy said.

Alice thought of telling them the whole story, but she couldn't do it.

"I saw her there and I don't think she came out," was all she could manage. "I was already outside when the fire started. I couldn't get back in."

"Maybe she left before you," her mother said. "Maybe you just didn't know."

Alice sobbed. She could not tell them the truth. "I hope so."

At the mortuary the next day, a freezing rain fell, and Mayor Tobin himself read the names of the dead. Their father didn't come. It was only Alice, her brothers, and their mother. After almost every name, someone screamed, the most shrill and awful sound Alice had yet to hear in her life, or ever would. The rare name that was met with silence made her wonder whether that person's loved ones had no idea yet. Maybe they were on the Cape, walking along a frigid beach with a thermos full of coffee, and they hadn't switched on the radio all weekend long. She wished that for herself, for her mother.

The mayor finished the list off after an hour, but Mary's name wasn't mentioned.

"That means she might still be alive," their mother said, hopeful. Alice wanted to believe it, but she saw the looks on her brothers' faces and knew.

They drove from one hospital to the next,

searching.

Those who had died on the way to help the night before had been piled in hospital lobbies while doctors and nurses scrambled to save the living. The bodies were still there. The stench made Alice ill as she passed through. She had to cover her nose with the sleeve of her coat.

Hundreds of people were lined up on gurneys in the halls of Boston City Hospital, some of them burned beyond recognition. Every medical examiner in the state was brought in to help identify the dead. It was hardest to figure out who the women were. Most of the men had their licenses in their wallets. But the women, dressed in gowns, had nothing that revealed them.

They walked in silence up and down those hallways for hours. Alice looked only at the gowns, telling herself that it was because she knew what Mary was wearing. In fact, she did it because she could not bear to look at the faces. She had always bossed her sister, but she had protected her too. Now Mary was probably dead, and it was Alice's fault.

A nurse told them that there was the threat of a blood shortage, so the government had allowed access to the emergency blood banks that had been set up for air raids. And, she said, the police were using the method set in place for an air raid, of receiving calls from relatives and loved ones, of assigning cards to the victims: white for the missing, green for the injured, and pink for the identified dead. Everyone had been focused on the war for so long, expecting a catastrophe tied to it somehow. Now something else entirely had taken its place.

Alice tried to bargain with God: if they found Mary alive, she would never eavesdrop on Trudy again; she would never have one of her temper tantrums; she would learn to cook and to be quiet. She looked at the sky and told Him that she knew her sister had sinned in one of the very worst ways, but if He would just let her live, Mary would redeem herself. She would marry the man she had sinned with and raise a good Catholic family.

In the days that followed, they would learn that the fire got started when two young lovers kissed in a corner of the Melody Lounge and, perhaps as Alice herself once had, the girl said it was too indiscreet, too bright under the lights like that, with a hundred other people in the room. So her date reached up over their heads and removed a lightbulb from where it hung on a wire stretched from one palm tree to another. Minutes later, they had forgotten it — they were interrupted by a teasing friend, maybe, or drawn out to the dance floor, where the piano player had just started another verse of "Bell Bottom Trousers."

Meanwhile, a bartender instructed a sixteen-year-old busboy to replace the missing lightbulb, so he climbed onto a chair and lit a match to see by, wobbling a bit as he held the match in one hand and the bulb in the other, and accidentally setting fire to one of the artificial palms.

Holiday ornaments, newly strung around the basement bar, caught fire. Flames flew up the stairs and tore through the flimsy silk draping, all the way up to the roof. Fireballs dropped down onto the tables and the bar and the bandstand and the floor, where seven hundred people were crammed in, dancing, drinking, flirting, and then — a moment later — pushing toward the doors, fighting to get out alive, which precious few of them did.

The room was dim enough on its own and quickly filled with smoke.

At the auxiliary doors, people were crushed to death, pushing in vain to get out. The doors had been bolted shut. Others ran aimlessly in all directions, scrambling like mad to escape before they died of smoke inhalation or were trampled where they stood. By the end, bodies were piled six feet high at all of the entrances, to the tops of the doors. There were bodies everywhere. They fell into the stone basement when the ballroom floor collapsed.

Later, four hundred fur coats and evening wraps were found in the coat check, destroyed by water and smoke. The redheaded gal with the crush on the Boston College fullback lay dead in the midst of them.

The fire chief told the *Globe* that really, the fire hadn't been so particularly bad. If people hadn't panicked and flooded the sole exit, if they had allowed the firemen in, if they hadn't had to dig through heaps of bodies at every door to reach the fire, he estimated there would have been at most a handful of deaths.

The chief loss of life resulted from the screaming, clawing crowds that were wedged in the entrances of the club, the paper read the next day. *Smoke took a terrific toll of life and scores were burned to death.*

Four hundred ninety-two people died in all.

Mary's body was identified after five days of searching, at a morgue in Scituate. She had been trampled, her face crushed by the boot of a man twice her size. It was impossible to say how long she had lived that way, or how much she had suffered.

At home that night, Alice drank half a bottle of whiskey, stolen from her father's secret hiding place under the basement steps, and passed out in her bed upstairs. Mary's bed, beside it, stood empty, and Alice had to turn her face to the wall. She woke up long after dinner had ended. She went to the bathroom and threw up, the whiskey like gasoline in her throat, her temples throbbing. Down on her knees, she noticed a pearl hair comb of her sister's that must have fallen behind the sink. Alice took it in her hand, sat down with her back against the tub, and ran her fingers over every inch.

She was positive that she would go to Hell for what she had done. She felt desperate to tell someone — her mother, her brother Tim — that it was because of her that Mary was inside the club to begin with, that she had murdered her own sister in a way.

Their father wept openly at the kitchen table and glared at Alice through drunken eyes. The sight of him terrified her.

The day after they discovered Mary's body, she went down the front hall early, her throat tightening, her hands shaking. She wanted to hide the newspaper before her father saw it and searched for Mary's name in the listings, as if this might make him forget.

When Alice opened the door, a burst of cold wind shot through her. She shook open the paper and saw his picture there, right on the front page: Mary's Henry, a formal shot from his college days.

Alice began to read the story's first paragraph, and her chest locked up: *Henry Winslow, son of Charles Winslow III, died of smoke inhalation,* the story began. *Mr. Winslow, who lived through a 1931 bus crash that killed two of his fellow Harvard students and a driver, was an executive with Winslow Shipping Enterprises. A diamond ring was found in his shirt pocket after he collapsed at Boston City Hospital. His sister, Betty Winslow, says that he was planning to propose to his girlfriend, Mary Brennan, the very next day. Documents indicate that Miss Brennan perished in the fire as well, and so she will remain, evermore, Maiden Mary.*

At that moment, grief filled Alice completely. She thought she might not be able to go on living. She still attended the early Mass each day. But the sermons and prayers that had always roused her, soothed her, helped her understand the world, now seemed like only hollow words. She felt nothing and always left the church thinking the same thought: she wasn't worthy to receive God's love now; she had committed a sin worse than any other.

Alice had failed her sister. She prayed, not for forgiveness, but for a sign, a signal from God as to how she could repent. She vowed to stop wishing for something better than she deserved. She would behave from now on, and expect nothing in return.

When, on the morning of the wake, her aunt Emily said, "Now, Alice, it's time for you to grow up. You will care for your parents and bring them some joy, I hope," Alice realized fully that her dreams were done for, and only answered, "I will." She wondered what this would mean, how she could best serve them. She pictured a lifetime of being alone, but not in the way she had wanted. She'd be working her days away at the law office, spending her nights in front of the radio while her father got drunk and angry, and her mother ignored it all. She would spend her life fixing them dinner and caring for them in their dotage, all the things that Mary would have done.

That same morning, a letter arrived, addressed to Mary and Alice. It was a cheerful note from their brother Jack, written on Thanksgiving, two days before the fire.

Greetings from the Tin Can! Happy Turkey Day! There's a festive mood on board today, despite the fact that we are all so far from home and missing our families. The dinner menu is fit for a king, or at least it seems that way from the way they dress up the names of everything: Hot Parker Rolls du Lyautey, Baked Spiced Spam à la Capitaine de Vaisseau, and for dessert — apple pie, strawberry ice cream, cigars, and cigarettes! The captain told us we've survived so many attacks "due not alone to skill or to good luck, but unquestionably to the intervention of divine providence." So don't you worry about me, my lovelies. I've got God on my side.

Your Jack

At the wake, Alice walked to the ladies' lounge every half hour or so and drank a long sip of vodka from a flask her aunt Rose had brought.

They had been forced to use a closed casket, and Alice was happy for that. Still, it felt torturous, standing beside that cold wooden box, calmly shaking the hands of so many neighbors and cousins and friends.

"I'm here for you," they'd say, or "I'm sorry for your loss."

Alice wanted to tear their hair out. She wanted to tell them that they could never understand this. She wondered how many of them were there merely to be a part of the tragedy — *I knew a girl once, from Sunday school, who died at the Cocoanut Grove,* they might say years later. *I was at her wake. She was so disfigured they couldn't even have a proper viewing.*

She stood by the casket with her family. Her brothers were still as stone in their dark suits, rarely speaking a word. Her mother couldn't even stand, and had to sit in a folding chair with Aunt Rose fanning her. Their father was at the end of the receiving line, with tears at the corners of his eyes that never once fell.

The afternoon wore on. Alice tried to focus

on a window at the back of the room, a thin slice of blue sky. Her head swam with dark thoughts that she wanted to scream out loud. They were here, burying her sweet young sister, and it was Alice's fault. For most people in the world, today was a day like any other. Out there, women were buying groceries and teaching children how to ride bicycles and getting dressed for a movie. But Alice would never have another pure day like that; she didn't deserve to. Her life was as finished as Mary's.

Then she saw them come through the door: Daniel Kelleher, the scarecrow she had met at the Cocoanut Grove, and his brother.

Alice moved out of her place at the front of the room, feeling her family's eyes on her. She walked through the winding line of mourners, past a long table of cold sandwiches and cake. She met him at the back wall, reached for his hand, and whispered, "Come outside for a smoke?"

He squeezed her hand tight. Though his palm was clammy, he didn't let go.

Out on the sidewalk, the bright sun hit her eyes, and she had to squint. He wasn't a handsome man, not by a long shot, but he was here. She was surprised to feel something like elation at the sight of him, something like gratitude.

"It was good of you to come," she said, as he lit her cigarette.

"Of course," he said. "How are you holding up?"

She shrugged.

"I'm so sorry for your l—"

"Please don't say it," she said.

He nodded. "Then I'll just say thank you."

"For what?" she asked.

"By finding me one hundred percent resistible, you saved my life."

She smiled weakly.

"Your sister knew you loved her," he said.

"How do you know?"

"Because sisters always do. You shouldn't blame yourself."

"What makes you think that I — ," she began, but she started to cry and couldn't complete the thought.

"Put that bad conversation you had before we left out of your head," he said. "It never happened."

"It wasn't just that," she said.

She wanted to tell him the rest, but she could not manage. She needed someone now, and if she told him, there was no way he would stay.

"It should have been me," she said through her tears.

"No," Daniel said.

"I killed her."

"Now, listen," Daniel said, more stern and strong than she would have thought him capable. "It was a terrible accident. People all over this city are wondering right now what they could or should have done. But it's not your fault."

She sniffed. "Thank you."

"Let's get back inside," he said.

She wondered if she could possibly love this person, who seemed excessively kind, but not much of a man in her opinion, nothing like she'd ever imagined for herself. At best, he could give her the common sort of life she had come to fear. Though it seemed only marginally better than living with her folks, that was still something. She remembered her aunt's words: *You will care for your parents. It's time for you to grow up.*

Perhaps this was what God had been trying to tell her all along. She hadn't listened when her mother told her to stop putting on airs. She had seen her sister's love affair as having to do with her own happiness — selfish even then — and now God had taken her sister away. Finally, she had been punished.

Daniel wrapped his arms around her, and she let herself sink in.

They were married six months later. Daniel was allowed a week's leave after the wedding. They moved into their first tiny house in Canton, where their honeymoon consisted of unpacking boxes and listening to Tommy Dorsey records for six days straight before he had to reboard the ship.

Daniel wanted to talk constantly and he wanted to make love nearly every night, when Alice just wished not to be touched. He asked her what felt good to her, which she happened to know from talking with Rita was a rarity, and a first-class thing. But Alice couldn't imagine saying the words, even if she knew what they were. It all felt wrong — sweaty and hot and uncomfortable, unholy. It wasn't painful, not after the first couple of times. But it never once compared to a good warm bath. When he had to leave at the end of that week, she was almost happy to see him go. She was pregnant, but it didn't last.

She joined St. Agnes, their local parish, and got to know other war brides. They'd gather on Thursday evenings to pray for safe returns or for the unlucky among them whose husbands had already been killed.

The war carried on for two more years. Alice did her duty — saving the drippings from the frying pan and bringing them to the butcher shop every Thursday morning; trading ration coupons for butter and sugar and coffee with the other women on the block; darning old stockings she had worn for years, even though they bunched at her ankles and sagged around her waist; drawing all the curtains at dusk when she switched on the lamps, so German subs wouldn't sink the ships in Boston Harbor, miles away.

She walked around in a state of despair that

felt like it had actual weight, pulling her down, making her feel exhausted. No one took much notice, but she grew nervous wondering what it would be like when Daniel came home.

She knew girls who were taking highly paid defense jobs — building bombers with such excitement you'd think Jimmy Stewart himself was going to fly them. Rita would call her in the evenings, gasping with excitement over wearing slacks to work, and having to pick specks of steel out of her hair and wiping grease from her cheeks.

Alice kept her job at the law firm, preferring to be solitary. She didn't understand the exuberance all around her, as if war were the Macy's Thanksgiving Day parade. On her lunch hour, she declined to join the others for sandwiches and frappes at Brigham's, and instead rode the streetcar to the Gardner Museum and walked from room to room, each of them so familiar to her after a time that she felt as though she were in her own home. She'd watch other women make a beeline for the Tapestry Room, or the courtyard, with its palm trees and flowers and pretty mosaics, but she herself was there for the paintings. She could spend the entire hour just gazing at John Singer Sargent's *El Jaleo* — a woman dancing, the flamenco perhaps, as female admirers and men with guitars cheered her on from the sidelines. It hung alone in the Spanish Cloister, a room that Isabella Stewart Gardner had built specifically for the painting, years before she even owned it.

A year after they married, Alice had her second miscarriage. Daniel cried, but in a way she felt relieved. She told him in a letter for the hundredth time that she wasn't made to be a mother, though he didn't understand what she meant and only responded, "Everyone worries they won't know what to do, darling. It's natural."

He wrote to her almost every day, sending jokes and stories and poems he had copied from a book of Yeats that his bunkmate kept under the bed. He told her tales of his childhood and his teenage years, and over time Alice began to feel that she was falling in love with him. Of course, she couldn't say so out loud: *I'm falling in love with my husband.* What sort of a comment was that? Still, it brought her some degree of comfort.

She grew terrified that he, too, would die. Having the house to herself was a gift, Alice realized that. But it felt lonesome there, not at all what she had imagined on those nights when she listened to Trudy and her fellow bachelor girls gabbing away on the telephone.

One night after dinner at her parents' house, Alice went up to her old bedroom. The twin beds were neatly made, as if she and Mary might slip into them after their baths like always. She took her paints down from a high shelf in the closet. Next to them lay her earmarked copy of *Live Alone and Like It*. She held the book in her hands for a moment, before throwing it into the back, behind Mary's old tennis racquet and all of her beautiful gowns, which Alice's mother had stupidly urged her to take.

After that, Alice began to do watercolors in the mornings before she left for work, small pieces, depicting the teakettle or Daniel's fedora or a single wineglass with a tinge of purple left over from the previous night. She painted on bits of scrap paper she had saved for the war effort — the backs of envelopes, receipts from the drugstore. She'd let them dry on the windowsill before laying them flat in a line on the counter. The sight of them cheered her and she imagined showing them to Daniel. But one morning a few weeks after she started, as if coming out of a trance, Alice looked at what she'd done and burned with shame. She needed to put that childish part of her away now, the part that had believed she deserved more.

She stacked the pictures into a pile and tossed them in a burlap sack for the scrap drive at Town Hall. She threw the rest of the paints in the rubbish and told herself to stop being self-indulgent. She went to confession. She joined the St. Agnes Legion of Mary. She ended her visits to the museum, and took to eating lunch alone at her desk.

When the war ended and Daniel returned from overseas for good, Alice tried to be a model wife: sunny and cheerful and domestic, as she imagined Mary would have been. She managed fine in the kitchen and she took on more and more responsibilities at the church, but she could never quite shake her moods.

On his first Saturday back, as she did the ironing in the living room, listening to the same radio melodrama she had once teased her mother for loving, Daniel sat in an armchair reading the newspaper.

"This is swell," he said. "This is what I've been imagining all these months away from you."

She had wanted him home, but now tears sprang to her eyes. She quickly pushed them away. She thought of all she had lost.

"Oh gosh, did I say something wrong?" Daniel asked.

"No. I'm sorry. I'm feeling a bit sad today, that's all."

"You've been through a lot," he said, getting to his feet, coming toward her and wrapping her in his arms. "Your sister, the pregnancies. It's all just going to take time. And I'm sure it's been made all the harder by the fact that your husband was hardly ever here. But the war is over, and it'll get better now, you'll see."

"I know," she said. It seemed like the easiest thing to say.

Early in their marriage, Daniel's idea of a big night out was going to a Red Sox game with his brothers and their boring wives, or taking the children on a long car trip, even though Kathleen whined and Clare always got nauseous.

Not that he didn't try; he did. But even that often caused Alice pain. They might go dancing or to a party, and she would have a wonderful time for a few hours. But afterward she only felt guilty that her sister would never again know such a night.

In Maine one evening when she was eight months pregnant with Patrick, Daniel took her out to dinner while his sister watched the girls back at the cottage. Afterward, he told her he had a surprise, and they drove out to the Cliff Country Club, where an enormous crowd had gathered in the parking lot.

"What on earth is this?" she asked.

"It's the Artists' Ball," he said with a big smile. "Mort and Ruby told me about it. They have it to raise tuition for poor students in the art school. It's supposed to be a real gas."

Daniel remembered what she had told him about her dream of becoming an artist, and he mentioned it an embarrassing amount, to strangers and co-workers and friends. He tried every summer to get her to take a class in the Perkins Cove school.

"A ball?" Alice said. "I'm not dressed for that."

"No, no. It's a costume party," he said. "Besides, we don't go in, we just watch the artists on parade. Apparently they do it every year. I've never heard of it before, have you?"

She said no, though in fact she had seen the signs around town and heard that it was near impossible for summer people to get in. She remembered from the posters that tickets cost two dollars and forty cents apiece. Herb Pomeroy's sextet would perform and cocktails would be served. It sounded like heaven.

"I want to go home," she said. "I don't feel well."

"Honey!" he said. "I thought you'd be excited. These are real live artists!"

They got out of the car and joined the pathetic mob, looking on as if at a bunch of Hollywood stars. There they were — the real live artists, men and women dressed as pirates and fairies and oversize babies, laughing gaily, soaking in the night, resting in Maine for a spell before going back out into the wide wide world. And there was Alice, with her swollen belly and her two children in bed down the road, waiting with their ears perked up for her to return home.

In the early sixties, they dredged the riverbed in Perkins Cove to allow bigger boats to come through. The dredging brought up gold-rich alluvial gravel, causing a small gold rush in Ogunquit that year. By the time the expansion was done, some of the fishermen's cottages had been torn down, and a big tar parking lot went up smack in the middle of the Cove. The artists' colony disbanded then, and though everyone else said it was a pity, Alice was happy enough to see them go.

MAGGIE

Rhiannon left before seven the next morning.

"I hope I didn't make the Gabe situation worse," she whispered to Maggie, who was still lying in bed.

"No, it's good that you told me," Maggie lied. She didn't get up and walk Rhiannon out. She knew she ought to, but she was still feeling injured by what Rhiannon had told her the night before.

Maggie hadn't slept much. She kept thinking that she was going to be a single mother, the young woman in the doctor's waiting room with a swollen belly and no wedding ring. Could she afford it? Would Gabe pay child support? Maybe his dad would write her a check for a million dollars in exchange for her going away forever. That would be fine by Maggie. Even scarier than the thought of doing this alone was the thought of some custody split with Gabe, not knowing what he was telling their child.

Note to self: Next time, don't procreate with

an asshole. Perhaps get married first.

He hadn't responded to her e-mail. It had only been eight hours and she had specifically told him to leave her alone, but still. An hour ago, she had thought of getting up and logging into his e-mail account to see if he'd read it. If not, maybe she should delete the message. Then she decided that that would be going too far — she should not lower herself to that level. And then she did it anyway, but the bastard had changed his password. She knew it was crazy of her to feel this way, but she was actually kind of offended by that.

Maggie didn't want to return to Brooklyn, afraid to reenter her real life without Gabe in it. Would she stay there? Move to a crappy but cheap rental apartment in the suburbs somewhere?

By the time late morning rolled around, she wanted to spend several hours lying in a ball on the hardwood floor. But she had to get up and puke anyway, so she dragged herself into the shower afterward to ward off the fear that had gripped her during the night.

Maggie remembered standing in that yellow plastic stall with her mother when she was four or five, the two of them peeling off their bathing suits, sand slipping from their bodies and gathering around the drain. They giggled as Kathleen mashed shampoo into Maggie's scalp.

She missed her mother.

Now she let the water fall warm over her shoulders, and rubbed her palm gently across her stomach. Beneath all the fear there was something unexpected and beautiful, like a crocus bud peeping out of the snow in early spring. She was going to be a mother. Her life was about to change.

She stepped out of the shower and glanced in the bathroom mirror. The skin around her eyes was gray and lined. She really ought to apply some concealer, but she couldn't be bothered. She decided not to blow-dry, either — she was at the beach and her life was falling apart. Who did she have to impress? She toweled off and slid into a pair of jeans, taking note of the dresses she had pulled from Gabe's closet a few days earlier. Life could change so quickly; you learned that as you aged. Yet it never ceased to surprise her.

Maggie glanced at the pink alarm clock on the nightstand. Had it once belonged in her mother's old room at her grandparents' house? She thought she remembered seeing it there. She felt like lying down, but instead decided to take a walk on the beach. Staying in motion seemed the best way to ward off insanity.

It was after eleven now. Maggie sat on the jetty, her feet immersed in the chilly water. A busted-up lobster trap had washed into shore and landed on the rocks. New York seemed a million miles away.

All around her were tide pools full of periwinkles and algae, which turned the water brilliant shades of red and green. She thought of childhood days, when Chris and her cousin Daniel would wrest the periwinkles from where they lay, grabbing hold of their shells and dropping them into iced-tea bottles full of salty water, shaking them hard for no apparent reason, other than the fact that little boys sometimes got a strange kick out of being cruel.

The ocean stretched out before her, with nothing in the distance but a lone sailboat. Behind her, the cottage and the big house next door sat quiet and still. This place had been one of the few constants in her life. Perhaps next summer she'd be sitting on these rocks with a baby in her arms. Maybe she could even stay in the cottage through the off-season, as her mother had done leading up to the divorce. It wouldn't be as gruesome as that spring had been. She could spend afternoons writing at the big table in the living room, while her child slept in a crib by the window, bathed in sunlight.

Maggie held a cup of herbal tea in her hand as she looked out over the choppy water. She wanted to tell her mother, but she felt terrified. Maggie knew all too well that Kathleen saw motherhood as the end of independence, growth, fulfillment. And yes, yes, we were at war, and terrorists might kill us all, and it seemed like a dreadful world to bring a child into. But when had the world been any better, really? When was it ever a safe time to create a life?

She took in a deep breath of ocean air and climbed to her feet, brushing sand from her tree-trunk legs, which were entirely resistant to the elliptical machine, thank you very much Great-grandma Dolan. As she walked back toward the beach, she saw an elderly couple in the distance practicing Tai Chi. They looked ridiculous, adorable. Some annoying reflexive part of her wished Gabe were there to see them. He would have taken their picture, preserving the sight forever.

She went up toward the cottage, planning to enter through the side door so she wouldn't have to pass by her grandmother's porch, where Alice was probably chain-smoking and reading a library book. Maggie felt guilty for avoiding her, but told herself she'd go visit Alice later in the afternoon, maybe bring some fresh cherries from Ruby's Market.

As she came up the path from the beach, Maggie heard a repetitive banging sound that seemed to get louder as she approached. Then she saw him: a handsome, dark-haired guy about her age, wearing a blue sweater over jeans. He was standing at the side entrance's railing with a hammer in his hand.

430

This must be the handyman Alice was yapping on about at dinner the night before, though he didn't appear to be Mexican. He looked like one of those dashing Englishmen Alice so loved in BBC adaptations of Jane Austen books.

"Hi," Maggie said, feeling her cheeks blush.

"Hello there," he said with a wide smile. "Gorgeous day, isn't it?"

"Yes," she said slowly.

"Connor Donnelly," he said, extending a hand.

"Maggie Doyle."

"So nice to meet you," he said.

Attractive straight men rarely came across as friendly — they usually either flirted or ignored you. Maggie felt skeptical.

"Have you seen my grandmother?" she asked.

"Oh yes. She's around front," he said.

"Uh-huh. Thanks."

Maggie turned the corner. Alice was down on her knees in the garden a few feet away, tending her roses and wearing a netted hat to ward off mosquitoes.

"Hello there," she said when Maggie approached. She struggled to get up, and Maggie rushed forward to help her.

"I'm absolutely fine," Alice said. "Don't make me feel like an old lady, please."

Even though Alice would never say exactly how old she was, Kathleen put her age somewhere around eighty. She didn't ever seem to change much. ("Too evil to grow old," Maggie's father often joked.) But here in this moment, she appeared frail, fragile.

"You look too thin, Grandma," Maggie said, fully aware of the risk involved in making such a statement to Alice. "Are you eating enough?"

Alice scoffed. "There's no such thing as too thin."

"Seriously, are you eating enough?" Maggie asked.

Alice sighed. "Okay, you got me. My secret's out. At the age of one hundred and five, I've decided to become an anorexic."

It was a horrible joke, but Maggie couldn't help but laugh.

"Where's your friend?" Alice asked.

"She went back to New York," Maggie said.

"Yes, I saw her drive off very early this morning. Did you two have a spat?"

"What? No." *How did she know?*

"She slept over; I saw her car," Alice said.

"Yup. It got late."

Alice nodded. "How is it down at the beach?"

"Glorious. Cold, but glorious."

"Well, that's good," Alice said. "Did you meet Father Donnelly on your way back?"

"Father Donnelly?"

"My priest. He's an absolute peach," Alice said. "He helps me with whatever I need done around here. He takes me to lunch."

He hadn't been wearing a white collar. Weren't they supposed to wear those at all times?

There were people, even now, who trusted a priest implicitly, based only on his vocation. And then, based on the same fact, there were those who instantly found everything he did suspect. Maggie fell into the latter category. Since when did priests make house calls to fix a wobbly banister? For less than an instant she envisioned him and Alice, wrapped up in some sort of intergenerational love affair, but then she willed the revolting thought to vanish.

"We're going to a new place in Kittery around one o'clock if you want to come," Alice said, smiling now, in one of her good moods.

Maggie exhaled a bit. "That would be nice."

"Good. That'll give you time to change out of those play clothes."

Maggie didn't see a reason to change out of her jeans and tank top in order to have lunch with her grandmother and a priest, but she responded, "Yup!"

Then she added, "I'm sorry it got so tense last night. I should have warned you more directly that Gabe wasn't coming and Rhiannon was."

Alice waved her hand through the air in front of her, as if shooing away a fly. "Water under the bridge," she said.

The three of them drove to Kittery Point at one o'clock sharp. Maggie sat in the backseat feeling a bit like a little girl, not minding the sensation at all. While Father Donnelly and Alice spoke about the women in Alice's prayer group and their assorted ailments, Maggie stared out the window at the houses — white and blue and pale yellow with American flags flapping in the breeze.

The restaurant they had chosen was right on the beach, with pink picnic tables out front. They ordered lobster rolls and chowder and iced tea. The waitresses wore crisp white shorts and pink polo shirts. Instead of MEN and LADIES, the signs on the bathroom doors read BUOYS and GULLS.

They took a table overlooking the water.

Maggie thought it sounded like the perfect setup for one of her grandfather's bad jokes: *An unwed mother, a priest, and an old biddy walk into a lobster pound . . .*

When the wind whipped up, threatening to blow the napkins away, the priest covered them with a saltshaker. Inside the glass shaker were grains of white rice. Maggie remembered asking her mother about this when she was a kid: the rice soaked up the moisture in the air, Kathleen had explained, leaving the salt dry. (*But why?* Maggie thought now. And how was she supposed to imbue herself with all that motherly knowledge? How did it happen?)

Alice started in on the current family gossip, while Father Donnelly ("Call me Connor") went to ask for more tartar sauce for her sandwich. Little Daniel was getting married to someone named Regina, who everyone loved, though it seemed to Maggie that he had known her for all of nine minutes.

When she said this, Alice smiled curtly and replied, "Well, he's always had such a good head on his shoulders. I think he's the type who really understands what he wants from life. He's settled, professionally speaking. Ready for the next step!"

Unlike me, you mean, Maggie thought, but she pressed on, reminding herself that in her grandmother's eyes, Ann Marie and Patrick's three kids could do no wrong.

"How are Aunt Clare and Uncle Joe?" she asked.

"How should I know?" Alice said. "They never call me. They've always kept to themselves, you know, but lately they've been worse than ever. Ann Marie told me she's invited them over twice in the past month, and they haven't even called her back. So rude!"

Maggie nodded. "Are they coming to Maine this summer?"

"No one tells me a thing," Alice said grumpily, then, "As far as I know, yes, they'll be here in August as usual."

Father Donnelly returned with two miniature paper cups full of tartar sauce.

"Oh, thanks, Father, you're a doll," Alice said. She gave him her brightest smile. She always was at her best around good-looking men. Maggie thought of her grandfather: even when he was young, he was never particularly handsome. She had seen old pictures. The women in his family came up thick and freckly. The men were spindly, pale. She wondered why Alice had picked him. Surely someone so vain would have been disappointed by such a plain-looking husband.

"Will you lead us in grace, Father?" Alice asked.

Maggie glanced around at the other patrons in their shorts and sandals and flimsy plastic lobster bibs. *Grace? Really?*

"I'd be honored," he said. To Maggie's horror, he extended his arms. They all joined hands.

Luckily, he spoke fast: "Bless us, O Lord, and these thy gifts, which we are about to receive from thy bountiful hands through Christ our Lord, Amen."

They dropped hands. He immediately turned to Maggie and said, "So how long will you be visiting?"

She shrugged, glad that was over, at least. "Not sure. A few days, maybe."

"Is that all?" Alice asked. "I thought it was two weeks."

"Well, my plans changed, as you know, and I'm not sure exactly what I'm going to do."

"She broke up with her boyfriend," Alice said happily. "She's hiding out."

Maggie laughed, because it was sort of true, and because laughing was really the only alternative to getting pissed off at the comment. Besides, it was nice in a way, to pretend for a moment that the breakup was the worst of her worries.

"I can't think of a better place for it," he said. He bit into his lobster roll, leaving a speck of mayo on his bottom lip. To Maggie's great amazement, Alice reached over and wiped it off.

"Thanks," he said.

Maggie wished she could stop time then and there, just to be able to call her mother and report on this immediately.

"When do you have to get back to work?" he asked.

"Technically I'm only on vacation these next two weeks, but my boss doesn't care if we work from home as long as we show our faces in the office, say, once a month."

Though I do have to be back in New York by July eighth for my next gynecological visit. You see, Father, I'm knocked up.

"That sounds like quite a job," the priest said.

"It is nice. Though I pretty much always go into the office anyway."

"What kind of work is it?" he asked.

"Well, it's a TV show, um, a crime show," she said. Talking to priests was incredibly weird. Every word you uttered had to be filtered twice through an appropriate censor. You could basically talk safely about Care Bears, Jesus, or the weather, and that was it. "I'm a fiction writer, too, though."

"Oh, I know; your grandmother's told me all about it," he said.

She had? Maggie felt so touched she might cry, and then she was immediately annoyed at herself: Why were her own affections so easily won? It wasn't really such a grand gesture on Alice's part.

"I think it's fascinating you're a writer," he said. "I dabble in fiction myself."

"Really?"

"Yes. I used to write lots of short stories. I still write them once in a while. Though the fact of it is, I'm too thin-skinned for your line of work."

"Thin-skinned!" Alice said. "I don't think so. You should see him with the sick parishioners, Maggie. He's a saint."

"Sainthood aside, it's true," he said. "I submitted two or three stories to *The New Yorker* and I got these form letters back. They really bummed me out. I knew *The New*

Yorker was a long shot, but all my hard work, and then *a form letter?* I didn't write again for months. And I sure as heck never submitted anything."

"Ah yes, I'm very familiar with the form letters," Maggie said.

"I could picture myself going crazy, gluing them all over the walls of the rectory, scaring the other priests."

"I once considered decoupaging a table with mine."

He laughed, a real, deep belly laugh. His smile was warm. There was something almost old-fashioned about his looks. Or maybe *classic* was a better word.

Perhaps she'd underestimated him. He seemed friendly and genuine, though she reminded herself that now would be an especially inconvenient time to fall in love with a Catholic priest.

"You write such lovely sermons, though," Alice said.

"Yes, and not a one has ever been called derivative or stale or not quite plumped up."

Maggie grimaced. "They said all that, huh?"

"Yup. That was the only non–form letter I got."

"Never mind those ninnies. What did Gabe *do* is what I want to know," Alice said, dragging out the words. She was a champion subject changer and apparently she was bored.

"He made promises he couldn't keep," Maggie said.

"He wouldn't give you a ring!" Alice said proudly, like she had just guessed the correct answer in Double Jeopardy.

"Ha, no," Maggie said. And though it was by all means the wrong crowd for talk of cohabitation, she continued, "We were supposed to move in together and at the last minute he changed his mind."

Alice's face crumpled. She looked genuinely injured. "That little — ," she started, then, looking over at the priest and perhaps deciding to tone down her language, "What a rat."

"I thought you were going to say we shouldn't be living together before marriage anyway," Maggie said.

"Oh, pish posh," Alice said. "I think it's essential! You have to get to know a person. And that city is so expensive, why not have a roommate? As long as you'd be sleeping in different bedrooms."

Had she meant that last part as a joke? Maggie couldn't be sure.

"A lot of girls in my generation married a man just because he was going off to war," Alice said. "They hardly knew those fellas to begin with, let alone what they became once they returned. And most of us went straight from our parents' houses to our husbands'. We never got the chance to live alone until we were decrepit old ladies. Young people are smarter now. Although I think you all get love backward."

"How so?" Maggie asked.

"You all seem to think that you should marry someone when you feel this intense emotion, which you call love. And then you expect that the love will fade over time, as life gets harder. When what you should do is find yourself a nice enough fellow and let real love develop over years and births and deaths and so on."

Maggie looked over at Father Donnelly.

"Pretty impressive, isn't she?" he said, giving Alice's arm a friendly squeeze. "I keep telling her she should get a TV talk show."

"Is that what you did, Grandma?" Maggie asked, holding her breath, remembering Alice's closed-offness at dinner with Rhiannon the night before.

Alice looked thoughtful. "I suppose so, yes, to some extent." That was all she could give, but that was enough. She switched the topic then, to a news item she had read about the inventor of Silly Putty.

Maggie sat back and listened, feeling more content than she had in weeks. This was exactly what she had come for, one of those Alice interactions that was actually fun, that made her feel welcome. She considered staying longer — the cottage would sit empty for the rest of June otherwise. And perhaps there would be more lunches like this, and time to

441

write and to plan. Her child could grow in the salty sea air, under a roof where generations before had spent their happiest summers.

She looked out over the water. "I love it here," she said.

"So do I," said Father Donnelly. "I can't imagine why anyone lives anywhere else."

"Did you grow up in Maine?" Maggie asked.

"Yes, further north. In a village about three hours toward Bangor."

"Sounds nice."

"It was a simple, no-frills kind of house," he said. "No TV or anything like that."

"His parents were in the Church too," Alice said. "His father is a deacon."

Maggie started to romanticize his childhood: a log cabin in the woods, a young boy reading the Bible by a crackling fire.

"Naturally, my brothers and I raised Cain," he said with a smile. "We would speed down these long country roads and bash people's mailboxes with baseball bats."

Maggie wanted to know how on earth he had gone from that to becoming a priest, but it seemed rude to ask.

"Sounds like my three," Alice said. "Did they put me through the ringer! Especially Patrick and Kathleen. Clare was the quiet one. But sometimes the quiet ones are the wildest, and you never even suspect. I know

442

she smoked like a chimney in high school. Always out the bedroom window. She ruined my white curtains!"

Maggie had heard all the stories of late-night parties at the house in Canton when her grandparents were away, and the time her mother and Uncle Patrick were pulled over with two open beers in their hands. There was the incident of Daniel tossing and turning one night and deciding to take a late walk around the block to cure his restlessness — as soon as he made it to the front lawn, he heard a noise from above and saw a boy climbing the trellis toward Kathleen's open window. She was guiding him in whispers, as if she herself knew the route well: "Step to the right, now over toward the left." Then there was the time Uncle Patrick drove back drunk all the way from Cape Cod at midnight, pulled into the driveway, and promptly plowed Daniel's new Cadillac straight through the garage door. (To this day, whenever the story came up, he maintained that in that light, the door had looked open.) It sometimes seemed to her that previous generations had had more opportunities to mess up big and still bounce back. Whereas Maggie had always felt like one misstep, and she would be ruined.

"We torture our parents," Father Donnelly said. "But then we get older and wiser and we give them the adoration they deserve. At least, we ought to."

Alice beamed. "I'd like to meet your folks one day. They really raised you right."

The conversation wound on, and Maggie tuned out for a few moments, watching a toddler and his father launch a toy sailboat at the edge of the bay. When she tuned back in, it was because she heard her name. Somehow they had arrived at the topic of the cottage schedule.

"Maggie's mother, Kathleen, gets June, but you won't be seeing her because she hates me," Alice said.

"Grandma!" Maggie said. "She does not! She lives all the way across the country, that's all."

Father Donnelly grinned. "Well, Maggie, if you have the whole of June set aside for your mother and her kin, I don't see why you wouldn't stay all month. It seems like the perfect place to get your writing done."

Was he flirting? No, that was ridiculous. He probably had old ladies and young ones all over town imagining that he was desperately in love with them. For some, she thought, the priest was the ultimate sex symbol: a really consistent, kind man, who was always happy to see you or to listen to your worries. Completely unthreatening, yet vaguely sexual, his vow of chastity serving the opposite of its intended purpose in that way, making everyone think about sex.

"I've been thinking the same thing," she said.

"Well, that's good," Alice said. "You'll stay! I'm glad."

History had shown that when Alice was kind, she would soon be something entirely different. But right at this moment, she wanted Maggie here, needed her, maybe.

They took the back roads toward home. A ways out of town the houses got shabbier, closer together, and every so often there was a trailer wedged between two trees. In front of one little house, Maggie saw a man and a teenage boy sawing at what remained of the trunk of an old pine. It looked like they were sculpting a giant squirrel.

Alice swiveled her head, gesturing toward them. "Year-rounders," she said, and shrugged her shoulders like, *What can you do?*

The houses eventually gave way to a field of wildflowers on the far side of a low stone wall. Off in the distance stood a stately red barn and a roofless silo that had been struck by lightning the summer Maggie turned ten.

Soon the two-lane street became a narrow dirt road. There were no streetlights here, only a wall of pine trees on either side that nearly blocked out the sun. She wondered if the locals realized how beautiful it was, or if they were immune. In New York, icons faded into the background most of the time — then one day you'd look up and notice the Empire State Building and it would take your breath away.

They drove until they came to the turnoff for Route 1, and there they sped up, joining the motorists rushing in both directions. Suddenly the world changed. The trees vanished. Two bright yellow lines popped out against black tar. Here the quaint and the garish were entwined in a decades-old wrestling match, so that the stately Ogunquit Playhouse with its forest-green marquee and white clapboard walls was offset by a strip of neon motels with pools out front, enclosed by chain-link fences. There was a massive liquor store, a place selling homemade quilts, Flo's hot dog stand, and a junk shop with tables out front, which were crowded with hundreds of glass bottles. At night, a wooden box by the curb said, BOTTLES, $2 EA., PLEASE OBSERVE THE HONOR SYSTEM.

They took another turn, and a few minutes later they had arrived at the fork where Perkins Cove met Shore Road.

"Shall we walk in the Cove for a bit?" Alice said. "I don't feel quite ready to go home."

The place had once been a quiet fishing village, but now the lobster men unloading their traps on the docks were outnumbered by tourists waiting in line at the old-fashioned ice cream shop and buying magnets and candles and trinkets in the gift stores. Maggie bought a giant box of saltwater taffy to mail to Kathleen and a necklace made of pure blue sea glass for Alice.

They ambled toward the entrance to the Marginal Way, chatting as they went. When they reached the mile-long path that wove through the shoreline cliffs, Alice said to the priest, "Way back when, this was just a stretch of dirt for farmers to walk their cattle on. Then some nice local bought it and dedicated it to the town, and the path was built. That happened the year after we got here. There was a big to-do."

"Were you there?" Maggie asked.

Alice shook her head. "It sounds silly now, but I was tired, I'd been up all night with a baby. I think your grandfather went, though."

They hardly said a word to one another as they walked the path, humbled by the natural beauty. You couldn't come here and not be absorbed by it. Off to the left on the other side of a fence stood stately homes with big front porches and Adirondack chairs on the lawns. To the right there was nothing but the pounding surf below, crashing against the rocks, the tide swaying back and forth like a dance. It made you feel as though you were a part of something more important than just you. Like even if there was no God there was always the ocean — before you and after you, breathing in and out for all eternity.

Maggie and Gabe had walked the Marginal

one night last summer. It was darker than any night she could remember. There were so many stars. A Jimmy Buffett song drifted out to the path from the poolside bar of a resort in the distance, and they danced to the sound, laughing and singing along. Part of her wished she had never brought him here.

Alice's knees were sore by the time they reached Ogunquit Beach, so instead of turning back on foot, they hopped one of the trolleys that puttered around town. The last time Maggie had ridden one was when Pat and Ann Marie rented the entire Ogunquit fleet for her cousin Patty's wedding. Maggie thought now of Patty's husband, Josh. He was a sweet guy, and he had been so happy on that day. "I just married my best friend and my dream girl," he had said when they pulled away from the church, as if he simply could not believe his own good fortune.

When they got back into the car, for the first time in three days, Maggie didn't bother to look at her phone.

After sunset, she walked the beach in front of the cottage alone. In the city, Maggie almost forgot about stars; you could hardly see them against the glow of the streetlights. But here there seemed to be millions, sparkling everywhere she looked. Her grandfather had made a big show of pointing out constellations to them when they were kids — the Three

Sisters, the Four Leaf Clover, the Big Dipper, Maggie's Pigtail, and Fiona's Big Toe. She couldn't recall when she had realized that half the names were made up.

The night air was chilly. Maggie pulled her sweatshirt tight around her shoulders.

She was really going to do this, and do it alone. It felt exhilarating and terrifying. She walked faster. Soon she had passed a dilapidated jetty. The jetty was a mile and a half from the cottage. Had she really walked that far? The Kelleher children rarely went to the public beach on the other side, but Maggie kept walking now. It was low tide, and all around her feet were nests of seaweed full of tiny shells. She picked one up, rubbed it between her fingers.

Up ahead there was a lifeguard's chair. At the height of the season, two tanned and toned teenage locals (always a guy and a girl, who you could only assume were sleeping together) sat there in the afternoons in their red bathing suits, occasionally looking up from their conversation to blow their whistles at some kid who had swum out too far. As adolescents, Maggie and Patty had worshipped the lifeguards from a distance, and sometimes after dinner they would climb up into the chair and look out over the ocean, silently pretending to be two gorgeous beach creatures with perfect thighs.

Maggie walked toward the chair. At its

449

splintering bottom, she climbed the ladder slowly, one rung at a time, until she had reached the top. The wind whipped against her face, blowing her hair back. She listened to the waves, feeling like nothing could ever get to her as long as she had this to come home to.

After a while, she felt sleepy and knew she ought to return to the cottage. But she decided to wait a bit, remembering how creepily quiet the house was at night. It was funny how a place could represent both your best and worst memories. The cottage was where she had been happiest as a child, happiest with Gabe. But it also reminded her of the painful months that had led up to her parents' divorce, spent here between those four walls, praying to the Virgin Mary to keep them all safe.

They lived in the cottage for the entire spring and summer before the divorce, because they'd had to sell their house.

For three months, Maggie and Chris didn't go to school. They hardly ever took baths or brushed their teeth. Kathleen didn't seem to notice. Uncle Patrick and Aunt Ann Marie had offered to take Maggie and Chris in through the end of the school year, but Maggie knew her mother wasn't speaking to them, and she had thrown such a hysterical fit at the prospect of staying with them that

450

Ann Marie seemed terrified she might burn their house down. It wasn't that she didn't want to: Maggie loved the thought of sleeping in her cousin Patty's bunk bed, under flowered sheets that Ann Marie had just pulled from the dryer, and the possibility of waking up to waffles and Hi-C, which her aunt served every morning of the week.

Maggie liked the way Ann Marie kept house and praised normal behavior, rather than constantly trying to stir things up. Kathleen always told her, "Don't be a sheep." Maggie hated that phrase. She wanted to be like everyone else.

But Maggie knew, even at ten years old, that her mother couldn't be alone. And so they went to Maine.

She still vividly recalled that spring, chasing her brother through the rooms of the cottage, which made a perfect circle, a sort of track for them to scuttle through. She remembered running on the beach, making forts in the dunes, dashing into the frigid ocean and right back out in her jean shorts, her lips tinged blue. They kept moving all day long, as if they might outrun the reality of what had passed: Their father had left, seeming not to care what happened to them. Their mother was falling apart.

At night, Maggie would grow terrified without her father there. Unlike at home, there were no streetlights to soften the dark-

451

ness from outside. If you looked out the window, all you could see was a meddlesome sheet of black. Giant white moths flapped against the lamps, somehow sneaking into the house, though she tried to plug up every crack. She could swear she heard footsteps in the loft overhead.

The cottage was freezing after dark. Even wearing long johns under piles of blankets, it was impossible to get warm. In the bedroom where Maggie and Kathleen slept — the one where her grandparents slept in the summertime — her grandmother had placed an Infant of Prague statue on the dresser. The two-foot Jesus stood straight, covered in an elaborate embroidered robe and a golden crown. In the daylight, Maggie thought the statue was funny: she pretended he was the king of whatever town her Barbies lived in. But after dark, he took on a sinister look, and she turned his face to the wall.

In the middle of the night she'd wake to find herself alone. She would creep from her spot in bed and into the living room, where her mother sat at the big oak table with papers everywhere and a bottle of red wine on the floor by her chair.

"Are you okay, Mommy?" Maggie would say. Or "Do you want to talk?"

Her mother would tell her everything: that they were broke, that Maggie's father was a lowlife, and that he'd been having an affair for a year, an affair that her uncle Patrick had known all about and helped to cover up.

"My own brother," Kathleen said. "Can you believe that?"

"I can't believe it," Maggie said, wrapping her hands in the long sleeves of her nightgown, wishing they could all go home again.

"And even my mother is against me — no surprise there," Kathleen went on.

"Why is Grandma against you?" Maggie said.

"She thinks I'm not trying hard enough in my marriage," her mother said, incredulous. "She thinks I'll go to Hell for refusing to let myself be walked on for fifty years. What kind of example would I be setting for you if I stayed? I'd sooner have us live on the street."

Maggie wanted to cry. She had heard about Hell in CCD, and her grandparents had spoken of a place called Limbo, where unbaptized babies floated around for eternity on tiny wings, unable to ever see their families again. She didn't want her mother in Hell. She didn't want her father to be with someone else. She didn't want to have to live on the street. She told herself to act like a grownup. She walked to where her mother sat and threw her arms around her, burying her face in Kathleen's thick sweater.

"Oh, hey, it's okay," Kathleen said. "We've got each other, kiddo. And we've got Grandpa. He'll take care of us, always."

The following autumn, the situation improved. Her father started paying child support, and they were able to move into a small house in Braintree. Her mother joined AA. She apologized to Maggie for asking too much of her, for treating her like an adult when she was only a child.

"You didn't treat me like an adult," Maggie said, sensing that this was what Kathleen wanted to hear.

"I did," her mother said. "Even though you're my little petunia, I think of you as a friend. But I should have known better than to drink like that around you. I still remember how scary it was when my mom used to drink when I was a kid."

"When did she stop?" Maggie asked.

"When I was eleven," her mother said. "About your age. My father threatened to leave her if she didn't sober up."

"Why?" Maggie asked.

"She was nasty," Kathleen said. "If I cried because I'd had a bad dream, she'd shake me really hard and tell me to get to sleep, or else goblins would come and get me. One time she drove me and your auntie Clare and uncle Patrick right into a tree."

"Did Grandma join AA too?" Maggie asked.

"No, sweetie," her mother said. "That's not exactly her style."

"Did not drinking anymore make her stop

being nasty?" Maggie asked.

"What do you think?" her mother said with a wink.

Two weeks went by without any word from Gabe. She had told him not to reach out, but maybe she hadn't meant it. Ironic that this was the first request of hers he had ever actually honored.

She passed the time reading and writing and eating the occasional meal with Alice and Father Donnelly — Connor, as he wanted to be called. She went to the beach, though it was still too cold to swim. She called Kathleen and her friend Allegra often from Alice's phone, just to hear their voices.

Every day, Maggie walked for hours to ensure that she would be exhausted by nightfall. One afternoon, she had traveled along Shore Road, past the Cape Neddick Lobster Pound and Connor's church, and fishermen casting their lines over the side of a bridge. She walked and walked until she found herself in the middle of York Beach, five miles away, a slightly seedy town bustling with color, full of T-shirts and movie posters and seafood places with red-and-white-checkered plastic on every table. She walked past the tattoo parlors and the chocolate shops and the tarot room, past the coin laundry and the Goldenrod, where a man was making saltwater taffy inside the window. And because it was what the Kellehers always did in York Beach, she made her way, zombielike, into the arcade, and played four rounds of skee-ball. She left the tickets she earned hanging from the machine like a long jagged tongue, for some lucky young kid to come across. She walked home without saying a word to anyone.

Usually the ocean air worked better than the strongest sleeping pill. But now, just like during those months after her parents' separation, she was up nights, worrying.

She tried to lose herself in work at night — she wrote a few dating profiles; she took on a freelance magazine assignment about how to lose your love handles in ten easy steps; and she had begun to look at the national news online for atrocious murders she could pitch to her boss at *Till Death Do Us Part.* But at some point, she had become obsessed with reading baby websites. She knew too much already and she was only two months along. By the third trimester, her baby was supposedly going to move once every other minute. She would feel punches and kicks from within. Her boobs would swell up and she would have stretch marks traversing her pale belly. Her body would never look the same again. When she gave birth, she should expect at least twelve to fourteen hours of excruciating labor.

And that was all while the child was inside

her. One night, watching the evening news with Alice, she saw a segment about two million cribs being recalled because they were crushing babies to death. If cribs weren't even safe, how would she ever manage to go a day without panicking about this child's well-being?

There were so many questions to be answered once she returned to New York, but Maggie couldn't face them yet. Maine never changed — the same faces, the same homes, the same blue sea. Here, she felt that she could float, as if in amber. Just stay still.

The next step was telling Kathleen. As the days passed, Maggie composed the letter in her head. She even sat down and started writing it, about seven different times. Finally, one rainy night as she watched a storm far out on the ocean, she sat down and typed.

Dear Mom,
When was the last time I wrote you a letter? Not just a birthday card or a silly note on the fridge, but an actual letter. I think it was that one summer you sent me to sleepaway camp, and I was absolutely miserable without you. I wrote you every day, and you wrote me just as often. I told you I was lonely, no one liked me. You responded that it was scientifically impossible for me to ever be alone, because I had you.

I've been thinking of writing you a letter lately, but I'm pretty sure I'd chicken out and never actually put it in a mailbox. E-mail is easier when there's something you're struggling to say. You just hit "send" and then give the regret and anxiety ten seconds to kick in.

I'm missing you in Maine. I know we have our phone calls, but as discussed, I barely get cell service here, and each time I call you from the landline in Alice's house, I know she's listening to every word I say. It's been over two weeks since I arrived, and the days are flying. Do you remember the way time moves differently here? A day goes by in an hour, and the nights seem endless. (Here, I find I am still slightly scared of the dark. It never actually gets dark in New York, now that I think about it. Maybe that's why I like it so much.) I love the simple routine of cottage life — I have twelve more days until I have to clear out, and I'm already dreading saying good-bye. Each morning I get up early and walk the beach alone. I walk up to Ruby's and buy tea, a paper, and groceries for the day. I have been frequenting Café Amore with alarming regularity. (I am often one bite away from a blueberry French toast overdose.) Then I go home and write for a few hours, maybe have lunch or dinner with Alice.

Sometimes we watch TV together at night. It's nice. She's still her crazy self, but we have had our moments. Most of the time I am alone, which I like. I've had a lot to think about.

There is something I've been trying (or, in some cases, trying not) to say each time we've talked these past few weeks, but I can't seem to get the words out, which is strange — I've always known that I can come to you with anything and you will support me, help me make it right. I've always known that with you I can be my true self, whatever that means.

The thing I've wanted to say (Jeez, I can barely manage to write it) is this: I'm pregnant. Needless to say, my emotions lately have run the gamut between terrified, bewildered, and elated, especially given my situation with Gabe. But I've decided to settle on the last of these feelings. I am having this baby, and I'm happy. Truly happy. Sitting here in the living room in the cottage, I remember so clearly that spring when we — you, me, and Chris — lived here. You were panicked then, but look what you made of it. I have no doubt that raising a child alone is beyond difficult. I've thought through all the challenges. But I know I won't be alone: I'll have you.

I thought by writing this instead of saying

it over the phone, I'd give you the time to really process it before reacting. I know you might be worried or freaked out or disappointed in me. Please think about it for a while, as I have, before you respond, okay? I'm here in Maine, tucked away safe, and I feel that (for now at least) everything is right with the world.

Love you always,
Maggie

P.S. I think there might be some weird sexual tension between Grandma and her priest.

Ann Marie

When the phone rang, Ann Marie was clip-
ping coupons from the Sunday circular at the
kitchen table, same as most Monday mornings, unaware that something big was about
to happen. She pressed the cordless receiver
between her shoulder and her cheek so she
could continue cutting out a three-for-one
special on Windex. She'd leave one bottle
here at the house and bring the other two
with her to Maine the next day.

If they had it to do over again, she would
have asked Pat to put less glass on the
architectural plans for the big house in Cape
Neddick. It got so dirty. Though it did have a
gorgeous view of the beach from almost every
room. *Focus on the positive.* That was a motto
of hers.

Someday that house would be theirs. Then
perhaps she'd make a few changes. The
kitchen, for instance, was almost too modern.
The cottage had to stay — Pat wouldn't have
it otherwise — but maybe they could do more

landscaping, allow for more of a real yard for the grandkids to run around in, and a proper driveway.

"Hello?" she said now.

"I'm calling to speak with Mrs. Ann Marie Kelleher," said a woman with an English accent.

"This is she."

"My name is Louise Parnell. I'm calling from the Wellbright Miniatures Fair offices with some wonderful news. Your dollhouse, entry number 2374, has been selected as a finalist in our annual worldwide competition."

Her heart sped up. Could this really be happening? In some ways, she had almost expected it, but then she'd tell herself not to be silly, that it was just a fantasy. She knew the decisions were being made this week, but she hadn't thought it would happen on a Monday. (After church on Sunday, while Pat went to get the car, she lit a candle for this very reason, and then felt ridiculous about it.)

"A finalist?" she said softly, as if she might have misheard.

"Yes. You should be very proud. Out of over two thousand contestants, you've made the top ten. The finals take place September first in London. All expenses paid for you, plus one guest."

God help her, she immediately envisioned herself walking hand in hand with Steve

Brewer down a cobblestone street.

"That's wonderful," she said, and then, almost as a sort of consolation to Pat: "My husband will be so excited. He studied abroad in London one semester during college."

"I expect you know all the rules and restrictions already, but we'll be mailing you a packet with the relevant information later today."

"Oh, I know them," Ann Marie said. She had practically memorized the competition section of the Wellbright website. The finals required you to submit a brand-new house. You couldn't have any outside help or even use a preexisting floor plan from one of the trade publications. You had to decorate it from the ground up. The grand prize winner got to have her house featured on the cover of *Dollhouse World* magazine, a five-thousand-dollar Wellbright gift certificate, and a brief lecture tour of craft fairs in the United Kingdom.

Last year's winner had been at it for decades — she owned two shops in Canada. And here was Ann Marie, with only a year's experience under her belt. After she hung up, she went to the dollhouse and actually kissed the front door. Then she removed the canopy bed from the master suite and kissed that too.

"Oh, you beauty," she said to the house. "Thank you."

Unsure of what to do next, she squealed like a child and bolted upstairs. Raul, her trainer, would be proud. She hadn't run this fast since high school.

"Pat!" she called. "Honey!"

He emerged from the bedroom in his suit, straightening his tie.

He chuckled. "Yes?"

"I won! I won! Well, I'm a finalist, anyhow. I just got a call from the Wellbright people."

"That's great," he said.

She tried not to let the fact that he sounded slightly underwhelmed stand in the way of her joy. This wasn't really his thing, she reminded herself. But she kept pushing.

"Out of two thousand applicants, they only picked ten."

"That's fabulous. I'm so proud of you. Why are we standing in the hall?"

"And we both get to go to London, all expenses paid, for the grand prize judging."

Now he nodded, his eyes widening.

"Look out, world, here comes my wife, the interior designer."

"Oh, I'd hardly call myself that."

"So you build it here and they judge it across the pond?"

"Right."

"Your dollhouse will make one hell of a carry-on," he said. Of all things.

"You send it ahead, silly," she said.

"Should we go out to dinner tonight to

464

celebrate?" he asked.

"That would be nice."

"It's our last night together before you ship off to Maine," he said.

"I know. I have so much to do before I can start working on my house."

"You're going to start today, huh?" he asked, sounding amused.

"There's not much time!"

She thought of everything she had to do: She needed to finish packing. She needed to go grocery shopping and pick up her mother's prescriptions and drop them off to her. Which meant she'd probably end up staying for lunch and helping her mother hang those blinds in the den. She had told Patty that she'd buy bathing suits for the kids at the Filene's sale. Then she had to come home and cook some meals for Pat to heat up while she was away. Plus maybe go over to Alice's house in Canton and retrieve whatever her mother-in-law needed from there. She had library books to return. The car was filthy. She should get it washed. She needed to remind the girl next door to water her plants while she was gone.

Ann Marie suddenly felt deflated. It was only a dumb contest. It couldn't fix the fact that Fiona was gay, that Little Daniel's life was a mess, that everyone expected her to do everything at all times. And she'd never have enough hours to make her dollhouse perfect.

She needed a break.

After Pat left for work, she cried. She sat at the kitchen table with her head in her hands and just let it out. Sometimes that could be good for a person. She allowed the pity party to continue for a few minutes, and then walked into the front hall. She looked at herself in the mirror on the wall and laughed. What was she crying for anyway? Maybe the news had been too good. Her kids always bawled at their own birthday parties when they were young, overwhelmed by the attention.

"Ann Marie Clancy, you need to get a grip," she said out loud. (Sometimes she still thought of herself by her maiden name, even though she had changed it to Kelleher nearly thirty-five years earlier.) "You're a finalist. A finalist!"

She felt a bit better. She went and looked at the dollhouse again. Then she called Patty at work. She dialed the office number, and Patty's cheerful secretary, Amy, picked up.

"Patricia Weinstein's office," she said.

Each time Ann Marie heard this name spoken aloud it was unrecognizable for a moment, even eight years after Patty had gotten married. She had to dig for it — *My daughter Patty Kelleher is now someone named Patricia Weinstein.*

"It's her mother," Ann Marie said. "Is she in?"

"Hold on, please."

Patty picked up, sounding frazzled.

"How's Foster feeling?" Ann Marie asked, before even saying hello. He had had a bad cold all weekend, a sore throat and a terrible cough. Patty had called her, worried as could be, on Friday night, and Ann Marie had told her calmly to make him a hot toddy with lemon and honey and a dash of whiskey, like her own mother used to make.

"He's okay," Patty said now. "He's on the mend."

"Are you making sure he gets plenty of fluids?"

"Yup."

"Good girl. And he's at school now?"

"Oh yeah."

"Hmm." Ann Marie probably would have kept him home for one more day to let him rest.

"I've got some big news," she said.

"Oh?"

"Remember I told you I entered my dollhouse in that prestigious competition?"

"Um, sort of."

"I'm a finalist! Daddy and I get to go to England for the judging in September. Which means I have to build an entire house by then, which is daunting, if you ask me."

"You do realize the house you have to build is only three feet tall?"

"What do you mean?"

"Just teasing. That's really cool, Mom. Congrats."

Ann Marie might have liked to talk about it a while longer, but Patty changed the subject. Josh's mother would be looking after the kids on Tuesdays and Thursdays while Ann Marie was in Maine. Patty was trying to find a polite way to ask her not to swear around the children.

"Josh says she was always this way. The woman talks like a truck driver. I really don't want to have to explain to Maisy what 'shit' means and why she can't say it at preschool."

"Patty!" Ann Marie exclaimed on instinct. She had rarely heard any of her children use profanity.

"What? I wasn't actually saying it."

A short while later, Ann Marie pulled her car keys off the hook beside the back door and hurried out to start her errands. The spring in her step was back, and it lasted all day — through traffic jams and department store lines and listening to some woman ahead of her at the deli yammering into a cell phone about her next-door neighbor's alopecia.

It lasted through an afternoon at her mother's apartment, where the dark carpets and thick old wallpaper made the rooms feel physically heavy, and the framed photographs everywhere were caked with dust: here were Ann Marie and her sisters at their First

468

Communions and on the beach, always with their little brother, Brendan, in the background, haunting them like a ghost. He was now fifty years old, if he was even alive. Ann Marie often wondered about that.

Her father had been born in that apartment, back when the rent was only thirty dollars a month. He had never lived anywhere else in his life.

After she left, the drive through the old neighborhood warmed her with its familiarity, but it embarrassed her too. The three-story wood houses looked as worn as they had during her youth. She had often brought her children here, and they had loved being so close to the beach, even though some of the rougher types made them nervous. They weren't built for this environment. Out in front of the L Street Bathhouse, a group of old Irishmen in their scally caps stood around talking and laughing. Each year on New Year's Day, they plunged into the frigid harbor, and everyone in the neighborhood came down to cheer them on. Ann Marie gave them a wave now, happy to be heading home.

All day she had been designing the new house — the grand prize winner — in her head. She thought it ought to be brick. She had seen some beautiful brick houses at the fair, though they were rare. She'd wire it for electricity herself, as she had learned. She would make sheets and facecloths from the best she had in the hall closet, the high-thread-count linens she reserved for guests. The kitchen should be all white. In the living room, she envisioned a stately family portrait over a fireplace, with maybe a couple of hunting dogs in the foreground. What if she commissioned a local Boston artist to paint it? That had to be worth a few extra points.

She felt so energized that she decided to launder all the bath towels in the house while she made Pat two chicken and broccoli casseroles, a roast beef, mac and cheese, and a ziti bake.

Late that afternoon, she showered for dinner. Afterward, wearing just her terry-cloth robe, Ann Marie decided to have a celebratory glass of wine. She poured until the golden liquid was almost at the rim of the glass. She took a big sip.

She went into the office and sat at the computer. At last. Pat wouldn't be home for a couple more hours. It was finally her time. She began making her purchases, AmEx in hand. Pat might moan a bit about the bill, but she would simply remind him that they were getting a free trip out of this, so really they were saving money in the long run.

A free trip. She felt terribly proud.

Ann Marie would have to have all the items express mailed to Briarwood Road, since that's where she would be for the next month. It wasn't ideal. She'd either have to finish building the house there and have it shipped from Cape Neddick (did she trust the sleepy little UPS Store in York, a few miles from the cottage?) or transport everything back home to Newton in the middle of July. All her tools were here.

But there was always a silver lining.

Ann Marie pictured herself on the screen porch of the cottage alone, opening each box, pulling out her treasures. She'd have hours to work in peace these next ten days before Pat and the Brewers arrived in Maine. That was something.

She focused on her shopping.

The house she had had her eye on forever was a three-story Newport brick, with shingles and white trim and a widow's walk. It had eleven rooms, a floor-to-ceiling height of ten inches, sixteen windows (two of them working bay windows complete with window seats), and a detailed staircase with a molded banister.

The house cost more than a thousand dollars. She thought it was worth it.

She bought gray shingle dye and a little doghouse and border plants for the yard, and then she added an old-fashioned push mower and a rake. She bought a Victorian hat vanity for a hundred dollars. (She had never even heard of a hat vanity before, but now she realized she most definitely needed one.) She bought a love seat and a dining table and a tiny iron and even an electric mixer, no bigger than a silver dollar.

When she looked at the clock on her computer screen, she was shocked to see that an hour had passed. She went to the kitchen for more wine, then came right back into the office.

She chose fabric for the window treatments, but decided to go down to the store in the morning and pick it up in person, rather than buy it online. That way she could make sure it was high enough in quality before she paid.

She went to a site that sold heirloom collectibles and bought a hand-carved desk and two newspapers to place on top. She added an antique umbrella stand.

Ann Marie imagined the father in this brick house coming in from a long day of work. Perhaps he was named Reginald, an Englishman. He might have a thin mustache. His wife (Evelyn?) greeted him at the front door each night in a pink gown, her cheeks rosy, her smile a bit mischievous. The children were already bathed and asleep. Dinner was on the table.

She watched the page load for Puck's Teeny Tinies, where she bought a little tin of coronation biscuits, a glass milk bottle, a dozen eggs the size of baby aspirin, a burlap sack of flour, a basket of ceramic vegetables, and a miniature box of chocolates, the top slid halfway open, a green ribbon cascading downward. Reginald would bring them home to Evelyn for their anniversary.

A thrilling wave washed over Ann Marie as she imagined how beautiful the house would be. It was silly, but she somehow felt more beautiful because of it. She wanted to share this with someone, someone who would understand. She sat back in her chair and got butterflies in her stomach, knowing what she was about to do. She typed in the familiar address for the Weiss, Black, and Abrams website, and as she so often did, she clicked on Steve Brewer's name. Then she did something she had never done before. She clicked on the *E-mail Stephen Brewer* link.

A message window popped up, and she wrote:

Hi there! Had to let you know . . . I think the *Life* magazine you sent was a good luck charm. I've just found out that I won the most important dollhouse competition there is. There are over 5,000 competitors, and I won it! So thanks, old chum. xo

Pat walked in at six thirty. It had been an hour since she had hit SEND and Steve Brewer still hadn't replied.

Ann Marie was frantic. Had she seemed

like a braggart? He could simply be busy. In a meeting, maybe. But why did she have to go and exaggerate like that? And, oh Jesus, that *xo?* What was she thinking? She blamed the *xo* on the chardonnay. She blamed the whole thing on the chardonnay.

They drove to dinner and Pat said she wasn't very talkative, and then he said he had run into Ralph Quinn, the father of one of Fiona's childhood friends, Melody Quinn, at the post office. Ralph had told Pat that Melody was engaged, and now Pat told Ann Marie as much. Her mood grew even more sour, but she tried to smile and act pleasant throughout the meal. It was sweet of her husband to take her to dinner.

She drank more wine, ordered a steak. While Pat talked about his business, she said a hundred silent Hail Marys, praying that Steve Brewer would have written her back by the time she got home.

He hadn't.

Ann Marie couldn't think straight. The wine made her a bit dizzy. She imagined his wife, Linda, reading the e-mail, figuring it all out. Linda might call Pat — or she might act like nothing had happened and then slap Ann Marie silly in front of the entire neighborhood at their next book club meeting. They'd have to move.

She thought of sending another e-mail to explain the first, but what could she say? *I*

474

was drinking at five o'clock in the afternoon and thought I ought to contact you? Oh yes, that would make her look much better.

What on earth was happening to her lately? She had trouble sleeping that night. Through the walls, she could make out the sound of Pat snoring down the hall, and she almost wanted to go to him for comfort. Instead, she decided to put her nerves to good use. There was no sense just lying there. She went to her craft room and switched on the light. Quietly, she began to pack what she'd need for Maine, transporting everything out to the trunk of her car: she carried towels and sheets and ribbons and stuffing in two giant beach bags. Silly, considering that she'd need only a tiny piece of each, but better to be safe than sorry.

Next, she brought out a stack of dollhouse magazines for inspiration.

She made three more trips. She hoped none of the neighbors could see her there, wearing her nightgown, lugging her sewing machine and glue gun and scrap basket and tiny cans of paint and brushes across the lawn, bathed in moonlight, the dewy grass cool beneath her feet.

By the time she woke the next morning, Steve had written back: *Hey, congrats! You're a wonder. This calls for a celebratory drink. Say, July 1?*

475

Ten days from now. The day he was coming to Maine with his wife. It wasn't the most romantic thing he could have said, but then she had written him on his work account. And now a conversation had begun.

You're a wonder. That was something.

She told herself not to respond, then immediately did so anyway: *Really looking forward to it! Heading up to Maine today to help my mother-in-law for the next couple of weeks.*

Though she had a lot to do before she left, Ann Marie sat in front of the computer for a long while to see if he might volley a short response her way. She cursed herself for not asking him a question. She had made it seem like there was no need to write back and so he didn't.

Now she'd just have to be patient, and focus on entertaining Alice, tidying up the cottage, and building her dollhouse. That was all the next two weeks required.

On the drive to Maine, she listened to the oldies station with the windows rolled down. Occasionally, she stretched her left hand out the window, feeling the air fly through her fingers. It was hard for her to let go — to leave her mother and husband and grandkids behind. But Alice was the one who needed her most right now. Alice didn't have anyone else.

The thought of ending up like Alice or like

her own mother, or most old women, terrified Ann Marie. They lived for years after their husbands died. Decades in some cases. She could not imagine living on after Pat. She had never been good at being alone.

So many years spent in the company of children made silence seem unnatural, and when she was driving, Ann Marie always imagined what they might say were they there. (Little Daniel: "Change the station!" Fiona: "Turn around! I think I saw a kitten back there!" Inevitably, it would be a squirrel.)

As she drove along 95, the seat belt digging into her stomach, Ann Marie told herself not to look down. This was one of her rules for self-preservation. She still looked okay in a tennis dress. But the sight of her belly in a seated position, highlighted by a taut piece of fabric, could only cause her pain.

She had last seen her trainer on Saturday evening. When Raul got her on those filthy Nautilus machines three times a week, she'd sweat and huff and puff, and swear that her body was transforming. But then she'd catch a glimpse of her belly and wonder if the workouts even mattered.

Ann Marie straightened up in her seat.

Until three years ago, she had been lucky with her figure. It always bounced back after a pregnancy, and she hadn't inherited her mother's tendency to pack on the pounds as she aged. But then came menopause. She and her sister Tricia were two years apart, but they started at the same time. It was nice to have someone to compare notes with, though Ann Marie thought Tricia treated the whole experience in a rather unseemly way. She went on an online message board full of menopausal women and chatted about symptoms and hormones and home remedies all day. She bought the two of them tickets to something called *Menopause the Musical.* Ann Marie had gone along to be a good sport. The show was funny enough, but she felt as though she ought to be wearing a sign around her neck that said I'M DRIED UP!

Then again, her body had done a good enough job of announcing that to the world already. A few times a week that year, Ann Marie had hot flashes. She might be standing at the register in the drugstore, or kneeling in a church pew beside her husband, and all of a sudden her upper body would feel flushed with intense heat and her face would start to sweat. It was mortifying. Her hair thinned slightly. She found clumps of it in the car and on the bathroom floor. Her body was betraying her in a million ways, none more awful than the fact that her belly swelled up and her breasts seemed to shrivel.

For Mother's Day that year, Pat gave her the sessions with Raul, and for a moment she had wanted to cry or stamp her feet — what kind of gift was this? A reminder of how horrid she looked was supposed to make her smile? But then she did smile. Because she knew Pat's intentions were good. And those sessions with Raul, which Pat had renewed every Mother's Day since, were a godsend, really. Who could say how lousy she'd look without them?

The hardest part of menopause for Ann Marie was knowing that she'd never have another child. She attempted to explain this to Tricia, but her sister just laughed and said, "I didn't realize you were trying."

She knew it was irrational. She was a grandmother, for goodness' sake. But it seemed so final.

Every day since Little Daniel had been born, the first thing she thought of when she woke up was her children, and they were still the last thing she thought about before she fell asleep at night. Parenthood by its very nature was the only job she knew of in which being successful meant rendering yourself useless. Who was she, if not the mother of Daniel, Patty, and Fiona Kelleher? That was something she thought about a lot lately.

She drove the speed limit, taking note of the staties parked on the shoulder, just chomping at the bit to catch some sucker with out-of-state plates going eighty. Her cousins were always willing to help get her out of parking tickets, but Ann Marie thought speeding was a different issue. She didn't want to set a bad example for the kids.

While she sat in traffic at the New Hampshire tolls, she called Little Daniel at home.

"How you doing, honey?" she said cheerfully.

"Okay," he said.

"Applied for any jobs this week?"

"Nope."

"Well, it's only Tuesday, right?"

"Yup."

"How's Regina, good?"

"She's good. We went to Nantasket Beach on Sunday. We rode the carousel."

"That sounds like fun."

"Yeah. Regina had never been before. And we went to Castleman's for lobster afterward."

That sounds expensive, she thought. But she only said, "Good for you. Did you go to Mass at St. Mary's while you were there?"

He chuckled. "Mom."

"It's a beautiful church, that's all. I don't think you've ever been. Which means you would have gotten three wishes."

She had no idea who had decided that a person got to make three wishes whenever he entered a new church. Probably some desperate mother whose child was throwing a fit in a church parking lot. It had always worked well on Ann Marie's children.

"I'm on my way to Maine now," she said.

"Going to head to the Cliff House at some point this week to do the food tasting so I can report back to Regina on what I like best. I'll just try to narrow it down for her to save her some time."

"Cool. Tell Grandma I say hi, and we're excited to see her in July."

"Will do. When are you coming?"

"Not sure yet."

She pulled the Mercedes through the toll-booth and sped up. It wasn't safe to be on the phone when you were accelerating. She hoped none of her kids would ever do it.

"I've got to go, honey," she said. "But one last thing. Maybe you should invite Daddy to have dinner with you some night this week. I'm sure he'd like that. He'll be lonely."

"I would, but I'm totally strapped for cash."

She thought about his lobster dinner the night before.

"You could go to our house. I made your favorite."

"Ziti bake?"

"Yes. And there's strawberry shortcake in the fridge, left over from Sunday. And plenty of wine. You could bring a bottle or two home if you want. Bring Regina too. I left those bridal magazines I told her about on my desk in the office."

"Okay, I'll stop by."

She hung up. The guy in the car beside her looked a bit like Steve Brewer — that sharp

481

chin and brown shaggy hair.

For the next forty minutes, she ran over their e-mail exchange in her head.

You're a wonder, he had written. *This calls for a celebratory drink.*

She wished it could be just the two of them, and then she could tell him how she was feeling. She imagined him nodding along, telling her he understood completely, telling her she had done a great job — with the kids, her figure, the housekeeping, the dollhouse, everything.

As she crossed the Piscataqua River Bridge, which connected New Hampshire and Maine, she thought of Pat's favorite road trip game: whoever spotted the bridge first would get a quarter. When her kids were small, you'd think that quarter was a hundred-dollar bill, the way they hooted and hollered and fought and accused one another of cheating. (*There's no way you saw the bridge yet — we're still in Boston!*)

When Pat tried the game on the grandchildren the previous summer, Foster said, "What do we win if we see it?"

"A quarter!" Pat had said excitedly.

Ann Marie glanced into the rearview mirror, to see her six-year-old grandson reaching down to the floor. "But I just found two quarters right here under the mat," he said.

Then he and Maisy started playing their handheld video games and didn't say a word until they reached Cape Neddick. Ann Marie knew she should be thankful for the peace and quiet, but she almost wanted to grab their faces and tilt them upward, holding them in place. Were kids these days too busy to look out a car window and daydream?

She turned off the highway and onto Route 1, where you still saw gas stations and the big Shop 'n Save and traffic lights every quarter of a mile. But after five minutes, she was in Ogunquit, where the streets were lined with gift shops and cafés. She followed the road to Cape Neddick, and within a couple of minutes she passed all the familiar houses and the big dilapidated barn at the end of Whipple Road. She looked out over the water, at the sailboats glistening white in the sun, under a cloudless blue sky. She had never loved a place as much.

When she arrived at Briarwood Road, she pressed harder on the gas. It was nearly ten. Alice would just be arriving at church. That gave Ann Marie a couple of hours to get settled in at the cottage and make them some lunch, and maybe she'd have a bit of extra time to get to work on her dollhouse curtains.

Her car zipped down the sandy street, pine trees blocking out the daylight. And then she had arrived, the sight of the cottage like seeing an old friend. Beside it stood the big house, and down below was their beach, empty, ready for her. She felt a giddy rush as she got out of the Mercedes.

Ann Marie opened the trunk and gathered her dollhouse gear first. She held the sewing machine in one hand, and hooked the heavy beach bag full of fabric over her free arm. Then she sort of scooped up her ribbons and paint and nudged them to the top of the pile. She was going only twenty feet, so she might as well take as much as she possibly could.

She pushed the cottage door open with her hip. It was never locked. She crossed the screen porch and then stepped into the front hall, inhaling the familiar scent of ocean mixed with the old, musty smell of the house itself.

She moved toward the living room, thinking that it was actually nice to be alone, and that's when she saw her niece sitting at the dining table in her underpants and a Kenyon Lacrosse T-shirt, typing away at her laptop. She looked chunkier than usual.

"Maggie." Ann Marie said it softly, so as not to startle her, but the girl gasped and clutched her stomach anyway.

"Oh my God, you scared me!" Maggie said. She climbed to her feet, smiling sheepishly. She reached for a pair of shorts that lay on the floor and pulled them on.

"I wasn't expecting anyone. Can I help you with that stuff?" Maggie asked. She looked it over. "What is that stuff?"

Ann Marie dropped everything in her arms onto the table, which was already strewn with papers and books.

"What are you doing here, dear? I thought you were going back to New York on the fourteenth."

"I decided to stay a while longer," Maggie said. "Didn't Grandma tell you?"

"No. No, she didn't."

"Are you just dropping this off?" Maggie said, gesturing at her dollhouse supplies.

Ann Marie took in a deep breath. It wasn't Maggie she was angry with; it would be wrong to take it out on her.

"I had arranged with Alice to be here for the rest of the month, since you and your mother couldn't stay," Ann Marie said.

"But I told her three weeks ago I was staying through the end of June," Maggie said. "Not that we can't both stay. That might be fun."

She was a polite girl, shockingly so given her upbringing, but Ann Marie could tell that Maggie found the prospect every bit as unappealing as she herself did.

"That's true," Ann Marie said.

"I'll help you bring your luggage in from the car," Maggie said.

They made small talk as they carried in her suitcases and bags of groceries and cleaning products.

"How are Patty's kids?" Maggie asked. "They must be getting big."

"They're adorable," Ann Marie said. "Foster has Big Daniel's ears! I'll show you pictures."

"I'd love that," Maggie said.

"Oh, and the baby's doing swimming lessons! He goes to his classes twice a week."

"What? How old is he?"

"One!" Ann Marie said.

"Wow."

"That's nothing. Maisy's four, and she's already in her third year of T-ball class. She knows all the moves. She's ready to start on a team next fall."

Maggie raised an eyebrow. "Is that typical, T-ball for two-year-olds?"

"They don't let them stay babies for long anymore," Ann Marie said.

"How much does stuff like that cost?" Maggie asked — a terribly odd question if you asked Ann Marie.

"I'm not quite sure," she said. "Not too much. Josh even takes her to these toddler batting cages they have now. All the dads go."

Maggie looked stricken. Should she not have mentioned fathers?

Ann Marie always felt a bit sad for the girl. She probably should have done more for her niece over the years. She had tried, when she could, to make Maggie feel special, loved. But she had her own three children to think about first, and any time she gave Maggie a nice gift just because, or offered to take her away with them to Disney World, Kathleen would fly into such an unholy huff that Ann Marie regretted ever getting involved.

"How's your mom?" she asked now.

"Oh, she's good."

"Life on the farm keeping her busy?"

"Yup. Hey, did you see that article in *The Times* a couple weeks ago about Peace Corps volunteers?"

Ann Marie felt her entire body contract. "No."

"It was great, all about famous alums. Sort of a 'Where are they now' kind of thing. It made me think of Fiona."

"Oh, that's nice," Ann Marie said.

"I thought I might send it to her."

"That would be sweet. I know she'd love to read it."

"She's been gone so long."

"Yes."

"Does she have any idea what she wants to do next?" Maggie asked.

Ann Marie tried to sound casual. "The mother is always the last to know." It felt like more than she had meant to say, but Maggie just smiled.

After they had brought in all the bags, Maggie worked on her laptop at the dining table while Ann Marie read her dollhouse magazines out on the porch. She tried to relax and

487

take in the view. But she was eager for Alice to get back and explain things. They spoke almost every day. How had her mother-in-law managed not to mention Maggie's presence? Ann Marie was struck with a fearful thought: Maybe Alice's memory was worse than they had realized. Maybe she had somehow forgotten about the overlap.

But when Alice walked into the cottage an hour or so later, that possibility vanished. She stepped out onto the porch, sliding the door closed behind her.

"Oh, good, you made it!" she said. "How was the drive?"

"Fine. I was sort of startled to find Maggie here."

"Oh?"

"Yes, and I think she felt the same way. I wish you'd have told me she was staying."

"Why?" Alice asked. "Would you not have come? In my day, people actually enjoyed going to the beach with their family. It wasn't a chore."

"That's not what I meant," Ann Marie said.

"Come out front and see my garden," Alice said. "It looks like a million bucks."

That night, the three of them ate dinner at Barnacle Billy's. While they waited in line to place their order at the counter, Ann Marie looked into the cloudy lobster tank, feeling somewhat sorry for the poor creatures. Their situation here was unpleasant at best, and when they finally got out they'd become someone's dinner. She had submerged live lobsters in a huge pot of boiling water dozens of times in her life, throwing on the cover and squeamishly listening to them clank around for a bit until they gave up the fight. Occasionally she had even allowed Little Daniel to stick a fork and knife upright into their claws, which were held closed with thick rubber bands. He would send them wobbling into the living room, where the girls would scream with delight. "They're having you for dinner tonight," Little Daniel would tell his sisters, and Ann Marie would laugh.

It had never once seemed cruel. But now, suddenly, she could not bear the thought of it. She ordered the clams.

The dining room was crowded with young families and couples holding hands. They took a table by the window, one of the only free spots left. There was a crackling fire in the fireplace, and outside, fishing boats bobbed up and down in the harbor.

When Maggie went to the ladies' room, Alice said, "Now, I know you're mad at me. Please don't be. I absolutely hate when you're mad."

"I'm not mad," Ann Marie said.

"Yes, you are."

She sighed. "Really, Mom, I'm not. It's fine."

"It was naughty of me not to tell you," Alice said. "But you know Kathleen and her kids — when Maggie said she was staying on, I figured she'd probably change her mind any day."

"But she didn't."

"No."

Alice's tone took on an edge. "Look. I told you not to come in the first place. If it's such a burden for you, why don't you go home?"

Ann Marie felt like a chastened child. She had changed all her plans to be here, yet Alice acted as if she were the ungrateful one.

"I want to stay," she said to keep the peace. "I'm sorry."

Alice smiled. "You'll stay in the big house with me. We'll put you in that front room with the best view of the water."

"That sounds nice," Ann Marie said.

Maggie came back to the table. Alice ordered two glasses of rum punch from the cocktail waitress.

"This one is becoming a killjoy like her mother," Alice said accusatorily, pointing at Maggie. "Doesn't drink anymore."

Maggie had never been much of a drinker, which was hardly a surprise. In Irish families like theirs, there was always a person or two so terrified of becoming an alcoholic that they never gave themselves the chance. In Ann Marie's case, it was her sister Susan, who hadn't had anything stronger than an

O'Doul's since college.

"I'm just on a health kick lately," Maggie said now. "Trying to lose some weight for summer."

Ann Marie tightened up, waiting for the inevitable.

"That's smart thinking," Alice said. "Obviously you don't look your best at the moment. But you're young. The weight will fall right off you." She paused. "Your hair looks nice, though."

"Thanks," Maggie said. She rolled her eyes at Ann Marie.

Alice switched gears. "Ann Marie, did you see that awful story on the news about the black boy in Dorchester who got killed by one of those scummy gangs? Two blocks away from the house I grew up in. What is wrong with these blacks? They're mad for murdering each other. It's their favorite hobby. They can't help themselves."

"Grandma!" Maggie hissed.

"What? It's true."

Maggie looked flummoxed. "There's a lot of history there. A lot of inequality and suffering."

"Oh, please," Alice said. "Our ancestors had to suffer horrible racism when they got to this country — there were IRISH NEED NOT APPLY signs in every window in Boston. Our people were treated worse than dogs. But they never made excuses. They helped themselves up, just the way the blacks should have done."

"It's different. African Americans' ancestors came here on slave ships and ours came here by choice."

"Do you really call dying from famine or going off to some unknown land a choice?" Alice said. "And did you really just compare the Irish to the blacks?"

"You shouldn't call them *the blacks* like that," Maggie said.

Alice looked genuinely confused. "What should I call them? Afro-Americans? Or Negroes, as we said when I was young?"

The couple at the next table swiveled their heads toward her.

"You shouldn't call them anything," Maggie said. "Let's change the subject."

Alice's face grew stony, a look that said she was going to the dark side. The Kellehers never did know how to handle her.

Before Alice could respond, Ann Marie whispered urgently, "Canadians! Call them Canadians."

Alice made an expression as if to say that it was silly, but she would indulge them.

"Fine. Canadians need to shape up. Better?"

Maggie shook her head. "I guess."

"And why do Canadians have such filthy mouths?" Alice asked. "I stumbled onto something on the radio this morning. And well, why?"

"I don't know," Maggie said, looking weary.

"Ann Marie?" Alice asked.

"No clue, Mom," she said.

Ann Marie flagged down the waitress and ordered another rum punch, even though her first one was still half full.

She called Pat from the phone in Alice's kitchen before bed. She was feeling slightly drunk and sorry for herself. No one ever told her anything. She tried to be an agreeable person, but what did it get her?

When she told him that Maggie hadn't left, Pat said, "Well good, then come home."

"No, I'll stay," she said. "There's still so much to do around here."

She felt like a prisoner. She knew it was an overreaction — anytime she wanted she could get in the car and go. But then what would she do for the next ten days? Patty had gotten another sitter for the kids. Her sisters were dealing with her mom. It was a bit disturbing how easily she could slip out of her own life without causing anyone much trouble. And anyway, all of her dollhouse furnishings were being sent here.

"Whatever you think," Pat said. "I miss you, though. The house is too quiet without you puttering around."

She smiled. "What did you have for dinner?"

"I'll plead the fifth on that."

"Patrick!" She knew it. He had gone to McDonald's. He was never allowed to eat fast food when she was present.

"I promise it won't happen again," he said. "Forgive me, I'm a weak man."

"Okay then," she said.

"Little Daniel called this afternoon," he said.

"Oh?"

"He said he misses his dear old dad and thought he might come over for dinner some night this week."

Good boy. "Well, isn't that sweet?"

"It really put a smile on my face, I have to say."

"I'm glad."

The exchange cheered her. She vowed to start tomorrow off right, to focus on the good. Before sleep, as always, she prayed. For her children and grandchildren, her mother and Alice, for Pat and the loved ones they'd lost. She said a special prayer for Maggie, who seemed so alone. She thought of her niece in the cottage next door, and had half a mind to go over there and tuck her in. Instead, she closed her eyes and listened to the crashing waves through the window.

Four days passed, more or less pleasantly. She went to the Cliff House and took copious notes on the chicken (very good) and the beef (a little tough) and the shrimp (her favorite) for Regina. She cooked dinners, some of which she froze for her mother-in-law to eat later in the summer. She jogged on the beach and helped Alice in the garden and chatted with her niece, who seemed overburdened — by her breakup, Ann Marie supposed. The arrangement was strange; not at all what she had expected, but that was life. Soon enough June would be over, Maggie would go back to New York, and Pat would be here, along with Steve Brewer.

On her fifth morning in Maine, Ann Marie woke with a jolt to the sound of the garbage disposal and Alice's voice coming from downstairs. It was only six thirty.

Alice sounded bright, happy.

"That's what I meant," she was saying. "I don't know if maybe one of the little ones put a marble down there or something."

"A marble?" came the amused voice of a man.

Ann Marie sat up in bed, straining to hear. Who was that? Her heart began to thump. She pictured Alice innocently answering the door, allowing some psychopath who claimed to be a plumber inside. Next, he'd be killing them both with a wrench and making off with their jewelry.

She pulled on her robe and went downstairs.

"Mom?" she said to Alice's back, and Alice

and the man swiveled around at once, like two teenagers who had been caught necking.

"Hello, darling," Alice said, full of pep. She was wearing black capri pants and leather flats and a short-sleeved red sweater that they had purchased together on sale at Eileen Fisher months ago. Her makeup was done to perfection.

"You remember Father Donnelly?"

"Of course," Ann Marie said, forcing herself to smile. There he stood, all in black, save for his white collar, looking about twelve years old. One of many things that disturbed her about aging was the fact that she could actually be twenty years older than a priest.

"How are you, Father?"

"Very well, thanks. I hope we didn't wake you."

"Not at all," she said, making her way toward the coffeepot.

"I told Alice that I'd come by and take a look at this sink," he said. "I'm saying Mass at nine, so we figured the earlier, the better."

"He's very handy," Alice beamed.

Ann Marie nodded. "How nice. But Mom, Pat can do all that stuff when he comes in a few days."

"It's no trouble," Father Donnelly said. "It's the least I can do."

Ann Marie's mother used to invite the parish priests over to their house for dinner one Sunday a month. She'd make an enormous roast and mashed potatoes and pineapple cake. Ann Marie had carried on this tradition for years. Her entire life, she had seen women catering to priests, providing them with the sort of warmth a wife would under normal circumstances. Leave it to Alice to turn the tables and put the priest to work for her.

The two of them headed out to church before long. Alice left her car behind. Did Father Donnelly provide chauffeur services too?

After they left, Ann Marie scrubbed down the kitchen counters and mopped the floor. She made a chicken salad from a cold roast chicken she had found in the freezer the night before, with only four or five bites taken out of it. (Alice still cooked for a big family, even though she ate like a bird. Ann Marie did the same, but it was somehow less sad when two people were eating.)

She showered and dressed, and then she set up shop at Alice's kitchen table, pulling out a large white towel and a slight floss of pale pink ribbon. She got to work, making half a dozen tiny facecloths and bath towels, sewing the ribbon on by hand. Maggie came over and they ate toast and blueberry preserves from a local farm stand for breakfast. Ann Marie told her about the dollhouse competition, and Maggie talked about her new novel. She didn't say anything about the boyfriend, and Ann Marie didn't mention him, not wanting to pry. But she thought to herself that by the time she was Maggie's age, she'd had three children. What would become of her niece?

"You know," Maggie said, "I don't think you and I have ever been alone together before."

Ann Marie thought of that New Year's Eve at her house when the kids were small. Kathleen and Paul, Clare and some boyfriend, and both of her own sisters and their husbands had come over for Chinese food, as was their tradition. Everyone was trashed, no one more than Kathleen, who had had so much gin that she was passed out on the couch in the den by ten o'clock. Ann Marie wasn't drinking. She had had maybe two glasses of champagne all night. Around eleven, she heard a thud from upstairs. She ran to Patty's room, following the sound of Maggie's cry. They had been roughhousing with the boys, and Maggie, only five years old, had fallen off the top bunk.

"She's fine," Paul had said with a laugh. "My daughter is tough as nails."

Since her parents were both intoxicated, it was Ann Marie who took the child to the hospital. It was Ann Marie who rocked Maggie in her arms, as patients and staff gathered around the nurses' station to count down to midnight. It was Ann Marie who told her stories over by the window, and tried to shield Maggie's eyes from the steady stream of drunks who came through the door.

They waited for four hours. In the end, the doctor said she had a severely strained wrist and should ice it as much as possible.

"I think taking her to the hospital was a bit of an overreaction," Kathleen said teasingly in the morning. Ann Marie wanted to take Maggie and Christopher and never let the woman see them again.

She didn't tell her niece this now. It was good that Maggie didn't remember it. She just said, "It's nice to spend a bit of time with you, sweetheart," and left it at that.

A while later, Maggie headed to the cottage for a nap. It really hadn't been that long since she'd gotten out of bed. Ann Marie was worried about her. She said, "Rest up and I'll come get you when it's time for sandwiches."

Maybe she'd try to talk to Maggie in the afternoon about whatever she had on her mind. Perhaps they could take a walk on the beach. Or Ann Marie could drive Maggie to Antiques on Nine and buy her something for her apartment to cheer her up, the way she had done with Patty before she got married.

Father Donnelly drove Alice home around noon and was quickly persuaded to join them for lunch, even though he had a two o'clock meeting.

"I've got it just about ready," Ann Marie said. "Give me fifteen minutes?"

Alice went out to the front yard to pick some daylilies for the table. Father Donnelly said he wanted to take one more crack at the broken garbage disposal. Ann Marie decided to serve the chicken on croissants she had gotten at the Shop 'n Save two days earlier. She cut all eight of them in half and placed them on a baking sheet in a warm oven.

"You're too good to us," she told the priest as she sliced a tomato. "But really, you shouldn't feel as though you have to do everything around here. Alice isn't alone, you know."

"It's no trouble," he said. "I enjoy it. And anyway, my helping out is the least I can do, considering."

Down on all fours, he fiddled under the sink for a bit. She placed the tomato slices on a plate and set to chopping a red onion. She thought his words over, rolled them around in her head. It wasn't the first time he had said it.

Finally she asked, "Considering what?"

"You don't know what your family's generosity means to the church," he said. "It's something we can count on, which is a precious gift, especially these days."

She smiled. She had no idea what he was referring to. Had Alice given St. Michael's a lot of money? Ann Marie felt uneasy. She wondered if Pat knew. She took a pitcher down from a high shelf in the pantry. There were so many fewer dishes here than she remembered. She felt pleased that Alice had finally taken her advice and decluttered a bit.

Ann Marie cracked a tray of ice cubes, plopping half of them into the pitcher. Then she took the pitcher to the sink.

"Okay if I turn the water on for a sec?" she asked.

"Absolutely." He climbed to his feet. "I don't think I have the right part for this anyway. I'll have to go up to the hardware store in York and see what they've got. I can come back after my meeting."

Three visits to the house in a single day? She said a silent prayer that Alice hadn't given the grandchildren's inheritance away.

"Have you always been so handy?" she asked. She filled the pitcher and set it on the table, alongside the tomatoes and onions and the bowl of chicken salad. She removed the croissants from the oven.

"Not until I moved into a rectory where the former guy in charge thought the way to deal with a leaky roof was to buy more pots."

She forced out a chuckle.

"Needless to say, moving into this house will certainly be an upgrade," he said.

Ann Marie felt her heart speed up. "I'm sorry?"

The strangest thought went through her

head: Was the priest somehow involved with Alice? She wasn't sure she could take that. Though her mother-in-law had always been flirtatious, she had never once seemed sexual.

His cheeks grew pink. "I apologize. I shouldn't have said that. Naturally we hope — well, we know — it will be many years. But being included in someone's estate planning is the best we can ask for. It was beyond kind of your family, that's all I'm saying. We're so grateful."

"Of course," she said, trying to understand. "So, you mean . . ."

Had Alice given him their home? She told herself not to look too bewildered, but he must have seen it in her expression.

He raised an eyebrow. "Please tell me this isn't the first you're hearing of it."

Composure, she thought. Sometimes it helped her to focus on a single word. *Composure.*

"It's okay," she said. "I'm sure that . . ." But she couldn't think of a thing to say.

"I am so sorry," he stumbled. "It was Alice's news to share, not mine. I must have gotten confused. I thought the whole family was in agreement on this."

She fixed her face with a plastic grin. "Don't be silly," she said. "It's fine."

Ann Marie felt like she couldn't breathe. She needed to get away from him. She needed to talk to Pat.

502

"The chicken salad!" she said, louder than she had meant to. "It needs paprika."

"Paprika?"

"Yes!" she said. "Just look at it! It's so bland. I usually add grapes but I didn't have any. Paprika will do the trick! I'll have to go over to the cottage and get some. I'm sure there's some over there. Things like paprika have a way of sticking around forever over there. Okay, well."

Before he had time to respond, she was out the door, making a beeline for her car, the only place she could get decent cell reception up here.

Her anger surprised her. She thought of the money they had spent to build that huge house and cover all the regular costs, the snowy days when her husband had driven out here to shovel off the flat porch roof, the hours they had both put in, the countless times she had bitten her tongue just to keep the peace. And this was how her mother-in-law planned to repay them?

The Lord never sends us more than we can handle, she reminded herself. But she felt like she might have a breakdown, right then and there.

She dialed Pat's cell instead of his work line. She was much too upset to have to make pleasantries with his secretary. When he answered, she told him everything in a rush.

"You must have misunderstood him. This

isn't the sort of thing my mother would do," Pat said, but Ann Marie could tell that the wheels in her husband's head were already turning. It was precisely the sort of thing Alice would do, and they both knew it.

"Goddamn it," he said loudly, giving her a start. "I'll drive out there after work tonight and we'll talk some sense into her."

She nodded. "Good. Oh, but Maggie's here."

"So?"

Ann Marie dropped her voice to a whisper, as if anyone could hear her out there in the car. "Is this really something we want to discuss in front of her?"

Maggie would no doubt tell Kathleen, and she didn't need Pat's sisters getting involved. It was hairy enough already.

"She'll be gone in four days and you'll be here," Ann Marie said. "Should we wait until then to talk to Alice?"

"Okay," he said. "Maybe it's a good idea to sleep on it anyway, and take a few deep breaths. I just wonder if she was in her right mind when she told him. Maybe she hasn't actually signed anything. I need to talk to Jim Lowenthal about the legality of all this."

His lawyer. Ann Marie began to cry. She didn't know how she could physically manage to get through the next few days, let alone lunch with Alice and that horrible priest. Having Maggie there would be a blessing. It would stop her from saying something she might regret.

As if sensing her thoughts, Pat asked, "Do you want to come home and we'll go back up there together on the first?"

If it weren't for the fact that her dollhouse was coming any day now, she might have said yes. But Ann Marie would have to stay.

She tried to sound positive. "No, it'll be all right. It's just — I don't understand why your mother would do this to us."

As soon as the words were out of her mouth, she realized there was no point wondering why Alice had done it. The Kellehers were crazy people, that was all.

Ann Marie felt crazy herself at the moment. She had the strongest urge to do something wicked. She remembered when her brother was a kid and used to put bags of dog poop on people's front stairs and set them alight. And the time he chopped the head off every tulip in their neighbor's front yard.

She wanted to say that this family would be the death of her, but there were Pat's feelings to consider, too, so she held her tongue for now.

KATHLEEN

Kathleen stopped at a gas station five miles outside Cape Neddick to buy cigarettes. She had already gone through an entire pack of Marlboro Lights and two Snickers bars on the drive from the airport.

Before yesterday, she hadn't smoked since eleventh grade, and even then only once or twice. Arlo would be shocked if he found out, but Arlo was home in California, the lucky bastard. He had been smart enough not to have children, so he would never know the peculiar sensation of caring terribly, insanely, for a person over whom you had no control; a person who was your responsibility yet no longer had to answer to you. This made Kathleen irrationally angry at him. She was angry at a lot of people right now. At Maggie, for dropping such a bomb on her in an e-mail. At Arlo, for acting like nothing was wrong. At Gabe, who was no doubt responsible for the whole mess. And most of all, in a vague way, at the Kellehers, who always found some method of drawing her back into the fray, of reminding her that underneath the AA mantras and the California calm, she was just the same old angry, overwhelmed girl she used to be.

Given the circumstances, she figured smoking was the least of many evils.

Kathleen drove slowly, trying to relax, reminding herself that life was messy, conflict inevitable. It didn't mean you had to fall apart.

When she read Maggie's e-mail five days earlier, she had sat still in front of her computer for several minutes, unable to move. She worried all the time about her daughter's safety in New York, about pickpockets and rapists and the diseases that could take young people out so fast. But this she had never feared, never pictured. Maggie had always been so responsible. Christ, Maggie had told *her* to go on the Pill when she was only a freshman in high school and years away from getting on it herself.

Kathleen had called down to Arlo in the den after a while, softly at first, and then louder and louder. She felt hysterical by the time she heard him climbing the stairs. When she showed him the e-mail, he whistled and said, "Oh, man."

"I have to go to her," she said.

"It sounds like she wants you to sit with this for a while, let it sink in. She knows you well," he said with a gentle smile.

"How can you be so goddamn calm about this?" she had snapped. She tried to take a deep breath.

"Because it's not the end of the world," he said, rubbing her shoulders. "A baby is good news."

She shook his hands off.

"I'm going out there to talk sense into her."

"Meaning what?"

She considered the options, none of them entirely pleasant. Maggie should probably have an abortion, but Kathleen doubted her daughter could go through with that. Adoption might be a better choice for her. Joni Mitchell did it, and she seemed to have recovered okay. *I bore her but I could not raise her.* Wasn't that how the song went?

But the thought of carrying a baby around inside of you for all those months and then having to say good-bye — she wasn't sure Maggie could handle that either.

"I don't know. Jesus. Why did this have to happen?" she said. "What does she expect me to do?"

"I think she just wanted you to know and to be supportive," Arlo said.

"I'm her mother. I know her better than anyone," she said.

"And?"

"And nothing. That's it."

Arlo frowned. "I wish we had some money

to give her, Kath."

She thought of the twenty thousand she had saved for the worm gin, but that was theirs; they needed it for the business. Even so, Kathleen felt guilty for not wanting to let it go.

They went to an AA meeting that night and a woman with gray-tinged skin and bottle-blond hair told a story about being so out-of-her-mind drunk that she left her kids in the car for hours one afternoon in the middle of August.

"I forgot all about them," the woman said. "I'm afraid they will hate me someday. I never thought I'd be the type to do something as awful as that."

Arlo held Kathleen's hand and she squeezed hard, imagining all the ways that motherhood could change a person, ways that you could simply never imagine for yourself until you were stuck right there in the middle of it. What if Maggie felt so desperate that she went back to Gabe? And if she didn't go back to him, how could she ever manage all on her own in that cold, unforgiving city? Both possibilities terrified Kathleen. She knew that it was Maggie's life, Maggie's decision, but she could not accept it.

When Kathleen had told Paul Doyle that she was pregnant with Maggie, he had seemed flustered at first, but then he said, *We'll just get married! That was our plan any-*

way. She remembered thinking, *Was it?* for a moment, before feeling relieved.

Kathleen thought of how lonely she had felt parenting on her own after the divorce. That had been the hardest part.

An idea crept into her head then: Maggie would have to come live with them. They could give her support, help her look after the baby. The child would have green fields to run in, and a family of caring adults around, and the healthiest food on the planet to eat.

Out in the parking lot after the meeting, she told Arlo what she'd been thinking.

"Would that be okay with you?"

His eyes grew wide, as if he couldn't believe she had to ask. "Of course!"

Kathleen loved him more than ever in that moment. She began to cry.

"What's wrong?" he asked.

"Our life," she said. "It's going to end. No more walking around the house naked, no more privacy. I can't believe it. Why did this have to happen to me?"

He cocked his head. "You do realize that you're acting as though one of us is dying. You need to get positive. A baby is coming!"

"Right," she said. "Right."

She pushed from her head the fear that maybe he was back on the dope. No, it wasn't that. He was just a good person. And he didn't know yet how hard it would be to have an infant in their house, crying at all hours.

She thought of asking Maggie to meet her at a hotel somewhere near the cottage. She could pay for a taxi. That way they could talk, really spend some time together, without Alice there poking her nose into things.

But she had been trying to call Maggie for days, and for days she had gotten voice mail. She responded to Maggie's e-mail, writing *CALL ME!!* in the subject line. But Maggie didn't write back. So Kathleen booked an overpriced flight to Boston, rented a car, and drove north without telling her daughter, or for that matter, her mother, that she was coming. And now here she was, driving down Briarwood Road, feeling so anxious that her insides seemed to itch.

It was after noon, which meant Alice was probably home from church and three-quarters of the way through her second bottle of wine. Kathleen hoped that she would see Maggie first and be able to talk to her in private right away.

As she made her way toward the cottage, she saw three cars in the driveway — Alice's and two others. Driving closer, she recognized the blue Mercedes.

"Shit, shit, shit," she said to herself. She pulled her car onto the property, and actually considered hitting the gas and plowing straight into it.

Maybe Pat had driven out to fix something.

Maybe he'd leave immediately. She could only hope.

Kathleen took the keys from the ignition and sighed long and hard. When she got out, she could smell the ocean air. For a moment she felt almost peaceful. But within seconds, the driver's-side door of the Mercedes flew open and Ann Marie stepped out. What, had she been spying from the front seat? Was she able to smell the enemy from a hundred yards away?

Her sister-in-law came toward her.

"Kathleen!" she said, sounding forced. "Well, this is a surprise."

It looked like Ann Marie had been crying. *What the hell was she doing here?*

Kathleen had a sinking feeling in her gut.

"Likewise," she said. "Are you up for the afternoon? Is Pat here too?"

"No, I'm here to care for Alice for a couple of weeks," Ann Marie replied. "I arrived a few days ago."

The nerve of her, concocting a schedule for their collective home and then not observing it herself. Of course, the rules wouldn't apply to the king and queen, only to their minions.

"During my month?" Kathleen said in a joking tone that she hoped Ann Marie knew was no joke. "I don't remember you consulting me about that." She smiled. "Just kidding."

"Well, actually, I did tell you I had concerns

512

about leaving Alice alone up here," Ann Marie said. "And no one told me Maggie was staying on."

"God, how is that possible?" Kathleen asked. "Everyone in this family is usually so good at communicating."

This was a bad way to start things off and she knew it. *God, grant me the serenity to accept the things I cannot change. God, grant me the goddamn strength.*

Kathleen tried again. "You look good," she said. "Have you lost some weight?"

Actually, Ann Marie didn't look any different at all. If anything, a bit haggard.

"Oh, thanks," Ann Marie said. "I'm seeing a trainer. I don't know if it's making a difference, really, but it feels good to at least try. Pat got me the sessions as a gift a couple years ago, but I've started going more regularly lately."

"How sweet of him," Kathleen said.

Ann Marie nodded. "Yes. He might have thought to say it with jewelry, but oh well."

They laughed in earnest. That was a good sign. One of the few things they'd ever bonded over was Pat's emotional cluelessness, though really his wife didn't seem any more plugged in than he was.

"Do you know where Maggie is?" Kathleen asked.

"Napping in the cottage, I think," Ann Marie said. "I was about to head over there to get her for lunch. You're just in time for chicken salad."

"Napping?" Kathleen asked. She hoped Maggie wasn't feeling nauseous or depressed, or some combination of the two. And she absolutely hated that Ann Marie knew anything at all about Maggie that she herself did not. Was it possible Maggie had told her about the pregnancy? Was Ann Marie dangling the information in front of Kathleen now, taunting her with it?

Kathleen needed to be alone with her daughter.

"I'll go get her," she said, starting toward the cottage's screen door. "We'll meet you over at Alice's in a bit."

But Ann Marie didn't take the hint. She followed close behind, saying, "Actually, I need to get some paprika from the cottage kitchen."

"I can bring it to you," Kathleen said.

"No, that's okay. You don't know where it is."

Kathleen sighed. She pictured herself slipping Maggie a note: *Meet me in my rental car and we'll get the hell out of here.*

She stepped into the screened-in porch, feeling as if she had stepped back in time. It was so much the same as it had been ten years ago, and ten years before that, and ten years before that. It even smelled the same. She hadn't expected to be here ever again. It

514

felt odd, and she thought of Sonoma Valley — the familiar road that cut through a vineyard and led to their house in Glen Ellen, with dog toys and bags of fertilizer strewn across the front lawn. That was home now.

She walked through the front hall. Her father's old Red Sox hat had hung on a hook by the door there for as long as she could remember, but it was gone. She wondered where.

Kathleen found Maggie in the living room, reading in the armchair. She still had a baby face, and Kathleen recalled her in this same position as a child — cozy and safe, curled up with a book. She felt that same old urge to protect her at all costs.

"Mags?" she said.

Maggie looked up, registering her presence. "Mom!"

Ann Marie buzzed around behind them. "Yes, your mom's here. Maggie, you didn't tell us she was coming!"

Maggie rose and hugged Kathleen hard. "I didn't know."

"It was a surprise," Kathleen said to Ann Marie, trying to sound cheerful, as if she did this sort of thing all the time.

"When did you get here?" Maggie asked.

"I flew into Boston this morning."

"Why didn't you tell me you were coming?"

"I tried. You never have your cell phone turned on."

"I told you the reception is crummy out here. You should have called on the house line." Maggie took a step back. "Have you been smoking?"

"What? No."

Kathleen had thought her daughter would be happier to see her. The usual ease between them was missing. Of course, that was because they both knew why she was standing here, but neither of them could speak freely.

She would have to be direct, but polite. "Ann Marie, could you give us a few minutes?" she asked. The words came out sounding harsher than she'd intended.

"I'd be happy to," Ann Marie said. "Except Connor's eating with us and he has to get back to the church for a meeting, so —"

"Connor?" Kathleen asked.

"The priest I told you about," Maggie said.

Oh. Well, naturally.

Maggie continued, "That's okay, we'll come now. We can catch up later."

Kathleen had to fight off the feeling that her daughter wanted an out.

"Yes, sure," she agreed. "We'll eat fast."

When they arrived next door, Alice was sitting at the kitchen table, smoking away, and talking to a handsome young guy in jeans.

She gave a dramatic start when she saw Kathleen standing there.

"My God, have you ever heard of a telephone?"

"Nice to see you, too, Mom."

Her mother's face changed, her lips curling up into a grin. Maybe she had just remembered that they had company, and male company at that.

"It's a surprise to see you here again, that's all. How long has it been since you were here? Five years?"

"Ten."

She had to know that Kathleen had stayed away since Daniel died, didn't she?

"This is Father Donnelly," Alice said. "Meet my older daughter, Kathleen."

He extended a hand. "It's a pleasure."

"Sit, sit," Alice said, suddenly in hostess mode. "Everybody sit. Ann Marie's made a gorgeous chicken salad."

There was a bottle of white wine on the table. *Really?* They needed it at lunch?

Ann Marie held up a dusty glass jar full of red powder.

"The paprika," she said knowingly to the priest. She began shaking it over the chicken as if it were her goal to empty the entire contents of the bottle right then and there.

"I think that's enough, don't you?" Alice said, looking to Maggie and raising an eyebrow in the direction of Ann Marie. "This isn't a curry house, darling."

Maggie laughed, and Kathleen was right back on that beach in the Bahamas, watching the two of them drinking rum, Alice trying to pull her daughter into all that Kathleen had tried to shield her from.

Alice looked Kathleen over. "You look good. You're keeping most of the weight off, I see."

Kathleen gritted her teeth. "Thanks."

"I've already sworn off chowder for the rest of the summer myself," Alice said, though she had never taken more than two bites of chowder in a sitting in her life. "We should probably all do that. So what on earth made you decide to come out here now? There's only a few more days in June, you know."

"I invited her!" Maggie said quickly, and Kathleen understood then that Maggie hadn't told them about her situation. She felt relief for the first time in days.

Alice poured the wine. When she got to Maggie's glass, Maggie placed her palm facedown over the top.

"Oh, right," Alice said, and rolled her eyes. "You know, Father, this used to be a dry town. My daughter and granddaughter here would have fit right in."

"Really?" he said. "I didn't know that."

"Yes! Can you imagine? Until the sixties, when you wanted to go out, you had to go to these silly Oriental tearooms. What a snooze."

"But you managed," Kathleen said. She turned to the priest. "She imported her whiskey from the local liquor store in Mas-

518

sachusetts. Until she stopped drinking herself, that is."

Alice shot her a look, but then said, "Guilty
as charged. We never had the money to go
out much anyway, in those days."

Across the table, Ann Marie began scoop-
ing the chicken salad onto the croissants.
After each scoop, she slammed the heavy
metal serving spoon against the china.

"Careful!" Alice said.

Ann Marie didn't respond.

"Are you feeling all right?" Alice asked her.

"Fine. Why?"

Alice shook her head.

The priest piped up then. "There may be
something Ann Marie and I should mention,"
he said.

*Sweet Jesus, was her sister-in-law sleeping
with the priest?*

"What is going on around here?" Alice said
gaily, as if perhaps this was all part of some
elaborate spoof. *Smile! You're on* Candid
Camera!

"Oh, it's nothing," Ann Marie said. "It's
just that I, um — I dropped a few of the
croissants on the floor when I was fixing
lunch and Connor saw me."

She sent him a scathing look, as if he had
just outed her in front of the pope.

Alice held up her sandwich. "This one?"
she asked.

"Oh no, no. The ones that landed on the

floor I threw straight into the trash," Ann Marie said. "It was only a little joke. Ha."

Kathleen sighed. That would be Ann Marie's version of a scandalous confession.

They talked about the weather and the crowds at Ogunquit Beach — parking was up to twenty dollars a day there, highway robbery if you asked Alice. They discussed the fact that cicadas were ruining half the birch trees in Wells this summer, and that the monastery in Kennebunk had received a visit from a conference of senior bishops last week. With each new benign topic, Kathleen clenched her fists in her lap, trying to be civil, reminding herself how much worse it would be if the rest of them found out about Maggie.

Alice asked if Kathleen had brought along any of her fertilizer.

"Why would I? Clare says you stockpile it in your basement and then throw it out."

"That is absolutely not true," Alice replied. "I've been raving about it all summer."

"Not to me you haven't," Kathleen said. She took yet another deep breath. "Sorry, Mom. That was nice of you to say."

"Of course, now that I have such gorgeous plants, the rabbits have decided to use my garden as their all-you-can-eat buffet," Alice said. She flitted her eyes at the priest. "The trials of a gardener never cease."

"You should try putting hair in the dirt,"

Kathleen said. "It works surprisingly well."

"Why hair?" the priest asked.

She opened her mouth to respond, but Alice spoke first: "Oh, I've already tried that. It didn't do a damn thing. And I've been spraying cayenne pepper juice all over the place, and they don't even seem to mind."

"You shouldn't do that," Kathleen said, horrified. She was glad Arlo wasn't there to hear it. "Their stomachs can't handle it. It tortures them."

"Oh, for God's sake, they're torturing me," Alice said. "And anyway, my rabbits seem to love their spices. Maybe I should feed them this paprika sandwich as a treat."

"Sorry if I used too much," Ann Marie said flatly. "I'm distracted today."

"Oh, it's fine, I was only teasing. And besides, I'm not very hungry," Alice said, putting her sandwich down on her plate and covering it with a napkin. "Father, Ann Marie made delicious oatmeal cookies yesterday. You should take some back to the rectory."

"Why not!" Ann Marie said, sounding almost shrill.

After a dessert of neon orange sherbet (again, Arlo would rather die), the priest said his good-byes, promising to return later with some new part for the sink.

Then it was just the four of them. Alice refilled her wineglass and Ann Marie's, emptying the bottle.

"That was an amazing lunch," Maggie said. "Thanks, Aunt Ann Marie."

God, all the woman had done was make a few lousy sandwiches.

"Yes, thanks," Kathleen said.

Ann Marie looked preoccupied, but after a moment, as if she were being fed a forgotten line from somewhere offstage, she said, "It was my pleasure."

"Well, we'd better be going next door, Maggie," Kathleen said, giving her a meaningful look. "I'm absolutely exhausted."

"You go ahead," Maggie said. "I'll do the dishes and be over in a while."

"Oh. Okay."

Kathleen walked to the cottage, crouching around the corner by the front door while she lit a cigarette, feeling like an eighth-grade girl. She took a few puffs, then quickly stomped it out. She walked inside and sat alone by the window in the dining room, in her father's favorite old chair. She would give absolutely anything to have him here now.

A half hour passed before Maggie joined her.

Her daughter flashed a great, warm smile. "Alone at last," she said.

Kathleen rose and hugged her.

She told herself not to rush. There was time enough to say her piece after she got settled. They talked about the farm, and the good writing Maggie had managed to get done

522

here. They joked about Alice and the priest, and about Chris's new girlfriend, whose entire back was covered in tattoos of Hanna-Barbera cartoon characters. All the while, Kathleen thought about the baby.

It was Maggie who finally brought it up. "So, I guess we should talk about —" She paused, looking like an embarrassed adolescent, and then pointed to her stomach. "This?"

Kathleen wanted to be composed, but she could feel the words pushing to get out of her, a flood of anger behind them. Even as she told herself not to, she blurted: "What the hell were you thinking, e-mailing me? You're pregnant and you send me a goddamn e-mail?"

Maggie looked startled. "That's what you came here to say?"

"I came here to stop you from making a huge mistake."

Maggie shook her head. "Look, I know that's how you see Chris and me, but we're not in agreement on this one, okay? I actually want this baby. I don't feel it's a mistake the way you did with us."

Kathleen felt like her daughter had just harpooned her with a sharp stick, straight through the heart.

"That's not true, Maggie," she said. "You were very much wanted."

God, she sounded like a robot. *You were*

very much wanted? How warm and fuzzy, Kathleen; why not go ahead and embroider that sentiment on a sampler?

She tried again. "I can't picture for a second what my life would have been like without you, Maggie, you know that. And I don't want to. But you can't imagine how hard it is, trying to provide for a child all on your own."

"We were provided for," Maggie said hotly.

"I meant provided as in putting you to bed each night and giving you your bath before dinner and cooking that dinner and waking you up for school on snowy days when school was the last place you wanted to go. I meant being a single parent. And yes, one of the ways I struggled was financially. I never wanted that for you."

"You struggled because you always thought you were too good for motherhood in the first place," Maggie said.

Kathleen blinked. Jesus, that was just the sort of thing she might have said to Alice. Had she really gone so far out of her way to do the dead opposite of everything her mother had done, only to be perceived as the exact same sort of woman?

"How could this even happen?" she demanded. "Aren't you on the Pill?"

"It's a long story."

"Please don't tell me you did this intentionally."

"You're the one who's always saying the universe works in mysterious ways."

Kathleen raised an eyebrow.

"I have it under control, okay?" Maggie said. "I wasn't asking your permission. I was just letting you know."

"Well, thanks so much for that. And I suppose Gabe is on board, all lined up to be a daddy? I suppose that's under control too."

Maggie moaned. "Shut up, Mom!"

"Shut up? I didn't come here to be talked to like that."

"No one asked you to come."

They had never spoken to each other this way, not even when Maggie was a teenager.

"I think hanging out with Alice is rubbing off on you," Kathleen said, trying to make a joke. Why was she being so mean? She had come here to help.

Maggie gave her a faint smile.

"You have to understand how difficult this is for me," Kathleen said. "I want to be a grandmother someday, but not now."

That part was a lie. She absolutely did not want to be a grandmother, ever.

Maggie's face grew stormy. "It's not about you. God, you'd think you were the one who was pregnant."

Kathleen sighed. "Nothing's coming out the way I want it to. Let's start over. I want you to come live with Arlo and me. I've thought about it a lot, and I think this will work."

"No," Maggie said with a laugh.

Kathleen was surprised. She had thought Maggie would be relieved by the idea.

"Well, wait a second. Hear me out."

"No offense, but your home is not exactly a safe place for a baby. I'd have to have a tiny pink or blue hazmat suit made."

"What is that supposed to mean?"

"I'm staying in New York," Maggie said.

"In case Gabe decides he wants to play house."

"No!" Maggie said. "But thank you for giving me so much credit. I'm pregnant, okay? That doesn't automatically make me an idiot. I'm the same person I was before."

Neither of them had heard the screen door open, but now a voice from behind asked, "You're pregnant?"

They turned to see Ann Marie standing in the doorway, affecting a look of deep concern.

"I wish you'd have said something," she said to Maggie. "I could have helped."

Kathleen tried to suppress a scoff. "That's why I'm here. I think I know what my own daughter needs."

The Kellehers prided themselves on coming together when something even vaguely resembling a tragedy occurred — anything from a funeral to a flat tire. Perhaps this was one of the benefits of having a large family,

526

but to Kathleen it always seemed slightly disingenuous, as if they were making up for the horrible ways they had treated one another over the years simply by taking someone's temperature or making a casserole.

Alice came bounding into the house now, wearing what looked like a beekeeper's hat, the veil still covering her face.

"What on earth was that all about?" she said sharply to Ann Marie. "You trampled two of my tomato plants!"

"Mom, what are you talking about?" Ann Marie said.

"I saw you! I was on my way out to the garden and I saw you step all over them and then come running in here. Why, Ann Marie? You know the trouble I've had with the rabbits."

"I have no idea what you're talking about," Ann Marie said meekly. "Maybe it was an accident."

"There's no way to accidentally step on a tomato plant." Alice set her gaze on Kathleen. "You always have a way of stirring everything up."

"Me? What did I do?"

Alice sighed. "I don't even know, it's just your way. When you're around, trouble starts. And Maggie starts acting like a pain in the ass too."

"Jesus Christ," Kathleen said.

"I'm going for a walk to clear my head,"

Alice said. "I need a break. You're all behaving like a bunch of Canadians today, and I'm not sure I can take it much longer."

"Canadians?" Kathleen said.

Maggie shook her head. "Don't ask."

Alice walked off and Ann Marie said, "Anyway. Maggie, I had no idea. What can I do to help?"

"You can leave us alone," Kathleen said. "Don't you think if she wanted you to know she would have told you?"

"It's okay. Everyone was bound to find out eventually," Maggie said agreeably. She was always so damn agreeable. She wasn't going to be any help when it came to getting rid of Ann Marie. She was too polite for that. Kathleen would have to take a new approach.

"So what happened with the tomato plants?" she asked casually.

Ann Marie blushed. "I'll be down on the beach if anyone needs me," she said, and turned on her heels.

Kathleen had hoped that she and Maggie could go to dinner alone, at the very least. She had read about a place in Portsmouth called the Black Trumpet in one of Arlo's food magazines. The restaurant was located in an old shipping goods warehouse, and the chef cooked with organic ingredients from local farms.

Kathleen imagined them sitting at a table

528

by the window and finally talking at length. She hadn't gotten a chance to tell Maggie that she knew exactly how they could arrange the nursery (which was now her home office), or that a farmer friend of Arlo's down the road had started selling homemade baby food. She had expected some amount of gratitude from her daughter, some acknowledgment that the last thing Kathleen would ever want to do was raise another child — but for Maggie, she would.

She hoped this would all come out at dinner. But when she mentioned it late that afternoon, Maggie said she had promised Alice she'd make a spaghetti sauce.

"If I'd known you were coming, I wouldn't have," she said apologetically. "It's just that she and Aunt Ann Marie have been doing all this cooking for me, and I wanted to repay the favor. Why don't you come over to Grandma's house with me now and you can help me cook?"

Somehow Kathleen felt like a child, an outsider. Maggie seemed to fit in so seamlessly here, unlike her. She could not imagine why Maggie wanted to go back into the belly of the beast next door after everything that had been said earlier in the day. *Thank you for shitting on my life, please allow me to cook you dinner!* But that was how the Kellehers worked. No one ever apologized for speaking harshly. They only wallpapered over it with homemade spaghetti sauce and tired old jokes and strong cocktails.

"You're going to start cooking now?" she asked. "It's four thirty. Why don't we take a walk on the beach first?"

"Alice likes to eat early," Maggie said. "Do you want to come?"

"I'll stay here for a while, I think," Kathleen said. "I have some work I need to do."

"Okay," Maggie said.

"Hey," Kathleen said. "Call me crazy, but are you sort of avoiding me?"

"What do you mean, Mom? We've been sitting here talking for the last three hours!"

Maggie didn't sound like herself. But then again, Kathleen wasn't herself right now either.

"You're right. Sorry. I'm being clingy, I guess."

Maggie gave her a kiss on the forehead. "Come next door soon, please."

"I will," Kathleen said. "Pasta for dinner, huh? Maybe that's why Ann Marie stomped the tomato plants. Maybe she got sauce making confused with wine making."

Maggie grinned. "Maybe so."

Kathleen made every conceivable work-related phone call she could think of, sitting on the hood of her car. She called Arlo and he asked right away whether Maggie was excited to come back to California.

"Not exactly," she told him. "I think it's going to take a bit of time to get her to realize it's the right choice."

"Well, tell her there's one old geezer, two aging dogs, and several million worms here who are eagerly anticipating her arrival," he said. "I started cleaning out the upstairs office this morning."

Kathleen knew she should feel grateful, but her heart seized up, thinking of her cozy, cluttered workspace emptied out. "Where are you putting everything?" she asked.

"In boxes in the shed," he said. "Kath, it's not forever. Okay? This baby adventure might just be our best one yet."

"You're wonderful," she said.

"Who knows? We might even decide to have one of our own."

"Okay, now you're just insane."

He asked about Alice.

"I am trying to be civil, but you know how it goes," she said. "And Ann Marie is here, too, as luck would have it. They were drinking by noon."

"Stay strong," he said.

After they hung up, she lit another cigarette, glancing toward her parents' house to make sure no one was watching. Then she looked around, taking it all in. The ocean and the sand and the look of the cottage itself, she remembered. But she had forgotten about the nature — the giant lush trees that shaded her mother's garden, the pines and the birches. The birds, with their bright red and blue wings, the hum of frogs off in the marshes on the other side of the street. The mosquitoes that had caused her to douse her children in Skin So Soft five times a day when they were young. (Ann Marie used OFF! on her kids, hazardous chemicals be damned.)

A few minutes later, the priest pulled his car into the driveway.

Him again? Already? Christ, was the priesthood really so bad these days that the guys had to moonlight as handymen?

"I got the new part for the drain," he said. He held up a brown paper bag.

Kathleen nodded. She stomped out the cigarette and hoped, absurdly, that he would not mention it to her mother.

"Is everyone okay around here?" he asked, sounding nervous. "I know it was tense at lunch."

"Was it?" Kathleen asked.

"Do you know where I can find Alice and Ann Marie?" he said. "I think we need to talk."

"Over at my mother's house," she said. She suddenly got the feeling that something interesting was about to unfold, and added, "I'll come with you."

In the kitchen, the smell of Maggie's tomato sauce filled the air. Maggie and Alice stood by the stove, talking about a book Maggie thought her grandmother would like. Through the archway that led to the living room, Kathleen could see Ann Marie sitting on the couch, sewing together swatches of fabric with a needle and thread for no reason she could fathom. There was an almost empty glass of wine on the coffee table in front of her.

"Father!" Alice said when she saw them there. Clearly, she felt no need to address Kathleen. "You didn't have to come back so soon! You're a saint."

"It's no big deal," he said. "They happened to have the part in stock. And I thought it might be good if we all had a talk. Is Ann Marie here?"

Alice pointed at her and said in a judgmental stage whisper, "She's drinking an awful lot today. She's acting very odd."

"I can hear you!" Ann Marie snapped from the other room, which was indeed extremely odd for her.

The priest frowned. "I'm afraid I might be to blame for all of this," he said.

"You?" Alice said. "Oh no, not at all."

"I'm afraid I mentioned our arrangement regarding the property to Ann Marie," he said.

Alice's eyes grew wide.

What arrangement? Kathleen thought.

The priest continued, "I hope we can all talk and I can help sort this out."

"That is rich," Ann Marie chirped, getting up from her seat now and storming into the kitchen. Kathleen felt a jolt of excitement and curiosity — a fight was brewing and it had nothing whatsoever to do with her.

"You're going to sort us all out, huh?" Ann Marie went on. "Why don't you start by explaining to me how you managed to con an old woman into giving you our family's summer home."

"What?" Maggie said.

The priest looked at Alice. "I don't understand."

Alice got up close to Ann Marie. Kathleen was positive it was the *old woman* part that had done her in.

"No one has conned anyone. And you're embarrassing me in front of my guest," Alice snarled. "This is not *our family's* home, Ann Marie. It's my home. Mine."

Ann Marie looked like she had been slapped. Kathleen almost felt sorry for her. She had tried to explain to Ann Marie many times when they were young that there was no sense trying to build up goodwill with Alice. If you displeased her once, that was it.

"When were you going to clue us in, Alice?" Ann Marie demanded, almost shouting now. "How could you give the house away without telling us? I don't understand."

Since she had no real stake in it, Kathleen felt like it was her responsibility to turn down the temperature on all of this, so she said in her calmest voice, "Why don't we take some deep breaths and all try to relax a bit?"

"That's easy for you to say," Ann Marie said. "You don't even care about this place. The only reason you've come here in ten years is to try to convince Maggie to have an abortion."

"How the hell is that your business?" Kathleen asked.

"It concerns all of us," Ann Marie said.

"Actually, no. It doesn't." Kathleen had only been trying to help, but now she felt her anger go straight from zero to a hundred and ten. "Just because you think your children are so goddamn perfect doesn't mean you need to go looking for extra credit with mine."

"You live across the country — you don't know the first thing about my children," Ann Marie said.

"Fiona's a lesbian and Little Daniel's a douche bag," Kathleen said. "Update at eleven."

Ann Marie looked like she might faint. She had probably never considered either possibility. Well there, give her something to chew on.

Alice narrowed her eyes at Maggie. "Is this true? Are you pregnant?"

They all turned to poor Maggie, whose face and neck were now covered in hives. Kathleen rubbed her daughter's arm. She glanced over at the priest, who was looking down at his shoes.

"Yes," Maggie said.

"Jesus, Mary, and Joseph," Alice said. "And you've been here all these weeks with me and you haven't said a word."

"Yes."

Alice stiffened. "What do you intend to do about it?"

"I'm having the baby," Maggie said.

"And Gabe?"

"He's not in the picture anymore."

Alice threw up her hands. "Well, that's that, then. Worse things have happened."

She seemed overly tranquil, and this pissed Kathleen off, since she knew that if it were one of Ann Marie's kids standing here breaking this news, Alice would be apoplectic. But she expected the worst from Maggie and Chris, since after all they were merely appendages of Kathleen herself.

"You're not angry?" Maggie asked.

"No," Alice said.

"Because Maggie's not one of your golden grandchildren, is that it?" Kathleen snapped. "How can you just say, 'Oh, it's fine. Go ahead and have a baby'?"

"What would you prefer I say?" Alice said. "That she's a little tramp like her mother, has absolutely no common sense, and has just flushed her chances at being a real writer down the toilet?"

Now the priest spoke up. "Alice," he said, as if her words had caused him physical pain.

Kathleen's hands formed two tight fists.

"None of that is true. You apologize or we're leaving."

"No. I won't."

"You are such a hateful person. God, I've only been here a few hours and I already want to kill you."

Alice raised her voice. "Do you know what I sacrificed to be a mother?"

"Oh, because you were going to be some great artist?" Kathleen shouted. "News flash, Mom, you really weren't that talented. None of us stopped you from becoming anything. That was a stupid childish dream like everyone has. Boo hoo, I never became an astronaut."

"Stop it," Maggie said softly. "You're being cruel."

Well, maybe so, but Kathleen had only been trying to protect her.

Kathleen turned to Ann Marie. "Thanks for butting in."

"I've been a part of this family for thirty-five years, in case you hadn't noticed," Ann Marie said.

"That's quite a claim to fame," Kathleen said. "Congrats."

"I don't ask for very much," Ann Marie said. "I'm here to take care of her all the time, while you're living out your strange boy-friend's dream in California. And for what? You've had it in for me since the day we met, admit it. You never thought I was good enough for your brother. You don't like the way I treat your mother. Well, she's all yours now. I wash my hands of this."

And with that, she stormed out of the house. They all watched her go. She got into the Mercedes and backed it out of the drive-way fast. Kathleen remembered now how up in Maine everyone left their keys in the car, a way to emphasize the safety of this place. Was it really such a burden to pull the keys out of your purse when you wanted to go some-where?

"Should she be driving?" Maggie asked.

"No," Kathleen said.

"I need a cocktail," Alice said. Then she smiled at Maggie. "Oh, *that's* why you haven't been drinking. Thank God."

The priest shifted awkwardly. "I'm so sorry if I've caused any trouble. Alice, should we talk about all of this later?"

Alice continued on like he had never spo-ken. "Well, I hope she'll come back so I can calm her down," she said, as if she were known for her calming influence. "Come along, Father. I'll walk you to your car. You've probably had enough of our family's insanity for one day. I'm sorry you had to witness that."

They walked off, and Kathleen said, "You must just be basking in the warmth of all the family support, huh?"

Maggie nodded. "That went better than I'd expected, actually." She paused. "Did you know about the house?"

"When do I ever know what Alice is up to?" Kathleen asked.

"Do you think she actually gave it to the church for real?"

Kathleen could see the worry in her daughter's face. Her only daughter, who she loved more than anyone. She hunched down, bending at her knees, so that she was facing Maggie's stomach. "You're coming into a very strange family, little one," she said. "Don't say I didn't warn you."

Maggie smiled and Kathleen wished it were that easy, that she could somehow just accept this, when she knew she couldn't. She wanted to tell Maggie she was grounded until she agreed to come to California and live there for as long as it took. But she told herself they could discuss it later. For now, they'd have something resembling peace.

"Will you let me take you to that restaurant?" Kathleen asked.

"Okay," Maggie said, looking forlornly toward her simmering pot of tomato sauce. She shut off the burner. "I guess we can have it tomorrow."

"Hurry up and let's run before Alice comes back."

"Mom, that's so mean."

"Oh, just come on."

When they returned home later that night, Ann Marie's car was back in the driveway. Either she and Alice had reconciled, or they had killed each other. Through the back bedroom window, Kathleen could see clear into Alice's den next door, but she couldn't make either of them out.

"So nice that the whole gang is here, bonding as much as ever," Kathleen said.

Maggie gave her a look, which Kathleen knew meant that she was at least partly to blame. Her daughter still wanted to be a Kelleher. Why?

She thought of her annual pre-Thanksgiving dinner in California. She held the party on the Tuesday before the holiday, for all her AA friends, and she cooked up a feast — two or three big turkeys, mashed potatoes, stuffing, homemade cranberry sauce, green beans. She bought pies at Kozlowski Farms, and everyone else brought a dish of their own. Maggie had come for the party a few times. They always stayed up telling stories and laughing all night. No one ever said a harsh word. For Kathleen, it was the highlight of the holiday season. Two days later, she'd be sitting in Ann Marie's living room, surrounded by her relatives, and she'd feel alien there, digging her fingernails into the arm of the sofa, willing herself back to that warm, friendly California house, full of her chosen family members.

The next morning, Kathleen woke early and went outside, barefoot, just as they had always done when they were young. She took note of Alice's garden, which she had to admit looked damn good. She would have to tell Arlo about it the next time they talked.

It was raining lightly, and she welcomed the rain, walking down to the beach with her face upturned.

She had forgotten that you experienced weather differently here. Rain and clouds were no longer an annoying distraction, but a welcome change in the atmosphere — a chance to curl up with a book and eat a grilled cheese sandwich by the window, and not get out of your pajamas all afternoon. Dampness hung in the air and clung to every surface. The waves lashed at the shoreline, getting frothy white and taller than any man, and everyone would go down to the beach and stand in awe as drops of water fell against their shoulders and the fog rolled in. Umbrellas seemed absurd.

Arlo would love this place. She wondered if it was sheer stubbornness that had made her never once even consider coming back.

In many ways, the past decade had been the happiest of her life, even though ten years earlier, she had lost her father and thought that she could not go on. But before long, she had met Arlo. Falling in love couldn't make up for what had happened; nothing could. But Arlo was her protector and her confidant, the same way Daniel had been. Sometimes she looked into Arlo's eyes and would swear she saw something of her father there. She wanted the same kind of love for Maggie.

After meeting Arlo, Kathleen had felt quite certain that her bad marriage and subsequent romantic disappointments had all led her to him. They were her blessings, disguised as burdens. Suppose she had stayed with Paul Doyle. By now, she'd be living on the south shore of Boston with a pickled liver, bickering daily, and probably up to two hundred pounds.

When Paul had an affair all those years ago, she had asked her father whether he thought Paul might somehow transform into a good husband.

"In my experience," he had said, "people can change, but most people don't."

He was right about Paul. But Kathleen had changed. At the age of thirty-nine, she reinvented herself, leaving a bad marriage, getting sober, finding meaningful work. She did it again at forty-nine when she met Arlo. She was fifty-eight now, so who knew what she'd do next? This was a life lesson she wished she had taught Maggie sooner — if you didn't like yourself, you could just become someone else. Of course, that wasn't exactly so when you had young children.

She wished Alice would understand this, too, but her mother was too far gone and bitter for life lessons. She'd rather just stew in it. She had certainly never had a suitor since Daniel's death, which in a way made Kathleen feel relieved.

It was strange to ponder, but Kathleen was fairly certain that her parents had actually been in love, right up until the end. At the top of Briarwood Road, her father had carved the initials *A.H.* into an old pine tree. (Kathleen had once drunkenly told her children that this tribute to her mother stood for Ass Hole.)

Alice's House. She imagined them young and in love when he did it, not a care in the world, just starting out and expecting life always to be perfect.

Kathleen heard footsteps behind her now. She clenched her hands. *Please let it be a brutal serial killer and not Ann Marie.*

She turned around.

"Hi," she said tersely.

"Good morning," her sister-in-law replied. "Do you know where Alice is? It seems early for her to be at church."

"I have no idea," Kathleen said. "You spent the night with her. Oh God, is this the beginning of your elaborate cover-up? You pretend you don't know where she is, but then we find the body in your trunk a week from now?"

"Stop that. I'm concerned."

She could see that yesterday's insanity was over, and Ann Marie had returned to her pod person self.

"I liked you better when you were acting nuts," Kathleen said. "Can I see some more of that?"

Ann Marie pursed her lips. "Let's try to be civil, okay? I'm sorry for how I acted. Pat will be here in a few days and you and Maggie will be leaving and we'll each have time to sort ourselves out."

Kathleen got a wicked thought in her head, the sort Maggie would say was childish and mean. She couldn't help it. "What makes you think we'll be leaving?"

Ann Marie's eyes grew big. "July first is in four days," she said.

"And?"

"And July is our month."

"Well, June is my month, and you're here now."

Ann Marie sounded panicked. "We've invited friends. It's going to be a full house, Kathleen. You can't just stay."

Kathleen grinned. "Watch me."

ALICE

Alice chose a table in the sun.

She assumed that's what Father Donnelly would pick, since given the choice, everyone always tended to want to sit outside. It seemed pointless to her in a setting like this — a busy Portland street, traffic flying by, smog in your pancakes. But when the waiter had asked, "Inside or out?" she immediately answered, "Out."

The one advantage was that she could smoke while she waited. It wasn't technically allowed, but no one had tried to stop her yet.

When Boston enacted the smoking ban a few years back, she had thought of her father, imagined him walking into a bar and being told to put out his cigarette. He would have been more likely to knock out the bartender. The older she got, the more she realized that while most girls grew up and turned into their mothers, she had become more like her father. Better to be an angry old bully than a passive little wimp, she supposed, though people were more inclined to pity the wimp. That seemed to be Ann Marie's approach.

The previous night, Father Donnelly had called and asked her to meet him for an early breakfast before Mass. He wanted to talk about the house, he said; he had some concerns. She couldn't shake the feeling of being sent to the principal's office: *Alice Brennan, did you steal the new pastels? Absolutely not, Sister Florence. I haven't a clue how they landed in my pocket.*

They usually ate somewhere close to home, but Alice had chosen this place — the closest thing Maine had to an anonymous city, far enough away from Briarwood Road, as if to distance herself from yesterday's mortifying scene. She had gotten used to Father Donnelly's company these past few months. She was furious with herself for how she had acted in front of him, how they all had acted.

Ann Marie had behaved as though Alice was robbing her of her ancestral home, and Alice had seen in Father Donnelly's eyes that he felt pity for her daughter-in-law. She hoped she could make him understand the reason for her decision.

They were meeting at eight, but she had intentionally arrived early. Now she drank her tea and looked out over the crowded sidewalk, hoping to see him first. He was such a polite young man, so sweet and understanding. He was probably scandalized by what had gone on at her house the day before. In a way, whatever he had to say would be a welcome distraction set against her family's problems.

Maggie was pregnant. Kathleen had accused Alice of not caring because of some lack of interest in the girl. But honestly, it wasn't that. It was the nerve of Maggie, coming to her home, stirring up the pot, asking questions about Alice and failing to mention her own circumstances. And all right, yes, it would have been more shocking coming from Fiona or Patty. Maggie was Kathleen's daughter, after all. There wasn't much she could do in the way of poor decision making to shock Alice.

Alice had enjoyed the past few weeks with her granddaughter. She may have gone a bit far calling Maggie a tramp, especially in front of the priest. That was one of the moments when she could actually feel Daniel looking down from Heaven, disapproving of her.

Ann Marie seemed convinced that Kathleen had come to persuade Maggie to have an abortion. If that was true, Alice might just be done with her daughter, once and for all. It sickened her that Kathleen would even think of it. Alice thought the only logical action for Maggie to take now was to marry Gabe. He wasn't all that bad when you got down to it. He was handsome, he came from money. He seemed to make her laugh.

547

Alice took a sip of tea. She felt exhausted. She had spent a long, hard night with her daughter-in-law, regretting ever having invited Ann Marie to bunk with her in the first place, regretting asking her to come back once she drove away.

And afterward, she was up thinking of what she'd say here this morning.

After their fight the previous day, after Ann Marie sped off, Alice had walked Father Donnelly to his car (calmly, as if to offset Ann Marie's insane behavior). She apologized. She couldn't stop talking. She didn't want him to leave with a bad taste in his mouth. When he had left, she thought she might talk some sense into Maggie. But once she got back to the house, she found Maggie and Kathleen gone. Shortly thereafter, she watched them drive off somewhere. Alice sat alone for a bit, thinking about it all and sulking.

Ann Marie had told Kathleen that Alice was her responsibility now, as if Alice were some drooling old invalid. It was an unforgivable thing to say, not to mention highly out of character for Ann Marie. She was in trouble with her daughter-in-law, that much was clear. But Ann Marie was such a big softie. How long could she possibly stay angry? Alice needed her, especially now, with Kathleen lurking around.

Eventually, she had called Ann Marie on

her cell phone.

"Where are you?" Alice asked.

"In Portsmouth. I stopped off for a minute, but I'm heading home to Patrick now."

"Don't go," Alice said. "Come on back here and let's have a glass of wine and calm down. Can't we laugh about this?"

"No," Ann Marie said.

"Please, darling. I can't have you angry with me. Especially after Kathleen just shows up, and considering this terrible news of Maggie's. I'm hysterical; I'm afraid something awful will happen if you don't come back."

She began to cry the sort of crocodile tears she had used on her mother as a kid, whenever she wanted to get out of some unpleasant chore, or when one of her brothers caught her snooping in his desk and wanted an explanation.

There had been a long pause before Ann Marie said, "Fine. Do you need anything from Ruby's? I'm going to stop for paper towels on the way back."

When Ann Marie walked in a while later smelling faintly of booze and something Alice could swear was men's cologne, she stiffly apologized for being so cruel, but said she was still very upset. Alice told her it was all right.

"I can't believe you sold the house," Ann Marie said.

"Donated it," Alice said calmly.

"I can't believe this."

"Yes, you mentioned that."

"Well?" Ann Marie had said.

"Well, what?" Alice said.

"Is there any explanation?"

Alice felt indignant, though she tried to suppress it. Who did Ann Marie think she was, demanding to know? How was it any of her business? Of course, there was a damn good explanation, but all the same, if she told her children they would only try to talk her out of it. She attempted to sound jovial, but she felt like telling Ann Marie to get the hell out.

"Calm down," she said. "At this rate, you'll be choking on your own tongue in a minute. Now look. The church doesn't get a thing until I croak, and you know mean old creatures like me live forever. By the time I go, that dashing son of yours will have made millions and bought you ten beach houses better than this dump."

Ann Marie didn't crack a smile. "I'm a good person, Alice. I don't deserve this."

Alice paused. "I know you're a good person. What I don't know is where Maggie and Kathleen have gone, but shall we boil up some spaghetti to go with that sauce for just us two?"

"Sure," Ann Marie said glumly.

After that, they didn't talk about the house. They spoke about Maggie's situation and

Ann Marie said she was furious — about that. Then they turned on PBS and pretended to be engrossed in a fairly bland production of *Pride and Prejudice,* which they had both watched in full only a month earlier.

The phone rang every hour or so, and Alice glanced at the display screen to see the number. Each time, it was Patrick on the line, and each time she ignored it.

"Go ahead and pick it up," Ann Marie said.

Clearly, she had asked him to do her bidding.

"No, I think I'll let it ring through," Alice said. "It's probably one of those lousy telemarketers calling from India."

The waiter came over with a basket of bread. Alice asked him for a Bloody Mary. The place was filling up. It would be rude to hold the table without ordering something besides tea. When he walked off, she unfolded the cloth napkin in the basket and pulled out three tiny jars of jam, which she promptly shoved into her purse. A moment later she gestured toward a busboy and said, "Could I get some jam, please?"

"Certainly, ma'am," he said.

A driver leaned on his horn, giving her a start. That got a few other drivers going, and soon the whole street was an ugly symphony of honks and shouts. She never came this far north anymore, even though she could remember darting around these streets as a younger woman, ducking in and out of shops with Rita in tow. Nowadays she couldn't always trust her eyesight. She had had to squint at the road signs all along 95 on her way here, especially near home, where it was misty and gray.

Alice felt a hand on her shoulder.

"Hi, there," Father Donnelly said. "Thanks for meeting me."

He looked as handsome as ever. He was wearing his collar. A couple of youngsters in suits at the next table stared. Had they never seen a priest before? Alice was embarrassed that she'd chosen this place. She hoped he didn't notice them.

She straightened up in her chair, turning her head. "I wasn't sure if you'd want to sit outside or in. We could move inside if you like."

"This is fine," he said. "This is lovely."

He sat down across from her. "How are you doing?"

"I've been better," she said.

He nodded. "I'm sure yesterday took a lot out of you."

"Yes. Once again, please let me say how sorry I am that you had to see all that. I, for one, am so embarrassed about how I acted."

He shook his head. "Not at all. Sometimes these things happen in families."

The waiter came by with the extra jam, and

filled the priest's cup with coffee. Father Donnelly paused, waiting for the young man to leave.

"Alice, I thought you'd told your children," he said a moment later. "And while I'm eternally grateful even for the thought, I'm starting to have reservations about accepting the house. I don't want to be the cause of strife."

"Don't be silly," she said.

"Your daughter-in-law seemed beside herself yesterday. I'm sorry that it had to come out that way, but —"

"My daughter-in-law is the hysterical type," Alice said. "Always has been."

"I'm confused about why you haven't discussed this with anyone," he said.

"They'll get used to it," she said.

"Well, that's what I mean. I'm not sure I feel right about that."

"It was a momentary shock for Ann Marie," she said. "But believe me, none of them value the place."

"Even so," he said.

"When you get old like me, you'll start to view your life as a whole," she said. "You'll see the things you did right, the things you made a mess of. I've always tried to do right, Father, but usually I muck it up somehow or another. Just look."

"At what?"

"Look at my children, for starters."

"I think you've raised a wonderful family, Alice. I've enjoyed getting to spend some time with Maggie these past few weeks."

"Maggie's pregnant," she said. "Kathleen hates me and so does my other daughter, Clare. Ann Marie only ever tolerated me because she wanted my house."

"That's not true," he said. "As for Maggie —"

She interrupted him. "Please. I can't talk about that now."

"Can I ask you a question?" he asked, and she nodded. "Why did you decide to give your house to the church in the first place? It wasn't to get back at anyone, was it?"

"Absolutely not," she said. She felt embarrassed that he would even think so.

"Then why?"

"That church is incredibly important to me," she said. "I gave a lot of thought to what you said about good deeds back when I called you about my sister last winter. This is a small way for me to atone. I know it's nothing, compared to my sin, but —"

"Alice, you can't blame yourself," he said. "There's no sin here. It was a fire. You had gone home before it even started."

"That's just it," she said softly. "There's a part I left out. If I tell it to you now, here, will you consider it a confession?"

"If you like," he said.

Alice knew she would only ever manage the

courage to say it once. For that reason, she wanted her brothers to hear it, but they were gone. She wanted Daniel, but he was gone too. As she heard herself begin to tell the priest the truth, in a way she felt like she was confessing to them all. She pictured Mary, twenty-four years old for the rest of time.

"I didn't go home," she said quietly. "That's what everyone always thought — even my husband — but I was there all along. I'm the reason Mary was in the club when it burned."

He looked confused, as if he was unsure of whether she was telling the truth.

"There was this blasted pair of gloves, and I refused to go inside to get them because I was angry about Henry proposing. Not that I should have been, but —" She stopped herself. "I'm not making any sense, am I?"

He gave her his warmest smile. "Take your time," he said.

Alice felt all riled up. Her heart pounded. She took a deep breath and started again. This time she told him everything. It surprised her how well she remembered exactly what she and Mary had said to each other, precisely how she felt watching her sister go back in to fetch her precious suede gloves. The high-pitched moan of the fire alarm.

As the words came out of her mouth, she was back on that frigid Boston sidewalk, immersed in chaos, taking in the sight of the dead and wounded, too fearful to do a thing for Mary, who lay dying on the other side of a plain stucco wall.

She recalled walking into her parents' living room and feeling filled up with relief at the sight of her brothers. And then, moments later, how she had told them that Mary was inside the club, though that was as much as she could bear to admit.

She spoke of how little she had felt for Daniel then, how cold she had been to him. But how his presence after the fact seemed like a way out of the horror and a means of living a more virtuous life.

She confessed that she had never told Daniel the truth about that night, never told a soul.

Father Donnelly was too young to remember that the Cocoanut Grove fire had remained a fixture in the Boston papers and in common conversation for years after it happened. She told him how she had devoured the stories, though they always made her morose, and Daniel warned her not to read or listen to them.

After she read about a victim, she could never forget. She carried all of them with her. A family in Wilmington lost four sons, all servicemen home on leave. They were buried side by side in Wildwood Cemetery. Girls who worked with Alice at the law firm, who'd never even met them, would go to their graves and visit every Saturday morning.

A twenty-year-old member of the Coast Guard named Clifford Johnson suffered burns over three-quarters of his body while helping twenty people to safety. He spent almost two years in Boston City Hospital. After hundreds of operations, he married his nurse and returned home to Missouri. In 1956, he was killed in a fire.

Each time she read one of the stories, Alice thought of her last words to Mary, and the look on her sister's face that night.

You shouldn't have gone to bed with him, she had said, planting fear in her own sister's head when she knew full well that Henry intended to propose.

She had allowed Mary to believe that Henry didn't want her, and because of something she had done. Perhaps it was the last thought Mary ever had. And now she would never know the truth.

When she finished talking, Alice looked across the table at Father Donnelly as if he were a stranger. She felt utterly exposed. She had thought of all of this over and over these past sixty years, but never said it out loud. Had it been worth it? She certainly didn't feel any better.

Her hands shook, and she had to place them in her lap.

Until now, it had been between her and God, and she had assumed that His wrath would be strong, which was all that she deserved. But the priest looked as if he might cry. She could swear she saw tears in his eyes.

He shook his head. "Oh, Alice, I'm so sorry."

"Sorry?"

"Here you've been, carrying this around all these years for no reason. You didn't do anything wrong."

"Of course I did."

He reached across the table and placed a hand on top of hers.

"I'm concerned that this still brings you so much torment," he said. "And you've never thought of talking it over with your children?"

What could she possibly tell her children about all of this? That her only sister had died just a few hours shy of her engagement? That the event was a tragedy, but everyone always said that it led to new fire codes across the country and innovations in burn treatment? That you'd never find a door in Boston that opened inward, or a revolving door anywhere that wasn't flanked by two regular doors, because of it?

That she had not met her husband's eye across a crowded room and fallen in love like in the movies, but rather, that she had seen him as a means of escape? That her sister had died because of Alice's stubbornness and anger, two things she could never let go of, even so, even now.

"No," she said.

"It might be a great comfort," he said. "They'd tell you the same things I'm saying here, I know they would."

She wondered if he hadn't understood. He was young, as young as some of her grandchildren, and maybe that made all the difference. Even though he was a priest, he wasn't one in the old sense of the word. He didn't believe in fire and brimstone. He probably didn't even believe in Hell. She wanted someone harsher here, someone to take a Brillo pad to her sins and scrub until she bled.

"I killed my sister," she said.

"No, Alice!" he said. He inhaled deeply. "Here's something to think about. You told me at your house last winter that before your sister died you never intended to marry or have children."

She thought of what Kathleen had said the day before — *you really weren't that talented . . . a stupid childish dream.* It was similar to something Daniel had said the night they met.

He went on. "Mary's death was a great loss. But consider how much joy — how many lives have come into being because of it. And because of you."

She felt uneasy with this sweetsy mumbo jumbo. If she had wanted positive affirmations that she was worthy and good, she'd be paying some cheerleader by the hour the way

Kathleen did.

"After she died, I promised God that I'd do better. I put all of my childish hopes away and tried, for Mary's sake, to do everything she would have done. But I failed miserably. My children don't respect me. They don't even have faith in God. It should have been me that died that night."

"You're being much too hard on yourself," he said.

"Please don't try to make me feel better," she said. "It's not what I'm after."

"What are you after?"

"I want to die in as close to a state of grace as I can," she said. "So that I can see my husband and sister again."

He shook his head. "I'll grant you an indulgence here and now if that will help, Alice. You don't have to give away your family's home for that."

"An indulgence comes from devoting oneself or one's goods to those in need," she said, snapping at him the way she might have at one of her children. "You can't just give it to me."

"Alice. If this whole thing is motivated by guilt, I can't accept it in good faith. You know that."

"It's not guilt," she said. "Giving you the house is my last chance to do something meaningful. It's too late for anything else."

She thought of St. Agnes, her comfy old

church in Canton, which was set to be demolished with a wrecking ball in the fall. How had she let that happen? Not since the months and years following Mary's death had she spent so many sleepless nights wondering how something so beloved could simply slip through her fingers like water.

"Understand the property is mine and no one else's," she said sternly. "Whatever hysteria you may have witnessed yesterday, no one loves the place more than I do. But let me be clear. I would burn that house to the ground today if it meant that St. Michael's could still stand. If it wasn't for the Church, I probably wouldn't have made it. I probably wouldn't be sitting here now. I don't even want to think of a world where people won't have that sort of thing in their lives."

He nodded. "I appreciate that. I just want to make sure you're doing this for the right reasons."

"It's done and it won't be undone," she said. "I gave it plenty of thought before I signed the papers."

"Well, then, I thank you again," he said. "Your kind of generosity is rare in this world, Alice. You're going to be the key to our survival."

She thought of an afternoon a few weeks earlier, when she had stood beside him in a hospital room, watching as he read a dying man his last rites. The man had been so truly comforted by it. She wished her children could understand that sort of power. She thought that perhaps she was being too hard on Father Donnelly this morning.

"I think you're the key," she said, and she felt more confident in her decision than ever.

MAGGIE

The morning after the fight, Maggie woke up to find her mother and Ann Marie sitting out on the deck, drinking tea. It must have rained earlier — here and there were pools of water on the wood, drying up in the hot morning sun. Kathleen was reading the paper and Ann Marie appeared to be gluing tiny buttons onto squares of blue fabric. For a moment, Maggie thought that perhaps a miracle had occurred and the two of them were getting along. If that was the case, she would swear right now that peace in the Middle East would be achieved in her lifetime.

But as soon as she slid the screen door open and said good morning, Kathleen looked up from her paper and said, "Mags, there's this amazing story about Whitey Bulger in today's *Globe*. You've got to read it."

Whitey Bulger was an Irish mobster from Southie who had risen to power mainly because of a shady relationship with the FBI. His brother had gone the other way — at-

563

tending law school and eventually becoming president of the Massachusetts state senate. They had grown up in the same neighborhood as Ann Marie; her brother was once some sort of low-level criminal in Whitey Bulger's gang. Kathleen loved mentioning anything vaguely related to this fact when Ann Marie was around, simply because she knew it would embarrass her.

Now Kathleen said, "Did you realize Whitey Bulger had a child? It says here that the little boy died of some rare disorder and that's part of what made Whitey and his boys so vicious. Fascinating, huh?"

Ann Marie had been smiling seconds earlier, but now she looked at her lap.

Maggie hated it when her mother went into bully mode. She shot her a look.

What? Kathleen mouthed, as if she had no clue what she had done.

This exchange, like so many other things lately, reminded Maggie of Gabe, even though it had nothing to do with him, really. Maggie had been obsessed with the Bulgers as a kid; she assumed everyone knew who they were. But when she mentioned them to Gabe once, he had laughed so hard that beer came out of his nostrils.

"What's so funny?" she had asked.

"Whitey Bulger?" he said, incredulous. "That sounds like something a frat boy would name his dick."

Kathleen put her bare feet up on a plastic cooler that had probably been sitting there since the previous August.

"Do you feel like going to the diner for breakfast?" she asked.

Maggie was famished, but she wasn't sure she wanted to be alone with her mother. She felt annoyed that Kathleen had come, and mad at herself for being annoyed. She kept trying to shake the feeling, but truly, it had been better here without her.

Kathleen wanted her to move to California. Each time they were alone, she brought it up. It was a preposterous idea, though Maggie wondered if it rubbed her the wrong way because she knew it was a real possibility. She was consumed by fears of not having enough money — in New York, she still struggled just to support herself. What if she couldn't afford this child, and actually had to move in with her mother? There she'd be, raising a kid alone, in the shadow of Kathleen's goofball hippie boyfriend and his worm farm; in the shadow of Kathleen herself, who would never be able to stop reminding Maggie of how little she wanted a baby around.

"Aunt Ann Marie?" she asked now. "The diner?"

"Oh, no, not for me, thanks, sweetie," Ann Marie said. "I'm trying to slim down for Fourth of July week."

"Why?" Kathleen asked. "You want to wow

Patrick with your hot bikini bod?"

Ann Marie looked down at her buttons again.

"What are you doing over there anyway?" Kathleen asked.

"I'm making a slipcover."

"For?"

"A couch."

"She's a finalist in this really prestigious house decorating competition," Maggie said.

"Yes," Ann Marie said. "Pat and I are going to London for the judging."

Kathleen stretched out her leg, pointed her toes. "House decorating?"

"Small-scale house decorating models." Ann Marie looked flustered. It seemed like maybe she was just making up terms now.

"Dollhouses," Maggie said, and before her mother could get a word in she continued, "It's so cool. There was an entire exhibition of them at the Brooklyn Museum recently. Amazing stuff."

Kathleen looked at Maggie. "So go throw some clothes on and I'll buy you breakfast, just the two of us."

"I'd love to, but I have to do some work stuff," Maggie said.

"Are you avoiding me?" Kathleen asked in a joking tone, though Maggie knew her well enough to know she was dead serious. It wasn't even the first time she'd said it in the last twenty-four hours.

They had gone to dinner the night before and then been trapped in the cottage together until they went to bed. Her mother had had plenty of time to lay out her absurd plan: Maggie should move to wine country and raise her child in the healthy surroundings of a teetotaler's worm farm. Delightful! Maggie didn't say that she thought Kathleen's lifestyle was odd, or that visiting for a week was enough to put her over the edge. She didn't say that Kathleen's house was so damn filthy she'd be afraid to raise a hamster in it, let alone a child. Maggie understood how to hold back.

Kathleen, however, had come in with guns blazing — with accusations and harsh words about Gabe, all of which might be true, but they still hurt. No one could ever injure Maggie with words the way her own mother could; that was just a fact. She'd rather not hear it, especially after the e-mail she had received from Gabe.

"Where's Alice?" she asked now.

"We don't know," Kathleen said.

"Do you mind if I ask what happened with the house?" Maggie said.

Ann Marie shook her head. "I'm so angry, I can barely talk about it."

She didn't seem angry. She sounded like her usual chipper self.

Ann Marie went on, "Alice has signed this

567

entire property over to St. Michael's in her will."

Maggie felt stunned. "When did this happen?"

"Apparently the papers were drawn up six months ago. But Pat's looking into whether we have a legal right to somehow undo it. We built that house next door, you know."

"Oh, we know," Kathleen said.

Ann Marie ignored her. "We must have some legal right to the place. Anyway, Pat told me to stay calm while he sorts it out with the lawyers. So that's what I'm trying to do."

Ann Marie smiled. Maggie wondered if maybe she was one of those women whose extreme agreeableness had to do with some sort of massive addiction to pills.

"The whole thing is classic Alice," Kathleen said. "I wish my dad were here."

The painful memory of her grandfather's funeral returned to Maggie then. Her uncle Patrick had given the eulogy. Chris and Little Daniel said the Prayers of the Faithful from the altar, reading aloud sheepishly like schoolkids. Chris's voice cracked as he said, "That we might *con*sole one another in our time of grief, just as Jesus needed *con*soling upon the death of Lazarus."

"Lord, hear our prayer," the congregation replied robotically, and Maggie thought of how Chris had pronounced the word *console* like he meant a cabinet where you store electronics, as if Jesus were a fifty-inch TV requiring a place to sit and collect dust.

They always turned to the men for strength in these moments, perhaps because they looked so invincible in their suits. The men pulled the cars around to the front of the church and dropped their wives and daughters off so they didn't have to walk from the parking lot; the men carried the casket up the stairs from the hearse. But in the end, it always fell to the women to do the hard work of putting everything back together again.

The choir sang "Ave Maria" as the gifts were brought up to the altar. Everyone wept. It was the sort of song that made you remember it all, your whole life a movie montage full of people who moved you deeply, and then were gone. She thought her mother must be crying to think of herself as a sort of orphan now.

Maggie cried for Daniel. She cried for the fear of ever losing Kathleen, and the fact that they would probably never have a perfect understanding between them, though there was love so strong it suffocated.

At the cemetery, there was an American flag draped over the coffin. The crowd of mourners stood still and silent as two young servicemen in uniform played a recording of "Taps" on a boom box, and then folded the flag into smaller and smaller triangles, snapping it taut with each turn. One of them presented the flag to Alice and said, "On behalf of a grateful nation, I present this flag as a token of our appreciation for the faithful and selfless service of your loved one for this country."

Maggie realized that she had never heard Daniel talk about the war.

She looked out into the swarm of faces as a priest led them in prayer, and thought that these Catholic customs, which were morbid in a way, served their purpose even so: let no one leave this world alone. There was still the question of who would come later. Who would visit Daniel's grave when it was bitter cold, or when his birthday arrived each year. One noticed in these cemeteries that certain graves were more tended to than others, that some were always heaped with fresh flowers. Maggie wondered whether these were the people who had been the most beloved in life, or the least. She imagined it could go either way.

Now, here in the cottage with her mother and aunt, she thought of the baby in her belly. She would have a life — a childhood, an awkward adolescence, a marriage and kids, like anyone — and then this baby too would die, and her grandchildren sitting in the church pews would probably not know Maggie, at least not as anything more than their feeble old great-grandmother. Kathleen would be someone they'd heard about in a story once, maybe.

Maggie heard tires on the road, and she craned her neck to see the plain brown top of a delivery truck coming toward the cottage. A moment later there was a knock from the screen porch, and all three of them went out to investigate. This was the sort of thing that happened when you were at the beach. There was something quaint about it. Back home, where televisions and cell phones and computers were all going at once, who would care enough to even get off the couch and answer the door to see what the UPS man had brought if someone else was already up?

All they could see was a pair of legs in brown shorts and hiked-up socks. The rest of him was obscured by an enormous cardboard box. His arms stretched out as far as they would reach.

"A delivery for Ann Marie Kelleher," he said from behind the box.

Ann Marie scurried toward him, opening the porch door.

"Oh, thank you! Please put it down right here. Gently, please!"

Kathleen rolled her eyes.

Ann Marie signed a piece of paper he held forth, attached to a clipboard.

"Have a nice day, ladies," he said, and was gone.

The three of them stood there for a moment, staring at the box.

"Is it a pony?" Kathleen asked.

"It's my dollhouse," Ann Marie said. She could not hide her joy, even if she wanted to. Maggie thought it was sweet. Her mother was into worms, for God's sake; couldn't she understand what it meant to have a silly passion?

"I'll just run to the kitchen to get a knife," Ann Marie continued, and then disappeared into the cottage.

"Oh God," Kathleen said. "A knife? I hope she's not planning to injure herself, having just realized how pathetic it is to be a grown woman with a dollhouse."

"Mom —"

"What?"

Ann Marie returned and sliced through the thick brown packing tape before pulling back the box flaps. They all gazed inside, where a miniature brick house was nestled in a sea of green foam peanuts. Maggie held the box down as her aunt slid the house out and rested it on the floor.

"Oh, it's beautiful," Ann Marie said. "It's even prettier than the picture."

It was rather lovely, the kind of thing that could stoke your imagination and make you believe that you belonged on an English hillside somewhere, raising sheep and reading poetry and permanently deleting your e-mail account. Maybe Maggie would get into dollhouses too after the baby came. She and Ann Marie could open a shop in Brooklyn. After all, it was every New Yorker's dream to own a home and most of them never would — perhaps this was the next best thing.

"I have to take a photo to send to Patty!" Ann Marie said. "My camera's in the car."

When she left to retrieve it, Kathleen leaned inquisitively over the dollhouse, tipping her mug until a thin stream of clear yellow tea poured onto the roof.

"Whoops," she said in a singsongy voice.

"What the hell is wrong with you?" Maggie asked. She quickly wiped up the spill with the bottom of her T-shirt.

"Oh, relax, it's herbal. It won't stain."

Maggie shook her head.

"Why are you so mad at me?" Kathleen asked. "Look, I'm sorry for getting us off on the wrong foot yesterday. It's just that I was worried about you for all those days and I couldn't get through. As soon as we were alone together, I just went for it."

There was really no sense in Kathleen apologizing, since she would only do the same thing again and again. There was an elasticity to their bond. Its limits were often stretched beyond comfort, but it always returned, unbroken.

I came here to stop you from making a huge mistake. That's how she had put it, and the words had crushed Maggie. She was annoyed at herself over the fact that she still wanted to please her mother so much. This had only gotten harder as she became an adult with a totally different set of values from Kathleen's.

"It's fine," Maggie said.

"Why don't we get away from this toxic environment? We could go to Boston and check into a hotel and have a mother-daughter getaway," Kathleen said.

"Nah. I need to get some work done. I'm officially back on the clock with *Till Death*."

"Oh," Kathleen said, clearly hurt.

"Not to mention, I have to write an online dating profile for a fairly unattractive woman with two toy poodles, whose interests include manicures, Pilates, and the Bee Gees. And she wants me to work in the fact that she has problems around jealousy."

She had said it to make Kathleen smile, but her mother said flatly, "Sounds like a real catch."

"Obviously I need to save my pennies," Maggie said.

"Right. Unless you take me up on my offer and come to the farm."

Maggie ignored the comment. "I think I'll go next door to Grandma's house, since it's just sitting there empty."

Kathleen didn't answer. Instead she said, "You and I have always told each other everything."

It was true. While Maggie knew that it wasn't the healthiest way to be, it was the only way they had ever been, and she believed it came from a place of love.

"I know."

"So how could you not tell me this?"

"I did tell you. You're the first person I told, other than Gabe."

Maggie decided to leave Rhiannon out of it.

"But how long have you known?"

"A month and a half."

"Oh, Maggie. The thought of you having to keep it to yourself. I wish you had come out to California right away. I'd like to think that's what you would have done in a situation like this. Not come here, to Maine, with all the family drama."

Maggie felt a mix of frustration and pity. Before she could stop herself, she said, "Until yesterday, there really wasn't much drama."

"So it's my fault."

"I didn't mean that."

"You know how proud I am of you, and how much I love you, no matter what," Kathleen said. "Sometimes I wonder why you feel such a sense of loyalty to this family. None of these people give a crap about us. It makes me so sad to see you let down by them, over and over again. Just like I've always been. When I think of what Alice said to you yesterday —"

Maggie had forgotten her mother's ability to turn every conversation about their extended family back to herself, and the ways in which she had been slighted by them. She had begun to make inroads with Alice and Ann Marie these past few weeks, and maybe it was stupid, but she felt happy about that. She knew her mother wanted the best for her. But she also knew this was one thing Kathleen could never let her have.

"No one's letting me down," Maggie said. She straightened up and lifted her computer bag off the table, carefully placing the strap on her shoulder. She muttered, "My boobs are killing me."

Kathleen nodded. "Right on schedule. They're getting bigger, too, you know."

"They are?"

"Yeah. I thought you'd had implants for a second when I saw you yesterday."

"Well, maybe that's what I'll tell people," Maggie said. "I'll be back."

And with that, she carried her laptop next door.

Each time she had opened her e-mail for the past four days, she told herself not to read the message from Gabe. And each time, she read it anyway.

When it arrived in her in-box and she saw his name there, just reflexively she got goose bumps, as if they had been out on one magnificent date and she was waiting to see if he would call her again.

But by then, she was already certain about what was to come. She was going to raise this child on her own. It was scary and sometimes sad, but she could do it. Women did it all the time. In some vague way, she had always pictured herself as a single mother. Maybe just because she had grown up with one.

Mags, I'm sorry to have taken this long to reply. Ever since I read your e-mail, I've been thinking about you and the baby and what I should do. I even went out one afternoon and looked at engagement rings in a panic. I was literally sweating on the jewelry case. But if I'm being honest with us both, the simple fact is I can't do this right now, at this point in my life. I don't know what the future holds — maybe I'll grow up one of these days. When you're back in the city, let's have coffee. I'm sorry. Love, Gabe

It was classic Gabe, exactly what she should have expected: Sorry I can't be a man and a father to our child, but hey, let me buy you a latte.

Maggie understood why he couldn't do it. Still, she felt like she was mourning the loss of something she had never had in the first place. In a different world, she might have been more trusting and he might have been trustworthy. She got that. But part of her missed him. She would never understand why logic couldn't conquer something as simple and commonplace as love.

Maggie sat down in Alice's kitchen now and decided not to turn on her computer just yet. She put in a call to the police department in a town called Tulip, Texas, where a bitter former prom queen had shot her cheating husband to death. It said a lot that this was a more soothing activity than going to breakfast with her mother.

"Can I speak to your press office please?" she said, fairly sure what the response would be.

"Our *what?*"

"Your press office. Public affairs?"

"Hold, please."

The hold music began. A country singer belted out that if given the chance, she hoped someone (her child?) would dance. It was some smarmy shit, but even so, Maggie felt a tickle in her throat. She sighed. She could not stand herself when she got like this, too cozy with her sorrow.

For the last several weeks she had thought about the horrors of giving birth, and all the terrible things that could happen to a baby, and how she could ever afford this, and whether maybe Gabe might show up in the final act and rescue her, having become another man entirely. But now she feared something else. It was about the way Alice and Kathleen and Ann Marie had all fussed

578

over her and what she would do next. Maggie was still a blank slate — childless, unmarried, and therefore yet to begin it. After this baby was born, she would never be that way again. She would cross to the other half of life, in which you yourself are no longer watched over, not in the same way. She couldn't take to her bed whenever she felt like it or allow herself to completely self-destruct.

That's what her own mother had done from time to time, and Alice as well, but Maggie couldn't; she wouldn't.

Sometimes she thought she would have been better off procreating at twenty-two than thirty-two. Back then, she had thought she wanted four or five kids someday. She was still young and dumb enough to think it possible. Maybe that's how mothers like Ann Marie were made — they plunged headlong into the whole endeavor before they knew any better. They weren't selfish or greedy with their time because as adults they had never spent several Saturdays in a row lying in bed watching Meg Ryan movies on cable. They had never passed an entire weekend indoors, just because they felt like it.

From everything she read online, Maggie had gathered that it was sort of in vogue for mothers to complain about their kids — there were entire websites devoted to mourning the objects and body parts their children had destroyed; there were Mommies Who Drink groups that met weekly in Brooklyn bars; there were forums where women could record every last grievance — every drop of apple juice spilled on the carpet, every time the nanny showed up five minutes late, every hideous temper tantrum that made them consider running away. They claimed they were miserable, and seemed pleased with themselves for admitting it. But then why have children at all? Maybe this sort of over-sharing was healthy set against generations of repressed American housewives, brightly smiling through the slog. But Maggie wondered if in some ways all the complaining only made matters worse.

She was still on hold. Now the country singer was telling her that living might mean taking chances but they're worth takin'. Lovin' might be a mistake but it's worth makin'.

She hung up the phone and put her head down on her grandmother's kitchen table. After a short while, she thought she heard footsteps out on the gravel path that led from the cottage. She felt certain it was Kathleen, so she picked up the phone again and held it to her ear, pretending to be mid-conversation.

Good Lord, had it come to this?

No one entered the house. When Maggie peeked out the window, she saw only two rabbits eating the grass.

"Thank you. Good-bye," she said to the imaginary person at the other end of the line, just in case someone was watching.

Maggie breathed in the mix of pine trees and salty air through the screen. June was almost over. Soon she would have to leave.

She could hardly picture going back to Brooklyn, to that same old apartment on Cranberry Street. She imagined that in some ways her life would be exactly as it had been — each morning she would sit by the window, watching the early commuters hustle down into the subway with their paper cups of steaming coffee. She'd admire the buff and energetic woman in spandex who always did her push-ups and step-ups on the bench across the road while she waited for the bus. But in other ways, everything would be different, unimaginably so.

Here in Cape Neddick, her life had quickly taken on a new rhythm — Gabe and Rhiannon and Allegra and her officemates had been replaced by Alice and Ann Marie and Connor. Less than a month had passed since she left, and already she felt like her city muscles were gone. In Maine, there was enough space to spread out. But in New York, you were surrounded by strangers all the time, living right on top of them. On the subway, the odors of their perfume and their sweat and their piss and their lunch all mingled together. They read over your shoulder, and while you might

581

find this annoying, you couldn't say much, because the truth was you were likely to do the same to them — you were all curious creatures.

Every day the city broke her heart: each morning she saw homelessness, illness, cruelty, right there in front of her. The brutality would sometimes spring forth from nowhere. Standing on the platform at Grand Central Terminal, waiting for the 6 train to arrive, she had once watched a young black man punch an old white man in the face, knocking him to the ground. The old man had said a hateful word that Maggie herself had never uttered, never would, but she still saw the young one as the coward.

She had watched mothers yank their children hard by the arm and yell at them to quit dropping crumbs or to hurry up. On other mornings, she watched the same mothers play twelve rounds of pat-a-cake with real delight in their eyes.

When she found herself crying on an East Village street after midnight, several people she had never met stopped to ask, "Are you okay?" as concerned as if they were her blood. When a guy grabbed her purse uptown one cloudy afternoon, she screamed for help, but no one turned and looked.

Everything, good and bad, was so much more predictable here. She wished she could stay. She imagined scenarios: Perhaps she could get a job cleaning at St. Michael's, picking up the rice in the church after a wedding, Eleanor Rigby style. Or she could write a best seller and become one of those novelists whose bio makes you swell with jealousy — *The author splits her time between Maine and Bruges.*

She wished she could stay until the baby came, at least.

It was impossible to believe that soon the house would be gone too. Maggie wondered if it was really going to happen. Had Alice actually signed away their rights to the place they all loved most? She had envisioned bringing her baby here, coming here until she herself was an old woman.

Kathleen had often said that Ann Marie and Pat made it clear that they wanted Alice dead sooner rather than later, so the house could be theirs. Was it possible she had done this on purpose so they would all have to want her to live forever instead? Maggie couldn't think of any other reason.

Ann Marie believed that Connor had somehow conned Alice, but Maggie knew to her core that that was impossible. He was a good man, an honest priest. (Leave it to her to develop a crush on someone who was already taken by Jesus Christ, but there you had it.) A recently dumped pregnant woman could spot a truly decent man from a hundred miles away.

A while later, Maggie decided to take a break from her research and walk up Briarwood Road. She tried to absorb the stillness, to focus on the sunlight coming through the pine trees and the birds chirping overhead. At the end, she looked back to see the cottage and the house in the distance, with the ocean glittering right behind.

She turned onto Shore Road, and a Jeep whizzed by, a surfboard standing straight up in the passenger seat. Eventually, she came to Ruby's Market, and she went inside to get a bottle of juice.

The place reeked of bleach.

"How are you today?" Ruby asked politely.

"Good, thank you, and you?"

"Fine."

Maggie walked toward the cooler in the back as Mort came down the aisle in near-limbo posture, struggling under the weight of a crate full of glass milk bottles. She felt like she ought to help him, but she wasn't sure if that would offend him, so she stayed still.

A woman came through the front door, and Ruby said, "Evangeline! How's the cold?"

They were always chatty with the locals, and with Alice. Maggie liked listening in on their conversations and wished she could earn entry into their club, though they never gave her more than a courtesy hello and good-bye. To them, she was just another summer person.

"We had a group of tourists in here this morning from Worcester," Ruby said to the woman. "They were taking one another's pictures out in front of the store like this was Green Acres, and then they came inside and wanted a picture with us."

"Oh my," the woman said.

"They said they were going to the beach in York and then they wanted to go berry picking. Back in our day you got paid to pick berries and then a month later it was string beans, and then corn after that, until you were begging for mercy. Why, the thought of paying someone else for the pleasure of bending over all day in the hot sun —"

"I hear you!" the woman said.

"Bunch of Massholes, if you ask me," Mort said, setting the heavy crate down.

Maggie laughed, putting a hand over her mouth.

Ruby shook her head, but she smiled, a look that said she loved this man, loved the life they had made together. They seemed utterly comfortable with one another, like they knew each other all the way through. Maggie wondered if she would ever feel that way about another person. She walked the half mile home to the cottage, wondering still.

When she arrived, Maggie found her mother and hugged her and invited her to lunch, despite the lecture she knew was coming. Because maybe Kathleen was as close as she was ever going to get.

ANN MARIE

It rained like crazy through the final days of June, but on the first of July, the sun broke through to reveal the finest morning of summer so far. Ann Marie stepped outside the cottage door, and the air was warm, the sky pure blue. She took it all in, looking down to where the ocean met the sand. Alice's lilies were thriving. A gentle breeze rustled the leaves of the trees overhead.

She hadn't minded the lousy weather. She mostly needed to stay inside anyway and focus on cleaning the cottage. Kathleen had been staying there for all of four days, and the place was a disaster. Newspaper pages were strewn across every surface. Cigarette butts had been hidden in the bottom of the bathroom wastebasket, leaving behind hideous black smudges and a smoky odor that took nearly forty minutes of scrubbing with a mix of baking soda and water to cover up. Kathleen seemed incapable of putting a glass in the sink once she had used it. There were business cards for California school superintendents in a stack on the dresser (why?), as well as handwritten notes that Ann Marie couldn't begin to understand: *Remind them that orchid will bloom faster/richer colors/longer life span with tea . . . liquid seaweed = increased fungal activity . . . With the gin we will need to start looking for more workers AND TRASH! . . .*

Ann Marie fastened all the pages together with a paper clip and shoved them into her sister-in-law's purse. Then she set to undoing the rest of the damage Kathleen had done.

Now there were freshly washed sheets on the beds and vases of Free Spirit roses on the kitchen counter and on top of the piano, blooming in orange and peach and yellow sunbursts. The grill out on the deck had been scrubbed down. The fridge was stocked with champagne and blackberries and pastries and fresh steaks, and corn on the cob, and three different kinds of cheese for the cheese tray. She had removed a lamp painted with seashells from the dining table and hidden it up in the loft, replacing it with her dollhouse, which now held the spot of honor smack in the middle of the living room.

This was exactly how she wanted the place to look when the Brewers arrived later today, the perfect start to her official month in Cape Neddick. Except for the fact that Kathleen and Maggie still hadn't left.

Kathleen refused to go, probably out of

spite. She said she had good reason: she hadn't convinced Maggie to move to California with her yet (*smart girl*), and she wasn't leaving Maine until she succeeded. At Maggie's insistence, Kathleen had finally agreed to vacate the cottage and stay at Alice's. So the two of them were bunking at the big house, and Ann Marie, Pat, and the Brewers would stay together in the cottage next door, as planned.

She had never seen Kathleen so badly behaved as she had been this week, which was really saying something. Her mere presence made Ann Marie nervous. She could picture Kathleen pitching a fit in front of the Brewers, embarrassing everyone to no end. Kathleen was in a state over Maggie's pregnancy, and while she claimed to have come here to help her daughter, she mostly seemed to have upset the girl ever since she arrived.

Ann Marie was distressed about it too. At night she lay awake thinking about poor Maggie, wondering how she could help. She wanted to impress upon her that while the situation was not ideal, God would provide. How many women could honestly say that their children's conceptions had been planned? It was not preparedness for a child that made the timing right, but the fact of the child's existence. *Begotten, not made,* that was what the Bible said. She feared that Kathleen was advising her niece to pass the buck, the way she would — to get rid of the pregnancy, or to get rid of the baby after he was born, as if this new life hadn't come along for a reason.

Her sister Susan's oldest daughter, Deirdre, had had a hell of a time getting pregnant. Maybe Ann Marie ought to tell Maggie about her. She spent thirty thousand dollars on in vitro, and gained forty pounds, only to have it fail twice. She attempted it a third time, and finally, after four painful years of trying, Deirdre had given birth to triplets.

Ann Marie's mother had nearly lost it, raging at Susan, saying that the Catholic Church didn't support such procedures, that they killed millions of innocent embryos, and that it was up to God to decide when a life came along. It was easy enough to think so when you yourself had effortlessly given birth to four children, as their mother had. Ann Marie considered herself a model Catholic, but she knew that if her only way to have babies had been through petri dishes and science labs, she would have done all of it in a heartbeat.

Her mother came from a generation of married Catholic women who had gone to the Church begging to be allowed to use birth control in order to keep their families at a manageable size. When the Church refused, they obeyed, and for that reason plenty of them ended up with ten, twelve, or fourteen children, as if they were cattle. So many of those women had died young, their bodies exhausted. Thinking on it now, Ann Marie wondered if it wasn't all a bit absurd, this business of celibate men deciding who got to be a mother, and when.

It was because of the Church that Alice believed Maggie should marry the awful boyfriend. Ann Marie had considered this — if it were her daughter, she might have felt that marriage was imperative, whatever the circumstances. But she couldn't really picture her niece settling down for a lifetime with Gabe. Maggie would probably be better off alone. Clearly, Kathleen thought so.

Ann Marie had told Pat about his sister's plan to stay on, and he was ticked off. But he didn't say anything to Kathleen, reasoning that they had bigger fish to fry with this business about Alice giving the property away. Pat had consulted his attorney, who said that the deed was in Alice's name, so it was her right to sell the property, or give it away, even though Pat had paid for the main house to be built, and paid the taxes and the homeowner's insurance since his father died. The only way around losing the house was if Alice changed her mind. It made Ann Marie more furious than she had ever been.

Alice had been avoiding Pat's phone calls all week and acting as if nothing had happened around Ann Marie. They agreed that they would confront his mother after the Brewers left, since they didn't want Steve and Linda getting mixed up in their family's business. It was sure to be an unpleasant conversation, and Ann Marie didn't need the whole neighborhood hearing about it.

When she first found out about Alice's arrangement with the priest, Ann Marie had gotten a bit out of control. She had actually trampled Alice's tomato plants. It was almost an out-of-body experience. One minute, she was standing there in the yard thinking of what Alice had done, and the next, she was pulling the plants by their green, leafy stalks, breaking them in two. The tomatoes fell to the earth and she stepped on the biggest of them all, digging the balls of her feet in and quickly moving them back and forth without raising them off the ground, as if she were dancing the twist.

After a few harsh words were exchanged later that day, she fled. It had felt thrilling to drive off, knowing they were all watching her from behind the cottage windows. But Ann Marie didn't have any clue where she was going. She drove aimlessly for a while and then crossed the bridge into Portsmouth. She parked the car in front of an Irish pub and went inside.

The place was dim, the dark floorboards and walls making her almost forget that it was daytime. There was a session going on at the back of the room — old men and young ones played away on their fiddles and uilleann pipes, filling the place with merriment. She thought of her daughters competing at every Feis in New England, Patty always taking the gold, Fiona rarely placing, though she didn't seem to mind. Afterward, the whole family would spend the afternoon at the festival, walking from tent to tent, dancing the Siege of Ennis with a hundred strangers while her daughters' banana curls bobbed up and down. Their dresses, heavy with starch and boning and rich with embroidery, had taken Ann Marie six months to make.

Now, already a bit tipsy, she sat at the bar and ordered a glass of white wine. She had never been alone in a bar before and didn't really know what to do. She stared at the bottles on the shelves, reading the labels one by one, feeling like she might cry.

For all intents and purposes, the house was gone. It would never be hers. Why would Alice do this to her? She couldn't begin to know.

Two stools down, a man with white hair said, "Oh, come on, sweetheart — smile. A pretty girl like you shouldn't look so gloomy."

How long had it been since anyone had called her pretty, let alone a girl? In spite of herself, she gave him a faint smile.

"That's better," he said. He scooted over to the seat beside her and patted her hand. He was the only other patron in the place.

He looked ten years older than her, but he was terribly handsome. And fit. His bare legs were tanned, with a light covering of fine blond hairs.

"What's troubling you?" he said. "Go on, you can tell an old friend like me."

"My in-laws are driving me insane." It wasn't the sort of thing she was used to saying. Other people complained about their in-laws all the time, but not Ann Marie.

"What are you drinking there?" he asked.

"Pinot Grigio."

"I think this calls for something stronger, don't you?" He looked to the bartender. "Could you get us two shots of Jameson, Christine?"

"Oh no, thank you," Ann Marie said. "I don't drink hard liquor."

The girl filled two shot glasses and placed them on the bar.

"Me neither," he said. "Except medicinally."

He handed her one of the glasses and took the other for himself. They clinked them together and then she swallowed the liquid down. It felt warm in her throat. She took a sip of wine to get the taste out of her mouth.

"Any better?" the man asked.

"I think so," she said. "Thanks."

His name was Adam. He told her he had retired early from a job in advertising and now he lived on a sailboat. His home base was somewhere off the coast of South Carolina, but every summer he sailed north and docked in Portsmouth for a couple of weeks.

"That sounds like a dream life," she said.

"And what about you?" he asked. "What do you do?"

She hated when that question came up at a dinner party or a work event of Pat's. She always answered "I'm a homemaker," which hadn't bothered her when the kids were living at home, but now seemed a bit silly.

She told Adam she was an interior designer based in Boston. It came to her so quickly, she almost felt it was true. Well, it was, almost. Then she mentioned her husband and three children.

He said he had gotten divorced five years back. He had a grown son in Florida who was thirty-eight and still single.

"Are yours all coupled up?" he asked.

"One married, one engaged, and my younger daughter is single," she said.

As far as she knew, anyway.

"Does she live near you?" he asked.

"She's been in Africa for the past several years. She's in the Peace Corps."

"Wonderful."

"Yes. She's a very special girl."

She craved Fiona then, the way you might crave a favorite food from your childhood. She wanted her daughter beside her instead of this stranger. Fiona had always been patient and good, yet utterly unsentimental.

That was why she could tell schoolchildren about the importance of condoms and the dangers of AIDS, while fully aware that half their parents had already died of the disease. Why she could sing the little sick ones to sleep and discipline them, too, the same as if they were perfectly healthy.

Fiona would know how to handle Alice right now; she was made for situations like this. Suddenly Ann Marie realized that it was the first time in months she had thought of her youngest child as anything other than just gay. It felt like an important step.

"Maybe we should set her up with my son," Adam joked, and Ann Marie felt a bit sad, but not as sad as she might have expected.

"Maybe," she said.

The group in the back began to play a song she recognized, "The Black Velvet Band."

"This is one of my favorites," she said. "I heard the Dubliners play it live in the eighties."

"Shall we dance?" he asked.

"No," she said, grinning.

He stood up, extended his hand. "Come on now, it's one of your favorites."

She got to her feet, both embarrassed and flattered. He was what her daughters would call smarmy, but she thought he seemed sweet. She let him put his palm flat against the small of her back, and she put hers up on his shoulder as they swayed side to side. It had been forever since she was this close to a man she didn't know.

The musicians gave a cheer, happy for the accompaniment.

Their voices rose, and Adam sang along with the chorus: *Her eyes they shone like a diamond, you'd think she was queen of the land, with her hair flung over her shoulder, tied up with a black velvet band.*

Ann Marie wanted to sing, too, but she felt self-conscious. If Pat were there, she would have. She closed her eyes and thought of their honeymoon, when they had traveled around the Ring of Kerry in a rented Peugeot, singing their way through Ireland, stopping into pubs in tiny towns where every person they laid eyes on looked like someone they knew in Boston. Pat had tracked down some of his relatives in Killarney, and when they met, each and every one of them hugged Ann Marie close as if she, too, were family and said, "Welcome home."

Ann Marie had been so excited for what she knew would come next — children, a nice house of their own. But she had never pictured what came after that. Some women she knew were elated to have their grown children out of the nest. Ann Marie felt worthless. She might have thirty years left to live, and she had no idea how she was going to fill them.

The bartender's voice rose over the music: "Ma'am? Your phone."

Ann Marie opened her eyes and saw that her cell phone was lit up and vibrating on the bar.

"Excuse me," she said to Adam, breaking away from him, suddenly feeling silly.

She picked up the phone and saw Alice's number on the screen. She inhaled deeply, said hello.

Alice didn't apologize for what she had done, but she asked Ann Marie to come home, and said she couldn't be alone with Kathleen.

"I'm afraid something awful will happen if you don't come back," Alice said.

Ann Marie knew it was manipulative, and she had no interest in seeing her, but she told her mother-in-law she would return soon.

She suddenly remembered that the paper towel dispenser in the cottage was empty and figured she might as well go to Ruby's Market on the way back. She asked Alice if she needed anything else, cursing herself for being so darn accommodating, even after what had happened. She was still upset, but what was she going to do — drive home to Pat and never speak to his mother again? There were people in every family who were capable of doing something like that, and people who weren't.

When she told Adam she was leaving, he tried to persuade her to stay for one more round, but the spell had been broken, and

Ann Marie just wanted to get home to the beach. He asked her for her card.

"I'm in the book," she said. "And online. Ann Marie Clancy Designs."

It sounded absurd once the words were out of her mouth. She could feel herself blushing at the lie. But if he could tell, he did not say so. He only said, "It was a pleasure dancing with you, Ms. Clancy."

Around three o'clock on the first of July, Pat called her from the New Hampshire tolls to say that he would be arriving in the next half hour, and the Brewers were two cars behind. Ann Marie made one last round of the cottage, making sure it looked perfect. She opened a bottle of wine to let it breathe. She set a tray of scallops in the oven. She had wrapped them in bacon that morning and dipped strawberries in melted chocolate.

There was one more thing she wanted to do before they arrived. She found the card she had bought at Shop 'n Save on the table in the hall and headed outside to find Maggie. She had meant to give it to her niece yesterday, but then she lost track of time, and anyway, Maggie was rarely out of Kathleen's sight.

Ann Marie stepped out into the sunshine. She didn't have to go very far. Maggie was sitting on the ground at the edge of the property, her back resting against a massive pine tree. She was scribbling in a notebook, occasionally glancing out over the water. Ann Marie wondered what she was writing.

"Maggie!" she called.

Her niece turned her head.

"Don't get up," Ann Marie said, but Maggie was already rising to walk toward her.

"Isn't it a gorgeous day?" Maggie said when they met in the grass. "It seems like July arrived today and boom — now the weather is acting in kind. I haven't seen it so warm here in years."

Ann Marie thought about the cottage schedule and felt a bit guilty. She and Pat had originally thought of rotating the months each Kelleher kid got from year to year, but it just seemed too confusing. They wanted July for themselves. And since Clare still had a son in school, it seemed that August was the logical month for her. Which left June for Kathleen and Maggie and Chris.

"It is nice," Ann Marie said now. "It almost feels like you could get in the water without dying of hypothermia."

Maggie smiled.

"Your uncle and our friends are coming soon," Ann Marie said. "They should be here any minute."

"I'm sorry my mom's being so stubborn about us staying on," Maggie said. "I'd leave, but I don't trust her here on her own. I'm sure it's only for a day or so, to make a statement or something. You know how she is."

"Oh, it's okay. Anyway, honey, I wanted to give you something. Here," she said, awkwardly pushing the envelope forth.

Maggie ripped the paper and pulled out the card. On the front was a picture of a pink and blue rattle, with *CONGRATULATIONS* written underneath.

"Thank you," Maggie said. She began to tear up. "You're the first person to congratulate me."

A few seconds later she was laughing. "I'm so emotional lately," she said. "I cry at everything."

"I was the same way," Ann Marie said. "So was Patty. You two will have to compare notes. She's got it all down to a science now. And her attic is absolutely crammed full of baby clothes. They're not having any more, so — it's all yours. Next time you come up to Boston, we'll go through it."

"Thank you," Maggie said.

"Patty will be here next week, so if you're still around . . ."

She prayed that Maggie and Kathleen would be gone by then.

"Don't worry," Maggie said. "I'm already working on getting my mother out of here."

Maggie opened the card. Seeing the folded-up catalog page inside, she asked, "What's this?"

"Just a token from me to you," Ann Marie said.

Maggie unfolded the page and smiled strangely. "A stroller?" she said.

"It's called the Bugaboo Bee," Ann Marie said. She pointed to the description. "See, it says here that this model 'answers the call of the modern! Compact yet complete, for parents who live life on the fly!' It sounded like a good fit for a city gal to me. I had it shipped to your apartment. It should be waiting there when you get home."

"Oh my gosh," Maggie said, staring down at the glossy sheet of paper in her hands. "This is too much. Thank you."

Ann Marie had tried to cross out the price with a pen, but she had succeeded only at drawing attention to the figure: six hundred dollars — that's what these things went for today. On some level, the gift was a bribe. If, God forbid, Maggie was having any doubts about keeping the baby, then seeing a beautiful stroller in her apartment day after day would serve to remind her that she was carrying a blessed child and needed to stay the course.

"I have to go, honey. I have scallops in the oven. Come over later and say hello to our friends."

"I will," Maggie said. She hugged Ann Marie tight and Ann Marie felt like she might cry too.

"Thank you so much," Maggie said.

"It's nothing."

She wondered what on earth had turned Maggie into such a good girl — she was so sweet and polite. It was probably because Maggie had had to look after herself a bit, same as Ann Marie had. Before she could think it over she blurted out, "You can come live with me and Pat, now or when the baby comes. I'll take care of you. If you want."

"That's really generous," Maggie said. "I guess we'll see how it all shakes out."

She nodded. "Fine."

Ann Marie went into the house to put on one of her new Lilly Pulitzer dresses. It was sherbet green, with pink blossoms printed all over. She hadn't even taken the tags off yet, and when she did so and pulled it on, she thought she looked pretty cute. She applied a bit of lip gloss and mascara, and then she waited.

They turned their cars onto the grass a short while later and got out, all three of them talking and laughing, changing the quiet energy in the air. Ann Marie walked outside to greet them.

"Hi there!" she said cheerfully. "Welcome!"

"Ann Marie," Linda said, hugging her. "This place is to die for."

"Oh, you're sweet," she said in a modest tone she had learned years ago when they first moved to Newton.

Steve came up behind his wife, with an oversize duffel bag on each shoulder. He gave Ann Marie an awkward hug, since the bags kept lurching forward, but he said, "You look great. I think this ocean view agrees with you."

She felt the same flutter that she always did in his presence.

"Well, come on in. I've got scallops and strawberries and a cheese plate and a bottle of wine with your name on them," she said, thinking about what it would feel like to kiss him.

"Always the hostess with the mostess," Linda said.

Pat was behind Steve. When he reached her, he gave her a long, hard squeeze.

"I've missed you," he said.

She patted his face. He had definitely been sneaking fast food every day since she left. His cheeks looked puffy, and there were a couple extra pounds around his belly. She'd mention it later.

"Me too," she said for now.

Inside the cottage, they left their bags in the hall and settled into the living room, where Ann Marie poured them all a glass of wine. She set the hors d'oeuvres on a big silver platter on the ottoman, like she had seen a hostess do in the last issue of *House & Garden*.

Steve sat at the piano bench, even though

the armchair was empty and there was plenty of room beside Linda on the sofa.

He ran his fingers clumsily over the keys.

"You play?" Pat asked.

"Oh yes, I'm a regular Ray Charles," he said. "You should hear my version of 'Heart and Soul.'"

Pat started talking about the traffic, and Linda praised the Gruyère, asking where Ann Marie had found it. Ann Marie responded warmly, but she was slightly ticked that none of them, not even Steve, mentioned her dollhouse, which was sitting right there on the table in the middle of the room.

Finally, she walked toward the house and said, "The funniest thing happened when the UPS man delivered this."

They paused before Pat said, "Oh? What?"

Drat, nothing all that interesting had happened with the UPS man.

"He couldn't fit it through the door," she improvised. "So he had to hoist it up onto the deck and then bring it through the slider."

"How could he — ," Pat began, but Steve interrupted, "Is that the one for that big competition you won?"

She nodded, pleased that he remembered.

"It's a beauty," he said.

"It is," his wife agreed.

"Thank you. I always wanted one in brick. They're very unusual."

"Is that right?" Linda asked. "Oh, I love

the little doghouse in the yard."

Ann Marie had painted it gray the night before, and she had made a white bone out of clay, which you could see only if you peered inside.

"I have a lot left to do on it," she said. "The curtains and rugs were my main projects this week. And the lawn."

"Sounds like you've been busy," Steve said. "Hopefully now you'll have time to relax."

Then he raised his glass and said, "To an unforgettable week!"

They all got to their feet and stood by the dollhouse. They clinked their glasses together, and Ann Marie felt grateful to be here with people who appreciated her. For a moment, it was as if the last few days had never passed.

The next morning, Pat and Steve went to play eighteen holes. Ann Marie and Linda slept in, and then decided to go down to the beach. For the first time since she could remember, Ann Marie didn't bother inviting Alice to come along. Not that she would have said yes — Alice hardly ever set foot on the beach, and she seemed to be avoiding them, staying hidden away in the house next door when she wasn't at church. She hadn't even stopped in to say hello to the Brewers yet. This was fine by Ann Marie, since she wanted to scream each time she saw her mother-in-law's face. But even so, the decision not to include Alice felt momentous somehow.

They placed their chairs on the dry sand up by the dunes, so they wouldn't have to move them when the tide came in. Between them was a tote bag full of sunblock and water and magazines, and a bottle of white wine with two plastic cups slung over the top.

"How marvelous to have this all to yourselves," Linda said, gazing up and down the shore as she untied her sarong. She looked better than she had last summer — her legs seemed more toned, her arms a bit less saggy. Ann Marie sucked in her gut and decided not to take her shorts off. "It must be so great to be able to just dash inside the house and get a snack or change out of your bathing suit if you want to."

Ann Marie nodded. "It's nice, especially with the grandkids. You can put them down for a nap up in the cottage and bring the baby monitor down here to the beach."

"How civilized!"

"I know."

They smothered themselves in sunblock, rubbing the white cream into their legs and arms until it disappeared, leaving a clear sheen behind.

"Gotta love the Irish skin," Linda said with a laugh.

"Tell me about it," Ann Marie said. "So, what have I missed in the neighborhood since I've been gone?"

"Not much," Linda said. She reached for the bottle of wine. "May I?"

"Please," Ann Marie said. It was only eleven o'clock, but what the heck? They were on vacation.

Linda poured the wine and said, "I hear through the grapevine that Josephine's husband might be leaving her."

"Ted? No!"

"Yes. And I'm not even sure I can tell you for who."

"Oh God."

"The babysitter. She's a sophomore at Tufts."

"Poor Josie!"

"I know. I told Steve if he ever humiliated me like that, they'd never find his body."

They giggled, though Ann Marie wondered for a split second if Linda was onto her and Steve. Was this her way of saying back off? For some reason, the thought of it gave Ann Marie a rush.

They chatted about their kids, and their neighbors, and how quickly the summer was passing by.

Eventually, they pulled a couple of magazines out of the beach bag and started talking about celebrities, pointing out funny stories to each other. They passed an hour pleasantly this way. And then, as if sensing Ann Marie's tranquillity, Kathleen came along to shatter it.

Ann Marie hadn't even noticed someone had approached them until Linda said cautiously, "Hello there."

When she looked up, Kathleen was hovering overhead in shorts and a T-shirt. She had a rolled-up towel under her arm, one of the threadbare brown ones from the linen closet in the cottage. Ann Marie never used those — she bought new towels almost every fall at the postsummer sales, and brought them from home the following season.

She felt like telling Kathleen to buzz off, but instead she said, "Linda, meet my sister-in-law Kathleen."

"Oh!" Linda said, putting a hand over her heart. "I didn't realize you two knew each other! You scared me there for a minute!"

The scariest part is that we do know each other, Ann Marie thought.

"What are you up to?" she asked, trying to sound cheerful.

"Taking a walk," Kathleen said. "You don't mind if I take a walk on the beach, do you? It being July and all."

Good Lord, here we go.

"Why don't you sit with us for a bit?" Linda said.

Kathleen raised an eyebrow. "Okay."

She spread her towel out in front of them and sat with her back to the ocean.

"Wine?" Linda asked.

Ann Marie cringed, but Kathleen seemed

to have come without her soapbox.

"None for me," she said politely. *Well, that was a shock.*

"Where's Maggie?" Ann Marie asked. She turned to Linda and, by way of explanation, added, "My niece."

"My daughter," Kathleen said. "She's up at Alice's house, working. I had to get out of there. Between Maggie talking on the phone about murder victims and Alice smoking like a chimney on the porch. . .Well, let's just say it's cramped. So! How do you two know each other?"

Ann Marie had already told her they were neighbors, but she replied, "We live on the same block."

"Ah, fellow Newtonians," Kathleen said. Maybe you had to know her to know that she was being snide, because Linda said cheerfully, "That's right. We're in the same book club, and we're on the ladies' council together at our country club. And we organize a wine and cheese night with the other neighborhood moms once a month."

Kathleen scooped up a handful of sand and then let it fall through her fingers. "Sounds like you two like to get away from your menfolk," she said.

"Sometimes a girl needs it!" Linda said, smiling. "Am I right?"

"Oh, I don't know. I actually enjoy spending time with my partner."

That did it! Kathleen was being rude to Ann Marie's guest. And why had she used that word, *partner?* It made it sound like she was a lesbian.

"Kathleen's not married, so her perspective is a little different from ours," Ann Marie said. "Her boyfriend is a lovely guy."

"Oh, thanks," Kathleen said. She looked straight at Linda. "I hate that term, *boyfriend.* We've been living together for ten years, but everyone in the family treats us like we just wrapped up our third date."

Linda seemed unsure how to respond, poor thing. Finally she said, "I was telling Ann Marie how jealous I am that you all have this beach to yourselves. It's wonderful."

Kathleen shrugged. "Personally, I'm ready to leave."

Ann Marie was relieved that Kathleen hadn't steered the conversation toward the topic of Alice giving the house away.

"When are you planning to leave, anyway?" she asked, hoping Linda wouldn't pick up on any friction between them.

"Not sure yet." Kathleen gave her a meaningful look, as if to say, *Just you wait.*

They sat in silence. Ann Marie looked out at the water and wondered when Kathleen would let them be.

A few minutes passed before her sister-in-law got to her feet.

"It's been lovely, gals, but I'm going to take

that walk now," she said.

"It was nice to meet you," Linda said. "We'll see you later."

Unless you get washed out to sea, Ann Marie thought. She gave Kathleen her biggest fake smile, because she knew Linda was watching.

When their husbands returned in the early afternoon, they gathered up the beach gear and headed inside. Ann Marie washed the sand off her legs and hands in the outdoor shower. It was finally warm enough for it. In the stall made of weathered wood, built on a raised platform, she ran the soap over her arms, looking upward. There was not a cloud in sight. She pulled off her wet bathing suit, slung it over the top of the wall. Afterward, she left it there to dry.

They decided to take a drive along the coast and maybe get a bite to eat. Linda wanted to photograph a lighthouse, so they got out of the car in York, and she snapped away at Nubble Light. It was a beautiful spot atop a grassy cliff — all white, with a white Victorian keeper's house attached. The house had a red roof and gingerbread trim. Perhaps Ann Marie's next project would be a replica of it. She imagined a battery-powered light that flashed every minute or so. But how would she do the water?

Her eyes met Steve's and they smiled warmly at each other. She wanted to tell him her idea. She thought of how he had remembered the big competition and mentioned it as a sort of nod to their secret e-mail exchange. She felt grateful. Their flirtation might be the only thing keeping her afloat right now.

"How long has it been here?" Linda asked, still looking at the lighthouse through the camera's viewfinder.

Ann Marie shrugged, but Patrick said, "It was built in 1879."

Now how on earth did he know that? She had married such a smart and capable man. She reached for Pat's hand and said, "Where shall we take these two for lunch, hon?"

They ended up at a new lobster shack on the beach in Kittery, where Alice and Maggie had gone with that schemer priest a few weeks back. Ann Marie felt uneasy just thinking about it, but once they started eating, she calmed down a bit.

After lunch, Pat went to get them a couple of milkshakes for dessert, and Linda headed to the ladies' room. Ann Marie was alone with Steve for the first time.

"Thanks again for inviting us," he said. "We're having a blast so far."

She smiled, but wished he wouldn't speak for them both.

"We're happy you came," she said.

"Pat told me his mother and sister have been giving you a tough time," he said. "How anyone could be mean to a sweetheart like you, I have no idea."

He reached across the table and squeezed her hand.

Ann Marie's entire body tingled in a way it hadn't in God knows how long. She would do anything right now to have an hour alone with him. But she could already see Linda coming out from inside.

The next two days passed uneventfully enough, though Ann Marie felt tense. She could tell that Pat felt the same way. As they went to the Cove Café for breakfast; as they pointed out the house that looked like a wedding cake, and the Bush compound with its Secret Service agents stationed out front; as she brought Linda to her favorite antiques shop and snagged an armoire that perfectly matched the desk in Patty's old room, there was a constant undertone of waiting — waiting for the Brewers to leave, waiting to see what Alice would do once Pat spoke to her about the property. And waiting for Kathleen to pull something.

But on the Fourth, Ann Marie tried to put all of that from her head because, other than Christmas, it was her favorite day of the year. From the time she and Pat were dating, they hadn't missed a single Independence Day fireworks display in Portsmouth. When her children were small, she dressed them in red, white, and blue and gave them American flags to wave. She always prepared a great big picnic, and they made a point of arriving early so they could stake out the best possible spot. By seven o'clock, the entire field behind the high school would be full of blankets, their edges pressed up against one another so that it looked like an enormous quilt.

Ann Marie, Pat, Steve, and Linda spent the first part of the day sunning themselves and taking quick dips in the ocean when they got hot enough, though the water was too frigid to stay in for long. Around four, Ann Marie left the others on the beach and went up to the house to prepare. She felt almost drunk from the sunlight, calm and sleepy and a bit light-headed. In the cottage kitchen, she poured herself a tall glass of water and drank it down as she looked out the window.

She fixed a shortcake with strawberries, blueberries, and homemade whipped cream on top, arranged to resemble the Stars and Stripes. She had bought fried chicken drumsticks at the market, and made potato salad, pasta salad, and hummus early that morning. She placed it all in a picnic basket, along with bug spray, binoculars, utensils, and a big bag of potato chips.

She wanted to look nice for Steve. Beach attire was clearly not her strong suit, but now she had the chance to shine. She put on a new red shirtwaist and the blue sandals she had chosen to go along with it. And then she dabbed on a bit of makeup, though not enough to make her husband ask why she'd gone to the trouble.

After a while, the rest of them trickled inside to get ready.

"Should we bring two bottles of champagne, or three?" she asked Pat before they left.

"Bring four," he said. "My mother's coming."

"Oh? How did that happen?"

"I went over and invited her." He paused, looking guilty. "She comes every year."

His tone said that he was trying to explain himself, which made Ann Marie feel like a terrible wife. Alice was his mother. Of course he had to invite her.

"It's fine," she said. "I was just surprised she accepted, since she's sort of been hiding from us."

"I think she figures we'll be less likely to off her in a really crowded public place," Pat said, a comment Ann Marie would have expected from one of his sisters, maybe, but not from him. It made her sad that it had come to this.

"We'll make the best of it," she said.

After he left the room, she removed an open bottle of chardonnay from the fridge and filled a big glass, drinking it down quickly before anyone could see.

The five of them took one car, since they knew it would be tough to find parking. Alice, Linda, and Ann Marie sat shoulder to shoulder in the backseat of Pat's Mercedes.

"I told Maggie and Kathleen to meet us there after dinner," Alice said. "I'll bet they don't have fireworks like this in California."

Oh, so now she was using Kathleen for backup? That was rich.

But Ann Marie just answered, "Great." She was already feeling the effects of the wine, which, mixed with a long day in the sun, had gone straight to her head. She rolled the window down a bit to try to get some air. She lost herself in the sound of cars whizzing past, not paying attention to the conversation.

When they arrived, they moved slowly through Market Square with the crowd all around, and Ann Marie tried to feel happy. She reminded herself that nothing terrible had happened yet, and who knew — maybe Alice would change her mind after all. But she felt weighted down all the same, like this might be the last time they would ever come here. Everything seemed temporary now.

As if intuiting her thoughts, Alice whispered, "Perk up, darling! You're acting like a real party pooper."

She was in one of her moods, which usually scared Ann Marie into being sweet and

617

obedient, but now, for the very first time, she couldn't care less.

"No one likes a droopy hostess," Alice continued, clearly looking for a fight.

Ann Marie ignored her. They reached the edge of the field and she said in her most upbeat voice, "This spot looks perfect." They spread the blanket out and she wondered if Alice was right — was it clear to the Brewers that her family was a mess, that she herself was floundering? Perhaps, but then again Steve had told her she looked great, and they had both been complimenting her cooking since they walked in the door.

She popped open a bottle of champagne as they got settled.

"Bubbly?" she said to Linda and Steve.

Ann Marie could hardly pour fast enough, she wanted a drink so badly. After she had filled everyone else's glasses, she filled one for herself, drinking it down in under a minute and refilling it right away. She had meant to place a raspberry and a blackberry in each glass, but it had slipped her mind. *Rats.*

By the time darkness fell an hour later and the band in the gazebo began to play, three bottles were empty. Ann Marie hoped she was the only one keeping track, because she herself had had a bottle and a half. She closed her eyes, feeling faint, but in an almost pleasant way. She opened up the Tupperware that

618

contained her homemade hummus and dipped a big hunk of pita bread right in, hardly even caring when a dollop of it fell onto the blanket.

Her eyes met Steve's as she looked up from the spot.

"Whoops," he said. He gave her a bright smile. "Hey, everything tastes great."

Pat was typing away on his cell phone's keyboard, either frantically tying up loose ends on a business deal or just trying to avoid his mother. Alice was droning on about some local newscaster who had taken up with the married head of the station, and Linda was trapped, listening and nodding along as if it were the most fascinating story in the world. Maybe she even was fascinated. Alice had a way of captivating people. She had captivated Ann Marie once too.

Ann Marie thought back to a time before the Kellehers. She had been a different girl completely. What would her life have been if she had married someone else? Of all possible paths, she had taken this one, and now she wondered how she had ever been brave or stupid or *something* enough to choose.

The fire station bell rang to signal there were only thirty more minutes before the fireworks began.

Steve got to his feet. "Excuse me a minute," he said, looking straight at Ann Marie, giving her a wink. No one else was paying attention.

"Save my spot?"

He walked off into the crowd and she was seized with a realization. That wink. He wanted her to follow him.

"I'd better run to the ladies' before the festivities get going," she said to no one in particular. She felt giddy beyond belief, like a high school girl before a big date.

She stood up on wobbly legs, only now noticing just how drunk she was. She pushed past families and young couples and old ones, unsteady on her feet. Ann Marie anchored herself on the shoulders of strangers as they passed by.

She found Steve in the long Porta-Potty line in the parking lot, standing behind a group of teenagers who were cramming glow sticks into their mouths, their cheeks lighting up in a sickly green hue.

He saw her and grinned. "Ah, thank God. Some adult company."

Her heart was actually thumping. She needed to calm her nerves. She wished she had brought the champagne. She noticed a flag pin on his lapel and raised a finger to touch it.

"I like this," she said, taking a step closer so that when he spoke she could feel his breath on her cheek.

"Thanks. I got it when we took the kids to D.C. Gotta show your American pride, right? But look who I'm talking to." He gestured toward her outfit. "You're basically Miss America tonight."

That was her cue. Ann Marie placed her hands on his face. She leaned forward and kissed him, feeling the warmth of his lips, gently pushing her tongue between them. For a moment, it was everything she had imagined. But then he pulled back hard.

"Ann Marie," he said. "What are you doing?"

He turned his head quickly to the left and the right, as if looking for an escape.

"I thought —" she said. And suddenly, it all crashed down around her. The house was gone and her children were disappointments. She would never be rid of her mother-in-law, or of Kathleen. There was only one person in her life who brought her any excitement anymore, and now she had ruined that too. She wanted to be able to wake up and discover that it was all a bad dream; she wanted not to exist.

"Please," she said softly, not even sure what she was asking him for.

"You've had too much to drink," he said, his face turning hard in an instant. "I'm going back to the others, okay? Will you be all right here on your own?"

She nodded, her belly filling up with dread as he rushed off. And then, at the moment when it seemed like her life could not sink any lower, she looked up and saw Kathleen standing maybe fifteen feet away, staring at her. It was clear that she had seen the kiss. Her mouth was actually hanging open.

Ann Marie wanted to run. Had she ruined her marriage in an instant? Would she live out the rest of her days in some sad one-bedroom apartment, or would she get to keep the house?

She walked toward Kathleen. She spoke quickly, almost unable to breathe. "Oh God, please, Kathleen, don't tell Patrick what you just saw."

Kathleen straightened up. Her expression changed, and she looked genuinely warm for perhaps the first time Ann Marie could remember. She said slowly, purposefully, "I didn't see anything. I'm just waiting for Maggie to get out of that disgusting bathroom. She's been in there for ages."

Ann Marie wasn't sure whether to believe her.

"Please," she said again. "I can explain what that was."

"Here she comes," Kathleen said, waving to her daughter. "Now, where are you guys sitting and what did you bring for dessert?"

The next morning, Ann Marie awoke with a terrible headache. Watching as she popped a couple of aspirin with her coffee, Steve said charitably, "I think we all had way too much to drink last night. The whole evening is a bit of a blur to me."

His generous behavior only made her feel worse. She wanted the Brewers gone. She started cracking eggs for a quiche.

Ann Marie knew it was pointless, but she kept going over the events of the evening in her head: Why had she drunk so much champagne? How could she have misread all the signs? Or maybe she hadn't misread them. Maybe it was just that the moment was wrong, but now she had ruined it for good.

Kathleen had been bizarrely kind all night, chatting like a normal adult with Linda and Steve, hardly picking any fights with Alice, and declaring that the Portsmouth fireworks display was among the best she had ever witnessed. She seemed to be going to great lengths to tell Ann Marie that her secret was safe. But Ann Marie knew her sister-in-law well. There were years ahead of them, and now Kathleen had this on her. Would she ever be able to exhale, knowing the havoc Kathleen could wreak now, anytime she liked?

After breakfast, though everyone was full and she herself was painfully hungover, Ann Marie decided to bake a three-berry pie. At least shopping for the filling would get her away for a bit. On her way out to the farm stand, she found Alice in her garden.

"Kathleen and Maggie left," Alice said.

"What? When?" Ann Marie asked.

"Early this morning. Kathleen took Maggie

home to New York. I don't get the impression Gabe's coming back around, the pig."

Ann Marie nodded solemnly. It was comforting to consider someone else's bad decisions for a moment.

"Kathleen said to tell you she was sick of the ocean and finally ready to get out of your hair," Alice told Ann Marie. She rolled her eyes. "That one."

Ann Marie hoped that Steve would create some work-related emergency and escape, but he did not. Nor did he avoid her, as she assumed he might. For the remaining three days of his stay, he went along as if nothing had happened. Each time he stroked his wife's hair or took her hand, Ann Marie relived the entire mortifying episode all over again.

And each passing day meant they were closer to confronting Alice. She and Pat whispered about it in bed at night, both eager to have it over with, both agreeing that their choice of words could mean everything. They should not put Alice on the defensive or make her feel attacked. Rather, they should highlight the generous spirit that her donation conveyed, while gently pointing out that she would break their hearts if she went through with it.

The Brewers finally left on the seventh. They probably hadn't even made it to the highway before Pat and Ann Marie went next door to deal with his mother.

They found her sitting at the kitchen table, smoking and reading a mystery novel that Ann Marie had gotten from her own mother and passed along.

"Mom, can we talk to you for a minute?" Pat asked. He sounded like a terrified child.

Alice was in charming mode. "Of course, darlings. Sit down! Do you want a beer, Pat?"

"No thanks," he said.

She held up the book. "This is a good one."

"I thought so too," Ann Marie said.

"Listen," Pat said. "We wanted to talk about this whole issue of your giving the property away."

Alice rolled her eyes. "Not this again."

"We think it was a wonderful gesture on your part, Mom," Ann Marie said. "We know how much the church means to you. But the house means so much to us."

"I know," Alice said. "It's not like I'm giving it to them this second. If the women in my family are any indication, I'll probably live another ten years."

You'll probably live another thirty the way my luck is going, Ann Marie thought.

Alice went on, "Ten years! You'll both be sick of this old place by then."

Pat piped up. "Think of the position that puts us in, Mom. None of us want to think about the number of years you have left in

625

relation to a house. We want you here for-ever."

He seemed genuinely choked up. *Mothers were the oddest creatures,* Ann Marie thought. *Their children tended to love them even when it made no earthly sense to do so.*

"The decision was made six months ago," Alice said. "I can't go back on it because of some sentimental attachment. Believe me, this is hard for me too."

"Why didn't you tell us?" Pat asked. "And what if that priest hadn't —"

"He has a name," Alice said.

"What if Father Donnelly hadn't acciden-tally told Ann Marie? Were you ever going to tell us this had happened?"

"Of course I would have," Alice said.

"When?"

"When the time was right." She sighed. "I didn't just rush into this. I hope you know that. I gave it plenty of thought. But the fact is that this place isn't what it used to be. You and your sisters can't even stand to be here at the same time as one another."

"That's not true," Patrick said. "Mom, we love this place. Our kids love it. Our grand-kids love it. Please don't take it away." He was begging now, but Alice was unmoved.

"I refuse to be bullied," she said. "And anyway, there is absolutely no way I could go to Father Donnelly and tell him I'm backing out. The church is depending on this."

"What if we just gave St. Michael's an acre?" Pat said.

"Let's stop," Ann Marie said. "She's not going to change her mind."

"That's right," Alice said triumphantly, as if they were talking politics and she had just won the debate. "Now let's change the subject. What time will Patty and Josh be here tomorrow?"

That night Ann Marie and her husband drove to the big public beach in Ogunquit to get away from her. They sat in the massive parking lot near the building that housed the showers, not even bothering to get out of the car. Ann Marie thought of how spoiled they had always been to have their own beach, a few steps from the front door.

She thought of those depressing rented houses her sisters went to on Cape Cod, where you had to bring your own ketchup and mustard and napkins at the beginning of the week, and clear out some stranger's tea bags and crackers from the cupboards before you could start your vacation. Those places were always cluttered with someone else's knick-knacks. They smelled stale, and were right on top of one another. Through the open windows, you could hear the voices of the renters next door.

No one but their family and dear friends

had ever put their heads down to sleep in the cottage on Briarwood Road, or even so much as taken a shower there. And soon it would belong to someone else. It seemed impossible. She felt as if a close friend had died.

Pat said that down the line they could get a place of their own. But she knew they could never afford anything as nice as the spread at Briarwood Road. Certainly not waterfront property. Pat had had it appraised for 2.3 million. And anyway, that wasn't the point. The point was, it was their family's home. Ann Marie and her husband had done as much as anyone — more — to keep it thriving. And now this.

Ann Marie cried, sitting there in the passenger seat. Pat rubbed her shoulder.

"I'm sorry she's like this," he said. "I wish there was something I could do to change it all."

"It's not your fault," she said.

"I keep wishing my dad were here to talk sense into her. He was really the only one who ever could. Well, him and you."

His eyes followed a mother and two boys with bright blue zinc smeared across their noses. They were all carrying pails and shovels and towels and flip-flops, hopping around on the hot pavement, trying not to burn their feet.

Ann Marie looked at her husband. "I feel lost, Pat."

"It's been a tough year," he said.

"Yes."

He raised his voice, trying, she imagined, for an upbeat tone. "I, for one, cannot wait to get to London in September and see you get your gold medal."

She smiled weakly. "And then what?"

"And then — who knows? It feels like we ought to start thinking about a new chapter, me and you."

She nodded. The idea made her feel slightly tired, but hopeful, too, in some small way.

"Maybe after London, we could go back to Ireland. A second honeymoon?" He raised an eyebrow suggestively, and she laughed.

"I was just remembering that trip," she said. "I'd like that."

"I missed you a lot while you were up here with my mom," he said. "It got me thinking."

They sat in silence for a few moments, each with certain private thoughts that the other could guess in an instant, and thoughts that the other could never imagine.

"Do you want to get a drink somewhere?" he asked.

She wiped the tears from her cheeks. "All right."

They got out of the car, and he took her hand as they made their way toward town.

The next morning, Patty and Josh arrived, their station wagon so full that Josh couldn't

629

see out the back windows as he drove.

"We're here!" Patty said, stepping onto the screen porch, where Ann Marie and Pat were waiting. She held the baby on her hip.

"Come to Grandma," Ann Marie said, taking the child into her arms, the warmth of that little body like a balm to her soul. She hadn't seen her grandchildren in seventeen days, which was exactly thirteen days longer than she had ever gone before. To think that her reason for leaving was concern over Alice's welfare.

"Did you hit a lot of traffic?" Pat asked.

"Not really," Patty said. She reached into her pocket and pulled out her cell phone. She was just like her father. Ann Marie had to fight the urge to tell her to turn the darn thing off.

"There's still no signal out here?" Patty asked.

"What took you so long?" Pat said. "I thought you were leaving at seven."

"We did, and we hit a new record for number of times we had to stop for someone to go to the bathroom," Patty said. "Seriously. Seventy-five miles, five bathroom breaks. I'm contacting the Guinness people. I really think we might have something special here."

Maisy and Foster burst onto the porch like Mexican jumping beans.

"Grandma!" they shouted, and Ann Marie hugged them with her one free arm.

"They missed you," Patty said. She dropped her volume. "And they've learned all kinds of colorful new language from their other grandma."

Apparently Foster heard this, because he piped up then, "Our Grammy Joan lets us drink tonic."

"What kind of tonic?" Ann Marie asked with a frown.

"Coke and root beer," Foster said.

"That stuff will rot your teeth," Ann Marie said, actually feeling a bit annoyed about it. "You don't want that!"

"No," Foster said.

"We already put our bathing suits on," Maisy said. Last summer she had pronounced it *babing suits.* "They're under our clothes, see?"

She pulled up her T-shirt to reveal the purple polka-dotted one-piece Ann Marie had picked up at the Filene's sale a few weeks back.

"I slept in my suit!" Maisy said gleefully.

"Don't tell Grandma that," Patty said.

Maisy went on, "Foster says the water might be too cold for me like last time, but I said no, because you get used to it once you're in."

Ann Marie smiled. Where had Maisy heard that? They had all said it so many times over the years. Her own children, never content to play with just one another, would call to her on the shore as she tried to read a magazine in peace — *Come on, Mom, come swim! You get used to it once you're in.* Never mind that the water never once got above sixty degrees, even at the height of August.

"Will you take us to the beach, Grandpa?" Foster said, pulling at Pat's shorts. "Can we bury you in the sand like last time?"

"Wait a minute, you two," Patty said. "Let's let Grandma and Grandpa adjust to this invasion before we start making demands."

Josh was walking up from the car, laden down with bags and beach chairs and a plastic cooler.

"Foster, go help Dad," Patty said.

He did as she said. Father and son returned a few moments later, though Foster's hands were empty.

"He said he had achieved perfect balance and would topple if I took anything," Foster reported.

"Okay," Patty said. "Well, it was nice of you to ask."

"When can we see the bears eating out of the Dumpsters?" Foster asked.

Maisy covered her eyes with her hands, as if the bears were right there on the porch. "I don't want to see them at all, please!" she said, and everyone laughed.

A few moments later, Maisy started shuffling from one foot to the other.

"You need to hit the bathroom again, bug?"

Josh asked.

Maisy shook her head no, and then nodded yes.

"Dad, you gotta help me get my suit off!" she said.

"Okay, okay, let me put everything down."

Ann Marie thought of how they were just as likely to go to Josh as to Patty. She had never wanted Patrick to understand the children like she did, preferring that the mystery of child-rearing be mostly her domain. Perhaps that had been a mistake, but it still seemed strange for a father to take his daughter to the bathroom, especially when the mother was standing right there.

"Little Daniel and Regina are coming up for dinner," Patty said now.

"Oh?"

"They just called me in the car to say so. They called you, too, but it went to voice mail."

"Well, that's wonderful," Ann Marie said. "What should we have?"

A debate ensued over whether to drive up the coast toward Kennebunkport or to stay at home and cook hot dogs and hamburgers on the grill.

Ann Marie's spirits were high. Here was her family, swirling around her, just as she liked, only beginning a week away at their summer home. She knew that it would go by in a flash, but even so she said a silent prayer, asking God to help her enjoy whatever time they had left.

KATHLEEN

On the fifth of July, Kathleen went to her
sleeping daughter and gently shook Maggie's
shoulder. Through the open bedroom window, she could hear the sound of the surf,
seagulls calling to one another.

"Mags, wake up, we've got to go," she
whispered.

"Go where?" Maggie asked, her eyes still
closed.

"Home. I'm taking you back to New York."

Maggie opened just her left eye. "Why are
we leaving in the middle of the night?"

"It's seven thirty in the morning," Kathleen
said.

Now Maggie opened the other eye, and
said, "For you, seven thirty in the morning is
the middle of the night. What's going on?"

"I'll tell you in the car," Kathleen said.
"Hop in the shower. I want to get out of here
before Ann Marie wakes up."

"Did you do something bad to her?" Maggie asked.

"No, as a matter of fact, I didn't. Now come on!"

Kathleen had been up all night trying to decide how she should handle the situation. Should she write Ann Marie a note letting her know that her secret was safe, and then stick around for a couple more days to make things look normal to everyone else? Should she try to get that asshole Steve Brewer in private, and tell him that if he didn't keep his mouth shut, he'd have her to answer to? Or should she simply go away, sending Ann Marie the silent message that the whole silly episode could now vanish too? Kathleen decided that if the roles were reversed, she'd want Ann Marie to leave.

She had never felt protective of her sister-in-law before. It was a strange sensation. It felt nice when you saw yourself evolving a bit; it felt better than any bitchy comeback or snide remark ever could. She wished Arlo were there so they could discuss it.

She had called him before she went to sleep, but instead of mentioning Ann Marie she said, "I took a step back tonight and I finally realized Maggie really doesn't want to live with us."

"And how do you feel about that?" he asked.

She thought this over. "Sad. Scared. Thankful."

"She's going to make it," he said.

"I know."

"Remember that there's a gray area between having her live with us and having her all alone," he said. "You can go back and forth for a while. Maybe she can bring the baby out here for the summer. We'll figure it out."

"Yes."

"You raised a really smart, tough daughter," he said. "A girl like you."

Kathleen thought to herself that Maggie was nothing like she had been at that age. It had taken Kathleen so much longer to find herself, because she had spent twenty years trying to be someone else. Maggie had gotten straight to the good stuff — her chosen career, her city, even the men she dated were exactly what she wanted. You had to give them that, though not much else. Kathleen felt proud, even as she knew it might have less to do with her parenting skills and more to do with the time. Maggie had been born at a point when girls were told they could do anything. God knows that hadn't been the case for Kathleen, never mind Alice. She imagined the world her granddaughter might inherit, incrementally better than the one they lived in now. The thought of it excited her more than she might have expected.

The previous night, she had grudgingly gone along with Maggie to watch the Fourth of July fireworks in Portsmouth after dinner.

Within minutes of their arrival, Maggie had to pee, and so they went to the Porta-Potty lines, and got into what looked like the shortest one. They stood there, barely speaking. At the restaurant, Kathleen had once again pleaded her case — Maggie should move to California and live with her. Once again, Maggie had refused. She had been a bit mean about it, really. Kathleen worried that this was Alice's influence. She had to remind herself about all the hormones that were coursing through her sweet daughter's body.

"Your place is a pigsty," Maggie had said, as Kathleen paid the bill. "I can't imagine a worse house for a baby to crawl around in."

"Babies don't exactly come out of the womb crawling," Kathleen said.

"Fine. I can't imagine a worse house for a baby to live in, crawling or not. Gabe was afraid to sleep there, for God's sake."

A moment later Maggie apologized, but the damage was done.

Her house wasn't *that* bad. Was it?

"So sorry to have offended that darling Gabe with my filth," she said.

They didn't talk in the car on the way to Portsmouth. But standing there by the portable toilets, Kathleen said, "When my brother was at Notre Dame, he and a few other guys once got suspended for tipping one of these over while a friend of theirs was inside."

"That's awful," Maggie said.

"Yeah. Pat was kind of a bad boy before Ann Marie came along and sucked all the fun out of him."

"I don't know if I'd call that fun," Maggie said.

"Good point," Kathleen said.

"I can kind of picture Chris doing that," Maggie said.

"I know. It's scary, but I know." She put an arm around Maggie.

Maggie nodded. She held on until it was her turn to go in.

"Don't you dare tip me over," she said over her shoulder as she moved toward the stinking plastic enclosure.

"Well, you shouldn't have called my house messy," Kathleen said, and stuck out her tongue.

She stood there, watching the crowd for what seemed like ages. Teenage couples kissed, and gaggles of girls ran around giggling. Young parents chased their offspring down the path, and older parents read books on blankets in the grass, eating pizza or submarine sandwiches wrapped in tinfoil while their children texted away on cell phones. A group of high school kids competed to see who could shove the largest number of glow sticks into his or her mouth. Well, that was charming.

Kathleen glanced over at the Porta-Potty

Maggie had gone into. What was taking her so long? She wondered if something was wrong. She pictured a gunman lurking behind the flimsy door, covering Maggie's mouth with a gloved hand.

She shook off the thought.

When her children were small, she'd experience a miniature panic attack at least once a week, thinking one or the other of them had been snatched. In the grocery store, she would turn her head this way and that, looking for Chris, her heart pounding, imagining the most gruesome possibilities — and then, a moment later, there he'd be, clutching a package of Oreos, which she gladly let him have as a sort of reward for not getting kidnapped and ruining both their lives.

Kathleen looked down at her watch. When she looked up, she noticed her brother's friend, Steve Brewer, standing two lines over. She hoped he wouldn't see her. She wasn't interested in making small talk with anyone who would consciously choose to socialize with her brother and sister-in-law.

Right on cue, she saw Ann Marie come through a wall of people. She was wobbling, and she looked plain drunk. Not tipsy, or just over the limit. Drunk. Some tiny part of Kathleen had softened to her sister-in-law this week. It had probably started with Ann Marie trampling Alice's tomato plants, and her all-out meltdown around the priest. You couldn't exactly wish more unhappiness on somebody who was so clearly coming undone, even if she was your mortal enemy.

Ann Marie approached Steve with a smile and said something to him. She fingered his lapel. Her face was dangerously close to his, as if they were two lovers about to kiss. As the thought struck Kathleen, she saw her sister-in-law lean forward and plant her lips on his.

"Oh my God," Kathleen said out loud, putting a hand over her mouth, feeling almost giddy, as if she were watching the season finale of her favorite soap opera. Her sister-in-law was having an affair with her neighbor's husband. It was almost too good. She had a momentary vision of all of them squeezed together, watching the fireworks, and hearing herself say, *So, Ann Marie and Steve — when did you two get together?*

She remembered when she had found out about Paul's infidelity all those years ago, Ann Marie self-righteously saying, "I think you'd better take it up with your husband."

How stupid she had felt then. How powerless. And now this. Maybe if you only waited long enough, all your life's wrongs would right themselves one way or another.

But then, quite suddenly, Steve pulled away. She couldn't hear what he was saying, but she understood from his expression that he had been taken by surprise, and not in a good way. The two of them exchanged words, and he stormed off, leaving Ann Marie standing in place, in tears. Some gentleman, abandoning a clearly intoxicated woman in the middle of a crowd.

Kathleen instantly felt sorry for Ann Marie. It was the excruciating expression on her face that did it, a look of embarrassment, shame. Kathleen felt a sense of pride, realizing that that was all she wanted. Not to hold it over Ann Marie's head as some sort of threat, but just knowing that Ann Marie herself knew she was not perfect.

At that moment, Ann Marie saw her. *Shit.* Kathleen almost hoped she would walk away, but instead Ann Marie came toward her.

"Oh God, please, Kathleen, don't tell Patrick what you just saw."

Ann Marie spoke in a rush, sounding desperate.

Kathleen had to remind herself that Ann Marie was drunk; that was probably part of it. She felt like being kind. Not her Kelleher self but that other, better version of her she thought she had left behind on the farm.

"I didn't see anything," she said. "I'm just waiting for Maggie to get out of that disgusting bathroom. She's been in there for ages."

Ann Marie looked skeptical.

"Please," she said again. "I can explain what that was."

Maggie finally came out of the Porta-Potty

642

then, thank the universe.

"Here she comes," Kathleen said, waving to her. She wanted to make it clear that she posed no threat. She put on her sweetest voice, the type she'd use with a school superintendent she wanted to charm. "Now, where are you guys sitting and what did you bring for dessert?"

The rest of the night whizzed by, Kathleen feeling almost giddy. For all time, she would now be the bigger person. Goddamn, it felt good. She talked to that slimy Steve about golf and the Grateful Dead (these middle-aged Dead Heads could surprise you with their Brooks Brothers polo shirts and Nantucket Reds). She talked to his wife about a trip they were planning to San Francisco. She praised the gloppy, over-sweet dessert, and she oohed and aahed over the fireworks until Maggie grabbed her sleeve and said, "You're kind of freaking me out, Mom. It seems like you're actually having fun."

While Maggie showered, Kathleen finished packing. She hadn't brought much. She had worn the same faded T-shirt of Arlo's for the past three days.

Eventually, Maggie came out of the bathroom wrapped in a towel, a wall of steam floating around her.

"Did you make the bed in your room?" Maggie asked.

"Yes!"

"Did you wash the sheets?"

"No. What is it with you and the sheets? Do you think I was performing an animal sacrifice in my sleep or something?"

Maggie sighed. "I'll meet you downstairs."

Kathleen found Alice in the kitchen washing dishes, already dressed in a dark blue pantsuit, her makeup done to perfection, her black bob sleek and in place. She looked like she was going to a funeral.

"We're taking off," Kathleen said.

Alice frowned. "Oh? Where to?"

"I'm driving Maggie back to New York."

"Is that right?"

Kathleen opened the fridge and pulled out a pitcher of water. Beside it, dripping onto a saucer, was a tea bag.

"Maybe you should start living a little and stop reusing the tea bags, Mom."

"Waste not, want not," Alice said. "So, has Maggie come to her senses about Gabe? Are they getting back together?"

"No, thank God."

"How can you say that?" Alice asked. "It's always better for a child to have married parents. Do you know what children call other children who don't have fathers?"

"It's not 1951, Mom."

"Yes, I'm aware of that." Alice paused. "If she's not going to make up with Gabe, what's the point of going back there?"

"To start getting ready, I guess," Kathleen said.

Alice fiddled with the spray nozzle on the sink.

"Now this thing's acting funny, as well as the disposal. And Ann Marie has succeeded at scaring Father Donnelly away from the place for as long as she's still here."

Neither of them mentioned the reason. Kathleen wasn't sure whether she cared that her mother had given the property away, but she knew her siblings were upset. The whole situation was absolutely bizarre, Alice at her most Alice-like.

"Speaking of Ann Marie, will you give her a message for me?" Kathleen asked.

"That depends." Alice's tone was cautious, as if Kathleen were some traveling salesman asking her if she was in the market for an overpriced vacuum cleaner.

"On what?"

"The message! You can't expect me to agree to say something before I even know what it is."

Kathleen shook her head. "Oh my God. Okay. Tell her I was finally ready to leave the beach and get out of her hair."

"I don't understand."

"Just tell her."

"Fine."

In the car, Kathleen told Maggie about the

kiss. She had to. In fact, she was surprised she had been able to hold it in for that long.

"You can't tell Arlo," Maggie said.

"Why not? He's not going to spill the beans."

"I know, but once you've told me, and then him, it's a hop, skip, and a jump and you're telling Aunt Clare, and then it's out to the family. And that's dangerous."

"Why are you such a Goody Two-shoes?" Kathleen asked, genuinely curious, though she knew Maggie was probably right.

"Promise me," Maggie said.

"Okay, I promise. Sheesh."

"I still don't really understand why we left so abruptly," Maggie said.

"It was time," Kathleen said. "I'm not going to try to talk you into moving in with me anymore."

"You're not?"

"No. You've done a great job of convincing me that my house is a shit hole and no self-respecting person would ever want to live there with us."

"I'm sorry."

Kathleen smiled. "It's okay. You're an amazing young woman, Maggie. And if what you want is to stay in New York, then I support that."

Maggie stuck out her bottom lip. "Thank you."

They listened to the radio for a while until

the station faded out of range.

"Aren't you even going to mention how virtuous I'm being about this Ann Marie situation?" Kathleen asked.

Maggie didn't respond.

Kathleen turned to look at her. She was fast asleep.

She brushed a dangling strand of hair behind Maggie's ear and kept driving.

When they arrived in Brooklyn, there was a huge box blocking the door to Maggie's apartment. Kathleen's first thought was that it was from Gabe. She looked at the address label.

"It says it's from Bugaboo," she said. "What the hell is Bugaboo?"

Maggie looked embarrassed, and Kathleen pictured a sex swing or something crazy like that.

But Maggie responded, "It's a gift from Aunt Ann Marie."

"Tell me she didn't buy you a dollhouse."

"No! It's a stroller."

"A stroller."

"Yeah, a really trendy one, I guess. It cost like six hundred bucks."

"Oh, well that sounds practical. Nice of her to let you know what it cost."

"She didn't let me know. I saw it in the catalog."

Kathleen felt her goodwill toward Ann Marie slipping a bit. She would probably end up telling Clare about the kiss, but that was all. No one else. Clare wouldn't tell anyone besides Joe.

They heard footsteps on the staircase behind them then, and a moment later a gorgeous young thing with mile-long legs was saying hello.

"Maggie!" she said. "You're back!"

Kathleen remembered the first time she had visited her daughter at college, how pleased and reassured she had felt to see that Maggie had built her own community there, full of friends Kathleen had never laid eyes on. Now Maggie had done the same here in New York. Her daughter was okay on her own. In fact, she thrived on independence, just like Kathleen herself.

"Rhiannon, hi. This is my mom. Mom, Rhiannon lives next door. She's the one who drove me up to Maine."

"Oh," Kathleen said. "It's nice to meet you."

"Likewise," the girl said. "I've heard a lot about you."

Kathleen wasn't sure she liked her tone.

"How's everything been around here?" Maggie asked.

"Same old, same old. I went to Governor's Island for the first time yesterday."

"Cool," Maggie said. "Listen, I should have called you sooner, but I've been kind of a mess, as you might imagine."

It was strange how easily these words came out of her mouth when she was talking to an acquaintance in the hallway. It was something she hadn't yet said to Kathleen.

"I'm sorry for how I reacted when you told me —"

Rhiannon interrupted. "Oh no, I'm sorry. I never should have said that. I'd just had too much to drink. I didn't think it through."

"You probably saved me from begging him to take me back with that piece of information," Maggie said.

What the hell were they talking about?

The two of them hugged. Rhiannon put a hand on Maggie's belly.

"Hello there, teensy neighbor," she said.

So Maggie had told her first. Kathleen tried not to let this bother her.

Inside the apartment, she asked, "What was that about?"

Maggie sighed. "She works in this restaurant, and Gabe and I went one night for dinner. Apparently while I was in the bathroom, he grabbed her butt and tried to kiss her."

Kathleen nodded. In a way, she wished she still drank, because then she might have downed half a bottle of gin and driven over to that little shit's apartment, and egged his car, or calmly asked him to come down to the street and then beaten the crap out of him with her purse. *Ah, the good old days.*

649

"He pretty much sucks," Maggie said.

"Yeah," Kathleen said.

She was somewhat relieved, realizing that Maggie was smart enough not to go back to him. But she felt sad for her daughter too. Through her child, she would be linked with Gabe for the rest of her life. They had so much to sort out, but most of the questions probably wouldn't even be clear until they were in the midst of it, never mind the answers.

"Can I ask one thing?" Kathleen didn't wait for Maggie to say yes. "Was this an accident, or did you get pregnant on purpose?"

"Something in between those two," Maggie said. "I guess you could say I sort of tempted fate. I was stuck. I needed a push, one way or the other. That probably sounds insane."

"It's going to be okay," Kathleen said, maybe more to herself than to Maggie.

Maggie nodded. "It has to be."

For lunch they ate tomato soup and peanut butter crackers, the closest thing to an actual meal that Maggie had in her cupboards. Maggie sorted through her mail and pulled the stroller from its box. They watched sitcom reruns on television, though Kathleen wasn't paying attention. She was thinking instead about what came next.

At three o'clock, Maggie had to get on a conference call for work, so Kathleen decided to take a walk around the neighborhood. Brooklyn Heights was beautiful, with its rows of perfectly preserved brownstones and federal houses. She walked to the Promenade, where the view of the Brooklyn Bridge and the Manhattan skyline never ceased to take her breath away. She almost felt jealous that she herself hadn't discovered it as a twenty-something. She could see why Maggie didn't want to leave.

They were hungry again by six. They ordered Thai food. While Maggie went downstairs to pay the deliveryman, Kathleen took the chance to really look closely around her daughter's apartment. She had thought the place was cute the first time she saw it — a jewel box, she had said. But that was years ago, when she was envisioning it as just a little hideaway for Maggie alone — a room of one's own, where she might write two or three great novels before moving on to a sprawling country house out west with her stable and appropriately aged husband.

Now Kathleen examined the tiny kitchen, with the window so drafty there was really no reason to close it. The refrigerator's long orange power cord was strung up over a series of nails toward the ceiling and plugged in across the room. The bathroom door never closed properly — half an hour earlier, the doorknob had come off in Kathleen's hand.

The dust that streamed in from outside could never be controlled, not even by an anal-retentive neat freak like her daughter. And there was the issue of those five flights of stairs. Five!

Maggie had said she could put a crib and a changing table in the living room, but that hideous yellow stroller Ann Marie had sent was already taking up a quarter of the space, so there went that idea.

When Maggie came up the steps with a large paper bag in her arms, Kathleen said, "I think we need to find you a new apartment. Something bigger."

"I can barely afford this one," Maggie said.

"Why don't you sit down?" Kathleen said. "There's something I want to say."

Her daughter looked nervous, but she set the bag of food on the coffee table and sat on the couch.

"You haven't changed your mind about trying to kidnap me, have you?"

"No. You don't have to come to California," Kathleen said.

"Oh God, are you planning to move here?"

"No, but thank you for your excitement over the idea."

"Sorry," Maggie said.

"I do want to come back — with your permission — when the baby's born, and help out until you get on your feet."

"I'd like that," Maggie said.

652

"You know your happiness is the most important thing in the world to me, right?" Kathleen asked. "Except sometimes I'm really selfish."

Maggie laughed, and Kathleen went on talking. "We both know that too. So. I'm kind of rambling here, but the point is, I should have done this right from the start."

"Done what?"

"I have some money saved for the farm."

"I can't take your savings," Maggie said.

"Yes, you can," Kathleen said. "It's twenty thousand dollars. And it would be my great pleasure to give it to you."

Even as she said it, she felt a deep sense of loss. Her father had made selflessness look so easy. But Kathleen would never be as good a person as he was, and she could not sit here and offer up her savings without thinking about how long she had planned on buying the worm gin, how diligent she had been in setting the money aside, month after month. The farm was doing fine, but now it would likely be years before any kind of meaningful growth could happen.

She felt sorry for Arlo. He had no idea how much she had socked away, but she'd have to tell him now. Her father had often bailed her out, and she had been grateful. But she had never once asked him what he would have done with the money if he hadn't given it to her. For the first time, she wondered how Alice had felt about all that.

"I couldn't take it," Maggie said. "Could I? Oh God. I'd pay you back, Mom."

Kathleen shook her head. "No, it's a gift. I wish I had more to give you."

And with that, she actually did feel somewhat selfless. Maggie needed her, and she had answered the call. Her father would be proud.

"You can use the money to take out a hit on Gabe," Kathleen said. "Or buy diapers. Whatever you want."

"That's a lot of diapers," Maggie said.

"You'll be surprised."

She stayed for a week. Just long enough to help Maggie find a bigger place — two bedrooms, right on the edge of a park, further into Brooklyn, Dominican kids running this way and that, an ice cream truck playing its tinny tune, ambling up the block. The rent turned out to be cheaper than her current apartment's. If Alice ever came here, she would probably say that the neighborhood wasn't safe, but Alice would never come. Maggie would have to bring the baby to her if she wanted her grandmother and her child to meet. No doubt, Maggie *would* do this, having inherited Daniel's belief in the importance of generations, of one person understanding life through the experiences of all the people who came before.

They packed boxes and listened to Beatles CDs. They ate a lot of takeout, and Kathleen began to feel her pants grow tighter. They shopped online for maternity clothes, which she was pleasantly surprised to find resembled real clothes — gone were the ridiculous muumuus and sailor dresses pregnant women had been forced to wear back when she was having kids.

She accompanied Maggie to her doctor's appointment and had to excuse herself for a minute so she could cry in the ladies' room. Kathleen wished Maggie had some handsome sweetheart standing by her side, holding her hand. That was what she deserved. When they walked out into the waiting room, crowded full of pregnant ladies wearing enormous diamond rings, Maggie looked like she might lose it — but a moment later she shrugged, as if to say that that was just life.

"What will you do when I'm not here to come with you?" Kathleen asked. "Come alone?"

"I can ask Allegra to bring me," Maggie said. "Maybe I should have a dinner party and break the news to all my friends at once."

"That might be a good idea," Kathleen said, and her heart swelled to think that this fearless young woman was her daughter.

At night, they slept side by side in Maggie's bed. Kathleen felt afraid to leave, though she missed Arlo. She missed her dogs. She missed working the farm and eating dinners made from ingredients they had grown right there in their garden.

She missed yoga. You couldn't throw a rock in Brooklyn without hitting three yoga studios, but her kind of yoga had nothing to do with svelte twenty-six-year-olds in trendy workout gear. Her kind of yoga included Arlo and her in the backyard, wearing sweatpants, gazing at the mountains in the distance, rather than looking out at a sea of taxicabs through a dirty window.

They both cried when she had to leave for the airport.

"I'm scared," Maggie said.

"That's just part of it. And you can change your mind anytime about coming to stay with us. Okay?"

"Thanks," Maggie said. "I love you."

"I love you, too, kiddo."

Several hours later, Kathleen sat barefoot at the kitchen table with Arlo, drinking ginger tea, telling him everything that had happened since they had kissed good-bye two weeks earlier. He had arranged white tulips in a vase on the counter, and made a pumpkin cake with the words WELCOME HOME etched unevenly across the top in white icing. Kathleen felt at peace.

The dogs sat at either side of her chair, as

if they were guarding her, as if to say *You're right where you belong.*

ALICE

Alice had been watching him all afternoon. He had reddish hair, unlike most of the others. He paused for a moment and looked her way to make sure that she was still sitting there on the screen porch, observing his work.

She gave him a wave and took a sip of her wine. He went back to eating the grass.

A few days earlier, she had decided to make peace with the family of rabbits who had been hanging around all summer. They had withstood every challenge she had given them since May. You had to admire the sort of gumption it took to break through a fence and stomach an entire bottle of liquefied cayenne pepper just to get a bite of good lettuce.

When she gave it some thought, she realized she was their type exactly: someone who seemed to bug everyone around her, when all she was trying to do was survive.

In recent days she had even gone so far as to put a few carrots out on the grass by the car, but the bunnies hadn't touched them, probably because they could smell the human scent she'd left behind.

This one was the father — at least she figured he was, since he was the biggest. She was worried about the little babies in this heat. She wished they would take a bowl of water. Father Donnelly told her this was the hottest August in southern Maine on record since 1893. He said it with a sort of awe for how long ago that seemed, as if dinosaurs might have roamed the earth that summer. Alice kept to herself that it was the year her mother was born, and so to her it didn't seem like such ancient history.

She still wouldn't let the rabbits near her garden, but there was hardly anything left there anyway. The strawberries and beans had been harvested. The lilies were wilting and brown. The tomatoes — well, she'd have to replant those next spring.

Kathleen was finally back in California. She and Maggie had left Cape Neddick so abruptly after the Fourth of July fireworks that Alice assumed she must have offended them somehow. They were both so damn sensitive. But Kathleen assured her she was just ready to leave — she had a lot to help Maggie sort out, she said.

Yes, like the pesky business of finding a father for her child.

In the month that had passed since, Maggie had sent Alice one letter a week, like clockwork. Most recently, she reported that she had moved further into Brooklyn, to a nice family-friendly neighborhood. The apartment cost less than her old one and it was twice the size, with a large bedroom and a second, much smaller room, which most people would use as an office, but which she planned to turn into a nursery. She had begun telling friends that she was pregnant, and her boss had agreed to let her work from home three days a week once the baby came. She had not seen Gabe since she got back, but planned to meet him for coffee in the next couple of weeks to sort out logistics. Imagine that. A coffee date with the man who impregnated you. It seemed a bit late for logistics.

Maggie wrote that she was fifteen weeks pregnant. Her morning sickness hadn't abated. She had read in her baby books that her child was now growing hair, and wasn't it strange but wonderful to think of someone sprouting a full head of brown curls inside your belly? Alice squirmed a bit, reading that part. Women had entirely too much information about such things these days. Maggie added at the end of her letter that in five weeks she would find out if she was having a boy or a girl. If the child was a boy, she wanted to call him Brennan, Alice's maiden name. *A baby boy named after our fearless matriarch!* she had written, and that at least had made Alice smile.

She responded to Maggie on small notepaper, so that she wouldn't have too much room to speak freely. She tucked a Mass card into each envelope. Alice was so worried about the girl — Maggie acted as if hanging a mobile and buying some tiny socks was all it took to raise a child. But Alice held her tongue.

Ann Marie and Pat's daughter Patty had been up for two weeks in July with her brood. Watching Patty and her husband, Josh, chase their three rug rats around made Alice think of Maggie and everything she had in store: the sleepless nights, the bad winter colds, the fights with a maddeningly obstinate toddler.

Patty's only daughter — Alice's great-granddaughter — was a four-year-old called Maisy. Who named their child Maisy? It was a name better suited for a beagle than a little girl. Anyway, this summer Maisy couldn't get enough of Alice. She'd be sitting alone on the porch drinking her morning tea in peace, and she'd hear a nasally voice at the door, "Great-grandma Alice, can I sit with you?" Or she'd be watering her flowers and Maisy would toddle up in her bathing suit and ask to help, plastic shovel in hand.

"She really loves you," Patty cooed, and of course Alice couldn't say anything, because it would be rude to tell her to go away. She was already in hot water with Ann Marie. But God help her, she found that child annoying. She wished Patty would have the good sense to realize that she didn't feel like being a damn babysitter. After they left, she found the remains of an oatmeal cookie under one of the chairs on the porch, absolutely covered in ants.

Alice had been alone for ten days straight now, fourteen if you didn't count Ann Marie's last visit, which had lasted only two hours. Alice had asked her if she wanted to go somewhere for lunch, but Ann Marie said she had a lot to get back to at home, which Alice assumed was code for "I'm still angry."

The silence in the house did not bother her one bit. She felt rather exhausted from the events of the summer as it was, and when Clare had called to say that Ryan was in rehearsals for a play the first three weeks of August, so they wouldn't be coming up until the twenty-first, Alice had felt almost relieved. Her world grew small again, as it had been before the Kelleher women descended on the place with all their drama and their worries and their strife.

Now she watched as Papa Bunny ran behind her rhododendron bushes and out of sight, back home to his family.

"Toodle-oo," she said out loud, and she felt good for having made amends.

She looked at the bottle of cabernet on the

side table, registering that it was now half full.

Aha. She had actually thought those words: *half full.* That meant she was an optimist, didn't it? Alice smiled. Daniel would have gotten a kick out of that.

"How do you like that?" she said. "You always said I failed to look on the bright side, but I think I just proved you wrong."

She poured herself a bit more wine.

Right after he died, she had talked to her husband out loud all the time, letting him know what the children were up to, how she was passing her days. At a certain point she had stopped, but lately she found herself doing it again. She had even told him how much she resented having Maisy underfoot, adding, "I only tell you this because I know you can't respond and scold me for being so awful."

Now she said, "I haven't heard from Patrick and Ann Marie for three days. The nerve of them. They didn't get their way, so now they're punishing me. Is that any way to treat your mother?"

She refused to feel bad about the house, no matter what they did or said. Really, she hadn't expected them to get so worked up about it. Patrick and Ann Marie were the most noticeably upset, but even Clare had called her in tears when she heard the news. Alice told them all that there was nothing she could do about it now. St. Michael's was counting on the money.

Ann Marie had asked how she could do this to them, how she could just go ahead and give their summerhouses to the Church, as if the Church were nothing. The Church was the only constant companion of Alice's life, the only thing that made sense, always.

She sipped her wine. Out in the distance, heat lightning flashed across the sky. Alice thought a little rain would help cool the air down, but the rain didn't come.

The next day was Sunday the fifteenth, the Feast of the Assumption. Alice was up early to get to the Legion of Mary's celebration. It was her job to bring the cinnamon rolls, and she had made a special trip to a bakery in Wells.

She wore a pale violet pantsuit that she had never worn before, and she took special care with her hair and her eye makeup. In a departure from their usual schedule, they were meeting before Mass to honor the Virgin Mother's assumption into Heaven and to prepare for their role in the offering.

As she walked to the car, Alice looked out over the ocean and remembered how the Catholic mothers of her generation — her own, and Daniel's, and Rita's, and everyone's — believed there was a blessing in the water on the fifteenth of August that would help any struggling young woman to get pregnant. Early on in her marriage, back when she was having all that trouble, Alice herself had been forced to head to the shores of Nantasket Beach. Before dipping in, she stood back for a moment to behold dozens of pretty young war brides with the same miracle in mind, immersing themselves in the cold New England sea with all the faith and determination of the saints.

That was a year before Kathleen came along. Daniel had called her their greatest blessing the morning she was born.

Alice got into the car and headed toward St. Michael's. The Irish Hit Parade was on the radio, Daniel's favorite. She left it on, even turning up the volume a bit. Five minutes later, she pulled into the parking lot and climbed up the front steps. The door was unlocked, and as she opened it, the smell of incense filled her lungs. She stepped inside. The church was vacant, and looked even grander than usual for that. There was still half an hour until her meeting began, and an hour before Mass.

She chose her usual pew and knelt down on the red velvet kneeler. She found her rosary in her purse, and then looked up at the stained-glass window behind the altar, a depiction of Jesus on the cross.

Troubling the glass beads between her fingers, Alice prayed for Maggie and Ann Marie, and for all the members of her family, the living and the dead. She prayed for her own soul, and for forgiveness for the things she could never undo. Over and over, she said the words that she had learned so long ago, words that had brought her comfort when nothing else could.

When she was finished and came to the final bead, she started again from the beginning. She prayed until she heard footsteps behind her, coming slowly down the aisle, a familiar voice softly calling out her name: "Alice? Alice. It's time."

ACKNOWLEDGMENTS

I am indebted to my fabulous editor, Jenny Jackson, and my incredible agent, Brettne Bloom, for their contributions to this book.

A million thank-you's to Hilary Black, Lauren Semino, and Eugene and Joyce Sullivan for reading the manuscript and providing such vital feedback. And to Laura Smith and Joshua Friedman for reading and editing everything else.

I am grateful to everyone at Knopf, Vintage, and Kneerim and Williams, especially Andrea Robinson, Jill Kneerim, Hope Denekamp, Leslie Kaufmann, Nicholas Latimer, Russell Perreault, Sara Eagle, Kate Runde, and Abby Weintraub.

The archives of *The Boston Globe* provided indispensible information about the Cocoanut Grove fire. A visit with the Held-Semino family gave me inspiration for the cottage, and Larry Ravelson gave me access to the very helpful book *Ogunquit By-the-Sea* by John Bardwell. Dorothy Joyce, M. Patricia

Gallagher, and Lawrence and Florence Sitterle were fantastic sources of wisdom when it came to World War II and the 1940s. And Beth Mahon, Noreen Kearney, and Caitlain McCarthy were kind enough to share their recollections of growing up Irish Catholic in Massachusetts.

Thank you to those who so generously offered me inspiring places to write: Jane Callanan, Amanda Millner-Fairbanks, Sudhir Venkatesh, Karla Adam, and Bennet Morris. You welcomed me into your lovely homes and said not a word when I accidentally killed your houseplants.

To the many members of my family, who mean the world to me — thank you Mom, Dad, Caroline, Trish, Dot, Jon, Jane, Mark, Mark Jr., Nancy, Michael, Pauline, Michael Jr., Richie, Tracie, Eugene, the Troys, the Joyces, the Gallaghers, the Radfords, and all the rest.

Finally, thank you Kevin Johannesen, for bringing so much love, laughter, support, and clean laundry into my life. I will never know how I got so lucky.

ABOUT THE AUTHOR

J. Courtney Sullivan is the author of the *New York Times* best-selling novel, *Commencement.* Her writing has appeared in *The New York Times Book Review, The Chicago Tribune, New York, Elle, Glamour, Allure,* and *Men's Vogue,* among others. She lives in Brooklyn, New York.